ANYBODY'S MIRACLE

By

Laura Hercher

HERRING RIVER PRESS
WELLFLEET, MASSACHUSETT

Herring River Press, 2012
Copyright © 2013 by Laura Hercher

This book may not be reproduced in whole or in part without permission of the author.

This book is a work of fiction. Any resemblance to actual persons living or dead, or events, or locales, is entirely coincidental.

For more information on the book or for inquiries on readings or appearances, please go to:
www.anybodysmiracle.com

Herring River Press ISBN 13: 978-0-9888140-0-4
ISBN: 0-9888140-0-5
www.herringriverpress.com

For My Mother.

Chapter 1

Spring came reluctantly to New England. It was April, but the winter chill was barely gone, and the air was filled with the damp, rich smell of thawing earth, ripe with rot and promise. Back home in Texas, Robin thought, it would be warm. Back home, the azaleas would be blooming, and not these sad-looking crocuses, hanging their heads over the remnants of dirty snow lingering in the hollows beneath the trees. She turned her eyes to the path and ran.

The park in Somerville was full of children punch-drunk on a few extra hours of weak Northeastern sunlight. Grimy, outgrown parkas pinched their shoulders and rode up their wrists as they chased one another around the playground. Their shouts and cries insinuated themselves beneath the pounding in Robin's ears that was the sound of her own heart beating. She ran faster, away from them, the sweat dripping in her eyes. She'd been delighted with the park two years earlier, when they first came here, when John made the decision that this start-up company in Boston was an opportunity that he would never find in Dallas. She took lovely photographs of tulip beds and budding branches as they walked, clutching the newspaper with the rental listings circled in red. She admired the swings and the brightly colored rocking ponies and a hopscotch board spray painted on the asphalt. It was a warm day then, and there were older couples strolling and dog walkers and teenagers congregating in corners, but all of them were invisible to Robin, who saw only mothers and babies.

Robin turned to the right and headed uphill. The path grew steep and rocky here, and the broken pavement very different from the neat sidewalks down below. Mommies with strollers did not come this way. She struggled to keep her footing on the uncertain terrain. Her ankles twisted and skid beneath her but she did not slow down.

Why on God's green earth, she wondered, was it so hard for her, and so easy for everyone else? There were pregnant women everywhere she looked. Girls who couldn't be more than eighteen or twenty, hiding a tiny bump under their boyfriend's baggy shirt. Working mothers headed downtown in pinstriped maternity wear, and women lounging on benches watching their other children play, in oversized tee shirts stained with food that had dribbled down the front and stuck to their bulging bellies. Everyone but her. Her thoughts, if she was not careful, gave way to bitterness. "God, grant me the serenity to accept your plan," she prayed silently, and then she thought, "oh Lord, why me?"

John hated it when she worried, as though her negative thoughts were the cause of all their problems and not the result. He was optimistic every month, and every month his confidence worked on her along with her own surging hormones until finally she allowed herself to hope that this time it might be different, that this time there would not be blood. And then the disappointment – always the disappointment, just like today. Robin ran along the ridge at the top of the hill until the path turned down again. The balls of her feet caught her weight with each stride as she ran downhill, and she felt a dull ache in all the bruised places where she slid the needles into the firm flesh of her upper thighs.

Stupid, useless drugs. Six months of treatment and nothing. Two weeks ago, she lay on that exam table yet again, dressed in yet another washed out gown hanging open in the front, while Doctor Aylmer stared grimly at the moonscape images on the monitor. Her ovaries should have been bulging with ripening follicles, but instead there was just one fluid-filled cyst, ready to release a single, elusive egg into the vast quantities of empty space that glowed black on the screen. What a joke it was that she had ever been afraid of getting pregnant. Afraid! She had forced herself to go to the drugstore even though she could just about feel Father Martin watching her as she walked down the family planning aisle, all because she was under the impression that having sex got you pregnant. Now she knew better. And it took her over a year to talk John into trying, wasted time they would never get back. "Don't worry so much about the money," she told him over and over again. "A child is a blessing. We will make it work."

"We're not seeing as robust a response as I would like to the stimulation drugs," said the doctor.

"Oh, they are certainly doing something," John replied. Robin glared up at him. The white paper crackled unpleasantly beneath her as she shifted her weight onto her elbows.

"He means the drugs are affecting my moods," said Robin. "I have been a little extra emotional." John's fingers stroked the back of her neck as his green eyes gazed puppy-dog at her. She smiled back at him, a small smile. It was true, after all. It was not easy for him either, the poor boy. One day, in a fit of pre-ovulatory rage, she had just thrown out his dinner because he was one hour late coming home. She knew how hard it was for him, how much pressure he was under, putting together that dog and pony show to impress the new investors. John stared at the pork chops in the garbage can for a long second before silently making himself a sandwich and going back to the computer.

"Mood swings are very typical," acknowledged the doctor. "Nothing to worry about. Well, let's finish out this cycle and hope for the best. It only takes one!"

"That's what I've heard," said Robin, "but it doesn't seem to work that way for me."

Dr. Aylmer nodded thoughtfully. "If there isn't a pregnancy this month, I think we should stick with the plan we discussed earlier and move on to IVF. It's a big investment, but we will do everything we can to optimize your chance of success in round one, starting with an increase in the dosage of the drugs."

Oh good, thought Robin, then I can be even more of a crazy ass she-devil. The technician ran damp paper towels across her belly, wiping away the warm jelly from the ultrasound. She vowed to herself that John would not see the worst of it, not this time. She would smile at him in the morning when he left and try not to cry when he called home during the day. Robin squeezed his hand and made a hopeful face. She had promised God faithfully every Sunday for two years that she would be a good wife – and a good mother, if ever he gave her the chance. She was keeping up her end of the bargain.

"How much of an investment?" asked John.

"The costs of a single cycle run from twelve to fifteen thousand dollars," said Dr. Aylmer. "If we have to go to a second cycle, that may be less, especially if we are able to produce some extra embryos the first time around and freeze them. You have a few additional costs associated with the freezing and thawing, and our success rates are a little better with fresh embryos, but for subsequent attempts, now or in the future, it does make the process a lot easier on Robin. If you want to. It's up to you."

"That's fine," said John quickly, "the money is not an issue. Do whatever is easiest for Robin."

"Can we really afford to do this?" Robin asked him as they left.

"Of course," said John. He paused, and she could see him calculating silently. "We can manage it. Don't worry. This money isn't going to matter at all in a couple of years, once the company is up and running and our options have vested. The meeting with the money guys last week was a complete home run. They loved the business model. They barely looked at all the work I did. You just say 'internet' to these venture capital guys and they throw dollars at you. I'll get a bonus when the next round of financing comes through, and that will cover one cycle of IVF, and maybe a second one too, if it comes to that. This is the most important thing, and you shouldn't worry about money. I'll take care of it."

That was the kind of answer she always got from John. He took care of things, not like the careless boys Robin had dated in college. They met in Austin during their senior year and she knew he was different right away. "He's a fine young man," her father said, grudgingly. "I don't know why a talented kid like that can't find a job worth having right here in Texas, but if you have to go north for someone, it might as well be him." Robin slowed to a jog as she left the park and headed back on city streets toward the two-family house with its many layers of brown paint. John's confidence was comforting to her. He was always certain enough for the both of them. He spoke like a man, but he stared at her like a lovesick boy, even now, when sex was something scheduled on their behalf by the Center for Reproductive Medicine. He still showed up on the appointed day with wine and flowers, as if he were trying to seduce the reluctant ovum. "A true romantic," Robin teased as she lay, hips elevated, brown eyes alight with distant memories of biology class. "I shouldn't be admitting it to you, but when it's baby-making time I am pretty much of a sure thing."

He brought her dinner in bed. "Don't get up yet," he said. "Let's not make the little guys swim upstream." He looked approvingly at the red painted toes peeking out from under the tangle of sheets and pillows. Their bed. His pillow. Three and a half years since their wedding and he still seemed surprised to find her there, as if she were not just another blond haired girl, but some exotic creature that he had coaxed here to live with him, in the cold and barren north. What a total geek he must have been when he was younger, Robin thought fondly. She wanted sons who looked just like him, tall and pale, with black hair and eyes that glinted emerald. She lay back and imagined sperm, tumbling over one another. The doctors told them John had an excellent sperm count with normal motility and good morphology. He was extremely pleased with himself when those tests came back. The lab did not find a problem with his sperm. The lab did not find any problem at all. They gave them a diagnosis of idiopathic infertility, which was just a fancy way of saying that something was wrong, but no one knew what the hell it was.

Robin closed her eyes and thought about a film she had seen as a child, a documentary about the miracle of life. It was so beautiful. It had no sex in it at all, this story of reproduction, none of the rawness, none of the sweat or the heat or the tenderness of the act itself. Fiber optics had transformed it into a thing that was clean and brightly lit, like an exhibit in an aquarium. It was as if God had created a window into something sacred and unknowable, only it wasn't God at all, but a tiny camera on a long, thin, snake-like stalk. In the documentary, everything went according to plan, and it didn't seem to matter that half the sperm ran off in the wrong direction, or that some sat immobile, or that one odd sperm with two tails was whirling away in a perpetual circle. In the video, that was only comic relief. But now it was her and John, the defective ones, dancing their stupid whirling dance, going nowhere twice as fast.

Robin walked the last half a block. It was past seven when she turned into the driveway that they shared with their neighbors downstairs, and she was surprised to see John's car was already there. She climbed the narrow stairs into the small front room. The leaded windows sparkled with a light that seemed to hover outside, unable to penetrate the absorbent darkness of the deep brown stain on the sills, frames and floors. Pink and flushed, Robin stood dripping in the corner of the spotless room. The indoor air felt warm and dusty in her lungs.

"Robin, is that you?" John walked in from the bedroom. "Where have you been? Do you have any idea how late it is?"

"I went for a run," she said, her lip trembling. "Am I supposed to sit here every afternoon waiting because once in a blue moon you might get home early?"

"But you told me to be home in time for dinner with your brother and Caleb."

"Oh!" It was Friday; she had completely forgotten it was Friday. They were supposed to meet Mickey in half an hour. They would be late even if she was ready to go right now. "Oh, damn it," she said. "Damn it." Robin sat down on the couch. Her head ached.

"Robin, c'mon, you need to hop in the shower. I don't know what you were thinking. Rob?" John looked more closely at his wife, "Robin? Are you alright? Is something wrong?"

"I got my period today." The tears she had been battling all afternoon seeped out, laying yet another layer of salt across her damp cheeks.

John sat down heavily on the sofa next to her. "I'm sorry, sweetheart." He put an arm around her shoulder.

"Don't!" she said, pushing him away. "I'll get you all sweaty."

"Shh," said John. She leaned her head against his chest. "It's alright. We'll just move on to IVF, like the doctor said. We'll get there."

"You don't know that. It doesn't always work. Lots of times it doesn't work." Robin wondered for a moment if John felt any disappointment himself, or only anxiety on her behalf. Did he ever see parents in the street and feel hungry, physically hungry, to have a baby in his arms? She knew that he disliked it when things did not go according to plan. Nature was hard on a computer programmer. "You remember my mother at Christmas, rattling on and on about that woman around the corner with the triplets? The test tube babies, that's what she called them. She'll be expecting two heads and a forked tongue."

"Kathleen will get over it. When it gives them a grandbaby, your mother and father will change their opinion of IVF in a hurry."

"Well, that's true enough. Did I tell you mother called yesterday? She kept telling me how she heard on the radio about how girls who exercise too much stop getting their periods." Robin laughed ruefully. "Thank you very much, mom, but that's not my problem. Every damn month I get my period."

"Did you tell her that?"

"No, of course not. I can't tell her anything about this. First she's going to tell me that it's all in God's hands, and then she'll be calling up every fifteen minutes, telling me about some magazine article on boxer shorts."

"I can't be discussing my underwear with your mother."

"That's why I don't tell her."

"Are you okay now? Should we cancel with Mickey?"

"No," said Robin, "he'll take it personally. You know how Mickey is."

"Then you had better get in the shower. I'll try and catch him to let him know we're running late."

"Alright," said Robin. "And you'd better change your shirt.

Mickey was digging an olive out of the bottom of his martini glass when the hostess showed them to their table. "You're late," he said to Robin, not unpleasantly.

"I am so sorry," she said, but Mickey had turned back to the hostess.

"These two need a drink right now," he said, gesturing at John and Robin. "What do you guys want? You'll take their order, right? They have catching up to do."

"I'll send over your server," she replied stiffly. Her long brown hair was pulled back severely and she wore a black trousers and a tight black button-down shirt that was not tucked in. I don't know why the girls up here like to be so drab, thought Robin.

"It's a desperate situation," said Caleb, swirling the ice in his empty glass. He looked appealingly at the girl in black. The smooth cotton of his dress shirt covered the broad arc of his shoulders without a crease or a pull. His blonde hair was cut short, so that it only showed a hint of a wave, and his teeth were very white when he smiled. "They may perish at any moment."

"I'll see what I can do," said the hostess, blushing.

"Do you have to be so charming all the time?" asked Mickey. "Is that something they taught you at boarding school?"

"Yes," said Caleb, "it was in our Intro to Running the Universe course."

"Seriously?" asked Robin.

"No," said Mickey. "Don't be an idiot." He looked more closely at his sister. "Are you alright? Is something wrong?"

"I'm fine," said Robin.

"How's Emoney?" Caleb asked John.

"It's coming along, thanks," said John. "We have most of the major retailers on board. Everything else will follow." They were just finishing up the website design; John was very pleased with it so far. "Our marketing studies look great. Everyone is looking for just this type of thing right now, something that's going to protect them and their privacy when they start to do business on line. People seem to want to feel a bit more secure before they give all these strangers access to their lives and their credit cards and their checking accounts. So we are going to provide that security. We can enable them to be out there spending money in cyberspace without taking any risk."

"Wait," said Mickey, "you can do all that, selling gift certificates?"

"Securitized transactions," said John. "The gift certificates aren't the main thing. They're just an added convenience."

"It's only been explained to you about a thousand times," said Robin.

Mickey shrugged. "I knew it had something to do with the internet, and making money."

"Speaking of making money," said John, "have you decided for sure to go with the civil liberties firm?" Mickey was graduating from Harvard Law School in May.

"Yup."

"And what does Daddy say about that?" Robin asked.

"What did you think he would say? 'Well, I expect yer goin' to do what yer goin' to do, son.' We all know what a terrible disappointment I am to him. Now I'm wasting my Harvard degree as well, when I could be raking in the big bucks. I believe he thinks it's crazy. Possibly even criminal. Just like the rest of my lifestyle."

"I think you are too hard on your parents," said Caleb.

"Well, you would," said Mickey. Robin rolled her eyes at her brother. She hadn't seen him for weeks, not since they helped him move into Caleb's apartment. His hair, hanging low on his forehead, was as dark as hers was blonde, and he was a little scruffy and unshaved, but not in a bad way. He had eyes like bruises – their mother always carried on about how no girl could resist those bedroom eyes, or she had done until last Thanksgiving, when Mickey finally broke the news that he was not interested in girls, whatever they might think of him. Mother hadn't said much about Mickey since, aside from telling Robin now and then to send her love. At Christmastime, when Mickey stayed behind to work on an article for Law Review, Mother asked her if she thought Mickey was taking care of himself, and then scurried away before Robin could answer, dabbing her eyes on her sleeve.

Robin had known her brother was gay since he was in the eighth grade and she was in ninth, long before he admitted it to her, in that semi-suicidal coming out speech the year before she left for UT.

Sometimes she had wanted to scream it at her mother, who was oblivious to anything except his smoky eyes and his perfect test scores. Mickey got A's in everything, even from the teachers who complained bitterly about his attitude in the classroom. Mother always insisted that he write letters of apology. He showed them to Robin to make her laugh. "Dear Mrs. So-and-So," he wrote, "I regret it extremely if my behavior did not accurately reflect the high esteem in which I hold your class."

"You are going to get in trouble," Robin muttered, when what she meant was that he was going to go to Hell. At first she worried about this all the time, but gradually less and less. She was very attached to her brother; it seemed natural enough to assume that God would love him too. It was easier now, since they had left Texas. Sometimes she still thought of him to herself as 'poor Mickey,' although often she did not even remember why.

"Which reminds me," said Mickey, "can I come stay at your place two weeks from now? Caleb's parents are coming to town for the weekend."

"Sure," said Robin.

"Thank you. I am grateful not to be put out on the street."

Caleb grimaced. "Could we cut back on the drama, Mickey? Robin and John are nearby, so it is not such a big problem."

"Well, I'm grateful to my brother-in-law for being such a genius with computers that the world would not let him hide his light under a barrel back in Dallas. Cheers, John."

John looked pleased. Mickey did not often go out of his way to acknowledge John's abilities, not that it would have bothered him, except that Robin cared so much what her brother thought. John knew he was good at what he did. He understood computers; they spoke to him. He had a knack for creating accessibility, for allowing those lacking the gene for html to tap into the power of the technology without having to understand how it worked. Mickey admired his proficiency, but it was not a talent that interested him.

As far as Mickey was concerned John was clueless, a fact he had determined the first time Robin brought him home. He seemed absurdly astonished that Robin had taken an interest in him at all. "That boy has no idea how good looking he is," Mickey told his mother. "My guess is he went through puberty about five years later than everyone else. But whatever his problem was, he grew out of it, and nobody bothered to tell him." Mickey looked amused. "No wonder he is so wild about Rob. I'll bet you anything, in high school, the closest he ever got to a girl was rescuing the princess in Nintendo."

The waitress came and cleared their plates. "Did you want anything else?' she asked, directing her question mainly at Caleb. They all had dessert except for Mickey, who ordered only coffee.

"I always eat more than you, Mick," said Robin.

"Perhaps that is because you run five miles a day, while I am sitting on my ass in the library."

"It wouldn't kill you to get to the gym," said Caleb.

"She's the athlete in our family," said Mickey. "Runner. Swimmer. Cheerleader." Mickey mimed the waving of pompoms.

"I only did that in junior high." Robin smacked him lightly on the shoulder. "But mother was so proud. It was nice to have her talking about me for a change, and not only about Mickey and what a genius he was."

"You were the little superstar, weren't you?" said Caleb, looking genial.

"He was the smart one."

"Also, I was the good-looking one," said Mickey. "Robin was always a troll. And I was the popular one. No one more popular than me." He looked at his sister. "Did you have friends? I forget."

"We were very different," said Robin. "It's funny how two children from the same family can be so different."

"Beware," said Mickey, "it's all buried somewhere in your DNA. The two of you could have a child like me. Be forewarned." Robin blinked, and her smile grew a shade brighter. Under the table, John squeezed her knee softly.

"I read a story the other day about what's buried in your DNA," said Caleb, who seemed to perceive a quaver in the atmosphere. "Not science fiction – a true story. It was about chickens. Apparently some researchers were trying to test a theory about development, and how the body knows where to grow added things like teeth and hair. Their idea was that there were two different layers of cells. One type of cell did the signaling –build a tooth here, for instance – and the other type of cell did the work. When they got the signal, the worker cells were supposed to pull a blueprint for tooth-building out of their DNA and construct it. They tried this out in a mouse, and by moving some cells from the jaw to the thigh, they got the mouse embryo to grow a tooth in its leg. But that didn't prove the theory about the two types of cells, so they decided to move the signal cells from the mouse into a chicken. According to their plan, nothing could happen because chicken's worker cells aren't supposed to know how to grow a tooth. It's right there in the basic definition of a bird: wings, feathers, beak – no teeth. So the signal cells would signal, but the builder cells wouldn't be able to build. Only, it didn't work out that way. The damn chicken grew a tooth."

"So they were wrong, " said Mickey.

"That's what the researchers thought – that their theory was wrong. But then they took a closer look at the tooth. It didn't look anything like a mouse tooth. So they compared it to various teeth, and that was the shock. It looked just like a pterodactyl tooth. Like the fossils of teeth from the dinosaur age. So it turns out, for all these gazillions of years, those birds have been carrying around a set of plans for building a tooth, just waiting for someone to ask."

"Wow." John gave an appreciative whistle. "I wonder what we're carrying around, hidden in our DNA?"

"I don't want to find out," said Robin. "You can't tinker with human beings like that. It's dangerous. Anything could happen."

"But it's kind of cool, just to think about it," added John. "It's like every time you have a child, you are handing down the whole history of the species."

"Talk about the weight of the world!" said Mickey. "And I thought it was enough of a burden carrying around just my own family history. It's a wonder anyone survives."

Chapter 2

This must be what it feels like to be a part of a team, thought Mickey, standing in a rustling sea of black and crimson robes. He liked the academic regalia, with its obscure and colorful iconography of intellectual achievement. Commencement! What a misleading term that was. Someone had pulled off a marketing ploy of historic proportions – just fucking with everybody, like those ancient Norwegians who found a chunk of ice in middle of the Arctic Ocean and named it Greenland. Call it what you want, graduation was always more about the past than the future. It wasn't like marriage or baptism, or any of the rituals that brought you into the fold. They were being ushered out into the world without any assurances at all that the world would embrace them. "*Good luck*," the speakers said. "*Do well*."

No, this rite was an ending, like a divorce or a funeral but without the rancor and the misery, another acknowledgement that time passes and life moves on. *We are done here. Thank you.* You felt all the weight of history and the great debt to those who preceded you at an event like this; the school made sure of that. Harvard loomed over you in brick and stone, and the speaker, the U.N. High Commissioner for Human Rights, exhorted a restless horde of future managing partners to go out and lead the world in productive ways.

Mickey had not felt so much a part of his class since the first days, when they were all lost together, bewildered over-achievers anxious to prove themselves once again. Tomorrow they would go their separate ways, and yet there was in passing this sense of something shared. It was a feeling he did not often permit himself to have – to relinquish, however briefly, the need to be better, to be smarter, to set himself apart. Sparing himself the burden of caring what anyone else thought.

Like tasting forbidden fruit, he thought, to imagine myself someone who belongs here. *We have been doing this a long time*, the walls told him. *We will continue on after you are gone*. Learning to disdain the desire to belong had been the great effort of his teenage years. It was the bargain he had made: you will not love me, but you will respect me. If he were to be honest with himself he would have to admit that the desire to wring some respect out of the world, more than any grander ambition, had brought him to this moment. He should have told them the truth in his admissions interview. *So, why do you want to come to Harvard Law?* To make my mother proud, of course: proud and not ashamed. So that she would brag about me to her friends, with their fat envelopes of baby pictures.

His mother, who was absent today. How could she possibly have been so surprised by his announcement last Thanksgiving? Was she really the only person in Dallas who didn't already know he was gay? Mickey remembered a stretch of time in college when he had made a stab at dating women. He'd brought them home for dinner, one after another, slim-hipped girls. His hetero-unsexual phase, Robin called it. For years, his mother asked after each of them by name. "Say hi to Melanie for me if you speak to her," she said. Melanie! He did not even remember which one was Melanie. Whoever she was, she was certainly not on speaking terms with him. Texas coeds took it very personally when their ex turned out to be gay, which was ironic, since it didn't have anything to do with them at all.

Probably it was just as well that his mother didn't come. What would he have done with his measly two tickets, if she had? He scanned the crowd, looking for his father and Caleb, sitting side by side. He wondered what choice he would have made, if they were all here today. Caleb would have offered up his seat as a matter of course, and that would have made Mickey angry. 'Oh - don't worry about me. The tickets are for the family.'

And what are you, Caleb? The thought of it provoked him intently. He felt his level of irritation rise as he imagined a suitable response. But this was all in his head, Mickey reminded himself. Idiot. He'd invented this scenario, and now he was genuinely mad at Caleb. Moments like this made him wonder if he was simply incapable of being happy; perhaps happiness was yet another thing he wasn't cut out for, like weight lifting or line dancing. Maybe it was something you could not change, like homosexuality. It was seductive to think about character in this way. It absolved you of all responsibility to be better. I am what I am meant to be, thought Mickey. I am what I am. Popeye the Sailor Man goes Calvinist.

Nonsense, Caleb would say. Biology wasn't destiny. It wasn't all black or white. Caleb was opposed to the tyranny of having to choose, when the world was painted in shades of grey. He might come from stern Protestant stock, but Caleb was negotiable. "You don't make it easy for your parents," Caleb said. "Can't you see that they are trying?" That was his point last night, after Mickey's father left the apartment. "Why did you have to bring it up again about your mother staying in Texas? Why can't you just appreciate that he is here? Change is incremental, Mick. People are complicated. Relax. There is a middle ground, a place where can they love you and still not understand. Can you never just take what is offered and be content?"

They had been down this road before. Progress came in stages, Caleb said. Labels, ultimatums, lines in the sand – these things were unnecessary. Good people did bad things. Bad people did good things. It wasn't as simple as right and wrong; everything depended on the context. Your life was full of competing interests; you sat them down at a table and worked out the best deal that you could get. Find a solution you could live with and get on with it. That was the real world.

Mickey's own world was full of dichotomies that Caleb did not believe in: good and evil; North and South; Democrat and Republican; smoking and nonsmoking; straight and gay. "I'm not gay," Caleb told Mickey the first time they had breakfast together. "I don't buy the whole package. I don't see myself that way. Why do I have to pick sides? Why can't I just happen to like you? If I slept with a woman, that wouldn't make me straight."

"Trust me it would not," Mickey replied, ruefully.

Caleb did not see that it was any else's business if he chose to keep his private life to himself. People at work had no right to know, and he had no desire to tell them. "How convenient for you," Mickey said. Caleb, defiantly refusing to out himself, would make partner in two more years. His secretary would go on doting on him in an unrequited fashion, and his mother would not have to resign her DAR membership out of embarrassment. If it didn't bother him, it certainly was easier. He was right about that, of course.

But Caleb was wrong about one thing – Mickey did appreciate his father's presence. Gratitude, in fact, was exactly what he had been trying to express. They had a couple of hours between the day's festivities and dinner with Robin and John, so Mickey suggested stopping in at the apartment. His father had never been there before. "Nice," he said, gesturing at the city view out the front window. "Very nice." He perched on the boxy edge of a black leather armchair, nodding solemnly as he looked around the room at the red granite breakfast bar, the oversized television, the dumbbells in the corner – anywhere but the closed bedroom door. He looked a little greyer than Mickey had remembered.

"Thanks, Dad," he replied. "I'm really glad you could make it for the graduation."

"You wouldn't have been thinking, would you, that I'd miss watching my own son graduate from Harvard?"

"Mother managed to keep herself away." Mickey felt as though the words escaped from him against his will. He saw them coming out of his mouth like words in a cartoon bubble, hanging in the air.

"Mick, you know your mother wanted to be here." His father looked pained. "She has not been feeling well recently. A plane trip would have been too hard on her sciatica."

If this were a court of law, thought Mickey, I could rip that argument to shreds. What evidence is there that my mother wanted to be here but couldn't manage it? Did you or did you not take a trip to Santa Fe in March? Come on. Are we not talking about my mother, the woman who walked three miles across town in the Texas heat when her car battery died, just to be in attendance for my first Little League game? The first game, one might add, of a brief and disastrous Little League career. Mickey remembered her, dusty but smiling, climbing awkwardly into the bleachers in her sensible heels for the sixth inning of a six-inning game. Just about the time they would have put me in, he noted. His irritation vanished, and he tried to take the sting out of his words. "I know. I'm sorry. I will give her a call this evening, after dinner."

But after dinner, when his father had gone back to his hotel room, Caleb gave Mickey his graduation present. He knew what it was as soon as he saw it, seeing its shape through all the layers of bubble wrap covered with cardboard and looped with twine. They had been to a show together at a gallery on Newbury Street, and both of them loved the same painting: a large, almost monumental, portrait of a single tree standing on the crest of a hill, caught between sunlight and shadow, silhouetted against an early morning sky. It reminded Mickey of the hills back home, and Caleb of the mountains in upstate New York where his family summered when he was a child. They sat on the couch and admired it, together.

"I like the way it sits alone," said Mickey. "It's beautiful, but it breaks my heart, the loneliness. I don't know how I stood it all those years."

"Before me."

"Before Caleb," Mickey agreed. "B.C."

"I thought about getting you one of those new Blackberries." A Blackberry was what Caleb wanted for his birthday; this was not his first hint. "But I decided I wanted to get something you would have forever." Forever. Forever was a loaded word.

"You know what I want forever?"

"What's that?"

"You. I want you forever."

"You have me, Mickey."

Mickey noted silently the omission of the operative word. "How do you think our lives will change, now that I've graduated?"

"You haven't actually graduated yet, right? I want to see that diploma." Caleb ran his hand through Mickey's hair. "I don't know – does everything really need to change? We'll have more money, obviously. I thought when the lease on the Acura comes up next fall we might think about getting a BMW or a Mercedes. But we could talk about getting a bigger place, if you'd like. Would you like to look for something bigger?"

"No, I don't mind – I am happy with the apartment. I guess I meant more big picture stuff. How do you see us in a year, or five years? Just the same, but in a nicer car?"

"Don't be ridiculous. In five years, I'm a partner. I should have a nicer car. Perhaps a really nice espresso maker. Definitely a Blackberry."

"Be serious."

"Mickey, I don't know. I hope I can work a little less. Take more weekends off. I would like to go on representing scoundrels, and it looks like you are going to insist on trying to keep the world safe for atheists and whistle-blowers. But they're still going to pay you something, right? You don't have to subsist entirely on good karma? I was thinking perhaps in a couple of years we could consider buying a place."

"Buying a place together?"

"Yes. We could buy it together, or I could buy it and you could contribute whatever you could afford – that doesn't matter to me." It matters to me, Mickey thought, but he did not interrupt. Caleb grew more animated. "We could figure that out. I would love to have something with some character, something we could really make our own. Maybe a old place we could fix up, if that's not too ambitious. With a little more room, and a yard."

"More room, a yard – sounds like a house out in the 'burbs, Caleb. All you are missing from this picture is a couple of kids and a white picket fence."

"I didn't say anything about kids!"

"But why not a couple of kids? Why shouldn't you have that? Are you really going to work like a dog your whole life so you can have heated leather seats and high end appliances? That's it? You would be a good father."

"I don't know. I – what kind of a family would that be for a child? What kid wants to be the child with two daddies?" He sighed. "It would be great, wouldn't it, to have a baby? And then, like, a little kid running around, going to school, going to summer camp. Going skiing. I wish – but it's not realistic."

"It has to be realistic, Caleb, because apparently people do it all the time. Take a look online – there's a whole cottage industry out there of egg donors and surrogate mothers making babies for people just like us. All of those children must live somewhere. We could live somewhere too."

"You know, I used to think all the time about having a child. I could see myself carrying the kid in one of those backpacks, and going to Disneyworld. I had these daydreams about Little League..."

"Are you sure it was a daydream? Because I seem to remember that as a nightmare."

"I like baseball, Mickey. You're the one who can't catch. Seriously, I always saw myself as a guy with a family. I never quite envisioned the wife – she was there, but not there, like Charlie Brown's mother. Of course, I knew I was attracted to men. But still, that was my fantasy – somehow, I thought maybe it would happen someday; I don't know, maybe it could have. And then I met you – and then I couldn't imagine being without you. I can't imagine being without you. But it was hard, y'know, because I had to give up on the imaginary life. Not that I gave it up to be with you – how could I give up what I never really had? It just felt a little bit like that."

"Like you were making a choice?"

"Asshole. Yes, like I was making a choice."

"But this time, I don't think you have to choose. We can have a family – we can be a real family."

"I guess. It's a lovely thought, Mick."

"But you know what the problem is, don't you?"

"Oh, we're back to that."

"Yes, well, how would you explain the little motherless tots to Grandma and Grandpa Dunhill? Perhaps if we move, we could keep the apartment and you can pretend you still live here when your parents come. Doesn't matter what it costs, it would be worth it. We could think of it as a shrine. The temple of self-loathing."

"Give it a rest, Mickey." Caleb looked weary. "I am sorry it is so difficult with my parents. I love them. I know you think I should be ready to give them up but I'm not. Look, you are mad at them because they can't accept me as I am – but doesn't that go both ways? Isn't it equally on me to accept them the way they are? My father fought in Vietnam. My grandfather was wounded in World War II. They made sacrifices. Mine are so much less. I don't want them to be unhappy. They would be crushed. I understand that you judge them for that."

"I don't judge them. I don't even know them. We've never met."

"I asked you to dinner last time they came."

"I am not going to sit through a meal with your parents pretending that I am some friend you met at work."

"You are some friend I met at work."

Mickey raised one skeptical eyebrow. He had caught a glimpse of the Dunhills when he dropped Caleb off at the restaurant that day. The mother was slim and imperious-looking in a red cloth coat belted at the waist. Caleb and his father shook hands, and the man's craggy face showed a small gleam of pleasure. "You have never even tried to tell them."

"I know the way they see the world. It's like how you see the world. Right or wrong. For them, it's wrong. Believe me, it's impossible."

"If it's impossible, so is everything else. I'm not trying to punish you; it's simply a statement of fact. We're stuck."

"I'm stuck."

"So I can move on, without you? Is that what you want?"

"You know it's not."

"Then don't say that. Don't say it like I could just walk out of here. Don't make it my choice."

"Okay. We are stuck together. Better?"

"Much." The single word was a bond between them, as though something had been resolved. They sat together on the couch and admired the lonely tree. Mickey thought with pleasure of the next four weeks, with nothing to do until his job began. Maybe he would test drive the BMW. Just for fun.

Chapter 3

The man in England who invented IVF wasn't even a real doctor, not a medical doctor. Robin read about it in a book she'd found at the library; it helped to pass the time between injections. Robert Edwards turned the eggs and sperm of small mammals into tiny embryos that grew in his lab, and then returned them to their mothers so they could grow into perfectly normal mice and bunnies. But there was no glory in improving reproduction for mice and bunnies. It was human beings who cried out for help.

The government committee that gave out grants did not support his research. You are moving too fast, they complained. There are too many risks. If you kill a rabbit while retrieving her eggs, you can put the fertilized eggs into another rabbit. If a baby mouse comes out wrong, you can euthanize it. But what about a baby? The government was afraid of all the unknowns. It was too soon, they said.

Still, Edwards never lacked for volunteers. Without a single baby to show for himself, and still the women came, begging to be a part of the grand experiment. It must have been hard, after a while, to stay upbeat. There must have been days when Dr. Edwards wished he was back with his bunnies. Rabbits did not weep or moan or clutch at you when their embryos failed to implant. But he was a confident man! He didn't tell Louise Brown how many times he had failed. She had no idea, when she got pregnant, that she was the first. She couldn't understand why writers from the tabloids were following her to the supermarket and hiding behind the potted plants in the hallway when she went to see her doctor, until finally she asked one of the reporters, and he explained that this had never happened before, not in the history of the world. She might have been angry at him, but she was not. She was too grateful to be angry.

Robin looked around the waiting room, and wondered how many of the women at the Center for Reproductive Medicine would hesitate if the doctor said he wanted to try something new, something that might help, although it had never been done before. Probably every single one of them would say yes. They all were in the market for a miracle. Nobody came to this waiting room who wasn't.

It was a very nice waiting room. She'd admired it the first time they came in, just about a year ago. The upholstery was unblemished, and the leather chairs were arranged in little groups of three or four, as though it were a place to sit and have coffee with your friends. There were paintings on the walls, real paintings, not posters. This was no ragtag operation of underfunded mad scientists. It was comforting, Robin thought, but John had looked around and said, "This is what you get when you pay out of pocket."

The magazines were nice too; there were plenty of copies and all of them were recent, not like at the dentist, where the issues of Newsweek were a year old, and the columnists were still speculating on whether or not Bill Clinton could get himself re-elected. The Center for Reproductive Medicine must have quite a budget for magazine subscriptions, between the ones up front and the ones in the back, in the little room behind the door marked "private." They kept that stuff current too; she knew from John, who had to give a sperm sample on day one. He'd turned red as a beet when they handed him the cup.

Robin picked up a copy of *Vogue* and leafed through the pages, glancing at photographs of a woman in a ball gown perched in a tree, and then put it down. She didn't want to see the great new looks for fall. She was hoping to be in maternity clothes by fall. The thought made her stomach constrict. It was better to expect nothing. Concentrate on today, she thought. *Please, God, let there be follicles. Please, God, let there be follicles.* How many should she hope for? There had never been more than five at this stage before. Could she ask for ten? *Please, God, let there be ten follicles.*

"Come on in," said the nurse.

The morning coolness had burnt away when she stepped back outside. She pulled out her new cell phone. John had programmed it, so she only had to hit the number one, and then the green button. Her fingers were trembling, and it took her three tries to get it right. The phone made its artificial trilling noise, and John picked up. "What's the news?" he said. She found it disconcerting the way he knew without asking that it was her calling.

"Fifteen!" she sang out. "At least fifteen. Dr. Aylmer says I have so many he wants to keep an eye on me. I have to come in Monday morning. And then we will be harvesting by the end of the week."

"What time is the appointment for Monday? I'll come with you, if I can."

"I don't know. The receptionist goes home early on Fridays. I am supposed to call tomorrow. John, isn't it so exciting?"

"Yeah, it's great. What are they monitoring you for?"

"Oh, the doctor said something about ovarian hyperstimulation something something. I don't know what it is. It's only a problem if you go over twenty follicles. Twenty follicles! Can you imagine?" Robin sounded thrilled at the thought of it.

"Is it dangerous?"

"He didn't say. I'm sure it's nothing. The bad thing is, if you get the syndrome, they freeze the embryos and make you wait a whole extra month. I would die. I would absolutely die."

"But you wouldn't have to go through the stimulation process all over again. So at least there's that. It wouldn't be so hard on you, not like this." John wondered how much more it would cost if they had to freeze and thaw all the embryos. Would they do the extra cycle for free? Doubtful.

"I bet I would still have to have some of the shots. They would need to control my cycle to know when to put the embryos in."

It would definitely cost more if they had to do another cycle of drugs. "It will probably be fine," said John. He could hear in the silence that Robin was waiting for more of a response. "Congratulations. This is great news."

"Congratulations to you too! They're your children as well." Eggs, thought John. They were eggs, not children. Follicles. She had gone to hell and back to produce these follicles, and he had done nothing but watch. They are all yours, he wanted to say, and you have earned them, but he couldn't say anything, not with all those hormones coursing through her veins. John checked his watch. "Listen, darlin', I have a meeting in about five minutes with lawyers about a new federal internet tax law. It goes into effect next month and nobody knows what we're supposed to do be doing with the existing state sales taxes. I don't know how these assholes expect us to be compliant when they can't interpret their own damn law."

"It's sales tax, John. Everyone has to pay sales tax."

"It's not quite that simple anymore. All the current laws are based on the old idea that a transaction occurs someplace in particular. But on the internet, the actual sale occurs in cyberspace, our company is in Massachusetts, the customer is maybe in one state, the seller in another. Depending on how you look at it, we are either nowhere at all, or in several places at once. The existing laws don't have the vocabulary to cover this. The government wants its money, but also they don't want to slow things down. They want the industry to push ahead as fast as the technology will drive it. So it's like, we're supposed to be solving everything on the fly, with no template and no directions. Now they're trying out a sort of three-year moratorium on all new internet taxes, but nobody knows what to do with the laws that already exist. And that's our dilemma of the day."

"Hmm" said Robin.

She wasn't listening, John realized. Of course she wasn't listening. It was stupid of him to try and discuss tax law with a woman incubating fifteen follicles. If it was only fifteen; if it wasn't more than twenty and a whole new set of issues to deal with. Not that he would dare say it right now, but it was this tedious bullshit that paid the bills, including the thousands of dollars for drugs and ultrasounds and examinations and blood work. Hell, they probably charged him for the privilege of jacking off into a cup. John wondered what that had cost, and how they would have described it on an invoice. Male gamete auto-extraction fee? He never looked too closely at the itemized bill, just glanced at the total and wrote a check.

Robin got off the phone and contemplated the question of what to do next. It was important to keep busy. There was a show at the Museum of Fine Arts by a photographer whose work she knew from her classes at UT. He took pictures of everyday things like worn-out shoes and old chairs in a warm, radiant lighting that made them look beautiful, even heroic. "What does it tell us?" said her professor. "That God, like the devil, is in the details." She would go see the exhibit. Maybe she could meet Mickey for lunch, if he could get away from that new job for an hour. She stared at the face of her cell phone as though it would tell her what to do. Just a few more days to get through before they gave her the go-ahead for the big needle – she had winced just seeing it there, with the rest of her supplies. John would have to do that shot. And then they were on the clock: twenty-four hours to retrieval time. Robin practiced breathing deeply to calm her racing heart. Her old swim coach had taught her that; you had to control your blood pressure to win a race. Mind over matter.

Dr. Edwards back in England liked to transfer the embryos into their mothers at midnight, as though to introduce an element of romance. The ladies dressed up for it too, in mascara and pearls, with their long white nightgowns buttoned up to the neck. Robin thought of them every night when she pulled back the plunger on her syringe, filling it slowly, so no bubbles would form. They dressed for him, combing their hair and brightening their cheeks, the way women dress for men who come in the night. And he came, their savior, with his test tubes and his turkey baster, and they shut their eyes and prayed.

It was a miracle, Louise Brown said. Maybe it was, for her. What Edwards did back then was a stab in the dark, but nowadays the doctors appeared to have it all figured out. Now it was medicine and not a miracle. They were definitely men and not God, these doctors with their expensive drugs and their fancy ultrasound machines. It was all a business. God would not give miracles only to those with means to pay. But that didn't make it wrong, did it? How could a child be wrong? Robin fingered the small gold cross that hung around her neck. She did not understand how the Church could be against IVF when it was a means of creating life. The child was still a gift from God, for those who were lucky enough to have the option. And for the rest, may God bless them too, thought Robin and she said a little prayer for those who could not afford IVF.

The weekend was interminable. It was hot, and Robin sat restlessly in the living room, in the small circle of cool generated by an inadequate air conditioning unit in the window. John drank a beer and watched the Red Sox, muttering to himself with annoyance because he couldn't get the Texas Rangers games in Boston. Robin began and then abandoned a novel, picking up her camera instead, and gazing idly through the viewfinder. "You know what?" she asked John, who was peering closely at the television screen, trying to make out the out-of-town scoreboard in the background.

"What?"

"I showed some photographs I took last Spring to Tom – the guy at the photo shop? He really liked them. He said he thought I could do a little freelance work if I wanted, with the right equipment."

"Really? That's great. Is that something you would want to do?"

"I don't know."

"I think it's a good idea. I love your pictures. Besides, it will take your mind off – I mean, you'll enjoy it, right?"

Robin sighed. "You don't have to be so polite about it. I know I'm just a little bit obsessed right now." John sneezed and Robin shot him a reproachful look. "You're not getting sick, are you?" she asked, sliding herself farther away on the couch.

"I hope not." He stared nervously into his beer. "A lot of people are sick at work this week. Some sort of stomach thing going around."

Robin made a mental note to wash her hands more frequently. Maybe it was just as well that John was too busy to come with her tomorrow.

John felt fine all week, except for a passing queasiness on Wednesday, when the order came to do the final injection. He shuddered as he pushed the large bore needle into her backside. Robin winced.

"Damn, I hate this," said John.

"That's not a nice thing to say about my ass," said Robin, arching her back to try and see the dark spot. She took a square of gauze and pressed down hard to stop the bleeding. She felt the soreness run deep, and her eyes shone.

The number of eggs at retrieval was twenty-two. "You should go home and rest for the next couple of days" the doctor told Robin. "You will probably feel sore and achy, with some cramping. Your ovaries are very large, and you will have a lot of tenderness from the retrieval process itself. That's normal. If you have swelling of your abdomen, fever, or extreme thirst, call us right away. Drink up! You should have lots of fluids. Keep off your feet and keep hydrated."

The nurse called the next morning to check on Robin and to give them a first report. They had embryos. Robin was thrilled to hear her use the word. Yesterday's twenty-two eggs were today's eighteen embryos. Thank the Lord. Her heart raced. *Slow down, slow down*, she told herself. Her own medical update was brief. She felt fine, sore, tired – just what the doctor had predicted. The nurse asked her if she had any cramping in her legs. "Just my belly," said Robin, laughing. Who cared about leg cramps when yesterday there were only eggs and today she had eighteen embryos? The nurse said she would check in tomorrow and got off the phone. Robin sat on the edge of the bed, still holding the receiver. She looked down at her stomach, the bloating easily visible across her taut midsection. She was nauseous again, but perhaps a little less. She needed to call John, but she would get something to drink first. Robin dragged herself into the kitchen, and opened the fridge. The big thing of Gatorade was almost empty. She poured herself the remains, and reached into the pantry for another.

It was all his fault for bringing home the stomach bug, John thought, staring at her greenish face in the morning light. He was fine but, just their luck, Robin had it. She said nothing about it to the nurse. "They don't need to know I have a touch of the flu," she told him. "It's just something that's been going around. The doctor is going to get all worked up about ovarian hyperstimulation syndrome, and next thing you know we won't be able to go ahead with the transfer tomorrow." It was most likely the flu, John thought. Only she looked so swollen – she looked like she was a few months pregnant already, which she couldn't possibly be, seeing as all of their embryos were still in little dishes at the clinic. Robin was probably just tired. She spent half the night in the bathroom, and then she was up again hopping around with that ramp in her calf.

"Hey Rob," he called out, "did you ask the nurse about the leg cramp?"

"I forgot. If it happens again, I'll call."

"Okay." She must know best, thought John. She would be able to tell if it were something serious. It would be such a disaster to cancel the transfer. Robin would be beside herself. "Do you want me to pick you up some bananas before I go to work? They're supposed to be good for muscle cramps."

"I don't think I could handle a banana just this minute, thanks. Could you just get some more Gatorade? We're all out."

Robin told him she felt better the next morning, although the swelling was worse. John didn't say anything when she came out dressed in a pair of his old sweatpants, her waistline visibly bulging beneath the tired elastic. It didn't look so good to him, but then it was not his call to make. If the doctor was worried, he could make the decision to wait a month, and he could deliver the bad news.

In the car, Robin took one long, slow breath after another. John glanced sidelong at her as they drove. Her face, thinner the last year or so, showed a gentle puffiness that smoothed and rounded her cheeks. She seemed younger, more vulnerable. She looked a little clammy but her eyes were bright and liquid, a color like melted caramel beneath the yellow bangs. She was so hopeful. It made John feel strangely sad and anxious. It would be too cruel if she were disappointed again. He tried not to look at her distended stomach, knowing how the fluid stretched the dark bruises around the injection sites into strange, elongated purple designs that looked like inky tribal markings against her summer tan. Her chest rose and fell, and he felt a tenderness suffused with desire. John reached out to take Robin's hand. Shaking her head, she pulled away, laying her hands across her stomach and continuing to inhale deeply. "Not now" she said, breathing out into the words. How long did you have to wait after the transfer, until it was safe to have sex again? John wondered if he could find a way to ask. It was ironic, really, that their method of making a baby should require so much in the way of abstinence.

Dr. Aylmer was not pleased with Robin's physical exam. "Your blood pressure is a little low," he said, "and there is more weight gain then I am comfortable with. I think we need to consider whether or not it is advisable to move ahead right now."

Robin nodded. She had been expecting this, John saw that now. If you didn't know her well, you might have thought that she was calm. "I see. Of course I don't want to do anything risky. But my blood pressure is always on the low side."

"It's true," the doctor admitted.

"And I think I may have taken your advice about staying hydrated too much to heart. I have been forcing myself to drink gallons."

"You haven't been unusually thirsty?"

"Not really. I just wanted to avoid any problems, so I kept drinking and drinking. I feel great."

The doctor flipped through the pages of Robin's chart for a long minute. He was going to call her bluff, John thought. No need to jump in. It was so obvious, looking at her, that she was ill. Another month. John sighed. More money, more aggravation, more misery for Rob. "It is a hard decision," the doctor said. John waited for the axe to fall. "There is some chance that symptoms of hyperstimulation may develop if we proceed today. On the other hand, I understand that there are drawbacks to waiting."

"I know our chances of a pregnancy aren't as good with the frozen embryos." Robin sounded so reasonable. "I don't want to do anything that would bring down the odds of succeeding, not unless it was absolutely necessary."

The doctor nodded and closed the chart. He seemed to have reached a decision. "Alright. In that case we will proceed with the transfer today." John exhaled lightly. His chest felt tight. He gripped Robin's hand, and she smiled at him, radiant. He smiled back, a pale moon to her sun. "As we discussed last time, I am going to put in three of the embryos and freeze the rest. We reviewed them in the lab this morning. Let me show you the pictures." He held out a file folder with a stack of black and white images printed out on little rectangles of glossy paper, curling at the edges, each stamped with a time and date. Dr. Aylmer laid them on the table one by one like tarot cards. "Selecting embryos is not an exact science. We look for ones like this." He pointed to a picture of a small, translucent ball, its sides pocked with tiny indentations. Pencil-thin black lines divided the sphere into pockets of clear fluid, varying in size but perfectly symmetrical right and left, up and down. It looked like a soccer ball made of soap bubbles. A darker, thicker ring that surrounded the whole was solid-looking against the ephemeral translucence of the interior.

"This embryo has shown good development and clean separation of the cells. We find we have less success when there is more fragmentation, like this." He pointed to a second embryo. Here the perfect geometrical shapes were interrupted by little bubbles in clusters that reminded John of the glycerine froth that burbled out of the plastic bubble pipes they played with as children. "But you never know. I have seen some great looking kids that started out as awful-looking embryos."

"Why did you use the bad ones?" asked Robin. "Did the parents choose them?" She felt oddly protective of the raggedy-looking little sphere. She could understand why someone might decide to give that less likely-looking embryo a shot.

"When you don't have a choice you use whatever you have." Dr. Aylmer looked tolerantly amused. "Not everybody has the luxury of eighteen embryos. Here is what I suggest. We have identified twelve embryos that appear to be growing well. We would like to transfer these three, and freeze the other nine. You often lose some in the thawing process, but nine should give you enough for several subsequent attempts, should that be necessary."

"What about the other six?" said Robin.

"If you want to freeze them all, you can," said the doctor. "I don't see the point, when you have nine high quality embryos,"

"Fine." said John. He could see that it was making Robin gloomy to part with any of them. It was perfectly understandable, when you thought about what she had been through to produce them. She ran a single finger along one of the photos, tracing the shaggy side of a smaller, less symmetrical ball of cells. John saw the glint of what might be tears forming in her eyes. Better to avoid the long good-bye. "Sweetheart, you know not every embryo develops properly. Let's trust Dr. Aylmer on this. I am sure he can identify all the embryos that are viable and we can freeze them. But right now, I want to move ahead with the transfer. Aren't you excited?"

The two week wait loomed in front of them as they went home with instructions to take it easy . No running, no hot baths, absolutely no sex. Worn out, Robin went to bed early. "I hope you feel better in the morning" said John, kissing her good-night, and the thought echoed in his head like a prayer: *please, please let her be better in the morning.* But on Wednesday there was no improvement and on Thursday her hands were puffy and her ring was tight on her finger. Friday, when he called from work, her voice sounded breathless. "I'm coming home right now," he said.

"You don't have to," answered Robin, sounding relieved.

"I do."

It was hard to tell if it was the added weight from all the fluid or the way she was curled up on her side so tight that her huddled mass seemed to have acquired greater density, but it looked to John when he walked through the door as though Robin was not so much lying on the couch as being absorbed into its worn upholstery. "I can't get up" she said, and he thought for a moment that perhaps it was true, that the indentation was not her body sinking into the ancient cushion but the fabric itself growing up around her like tweedy quicksand. He shook his head to clear the craziness.

"What do you mean, you can't get up?" he asked. The harshness of his own voice frightened and surprised him. "Literally? Sure you can sit up. I'll help you up."

"No, don't. I tried to sit up before. It hurts. Dizzy. I feel funny, John. I can't get any air into my lungs." Robin sounded exhausted with the effort of speaking. She did not try to stop him as he went for the phone. She heard him speaking as though it were in a dream, telling the after-hours answering service, *"Yes, it is an emergency. Weight gain, trouble breathing, abdominal pain. It has been going on for three days. No, wait, it has been going on for a week, maybe more."* I have to keep drinking, Robin told herself, staring at the cup of Gatorade sitting on the coffee table. It was very far away. John was here now, she thought. John would take care of her. Gratefully, she closed her eyes.

In the hospital, there was a bench across from Robin's room where John sometimes sat, away from the sound of his wife's labored breathing. He got in the habit of waiting there while the doctors were doing their exam. He thought it was more respectful of her privacy, not that Robin had any awareness of his coming or going. She showed flickers of wakefulness as they poked and prodded, fluttering her lids while the doctors spoke to her in low tones, saying she might feel a little pressure here, or a stick there. The nurses, on the other hand, talked to her in booming, cheery voices, as though her failure to respond was a matter of deafness or intransigence.

Dr. Aylmer came out and took a seat next to John on the bench. He looked worn. "How are you holding up?" he asked. John shrugged. He glanced down as if the sight of himself might give him an answer to that question. There he was in the same clothes he had arrived in – was it 48 hours ago? Then it must be Sunday, John reasoned. You wouldn't have guessed that a senior guy like Aylmer would be at the hospital on a Sunday evening. The thought frightened him and he refused to consider it further.

"She's very sick, John." The doctor spoke as though compelled, like a little boy told to say he's sorry. "She's leaking fluid from her bloodstream into the abdominal cavity. That's why there is all the swelling. At the same time, the loss of fluid is making her blood too thick. We've been trying to hydrate her aggressively, but she has not responded as well as we might have liked. When the blood gets thick and sludgy like this we worry about things like clots and strokes. Also, her kidney function is not good at all. I have to tell you honestly, this is a dangerous situation."

"What can you do?"

"We will try inserting a catheter to drain off some of the fluid. That will make her more comfortable and it should make it easier for her to breathe. Also, it may lessen the burden on her heart, because it won't have to pump against all that extra weight. But right now those empty follicles are continuing to dump hormones directly into her abdomen and until that stops, we can't make this go away. I'd like to tell you that I am sure it will get better, but frankly I don't know what to say. We've never seen a patient get so sick, so fast." John felt a tug of nausea. "And there is one other thing."

"What's that?"

"Generally ovarian hyperstimulation syndrome gets worse with pregnancy. So the fact that your wife is so sick is very likely a sign that one or more of the embryos has implanted."

"I'm sorry Dr. Aylmer, but let me get this straight. You are telling me that my wife could die. That is what you are saying here, right?"

"I think – it is possible. Not, I would say, likely. But possible."

"And you think I give a damn about whether or not the IVF was successful? When it could kill her? I don't – I don't appreciate the great irony that my wife may die pregnant." Tears stung his eyes.

"You misunderstand me, Mr. Hogan. My point is that if Robin is pregnant, it may help her medical condition if we terminate the pregnancy. I tried to discuss this with your wife. I believe that she understood what I was saying to her. I asked her for permission to terminate a pregnancy if necessary and she refused."

"She doesn't understand. Of course you have to end it. Can you do that right now?"

"With all due respect I think she did understand. I suggest you try to talk to her. If her condition continues to deteriorate and I can't communicate with Robin, I may ask you to make that decision on her behalf. But for now, we are obliged to follow her wishes."

"No!" John heard himself shouting and lowered his voice. "Dr. Aylmer, I don't think my wife is competent to make this decision in her current state. Even before she got sick. She's not rational on this subject anymore. She was sick as a dog for days before the transfer – I knew she was sick, and I didn't tell anyone. She was willing to risk anything to get pregnant and I didn't want to deal with it. If something happens to her now, I will have to live with that guilt for the rest of my life. But I am not going to make the same mistake twice. I am not going to go along with her craziness this time. If Robin is pregnant, I want it gone."

"I understand your feelings, Mr. Hogan, but there is nothing I can do. Talk to your wife. I can only suggest that you talk to your wife."

Chapter 4

John sat slumped in a chair in Robin's empty room, clutching his cell phone and staring into space. He had no idea how long this draining procedure would take. A nurse passing by stuck her head in the door. "You can't use that in here," she said, glaring at the phone as though it were a loaded gun, and John slid it into his pocket obediently. Later, he would need to call Kathleen and Michael. Perhaps by then he would have hit upon what to say. If he told them how serious it was, they might want to fly up to Boston. They might even help him talk some sense into Robin. But what would they think, when they saw her? They would stare at her, swollen and gasping, in the hospital bed. It was better, John thought, much better, if they did not come.

If Robin died, and they did not get a chance to say good-bye, they would never forgive him. But what would anything matter, if she died? They would sense his culpability in the event, John felt certain of that – everyone would. And it made no difference anyway; he was nothing to them if Robin was gone. Son-in-law. They were very fond of their son-in-law, or they had been until he dragged their daughter up to Boston. He'd caught a whiff of it then, the conditional nature of their love. If he lost his Robin, they would not comfort him, and he could not comfort them. They would look past his grief to a time when his life would move along, while theirs remained mired in loss. John tried to imagine himself at some future date, with only a lingering shadow that hung over a new life and a new family. No, it was not possible. This was his life. This was the life he had chosen, the one he was going to have, a life here, with the woman he loved, and not some sad tale of loss and second chances.

But this was crazy: crazy and pathetic and morbid. Twenty-nine year olds did not just die. Women didn't just die having babies anymore. This wasn't the stone age; this wasn't some godforsaken south-of-the-Sahara African village where the struggle for survival took the young and the fit as well as the aged and the weak. It would not happen. He would make Robin see that she didn't need to hold on to this pregnancy, not when they had nine frozen embryos waiting there. He would call Robin's parents later, when the crisis was over, and he could be calm and reassuring. *It was really scary*, he would admit. *Thank God Robin's feeling so much better.*

Robin did look better when they wheeled her back into the room. Almost fifteen pounds of fluid drained off, the nurse reported – a painful process, but the improvement was almost instantaneous. She could breathe again. She could talk. The doctor had cautioned her that she was not out of the woods yet. If she was pregnant – and he was sure she was pregnant – then she had to expect that her symptoms would recur, and perhaps even get worse. Recovery would be gradual and take a number of weeks; meanwhile, the IV drip and the oxygen supply would help. "I have to keep my oxygen on all the time, even if I feel better" she murmured, "because not enough oxygen in my blood might be bad for the baby."

"Robin." John sat uncomfortably on a corner of the bed. "About that. Listen. It was a mistake, going ahead with the transfer when you were already sick. I don't know if you understand how serious this thing is. If you are pregnant, we should end it right now. At this point, the only thing that matters is getting you well. Then, when you are better, we can try again."

"End it? It? This is our child, John. You don't throw that away and start again. I'll do whatever is necessary to save the baby. It's okay. I feel much better now."

"It's is not a question of what you can put up with, sweetheart. People have died of this. The risk is unacceptable. I know you hate the idea, but you have got to be reasonable. I can't let you endanger yourself. If you get worse – I can't even think about that. You have to protect yourself. It's not fair to me, or your parents, or anyone else who loves you. I won't agree to this, Robin."

"You already did agree to it, John. You knew when we started that there were risks. We signed off on it, both of us. Okay, maybe we shouldn't have done the transfer, but we did. Don't worry, darling. I will be fine. God will watch over me. I feel it. Have some faith, John. I have prayed for this baby for so long. This is nothing. It's nothing. The important thing is to protect the baby."

"Baby? There is no baby, not yet. There are three embryos, and we have nine more of them on ice in the clinic waiting to go. It's a few cells – a handful of cells. There's no person there. Robin, please. I can't live with myself if something happens to you. I have to insist, no. No."

"Don't yell at me, John. I will not give them permission to do an abortion. You don't think that's fair to you? To you? What about what is fair to the child? It doesn't matter how many cells it has. It has a soul. It's in God's hands now. Jesus will watch out for our child."

"Jesus? Jesus didn't make this choice. We made this choice, and we can change our minds. It's not too late. It's not a baby. It can't feel pain. It can't feel love. That's your soul you feel. That's your love. Whatever life you believe is in there right now is also in each of the other embryos. Please, Robin, think rationally."

"I am thinking rationally. If I am pregnant – God willing – then I will do everything I can to protect the baby. How can you ask me to have an abortion? I don't believe in abortion. It's wrong. I won't murder our baby, John. You can't ask me to do that."

"Robin, you are a million times more important to me than some dream of a child that does not even exist. Please. We will have a baby soon. I know we will. Do the safe thing. I can't risk losing you."

"I can't do it, John. It's wrong. I couldn't live with myself."

"If you are alive, we will have the chance to work that out."

"It's not your decision. It's my decision."

Well, that's the bottom line, thought John. It doesn't matter what I think. She would make the decision and he would face the consequences. "Dammit, Robin," he said, his hands slapping his sides in frustration. It was so unfair of her to put him in this situation. But then he looked at her white face, worn with the effort of talking. It was no wonder she wasn't making sense. It would be unkind to continue arguing with Robin in her current state. He needed to take care of her and regroup.

Mickey might help, thought John. She would listen to him. He would sweep all this bullshit aside and make her see what was necessary. In what way was one microscopic dot more like a baby than all the others sitting there in the clinic? Mickey would find some way to make her see. And Mickey could not be threatened like a guilty dog with the evidence of his own acquiescence: the scrawled signature on the informed consent; the inability to see what was right in front of his face; the failure to speak when he had a chance. Anyway, Robin looked pretty good right now. Maybe she wasn't even pregnant. Maybe the symptoms would not reappear. No use borrowing trouble.

But she was miserably ill by the time they got the pregnancy test back. "Positive," John whispered into her ear, and she nodded, her eyes staring straight ahead. Mickey came to visit prepared with a collection of unassailable arguments but was undone by the sight of her familiar, distorted self. Robin was happy to see him; her brown eyes lit up in her swollen face and she panted, "Mickey, you came" with something like delight. He stayed for an hour, talking about nothing, trying to make her smile.

There were better hours and worse hours. John, in retrospect, was never able to pinpoint the moment when he knew it was going to be okay

. She always felt better after they tapped the fluid; perhaps by the third or fourth time, the relief began to last a little longer. She sat up a little more easily. One evening he realized it had been a full day and more since he had looked at Robin gasping for air and felt panic slide its cold hand down his throat and squeeze his guts. Eventually, there were more good days than bad days. Four weeks after she was admitted to the hospital, Dr. Aylmer announced that Robin could go home the next morning. I can call her folks and let them know, John thought. A painless phone call, the first painless phone call, just checking in with some decent news at last. The idea of it gave him a spreading sense of pleasure. It would be so nice not to dread the sound of his own voice.

"Michael!" Kathleen trilled, "Michael, pick up the phone. It's Robin." Robin noticed that her mother's usual unhurried drawl had gone tremulous. "It's so good to hear your voice again, sweetheart. How are you feeling? Now, don't talk yet; wait for your father. Is something wrong? John was telling us yesterday you were feeling so much better. Thank God. I was so scared. I was as nervous as a long-tailed pussycat in a room full of rocking chairs. But you're alright now? Wait; wait! Okay, here's your Daddy."

"Okay, Mother? Daddy?"

"I'm right here, honey."

"We had our ultrasound today."

"Already? You can already see pictures of the baby, so soon?"

"Just to check for a heartbeat. You can't see much, just a dot, and a beating heart. Or, in our case, two beating hearts."

"The baby has two hearts? Oh dear, Robin, you know this is just the sort of thing I was worried about with the tampering,"

"Kathleen, don't be foolish." Michael's voice cut in, impatient and husky, "They're having twins. Two heartbeats means twins."

"One per baby, Mom." Robin sounded elated. "Thank the Lord." She had wept with happiness, seeing the first and then the second blinking signal on the screen, with the steady whoosh-whoosh echoing amplified through the room. Then came the long search for baby number three, and a collective sigh of relief when Dr. Aylmer announced that the final count was two. Silently, Robin felt a passing twinge of sadness for the one that didn't make it. But it was easier this way, for her tired body, and for the other babies, and for John, who looked excited and relieved and overwhelmed. His eyes glinted at her as he rubbed her neck and mouthed 'what have we done?' She watched the funny half smile on his face. She recognized the look, but could not remember when she had seen it last – that hyperactive delight, boyish and intense. It had been a long time.

This was it for him, Robin realized. All those weeks, and this was the first moment he had permitted himself to understand what it meant. But he was committed to them now. He would do anything for his babies now. All that stuff that he had said earlier – it didn't matter anymore; she would never mention it again. She made an effort to be sure that no trace of her smile said, '*I told you so.*'

Chapter 5

Meredith Schuyler was not, as she reminded herself, vain. Still, trotting past the mirrored wall of the duty-free shop, she was not entirely comfortable with her own reflection. Taken by surprise, she always turned out to be a little shorter and a little older than she remembered being – not old, of course, but not the sweet young thing she expected to see staring back at her. She was a pretty woman, with brown hair untouched by gray at age thirty seven, and a body that was petite but not without substance. Meredith smiled her most serene smile, and the lines disappeared. Still, she did not look zen. She did not look like someone who had been to yoga class every day that week. In fact, she was rather red in the face, and the tendrils she let escape from her pony tail no longer looked so charmingly pre-Raphaelite, all damp and sticking to her neck.

"Lindsey!" she called out to the woman in front of her, "slow down." The brisk rat-a-tat of her friend's heels on the airport floor stopped abruptly. The wheels of Lindsey's carry-on swiveled neatly as she turned. She raised a single finger to her lips and pointed at the phone attached to her ear. "Lindsey," Meredith whispered, "we have lots of time. No need to hurry." Lindsey smiled at her fondly and nodded. She took a few slow steps and then resumed her previous pace.

Meredith sighed, and shifted her heavy carry-on bag to the other shoulder, so that now she listed to the right. For the hundredth time, she wondered how Lindsey managed to move so quickly in three inch heels. "Of course I can walk in them," Lindsey said, when Meredith asked. "They are my shoes. Did you think I was going to wear tennis sneakers with the Prada pant?" Tall and whippet thin, Lindsey towered over Meredith even in stocking feet. Her hair was dyed an artful shade of honey-gold, and her roots were dyed darker brown to cover the grey. You couldn't have grey hair if you were the editor-in-chief of a magazine called *Twentysomething*.

Meredith tugged at her arm as they got onto the moving sidewalk and Lindsey moved reluctantly to the right, pulling her bag behind her to allow people to pass. "Yes," she said into the phone, "I am aware that it is difficult to do a story on Monica Lewinsky without mentioning the President's private parts. But not that word. I don't care. Nothing too cute, and nothing that sounds like pornography. And you absolutely cannot use the term blowjob." A man in a grey suit edging by gave her a startled look, and Lindsey stared back at him, her face impassive. "Try to do something different from what everybody else is doing. We want something our girls can relate to. Sex with the boss – bad idea! Forget the politics. Nobody cares." She smiled apologetically at Meredith as she paused. "Well, they can call it what they want, but it is still sex in my book. And I absolutely need to see finished copy on this before it goes in. Fax it. They must have fax machines in China." Lindsey hung up and grinned at Meredith. "Honestly, there is no roadmap to follow for some of this stuff. What would you do?"

"Me? Don't ask me. I don't think I could write about it at all. Imagine how hard it must be on their family members. Think how Monica's mother must feel. And Chelsea."

"Brutal," she agreed. "Well, you'd be one heck of a journalist. Remind me not to hire you."

"Lindsey," Meredith asked, "you never told me how things are going with that guy you were so excited about last summer."

"Done," Lindsey declared. "No chemistry. Zero. I was really surprised. He seemed like my type exactly. But he put his tongue in my mouth and I thought, oh my god, I have to get out of here. Which was a problem, since we were at my apartment."

"What did you do?"

"I developed a sudden overwhelming urge for a latte. We walked down the block and on the way home I realized that it had gotten late and that I had to be up early."

"You might have given him another try. Maybe it would have gotten better."

"No, I've gone down that path before. You can't manufacture chemistry. I've spent months trying, making out with absolutely lovely guys that kissed like St Bernard puppies, until finally you find yourself thinking that if he drools in my ear one more time I am going to smack him with a rolled-up newspaper. And by then, you have a whole history with the guy, so you can't just say thanks for the latte and stop returning his phone calls. You have to have long, dull, self-flagellating conversations and they want to know *why, why, why* – and what can you say? It's not you, it's your tongue? Seriously, it's just awful."

"I don't know," said Meredith.

"Did you feel something for David right away?"

"Yes, " she admitted. "I did. It was pretty primal."

"I rest my case. He's great, by the way. Not your usual type at all. Doesn't seem like he suffers under the compulsion to save the world."

"He cares. I know he cares. But he has a business to run and a lot of people depend on him. He does so much for the people who work for him."

"And they make lots of money for him. How lovely for everybody – including you. That's very nice birthday present you have on."

"This?" said Meredith, fingering the red stone set into a thick gold chain. "Do you think this was expensive? I hope he didn't spend too much."

"Ninny. Of course it's expensive." Lindsey frowned at her. "I shouldn't have told you. Now you will probably go sell it and give the money to all the poor sad girls at the Center."

"I won't! I promise. David made enough of a contribution at our last fundraiser. He really understands the value of legal services for women in transition."

"Oh I'm sure. It's not like he could have had any other motivation."

"If you are suggesting that David only gave money because I work there, I am certain you are wrong. He was very moved. It touched his heart."

"All I'm saying is, I'm not entirely convinced that his heart was the body part involved here. But it's very sweet of you to believe otherwise. And very sweet of him to care. So tell me, are you guys serious?"

"I think we might be." Meredith smiled. "I don't want to jinx it."

They reached the gate with an hour to spare. "Why on earth did I get here so early?" Lindsey asked Meredith. "You would think we were walking to China, I left so much extra time."

"You are excited," said Meredith. "It's very understandable. It's not everyday you fly off to the other side of the world to meet your child."

Lindsey nodded. "I can't wait to get on the plane, even if it means turning off my phone." She started to press a button and then stopped. "Do you want to call David before we board?" she said, offering the sleek silver rectangle to Meredith.

"Oh, no," Meredith said, and then reconsidered. "Maybe I should. He was so sad when I was leaving last night." Meredith turned slightly pink at the memory. She poked uncomfortably at the phone's tiny buttons. "Hey," she said, "we're at Logan. And I miss you already."

"I miss you too." David's voice was pleasingly gruff. "And two weeks is a long time."

"I can't believe I am going to be out of the country for the whole World Series."

"It's just going to be the Yankees again. You don't want to see that."

"I don't know what I would have done if the Red Sox had won. How could I leave?"

"Luckily for you, that was never going to happen."

"No," Meredith reluctantly agreed. "No miracles this year. Except Lindsey getting a baby. That's a pretty big miracle."

"Yeah," David agreed. "Good luck. See if you can help Lindsey figure out which end to diaper." She could feel him smiling. She said good-bye and handed back the phone.

"Pretty great, isn't it?" Lindsey asked, putting it in her bag. "You should get one."

"Oh no," said Meredith. "I would never use it."

"You'd be surprised," said Lindsey.

They were flying business class. Lindsey's treat, of course. Meredith's objections had been swept aside: Lindsey was not prepared to make the trip in coach, and she could hardly be expected to enjoy her champagne if her friend was languishing in the back. Meredith felt uncomfortable taking possession of one of the oversized leather seats, watching the rest of the passengers file by with their backpacks and their neck pillows, those with small children juggling bags full of food and distractions for the long flight. A few stared at her with a frankness that she found disconcerting; she wanted to stop them and explain herself. They have the wrong idea about me, she thought. I would switch with that woman with the baby if there was any way to do it that wasn't so awkward. She sat forward in her seat and waited for them to pass. To her right, Lindsey looked out the window at the ground crew. "God, I hope they don't lose anything. I will go ballistic if they lose my luggage. I have all this stuff in there I need – these cute little kimono shirts, special bottles and formula, the perfect sling that holds the baby just the right way. Good luck finding one of those in China if those knuckleheads lose my bags."

"What type of sling?"

"It goes around one shoulder like a little hammock. I was told it maximizes body contact. The woman at the information session said it was the best way to promote bonding. She seemed extremely concerned about bonding." The flight attendant leaned in to offer them a drink before take-off and then, a small handful of warm nuts later, they were in the air, settled in for flight number one, that would take them as far as Tokyo.

Three flights, and there was no accounting, after a while, for what time it might be back home, or when they might expect to be hungry, or how many naps it took to equal a full night's sleep. They had eaten dinner, and then lunch, and then breakfast, like time travelers on a particularly gracious trip back into the past. Now they stood on the tarmac in the city of Nanning blinking in the bright sunshine, moving through the routine bustle of disembarkation with a burst of nervous energy that felt precarious. Meredith was excited but she sensed exhaustion creeping in, and the likelihood that she would melt along with the morning chill of early Fall.

Everyone seemed happy to be off the rickety-looking airplane that had carried them from Guangzhou to Nanning. A bus brought passengers from the landing strip to the terminal, and following close behind them were a few battered trucks carrying their bags and a small army of men, all of whom jumped off the minute the truck stopped, grabbing the luggage and hurrying it to a central rack. Lindsey, eyeing them carefully, looked optimistic. She was okay now, Meredith thought. There was not a trace left of the anxiety that had surfaced midway through the dim facsimile of night on the plane, when Lindsey woke her shaking and near tears. "I am so afraid," she whispered. "I've looked at her picture a thousand times and she looks absolutely beautiful to me but what if I get there and it just doesn't happen? What if there's no chemistry?"

"You're going to love that baby, Lindsey. You're going to love the baby because she is yours. If you don't feel it right away, you'll just have to give yourself a little time. How can you not love her, when she needs you so much? You are going to be the most important person in that little girl's life."

"Maybe she'll hate me."

But that was impossible, Meredith thought. Babies love their mothers, and mothers love their babies. It would be fine. Smoothing the hair off her friend's forehead, she comforted her, talking in low tones amid the unhearing blanket-shaped mounds that were the other passengers nestled in their reclining seats, sleeping restlessly as the plane hurtled through time zones, whisking them, eyes closed, into the future.

And now here she was, back in action. She barely looked rumpled, in the sort of simple white shirt and black pants that looked stylish on Lindsey and just plain on anybody else. She strode off and then reappeared a few moments later, having recovered their luggage, found their guide, and rounded up the two other couples who were here with the same agency. "Come on, Meredith, there's a van outside." She waved her hand at a several Chinese men in orange vests. "Those guys will take the bags."

There was plenty of room in the van. The guide took the front while the six dazed looking Americans piled in behind. Two women in their early thirties sat in the back row. One was round-faced, with short brown hair and a friendly smile, and her companion was an athletic looking woman, bigger-boned and angular. The couple in the middle seat were older: a jovial, frosted blond in pink sweatpants that pulled tight across her wide bottom, and a man in a neatly tucked in button-down shirt, skinnier than his wife, with a head of hair as thick as sod. He had a face that probably had looked middle-aged at twenty-five; he looked middle-aged now as well, when he was perhaps forty-five. He'll look middle-aged at seventy, Meredith thought.

"So what is the plan from here?" Lindsey asked the guide. "How far is it to the hotel?"

"Oh no; we are not going to the hotel at this time." His English was very clear. "Now we will be driving to the village where is the orphanage. About one hour drive away."

There was a low murmur of surprise from the back. "To see the babies? We're going directly to see the babies?" Lindsey looked aghast.

"Yes" he continued cheerfully. "The foster parents have all ready for you with the babies."

"We meet the babies and then what happens? Then we go back to the hotel? Because we don't get the babies until tomorrow."

"No, everybody get their babies today."

"This is impossible." Lindsey sounded authoritative. "The agency told me that we would have twenty-four hours before we went to pick up our child. I think I would be better prepared with a good night's sleep."

"I am sorry." The guide pantomimed a face of great concern. "It is not possible to change arrangements now. Everybody has been gathered together for the meeting. Now you meet the babies and the foster mothers. If you come tomorrow, the foster mothers are already gone home. No opportunity to ask questions. You will have many questions about your baby."

Lindsey turned to face the others in the car. The two women in the back were holding hands, their faces pale and excited. "Did you expect to go straight to the orphanage?" she asked the others. No, they all agreed. They had not.

"Well my goodness" said the blond woman, looking unperturbed. "there's a good lesson here about life with children. You never quite know what will happen next."

"Do you have other children?" Lindsey asked her.

"Oh, yes. We have four."

"Four?" repeated Lindsey, dumbfounded.

"Yes." Her smile became more resolute in the face of Lindsey's amazement. "Charles and myself had three, and then two years ago we adopted a little boy from Paraguay. He is four years old now – doing so well, God bless him – but they gave us a lot of trouble with the paperwork down there."

"Very difficult," said her husband.

"So we heard this was a much more straightforward process and – well, here we are." She smiled again. Her eyes were shiny.

"You two don't have other children?" the taller woman in the back asked Lindsey and Meredith.

"I don't have any children," Meredith said in a puzzled voice, and Lindsey answered with a grin and a wave of her hand.

"We're not – I am adopting the baby by myself. I am Lindsey; this is Meredith, my best friend from home, and she was just so good as to make this trip with me." There was a little awkwardness to the silence, which Lindsey quickly filled. "This is my child. Here's a picture. Lily. She is nine months old."

"Oh, a little one" said the blond woman, introducing herself. Her name was Linda, and they were from North Carolina. Linda and Charles were adopting an eighteen-month-old they planned to call Kaylee. "She's what they're calling a 'special needs' baby, but the doctors here say there is nothing wrong with her except a little mark on her back from a fall." Linda pulled out her own pictures. The smiling baby looked small but her features and her shape were entirely normal. One picture was a close-up of her back; there was a small scar at the base, along her spine. In the most recent photo she was walking, a delighted expression on her face, arms raised high above her head.

From the third row, Mary and Louisa passed their pictures forward. The daughter they were waiting to meet was almost two. "We asked about a younger baby," said Louisa, the round-faced woman, "but the wait was too long. Next time, perhaps." The chatter in the van was animated, but died away as the minutes ticked on. Coming from the airport they had skirted the edge of a modern looking city, but as they passed further out, moving from valley to valley, the cars grew scarce and they saw fewer houses. They sped past bicycles, many with riders precariously balancing boxes, bales and passengers. The van pulled into a small town and passed a cluster of buildings with square fronts painted white. The roofs looked like wood but perhaps they were clay, corrugated and dusty with age. The eaves formed a pattern like an endless snake, adding an incongruous decorative touch to the flat simple faces of the village homes. Turning right, they headed down a rough road that was pitted and muddy. Everyone was silent as they lurched along.

The orphanage was two stories high, a nondescript grey concrete structure looming block-like over the small parking lot. They climbed out of the car. You could hear children shouting in the back, but out front it was barren, featureless and unwelcoming. The guide led them all to the entrance. He knocked and they heard footsteps running. The door was opened by a woman with a wide smile and a cheerful expression. "Welcome; welcome" she said, ushering them inside. "You have nice trip, I hope?" Meredith felt her heart beat faster, and she reached out to squeeze Lindsey's hand. Lindsey squeezed back but did not turn her head to look at her. She looked ashen. "Are you ready to meet the babies, all the babies?" asked the woman.

"Yes, ma'am" said Linda, and the others nodded mutely.

"Good; good." Does she always say everything twice, Meredith wondered? Maybe it was a Chinese thing. Or perhaps she was just excited. She asked them to wait in the entry and disappeared for two minutes or perhaps five; it felt like an eternity. When she came back, she led them down a long, drab corridor to the back of the building. "Come; come." Around the corner were a pair of doors, large swinging doors like the entry into an auditorium or some other public space. She had a small sheaf of papers in her hand. "Winsey?" she asked, looking at one of the forms.

There was silence. "Winsey?" she asked again.

"That is you," whispered Meredith, give her friend a gentle shove in the back. Stifling a half laugh, Lindsey moved forward, raising her hand. The woman pushed open the door and led Lindsey toward the far corner. Meredith trailed after them. A woman, perhaps twenty-five, sat on a couch holding a little girl in leggings and a clean, threadbare tee shirt. The child eyed Lindsey gravely as she approached. With one little fist she clung tightly to the young woman's arm. Lindsey sank down next to them on the couch, reaching out a hand, palm up. Lily stared back at her. Meredith wondered if Lindsey looked foreign to the child. Effortlessly, intuitively, the baby could recognize the unfamiliar architecture of this new face – that was obvious. Could she see the differences, or only the similarities? They would never know what she was thinking.

Lily looked from Lindsey's blue eyes to the hand stretched in front of her like an offering. Slowly, she reached out one arm. Meredith could see Lindsey's face as the baby's hand touched hers. There was no expression in it but yearning. She ran her hand along Lily's head, and the baby pulled back, stiffening. The young woman soothed her, murmuring in encouraging tones. Seeing the two of them together, Meredith felt a tug, imagining what she might be feeling. She spoke softly to the child and it was not possible to tell if her voice was sad.

In the near corner of the room Meredith saw a small basket of simple toys. She picked out several and brought them to Lindsey, who offered them, one by one, to the baby. "I wish I'd thought to bring the things from my bag," Lindsey said regretfully, but apparently the old toys were fine, because after a moment or two Lily's grip on her foster mother relaxed, and letting go of her sleeve, she lowered herself down to crawl along the couch. Lindsey held one toy shoulder-high, and the baby put a hand on her leg, leveraging herself up toward the small cloth ring. Laughing, Lindsey brought the toy down to the child's waiting hands, and was rewarded with a smile. She poked the baby softly in her stomach and said "you did it!" and both of them giggled. Quietly, Meredith began to cry.

Eventually, the woman who had led them in returned to translate so they could communicate with Lily's foster mother. Lindsey asked her about when she got up in the morning, which foods she liked, what time she napped. Was she very prone to cry? Not usually; once in a while. She was very sad if woken up too soon from her nap. What could you do when she cried? Hold her. The young woman, talking quickly, made a cradle of her arms, and the translator explained: "If she is happy, this baby wants to be always moving, crawling, already trying to stand up. But when she is sad or tired or scared, baby wants always to be held."

"Good thing I brought my sling" said Lindsey to Meredith, and she grabbed Lily around the waist and tried to pick her up, but the baby wrestled away, arching her back and twisting to get back on the couch. Lindsey laughed, and put her down. Lily climbed into her lap and walked her hands up the white shirt, grabbing Lindsey's cheek with chubby fingers. Lindsey ran her hand across Lily's wispy hair. "No pigtails for a while," she said, smiling.

Another baby's cry startled her, and Meredith realized suddenly that she had been oblivious to the dramas unfolding in other parts of the room. She looked up. On one side, a happy-looking toddler sat in Louisa's lap eating cookies and staring at Mary, who sat across from them, holding the little girl's toe. On another couch, Charles and Linda seemed engaged in a long conversation with their child's foster mother. The translator was back with them, and so was the guide. Linda held the baby, who was no longer crying. She jiggled her expertly with one arm as they talked, and the child's head was against her shoulder. Her free hand stroked the baby's face gently, but her expression was anxious.

That foster mother was not so young, and she spoke in an animated fashion to the guide. Her voice was loud. She pointed to the baby's back and shook her head. Her words came very rapidly, and

Meredith could see that little of it was getting translated. After a while, the foster mother took the baby from Linda and set her on the floor. She started to cry again, but the foster mother shushed her, pulling the child up to a standing position. With a finger tightly held in each hand, the little girl took several tentative steps as the woman walked backwards, urging her on. A smile spread over her little face, and Meredith was reminded of the radiant child in the photograph. Wasn't she walking in that picture? With a pang it occurred to her that they had misunderstood: the child's arms were not raised in triumph over her head. Some unseen figure supported her from above and, smiling, she walked towards them like a marionette with an invisible puppeteer, held upright so that she would not crumble back to earth.

Chapter 6

They had a little suite at the hotel, with a bedroom and a sitting area. "I think I will have them put Lily's crib there" said Lindsey, pointing to a small space by the sofa. She pronounced "Lily" in the self-consciously off-hand way in which a new bride might say, "my husband." The baby was still sound asleep from the car trip and Meredith was jealous. A nap sounded like a great idea.

The good-byes at the orphanage were hardest on Charles and Linda, whose baby cried desperately and pulled at her foster mother. The impassive woman detached the little hands from her clothes with gentle efficiency and gave Charles and Linda each a formal head-bob of farewell before strolling out of the room. All the Americans were unnerved by the intensity of the child's sobs. Mary and Louisa's daughter stopped eating her cookies and stared; her own foster mother spoke to her in a cheerful sing-song voice, and then gave the little girl a pat and slipped away. She held Louisa's hand, looking wary.

Meredith turned to watch Lily's foster mother, who was eyeing the baby intently, unsmiling. Meredith suspected she was struggling for self-control. She smiled ruefully at the woman, trying to convey without words how she shared and understood the terrible poignancy of this leave-taking, but the younger woman looked away as their eyes met, staring down at her feet. Hastily gathering her things, she ran her hand over the child's head, murmuring something in a low voice that might have been a blessing, and hurried from the room.

There was no ceremony in departure. They got into the suddenly crowded van, and with the whump of the door sliding shut, the three Chinese girls became Lily, Kaylee and Hannah. On the ride back, all the adults grew glassy-eyed despite Kaylee's continued screaming. The other women held their silent children, staring out the window and thinking, "thank god, thank god, thank god."

Meredith left Lindsey and Lily in the room and set off downstairs to rummage up some food. There was a decent looking restaurant in the hotel, with an English-language menu and little displays of fake food for the convenience of foreign guests. She ordered a couple of the more familiar looking options to go. Meredith spotted Charles across the room at a table by himself, and went over to say hello. "Sit down," he waved jovially toward the empty chair. "Join me!"

"I am just waiting for them to box some things up." Meredith sat, perching on the edge of her chair to highlight the temporary nature of the arrangement. "Lindsey is upstairs with the baby. We're starving!"

"Linda doesn't care for the Chinese food" said Charles pleasantly. "She finds the foreign food too spicy."

"What will she eat then?"

"I think there are some home-like places around in most of these Chinese cities. They have your McDonalds and so on. I'll get the hotel folks to help me find something. When we were in Paraguay, Linda could hardly locate anything she was willing to eat. Finally, we found this one little store that carried Snickers bars. She just about lived on those candy bars. Didn't think we were likely to get that lucky again, so this time round we brought along an entire suitcase full. She'll be very happy with that for now." Meredith wanted to laugh, but she felt constrained by the memory of the scene back at the orphanage, and the questions surrounding the health of their new daughter.

"How is she doing with the baby? Is everything okay?"

"Oh sure." Charles sounded sincere, although his face looked ragged. "She just cried a bit and went off to sleep. There's always a bit of crying with the older ones when they leave their home. A couple of days from now it'll all be fine. Never saw a baby yet that didn't take to Linda straight away."

But what about the walking? Meredith could not tell if his lack of concern was genuine or evasive. "Are you going to do her physical here or in Guangzhou?"

"We've got it all set up to do it there." Lindsey had made the same arrangements; all candidates for adoption had to have routine medical exams before the U.S. Embassy would issue their new passports and allow them to travel home. "Course we're not really going to know fully what's going on with her spine until we get her back to home. We tend to think, Linda and me, that she had some sort of surgery done. That little scar on her back don't look like the kind of thing you get by falling down. Everyone there at the orphanage was saying they didn't know, they couldn't say – whatever the cause is, it's from before she came to them. But we'll get her back to our own pediatrician and he'll get it all sorted out. He's a wonderful doctor. Took care of all our children. I don't imagine they have anyone like him over here."

Meredith wished him well and collected up her food. She wondered a bit at his attitude, hoping that Charles and Linda would not pay too heavy a price for being so cavalier. Didn't they even think of checking on the girl's condition now, when things could still be undone? She was glad Lindsey had been more careful. Also it was so much better having waited longer for a younger child – Lily seemed hardly to react at all to leaving her foster-mother. Everything was going according to plan.

Lily cried when she woke up from her nap. Meredith was in the bedroom attempting to get a little sleep, but the noise woke her. They both huddled around the baby, making soothing sounds. She sobbed against Lindsey's shoulder, burrowing her damp face into Lindsey's chest until she ran out of air and the crying became a rhythmic, hoarse catching of her breath; finally, lifting her head to look around, she returned to a full-throated wailing. It was an hour before she calmed down enough to accept the bottle. She was calmer for a time after she ate, until a hotel employee knocked on the door to deliver a fax for Lindsey. The baby crawled over when the door opened, staring at the new face in the room. As he closed the door behind him, she began to cry again. "Oh no, it's okay, little girl," said Lindsey, picking up the baby and tossing a cloth over her grimy shirt. She handed the papers to Meredith. "Can you stick this crap somewhere?"

Nighttime was a series of crying jags interrupted by periods of fitful, exhausted collapse. When they finally capitulated to the fact that it was morning and stopped pretending to go back to sleep, it was a relief. Meredith played with the baby while Lindsey took a quick shower to revive herself. "Didn't work," she announced, coming out in a towel. "I should have made it ice cold. I don't think I ever fell asleep in the shower before."

They staggered downstairs, Lindsey carrying the puffy-eyed Lily in her sling, and found the others already assembled at breakfast. Linda sat next to her husband with Kaylee ensconced in her lap, both of them looking content. She squeezed the little girl tightly with one arm. An empty Snickers wrapper was on the table in front of her. With a knife in her free hand she carved a second candy bar into thin slivers and transferred them delicately to her mouth. Louisa and Mary, looking battered, had Hannah perched on a chair between them, picking at some Asian cousin of the sticky bun. Lindsey asked them about their night, and the two of them groaned. "She was okay for a while," Mary elaborated, "and then it was like, visiting time was over and she was ready to go. She kept trying to tell us something, but of course we couldn't understand…"

"No question what she's trying to say," interrupted Louisa. "She wants to go home."

"True," agreed Mary. "She got so tired of us not understanding her, she finally just gathered up her little shoes and went to stand by the door. It was heartbreaking. She just stood by the door with her things waiting for somebody to come. We had to coax her away to get some food into her. Awful."

"You just have to keep believing that it will get better," said Louisa.

"I know. It's all for the best! At least, that is what I keep telling myself. Meanwhile I came over here with this idea that I was going to rescue some poor orphaned child, and right now I feel like a kidnapper. I swear, last night, if I had any way to get there, I would have taken the poor girl to her foster family and begged them to take her back."

"It always feels that way right at the start" said Linda soothingly. "I was beside myself with our little boy and all the screaming, I can tell you that. But you have to think about what kind of a life these children will have if they are not adopted. It's hard for a few days. But it is a blessing forever for these babies to come to the United States of America."

"Right, sure," said Louisa, giving Hannah a kiss as she wiped the sugar off the little girl's face. "We just need to get a decent night's sleep, and everything will seem better."

"Well, good luck with that!" said Linda, cheerfully skeptical. "I don't think anyone is getting much sleep this week!" She beamed at them as they packed up their gear and their daughter to head back upstairs. She turned to Kaylee, who held her blouse with both hands. "Say bye-bye to Hannah, sweetie. Can you say bye-bye?" The baby squirmed and clung tighter. "Can you say mama?" Linda pointed at herself. "Say mama?" Kaylee stared intently at her face. "Ma-ma," Linda encouraged her, smiling.

"Ma," said Kaylee.

"Good girl!" Linda cooed at the baby ecstatically. "Charles, did you hear her? She said 'Ma.' Good girl, Kaylee. That's right. Ma-ma." Linda put a small piece of Snickers bar in the baby's mouth.

"That's so wonderful!" said Meredith, pleased for her.

"Wonderful" agreed Lindsey, checking her watch, which was still set to Boston time. "Listen, Meredith, I'm done here. Do you think you could hold Lily for a bit while I run upstairs and take a look at that fax? Leave them alone for five more minutes and they're going to put references to penile anatomy in my magazine that will give my publisher a stroke." She handed the child and sling off to Meredith and waved good-bye to Linda and Charles with a friendly disregard for their appalled expressions.

Charles left the table as well, but Meredith and Linda lingered with the children. "It is so great," said Meredith, "that Kaylee is speaking already. That must be very reassuring."

"It is nice," Linda agreed. "But I wasn't very worried about that. They all start to talking sooner or later. Then you can't shut them up! Now we just have to get her up on her feet."

"What did they tell you at the orphanage?"

"Oh, they weren't too helpful there at all. I think they were mainly concerned with their own not being held to account for any problems she might have. And that foster mother! I didn't care for her. She didn't seem like a nurturing type of person at all. My goodness. Not what I was expecting in a Chinese person. She just kept saying 'We tell you special needs child. This special needs child.' But they told us Kaylee had hurt her back in a fall. You don't get this type of scar in a fall." Linda gestured Meredith closer, and raising Kaylee's dress, revealed a small, neat scar tracing vertically along the ridge of her spine, almost hidden in the elastic top of her diaper.

"You must be very, very angry at the people from the orphanage for putting you in this situation" said Meredith, patting her ample upper arm.

"Angry? Oh good lord no, I am not angry at them. I am so very grateful to them for helping to bring our Kaylee to us. When I think of what she would be if she stayed here – a crippled child, discarded by her own, no family, no Christmas, no love of Jesus to comfort her – it just makes me shudder. I could cry right this minute, thinking how easily that could have been her life. I am so grateful they brought her to us, so we can keep our little girl safe. I thank them for it. I thank them, and I thank the Lord."

With the hard exhale of a close escape, Linda sliced another morsel of Snickers bar and fed it into the waiting mouth of the little girl snuggled into her shoulder. What a lovely thing to say, thought Meredith. How stupid of me! Meredith reproached herself for assuming that their main concern would be to avoid getting stuck with a defective child. She had not been thinking like a mother. They were interested in protecting Kaylee, not in giving her back: that was how a parent would react. The more she thought about it, the more Meredith was convinced that she would have responded in just the same way. Lindsey might think she was a fool and a martyr – she could understand, naturally, that her friend would need to avoid situations that she could not handle. But her own impulse would have been to embrace the child. Of course; she could see that now. She smiled at Linda, anxious to convey how well she understood. "Thank goodness she has you. What a wonderful thing for her – for both of you." Kaylee bounced, pointing at what was left of the chocolate bar, and opening her mouth like a baby bird. Linda put one piece in the baby's mouth and one in her own. "Can you give them peanuts so little?" Meredith asked. "I thought I read somewhere that now they worry about peanuts and allergies."

"Well, it might be" said Linda with a laugh. "I can hardly keep up with all these new rules. But all my other children ate peanuts and it doesn't seem to have done them any harm. I imagine this one will survive the peanuts as well." Meredith shifted Lily in her lap and Linda looked warmly at the two of them. She was smiling. Despite the early hour, Linda wore thick pink lipstick and a dark liner around her eyes. "You're going to miss that one, when you get home" she said, nodding her head towards Lily. It was true, Meredith thought. It would be strange to say good-bye at the airport, and to recede into being what she was, a tangential figure in the child's life – one more of Mom's friends, insisting on a hug and a kiss. Linda interrupted her thoughts, leaning toward her with an air of intimacy. "Now I want to ask you a question." She lowered her voice conspiratorially, "Those other young ladies – I am having such a hard time figuring them out. Do you know which one is the mommy?"

Chapter 7

"Boys! Boys? Ya'all are awake, right? Because I want to get over to Robin's place and see those babies again before they are all grown up!"

Mickey stirred, turning towards Caleb, who opened one eye quizzically. Mickey shrugged apologetically. "My mother is in our kitchen in her pajamas," he whispered.

Caleb nodded. "What did you imagine would happen when you offered her the extra bedroom?"

"I imagined that she would say no. I had to ask, because she can't stay at Robin's place now that the boys are in the nursery and the living room is full of swings and little baby-holding devices. I just never thought she would actually do it."

"I'm glad she did."

"Yeah?" Mickey contemplated this. "I think we might have been better off with a bit less acceptance." He raised his voice, still sleepy-throated. "Alright, Mother, we were just getting up."

"Would you boys like some breakfast?"

Mickey made an uncertain face at Caleb, who looked blankly back at him. If Mom was going to try making herself at home, Mickey thought, they might as well play along. "Sure," he called out, taking care to sound enthusiastic rather than amazed.

Mickey was in less of a hurry than his mother to get over to Robin's house, having committed to spending the whole day admiring babies. Caleb, of course, could not be expected to join them for the marathon, but Mickey hoped he would make an appearance. It was hard to predict. He got funny about other people's children. He liked kids and they liked him; you could see that when he was with them, but there were always a lot of sighs and silences when they got back home. All the excitement around Robin's pregnancy and the birth of the twins had made Caleb moody and withdrawn. Well, it was his own damn fault if he couldn't have kids. Mickey had to make an effort not to fall into familiar patterns of recrimination and circular argument. One night last week they had spent an entire evening online looking at profiles of potential surrogate mothers. Neither of them mentioned any reason why this might not be a good idea. Instead, they debated about which of them was the fitter candidate for biological father. Caleb flexed his biceps and looked critically at Mickey's scrawny arms. Mickey mentioned his superior test scores. Caleb shook his head gravely. "SAT scores. Pathetic. That, in a nutshell, is the argument against you, Mickey. Standardized tests. I can't even believe you even went there. Frankly, it shows a serious lack of character. Now I have an excellent character and – I might add – I can thrown a baseball on a line from right field to third base."

There was a lot to be said for that, Mickey admitted. Perhaps that should count more than his own two inch height advantage. Really, it was almost impossible to decide. "What we should do," he said, in an inspiration that followed several glasses of wine, "is let fate decide. Let the sperm duke it out themselves. Mix the two samples together, and may the best gamete win."

"Wow," said Caleb, "I would so very much enjoy explaining that plan to whoever actually had to implement it. You have such a genius, Mickey, for making complicated things even more complicated. I don't know how you do it."

"It's a gift."

"Boys!" Kathleen Hanley trilled loudly over the sound of bacon frying. "How do you like your eggs?"

"Oh, about 25 years old," Mickey murmured, "and I am thinking perhaps Norwegian. I hear the Norwegians are tolerant. Tolerant and tall."

"Ssh" said Caleb, laughing. "Tell her scrambled. I think that's easiest."

"Tell her yourself. You can speak."

"No," said Caleb. "Too weird."

Mickey and his mother left for Robin's after breakfast without Caleb, who had some work to finish up. He did promise to meet them over there later in the day. Mickey must have looked skeptical, although he didn't mean to, because Caleb repeated his plan several times, as though his intentions were in doubt. "Give them my love," he yelled through the closing door. "Tell them I'll be there by early afternoon."

Mickey had seen the babies in the hospital, but he still couldn't tell them apart. "They don't look anything alike, Mick." Robin seemed genuinely perplexed. "Look. This is Ryan. He's much bigger."

"Robin, he is like six pounds. How much 'much bigger' could he be? They're both very little. They're very little people. Where are their hats? I liked the hats."

"I'll put a hat on Teddy, and then you don't have to keep asking me which is which."

"Well, they are both the most beautiful little boys," said Kathleen. "I don't have any trouble seeing the difference. I think Ryan is going to be darker, like his father. And Teddy might be a blonde like Mommy when his hair grows in. And I think they are both going to have your eyes, Robin."

"They were blue for a minute," said Robin, "but they are already turning brown." Teddy, wrapped like a sausage in his blanket and tucked in the crook of his father's arm, was starting to fuss. "John, do you remember if it was Teddy or Ryan I fed last? I know I nursed someone about twenty minutes ago. If that was Teddy, he needs to be burped. But if it was Ryan, Ted probably needs to be fed."

"I think it was Ryan, because I gave him the bottle during the night, and I noticed that Teddy was hungry earlier this morning. So I think that six am was Teddy and this guy waited until seven, and then Teddy again at eight. So the nine o'clock was probably Ryan."

"So he's hungry." Robin scooped up Teddy and went into the nursery. John followed her in. The two cribs took up most of the small room. At the far end they had tucked an upholstered rocking chair that was pale green with skinny white stripes. Robin sat down there and opened her shirt.

"Do you want something to drink?"

"That would be great." Robin stared at her swollen breasts, touching one and then the other appraisingly. "I can't remember which side I used last." From across the hall they heard Ryan begin to cry. Robin, adjusting the position of the baby on the pillow in her lap, looked up at John. Their eyes caught, and Robin gave a laugh that was half a groan, more exhausted than mirthful, not cheerful, but content. "Mother?" she called out, "could you get him?"

Her mother brought in the water, holding Ryan curled tight in one arm. "You didn't have to do that," Robin said. "John said he would."

"Oh now," said her mother, "he is busy talking to Mickey. Asking his opinion about some legal question that came up at work. It sounded very important."

"If it was important, he would ask Caleb. You don't go to Mickey for legal advice unless you are being oppressed. Mickey thinks John's business is without redeeming social value."

"Your daddy and I think it is so exciting."

Robin shrugged. She felt certain that her mother had no idea of the wild sums John and his co-workers tossed around, when they speculated on what Emoney might be worth this time next year. The price of tech stocks rose so quickly that it was impossible to put a figure on the real value of the company. The standards of comparison were all useless; the information, like the technology itself, was perpetually out of date. Robin had stopped listening months ago, when the numbers got so big that they ceased to have meaning for her. They looked at Amazon and Etoys and all the other harbingers of the future and argued about what it meant for them, but the truth was that no one knew. Not a soul.

"I think Mickey is real pleased that you wanted to stay at their place," said Robin.

"It was nice of him to ask," said her mother stiffly. "It didn't seem right to say no. He's my son. Why shouldn't I stay with him?"

"No reason."

"I have to say it is a nicer place than what I had imagined." Kathleen paused, remembering the disarray of Mickey's college rooms. "They have done a good job with the decorating. Nothing flashy." Robin wondered if her mother had been expecting disco balls and white leather upholstery. "And the new car is very nice as well."

"Yes," said Robin. "I like the BMW." She grabbed a cloth from the small table covered with pacifiers and stacks of diapers and a book called Mothering Multiples. Teddy had fallen asleep. Milk dribbled down his cheek into the warm folds of his neck and behind the perfect helix of his tiny ear. Robin dabbed at him softly. "Isn't he sweet?" she said.

"He is the sweetest thing I've ever seen, him and his brother. I can't believe you carried two babies at once. It must have been so hard on you."

"I don't know if it was hard," Robin replied. "I never did it any other way. It seems strange when you think about it, but when it happened it just felt normal. Besides, twins aren't that unusual anymore. It's the new normal."

"Well, it's like a miracle. I was sure there was going to be some problem. Between the IVF and how sick you were, it just seemed like there was bound to be something wrong. I drove your father crazy. But now they are here, and they are perfect."

"Perfect," Robin agreed.

"Two boys." Kathleen smiled. "Two boys is a handful."

"What will I do with all those old Barbie dolls we saved? That trunk must be still in the attic." She smiled ruefully at the thought. "Maybe next time."

Kathleen looked at her with alarm. "Darling, you cannot tell me you would think about doing this again, not when it almost killed you. You have two beautiful sons. I know you would have loved to have a daughter as well." But I already do, thought Robin, visions of soccer balls smaller than snowflakes floating through her mind. "Still, you cannot tempt fate. You have to count your blessings."

"They are a blessing," Robin agreed, yawning. "But oh my God, I am so tired. I could sleep for a week. I don't know how I am going to manage, when John goes back to work full time."

"Oh, sweetie, I hate to think of you being alone. He can't be spending all his time there, the way he was before the children came."

"He can do some work from home, but he's not much help to me when he's on the computer. He is going to slip out to the office this afternoon, since you and Mickey are here. There is so much pressure to get things done fast, because they want to do a big advertising blitz during the next Superbowl, and that means the site has to be up and running by this fall. Everything has to be perfect. God forbid you get your stampede of people trying to get on after the ads run, and the site crashes. That's what has John up in the middle of the night, worrying."

Mickey knocked and came in. He stood next to his mother, in the sliver of space between the two cribs. "Well, this is cozy," he said. "I thought I should clear out of the living room. John is on the phone about some emergency involving a virus."

"Really?" said Kathleen, alarmed. "I hope the babies don't get it."

"Computer virus, mom. The children are safe, unless he has downloaded something into them recently." He looked at Robin. "Is there anything I can do?"

"You can burp Teddy," said Robin, holding out the child, who was beginning to stir.

He stared at his nephew with a perplexed expression. "That sounds complicated. Is there anything I can do that doesn't involve touching a baby? They're squirmy, and they look breakable."

Robin laughed. "Okay. Why don't you run down to the deli and get us some sandwiches?"

Mickey looked relieved. "That I can do." His mother and sister were standing in the nursery as he left, jiggling up and down, each of them holding a boy tight to her shoulder. They were cute little creatures, thought Mickey, standing in line behind the lunchtime crowd at the deli. They appeared to require a great deal of attention for something with so limited a repertoire of activities. What would you do with one all day long? They had cribs and bassinets and little plastic seats covered in a bright blue fabric with trains on it, but both babies seemed to spend most of their time in someone's arms. How did Robin and John know what to do? When his sister handed him Ryan in the hospital, he was seized with a fear of dropping the child. "Watch his head," Robin said, and he did, staring at the tiny head and squeezing him so tightly that the baby started to cry.

It amazed him how badly Caleb wanted one of those. He had gotten more of a sense of it these past months, watching him as Robin and John talked about strollers and birthing classes and all that nonsense. At first he assumed that Caleb shared his own impatience; it did get boring, after all. But that wasn't it. Caleb was patient – too patient. It was sadness, Mickey thought. The silences were sadness.

Mickey felt badly, but then again, it might also be pointed out that this was a problem Caleb could fix, if he was willing to force the issue with his family. Otherwise, nothing would change. Their own conversations were like a child's game, just fantasy. *Let's pretend we are having a baby. I'll be the daddy. No, me.* It was pathetic. The thought that he could not have a child irritated Mickey, if only on principle, although given a choice he would have preferred one that arrived a little farther along the developmental path than these tiny, helpless creatures that his sister had produced.

Mickey had forgotten to take sandwich requests, so he decided on turkey for everyone, like Thanksgiving. That was appropriate. "Mayo on that?" the counter guy asked, his knife already thick with the glistening white spread. Mickey stared at it, and pictured small, wriggly bundles falling through greasy fingers.

"No!" he said. "No mayo."

What bothered him was that Robin and John might sense Caleb's reserve and take it the wrong way. The closeness that had developed between Caleb and his sister and brother-in-law made him very happy. They didn't merely tolerate him like his mother did. Tolerance was such a low bar. John and Caleb liked one another. Caleb was interested in what John did, which was more than you could say about Mickey himself. Business was a game to them, and they enjoyed it, the way people enjoyed doing things they do well, however fundamentally uninteresting they might be. Strategizing about how to make money reminded Mickey of gym class: a dull and bruising exercise that was necessary without being valuable.

They had circled one another warily at first, John and Mickey, the one suspecting disrespect and the other everlastingly on the alert for disdain. It was all easier now, with Caleb. Their differences were somehow amusing when Caleb was around. For this reason, it was particularly annoying that Caleb had decided to make Robin and John the object of his existential crisis. Mickey suspected they were beginning to notice; they both seemed disappointed when Mickey showed up without him.

Robin looked utterly mystified when she bit into her sandwich. "Mickey, there is no mayo on this. What were you thinking? Who eats turkey without mayo?"

"I didn't think it needed it."

"What kind of a Southern boy are you?" she replied, going to the fridge and taking out the mayonnaise. "It's not even fried! Of course it needs mayo."

She slathered John's sandwich and handed it to him where he sat, at the computer. "Thanks, sweetheart," he said. "Mickey, do you think Caleb is coming soon? I need to run into the office for a little while, and I was hoping to see him."

Mickey stared at his shoes. "I can try his Blackberry. He was working, and he said he had some errands to run." Caleb did not answer the phone. Mickey's foot jittered against the floor as he sat on the couch. It was inconsiderate, he thought. He could at least call and let us know. "I don't know where he is," he said. "You might as well go. Caleb won't mind."

"No, I'll stick around a few more minutes," said John. "It's fine.

John was in the kitchen cleaning up when the doorbell rang. Kathleen was holding a baby and Robin had stepped into the bedroom to fold a laundry load of tiny little shirts that buttoned at the crotch like Amish underwear. "I'll get it," Mickey said. He went down the stairs and opened the door. Caleb stood on the stoop, his arms full of boxes wrapped in blue and white paper covered with rocking horses. A large shopping bag hung from one wrist, and Mickey recognized the name of a bakery in the city. Two star-shaped mylar balloons said

"It's a boy." They fluttered in the breeze, and the ribbons that held them were wound several times around his hand. Caleb peered over the top of his packages.

"Are you going to let me in?" he asked. Mickey nodded apologetically, opening the door wider. Caleb moved past him to climb the stairs. Mickey stared after him, admiring his wide shoulders and narrow waist and the way he hesitated, and then moved, with quick, purposeful strides. It occurred to Mickey only in retrospect that he might have offered to carry one of the boxes.

Mickey watched his mother as Caleb walked into the living room. The balloons were a nice touch; she looked approvingly at them. She had brought the boys a pile of baby clothes – pajama things with feet, and two matching outfits decorated with horses and cowboy hats. Mickey found himself hoping that Caleb's boxes were not full of Swedish baby clothing or tiny hand-knit sweaters, but no – there were baby blankets, and sturdy little fleece jackets with pointy hoods and a full-sized baseball glove for each of the boys. "Wow" said John. "These are really good." He stroked the leather lovingly. "I wish I had a glove this nice."

"I guess they won't be able to use them for a while" said Caleb, looking at Teddy, who he was holding, swaddled, in one arm. "But in the meantime, they'll look good in their room."

"I think they might work well as recliners" said Mickey, measuring one of the gloves against Ted. "Baby Barcaloungers."

John stepped out of the room and returned carrying two baseballs. He put one into each of the gloves. "They should just about be broken in when the boys are big enough to put them on. Caleb – thank you, man." John stuck out his arm and the two of them shook, leaning towards one another in a half a hug over their clasped hands. "This is great. The gloves, the stuff, the cake – everything. I am so glad you made it here before I left, because Rob and I have something we want to ask you and Mickey." He looked suddenly solemn. "Robin and I have discussed this a lot, and we would be very happy if you and Mickey would stand as godfathers for the boys." Neither Mickey nor Caleb spoke. "You don't have to answer right away," John added. "You can think about it. We understand it is a big commitment."

Mickey crossed over to John and hugged him. "We'd be honored." He looked over at Caleb, who nodded. "No need to think about it. Honored." Mickey stole a glance at his mother, who looked like she might cry. He went over to give her a hug, and Caleb hugged Robin and then Robin hugged her mother. Caleb and John shook hands again, and Kathleen, who had sat down heavily on the couch, stood up again and came over to wrap her arms around Caleb in a brief and fervent embrace. Mickey, watching with something like wonder, put his arm over his sister's shoulder and squeezed, whispering, "Thank you."

CHAPTER 8

"There you are," said Meredith, as David slipped in next to her with a kiss. She gestured to the two empty seats, "Lindsey and Rick will be little late. She has some emergency at work."

"I'm shocked," said David.

"No, you are not," said Meredith. "But it gives us a few minutes alone. How was your day?"

"Great. We got the contract with Target for the mermaid swimsuits. Should be in the stores by May."

"That's wonderful! Do you make those here?"

"Darling, you know we don't. We don't make anything here but profits. Target will not even talk to you unless you are manufacturing overseas. They can't squeeze you enough on the price if you are making stuff here."

"Why do you have to work with them?"

"Why did Willie Sutton rob banks? Because that's where the money is. My workers would rather be underpaid and employed than fairly compensated and out of work."

"Which is always the rationale for treating people unfairly."

"Meredith, sweetheart, not everybody works at a non-profit." He smiled at her fondly. "We can't all be angels. You did want to renovate the kitchen, right? Wasn't that you last week, staring longingly at a Viking stove?"

"I've been thinking about that."

"Buy the Viking, Mer, it's all right."

"No, I've been thinking that we should put off the renovations. There's going to be dust and paint fumes and all that, and if I get pregnant, I don't think I should be exposed to that."

"So we wait until the baby is born?"

"Oh no! You can't do construction around a baby. Imagine what they could breathe in, or put in their mouth."

"So we can do the kitchen when the kid goes to college?"

Meredith considered this. "Maybe we should do it now, but fast. So it's all done before the placenta forms." She laughed. "Here I am planning around a pregnancy as though there was nothing more certain in the world. At thirty-nine."

"Thirty-nine is young," said David, who was ten years older.

"Easy for you to say," Meredith smiled at him. "Sperm don't age."

"Well, it looks like we missed an interesting conversation," said Lindsey, sweeping up behind them. "Now I'm even sorrier that we are late. It's all my fault. We had a crisis."

"Happy New Year," said Rick, leaning in to kiss Meredith.

"Happy New Millennium," said Meredith, rising to hug them both. "What was the crisis?"

"Oh, it was a disaster. We are doing this feature on creative drinking games, and it turned out that one of the models in the photo spread we did to accompany the article was underage. So we had to shoot the whole thing over again."

"What difference did it make?" asked Meredith. "It's not real alcohol you're using in the ad, right?"

"No, but those are real complaint letters I am going to get from Mothers Against Drinking Games if anyone notices. Besides, this girl looked about twelve, and if we used her we were going to get a ton of flack. So we had to reshoot it."

"Who do they think plays drinking games anyway?" said Rick. "Kids."

"No, Rick, this isn't Spin the Bottle we are talking about. We have some sophisticated stuff. We have a Sex in the City Drinking game. That's very hot with the college kids. Oh, and Merrie, you'll like this – we have one based on the election."

"How does that work?"

"Well if you are on Team Democrat you drink every time Al Gore says Lockbox."

"And if you are a Republican?" asked Rick.

"Every time George Bush says something ungrammatical."

"Team Republican is going to be Team Alcoholics Anonymous by November," said Meredith.

"Meredith," said David, "no politics at dinner. You promised."

"My fault!" said Lindsey. "I shouldn't have brought it up. I will change the subject. Meredith: Lily says hello."

"Darling girl! I wish she was here."

"Do you? Because I am very glad she is not."

"I'm sure you need some time to yourself," said David.

"I do. But that is not what I mean. I don't like taking her to restaurants. You know, she talks a blue streak at home but she won't say one word in public."

"She's just shy," said Meredith.

"Shy? Try selectively mute. I have to read the whole menu to her, and then it's like 'blink once if you want the chicken nuggets.' I mean, it's tons of fun if you really like charades. Which I don't. So we eat in."

"That's a real challenge for you," said Meredith. "I know you don't love to cook."

"No, Meredith. It's not that I don't love to cook. It's that I don't cook. Why would I cook? It makes no sense. You have to shop, and then make something, and then clean up. It takes hours. It costs money. And there are people all over the city happy to send me food that is already cooked and the plates to eat it on. I know you find it therapeutic, Mer, but as far as I am concerned cooking my own food makes about as much sense as knitting my own sweaters or distilling my own vodka."

"It wouldn't kill Lily to have a home-cooked meal now and then."

"It might, if I were the one cooking it."

The waiter poured wine for David, Meredith and Rick, and placed a cocktail in front of Lindsey. "You're drinking?" Lindsey said to Meredith.

"Not that," she replied. "It's pink."

"Don't judge my pink lemontini," said Lindsey. "It's what everyone's drinking in L.A.. But I was hoping you might be off the booze. No luck yet, I guess?"

"It's barely been a month," Meredith protested. "And there are no guarantees, at thirty-nine."

Under the table, David squeezed her leg. She worried too much about her age. "You could always adopt," Lindsey said.

"You know, we'll jump off that bridge when we come to it," David replied. "I just don't want Meredith to let this upset her. It will happen or it won't. It's not a referendum on her fitness."

"Oh, the ticking clock. This is exactly why I got Lily when I did."

"But it takes a while," Meredith said.

"It's true," said Rick. "What were you, thirty-four when that process started?"

"Thirty-five."

"Whatever. Why then? You didn't want to wait?"

"No. I knew I wanted a child. My second marriage had just broken up, and I wasn't interested in dating if I had to treat all my dates like they were potential sperm donors. We did an article on all the extra baby girls in China and I thought, I'll do us both a favor."

"You got lucky with her," David said.

"I did."

"You weren't worried?" David spoke casually. "You didn't worry if the kid was going to be very, I don't know, different from you?"

"You say that likes it's a bad thing, David. No, I wasn't worried about denying my child the great Evan's family legacy. Why would I? I come from a long line of alcoholics and chain smokers with anger management issues."

"Lindsey had all the drama growing up," Meredith said.

"I wouldn't have survived if I hadn't practically moved in with Meredith's family. So I figured a little dip into someone else's gene pool wasn't such a bad idea."

"Plus, you were so excited to get a baby with Chinese hair," Meredith reminded her.

"Yes, I thought, she'll never need to straighten it. And little Chinese girls look so cute in pigtails." Lindsey sighed. "Of course, Lily absolutely refuses to wear pigtails."

"Tragic," said Rick.

"You always take her side," Lindsey complained.

Lily was wonderful, Meredith thought. There was no reason they couldn't be just as lucky, and of course she of all people didn't care about having a baby who looked like her. Hadn't she worked for fifteen years now with girls of every color and faith, and taken each one of them into her heart? The girls at the Center were hard luck cases too, not always easy to love. That's why most of the staff came and went. But she thrived on it, accepting their excuses and their mistakes and occasionally some outright abuse, but most of them came around. All that bravado – they just didn't want to be judged. She accepted them all and they loved her, but at the end of the day she couldn't solve their problems, she couldn't really fix their lives, not like she could if it was her own child.

David would warm up to the idea; she wasn't worried about him. He would treat the adoption process like it was a giant favor for her, like it was the cooking classes she had signed them up for last spring. She knew better. He was a sucker for puppies and kittens. If she brought a child into the house, he would fall in love. Oh, but he would hate the vetting process like crazy, what they put you through. Twenty-seven year olds with social work degrees coming to your home to see if you could be trusted to feed and clothe an infant! Adolescent girls with abusive boyfriends weren't the only ones who didn't like being judged.

But what did that really matter? Lindsey as a single woman had made it through her home study – a minor miracle. "It will be fine," she insisted when Meredith expressed her concerns. "I just had the second bedroom repainted, and I put up those beautiful cove moldings, like I have in the living room."

"Honestly, Lindsey," Meredith said, "the home studies aren't run by decorators." But then maybe it hadn't hurt; money never hurt. Meredith had learned that lesson well in all the years when she didn't have any. Plus, Lindsey had her to help. She coached her about what to say in the interview. "I think they are going to be concerned about whether or not a Chinese child raised in a Caucasian home will feel alienated from her own cultural identity. Do you have any ideas about how to address that?"

"Puh-leaze," Lindsey replied. "She will grow up a normal Boston kid! She'll watch too much television and eat with a knife and fork. And she will root for the Red Sox even though they never win, and play with Barbies and purple glitter ponies, and when she is older she will wear outrageously expensive jeans and get her navel pierced and I will get a facelift and we will both look fabulous. And if this brings some anxiety to the shades of her ancestors, I hope it will oppress her not one bit, and my own parents, if they are watching from heaven, are no doubt still too drunk to care."

Meredith convinced her to tell the social worker she planned to educate her daughter about her cultural heritage and to find a playgroup with other babies adopted from China. The notion of a playgroup amazed her. "All the mothers go?" she said. "Can't one of us watch them play, and the rest of us go have drinks? That would seem to me like a much better allocation of resources."

And yet, the child was bright and beautiful and they were very happy together. Lily was thriving on take-out food. It was wonderful. Meredith sighed. It would happen for her too; she would be a mother one way or another. But she did want to get pregnant. She wanted to know what it felt like, to have a child inside her. She wanted David to watch her nurse her child. Their child.

Meredith's attention returned to the table as the food was served. Rick was on a rant now, something about a client. "He makes me fucking crazy. I made millions of dollars for this guy last year, and now I tell him I plan to cut back on the dot com stocks and he has the nerve to interrogate me like he is Gordon fucking Gekko. Knows fucking nothing, this kid. Inherited a few bucks and he thinks he's a genius. I figured fifteen minutes for the call, and a half an hour later he's still asking me questions. Then he says, 'Okay, now, for the coming year, I would like you to give me your best and worst case scenarios.' Give me a break. What a stupid question."

"Did you answer it?" asked David, laughing.

"Yeah, I answered it. I said, best case scenario – best case scenario, I take all your money to Vegas, put it on red thirteen to win, and it hits! Worst case scenario – worst case, I don't know, I guess some crazy asshole terrorist gets a hold of one of those leftover Russian nukes and blows up the stock market. Nuclear winter."

"That is a bad scenario," Lindsey agreed.

"So what did the kid say?"

"Who gives a shit. If he wants to go heavier into the tech stocks he can take his money somewhere else. It's making me nervous. Not one of those internet companies has made a dime – not yet. It's very cool stuff, and new, and everybody is certain there has got to be a gold mine in there somewhere, but I'll tell you what, we are completely out ahead of ourselves. People are way out over their skis. It's like yesterday somebody invented the wheel and today people are trying to tell you they're ready to go to market with a Ferrari. Bullshit. Show me a goddamn wheelbarrow first. Show me a wheelbarrow that works and then maybe we can talk about putting some money behind a bicycle."

"But you liked the dot coms a few months ago."

"I did. I was right, wasn't I? The stocks are way up. I've never seen anything like it – Nasdaq up eighty-five percent for the year. Eighty-five percent! No one has ever seen those numbers. We used to be happy if the market moved one percent in a week and now we expect it to go up a percent every day. You'd be crazy not to have been in those stocks, but that doesn't mean I have to like the business when everything is priced through the roof. The thing is, the market is assuming that anyone who knows how to use the technology is going to be a winner. But this technology is like a rocket – it can take you to the moon or it can burn your ass. There's a world of hurt coming for some of these companies. Someone is going to get a haircut. But it isn't going to be me."

Chapter 9

"Quiet! Everyone, be quiet," John called, watching the play clock tick down the final seconds of the first quarter. The Superbowl XXXIV logo appeared, cueing a cut to the commercial break. John smacked his hands together, startling Ryan, who sat down, whoosh, on his padded bottom. The baby looked around him, brown eyes open wide, as if surprised to find himself once more down here on the rug. He reached out with two hands to grab the coffee table and haul himself back up. "This could be it," said his father. As conversation ceased and the crowd gathered closer around the set. A sock puppet dog with mismatched ears came on, yammering about how to buy pet food and chew toys online. "No," said John. The dog batted its button eyes imploringly. "It won't be the next one either. Right after the break or right before you go back. We didn't want the ones in the middle."

"That's bathroom time," said Frank agreeably. Robin had met Frank's wife Lydia at a class for expectant mothers and they got together regularly with the babies. Robin adored baby Caitlyn, who was a easygoing little cherub. "Really," she told John, "it is so nice to have a baby around who sits still and isn't into trouble every other second." At eight months, Caitlyn sat plumply on a blanket and played with her toys, while Ryan cruised along the furniture hand over fist and even Teddy, who clung to his mother more than his twin, crawled like he was shot out of a rocket when he saw something he wanted. "Lydia just has no idea know how lucky she is," she said, smoothing Ryan's hair along his temples, where the ends curled up damply in the moist heat of his exertion.

The next ad was for beer, and then there was one for a website that helped you find new jobs. "Shit," said John, and Robin said nothing, although she did not like him cursing in front of the babies. He couldn't be happy with all these dot.com commercials coming one right after the other. The next ad opened with a shot of a teenage boy in front of a computer. "Here it is!" said John. The web site the boy was looking at said MISTER VIDEO GAMEZ across the top. A man with a gold tooth waved his hand at an assortment of games, their boxes decorated with knives dripping blood and buxom women spilling out of scanty clothing. The ad cut to a middle-aged man with a thinning comb-over and a wide, fatuous grin. "Dad!" the teenager called in voice-over, "I found the video game at a lower price! Can I have your credit card?"

"Sure!" said the man, looking relaxed in a shabby armchair. He flashed a smile with yellow teeth. "Great! No problem!" The picture changed to a girl a couple of years younger than the boy. Her computer was a bright bubble of pink. On the screen it showed a rectangular box with a unicorn and a rainbow on the front. The lettering along the bottom was Chinese. "Dad! The girl called, "They have the new princess movie for sale and it's not even out yet! Can I have your credit card?"

"Sure!" The father nodded like a bobblehead doll. "Great! No problem!" A blond woman next to him stared at a screen of her own. She was typing with intense concentration, pecking gingerly at the keys with nails long enough to curl inwards. "Honey!" she cried, "We might be the next grand prize winners! I put in your social security number."

"Great! No problem!" says her complacent husband, looking extra pleased.

"Worried about internet fraud?" The voice that broke in sounded serious but not grim. It reminded Robin of John: not glib, but confident. "Keep your credit card information secure with Emoney.com." The dot in the Emoney logo became a spinning globe, and the letters rearranged themselves into a net below it. "Emoney. A safety net for your internet." The group in the living room burst into applause, punctuated by a wolf whistle from Mickey. Teddy, in his mother's arms, joined the clapping.

"Did you like Daddy's commercial?" Robin asked, kissing him. "Good boy. Hooray for Daddy!" Ryan freed his hands from the coffee table to clap along with them and pounded his fat palms together three or our times before dropping precipitously to the ground once again.

"It was good," said John, "wasn't it?" He looked relieved. "I thought it looked pretty funny."

"Great! No problem!" said Frank, parroting the hapless Dad.

"It hits a nerve," said Caleb. "Everyone is worried about security and privacy. Who knows who these people are."

John nodded. "I am so glad the game is close. I was terrified the Rams would run away with it early and we would lose half our audience by the second quarter. But that thirty seconds alone was more than two million dollars, and the earlier time slots were even more. In the second half, we have one other spot. The time's a little cheaper and you can get lucky with the audience if they just keep the game close."

"Is it the same ad?" Mickey asked.

"No – it's the same family. This time they are getting all these terrible gifts – a too-small sweater for the son, and something babyish for the tweener daughter. The wife gets two of the same gift. The dad keeps saying, 'Great! Love it!' The voiceover is about our internet gift certificates –'Emoney.grams, good at thousands of Emoney.com shopping partners.' And then we have that tag line again, 'A safety net for your internet.'"

They had run focus groups on the ads and they worked; John felt confident of that. The problem was, Tennessee was getting completely outplayed. Every time John looked up, there was St. Louis in the red zone with the ball. "Come on, Titans," he yelled at the screen. Three times they held firm, and the Rams settled for field goals. It was nine to nothing at the half. "Not bad," said John, to no one in particular. "Could have been disastrous. This is okay. This is still a game." He figured anything over a ten-point spread and people would start to tune out. Reflexively, he opened a second beer, although his first sat on the table still half-full. John paced through halftime listening to the chatter and crunch of his guests and thinking about the Tennessee offense. He had several ideas for new plays. One quick score would change everything.

It was funny to care so much about the game and have no stake in the outcome. It wasn't like watching the Longhorns play back in Texas. The adrenaline was just the same, the sweaty palms and the shallow breathing, but the exhilaration was less and his stomach hurt more. Usually he enjoyed the way each play unfolded like a little drama of its own, but now he felt impatient with the players and their ritual high-fives after every catch or tackle. It seemed to him there would be plenty of time to celebrate when the ball was in the end zone. This must be what it feels like to gamble, thought John. This must be what it feels like to bet the mortgage money.

Not that Emoney was gambling; they had a marketing plan and they were sticking to it. Still, those two spots would take up a big chunk of their remaining capital. The game began again, and John turned up the volume. Ryan started to cry and Robin took him into the nursery where Teddy was already sleeping. He could hear some helpful soul in the kitchen washing glasses. John grinned. Mickey. He really hated football.

They were well into the third quarter before the Rams scored again. The young couple who lived next door cheered quietly. "Damn!" said John. He looked apologetically at their neighbors, whose parents lived in St. Louis. "I'm not rooting against the Rams," he said plaintively, "but it would be nice if Tennessee put something on the board."

Then Tennessee came back. They scored one touchdown, and then another. The score was sixteen to thirteen and Tennessee was getting the ball back when the ad ran. "Thank you, Titans'" said John, squeezing Robin's hand. Both boys were sleeping now. He thought of them there, the two cribs side-by-side in the semi-darkness, and was grateful for the hard work of the Tennessee offensive line. He was rooting for the Titans for real now, as they moved the ball down the field, as though the team had taken his company on their collective backs and carried it into a new age. The message was out there; the technology was ready. John had always hedged on what he thought their stake in Emoney was worth, but now if Robin asked he might say, "oh, a couple of hundred thousand, maybe more." He could picture the look on her face when he brought home that seven figure check.

A Titan field goal tied the game with two minutes and twelve seconds to go. Tennessee looked confident as their defense came back out on the field. The Ram's quarterback took the snap and stepped back and back, coming to a stop like he had nothing to fear from the large men closing in on him. With a stride forward he threw it long – the throw was a wish, a prayer. John's eyes followed it halfway down the field; remarkably, there was the St. Louis receiver, fifty yards from the line of scrimmage before you had time to blink. He caught the ball on the thirty-eight and ran it into the end zone.

John was stunned. "I thought you said you didn't care who won," said Robin.

"I didn't," said John. But now he did, desperately. Tennessee had almost two minutes left. They moved the ball steadily downfield as the clock ticked down. The Titans were in field goal range, but that didn't matter. Twelve seconds, and the Titan's quarterback looked like he was sacked but no – there he was, like a cat on its seventh life, spinning away to throw. The ball was caught on the ten yard line. When the Titans called time out, there were six seconds left. "What a ball game," said John.

Even Mickey was watching. "I think the QB is going to run it in himself," said Caleb. "I think he can do it." There was a long pause before the snap as each team hoped for a false move and a few cheap yards on a penalty. The quarterback rolled left like he was keeping the ball. One lone Titan stayed right as the pack moved. The camera followed the ball and missed the man, but a single St. Louis defender saw him there unguarded and headed back against the tide. The receiver was alone when the ball flew toward him and for a moment you could almost see it unfold: the catch, two long strides, the celebration in the end zone. But then the ball was there and so was the Ram's defender, flying in from the side, hurtling through the air like he ought to have been wearing a cape. Wrapped in a tackle that was like an embrace, the two of them rolled together, forward toward the goal line, downward toward the ground. For a long second the Titan player flew outstretched, his arm reaching to bring the ball across the invisible plane that separated winning and losing. And then he landed, the tackler bound to his legs like a anchor, and the ball inches from the end zone. The game was over. The St. Louis neighbors hugged.

"Well that was exciting," said Robin, clearing up. She could tell that John was distressed but she did not know why. "I thought everything went really well."

"It was a nice party," John agreed somberly.

"Mother called during the halftime. She was so excited. They watched with some old friends, and she said Daddy was all puffed up like a peacock, saying 'I told Kathleen the first time Robin brought this boy home, you keep your eye on this one. He's got big plans.' He's so proud of you."

"That's great. I'm glad I didn't disappoint him." John was anxious to get into work the next day and track the response. He dried off a platter as Robin washed. He was tempted to run into the office now, except that Robin wouldn't like it.

"I showed Lydia the pictures I took of the boys." Robin picked up the digital camera that John had gotten her for Christmas and looked at him through the lens. "She said they looked just like professional portraits. She says she wants to pay me to take pictures at Caitlyn's christening in May." She put the camera down and picked up a half empty bowl of chips. "She showed me the dress she bought for her. Oh my God, it is so precious. It's all lace and little pink ribbons. I told her I would take pictures. I won't charge her, of course."

"Absolutely not."

"But I could get a little experience, you know, maybe develop a portfolio. Buy a printer. It might be fun to do a little work as a photographer. I could take out an ad."

"Our ad budget's a bit tight right now." John made a face to make sure she knew he was kidding. "No, I think it's a great idea. Go for it." He looked quickly at his watch. It was late – too late to go out tonight.

Traffic on the website increased just as they had predicted. That was the good news from the marketing people at the monthly meeting in March; the bad news was that people were coming to look, but not registering to use the service. The staff had done some consumer research. Renee, the head of marketing, passed around copies of a bound report with color graphs and pie charts. It seemed that respondents liked the concept but continued to regard Emoney as an unknown, no more trustworthy than any of the hundreds of other new businesses that operated in the ether.

There was a murmuring of discontent from the technical staff. "Didn't you tell us that those Superbowl spots were going to give us credibility? Isn't that why we spent the money?" Renee exchanged a look with her assistant. You could see she was frustrated having to explain herself to people who did not understand the nature of her work.

"It's not an exact science," she said, remembering to sound calm and not defensive. "We couldn't have anticipated that there would be so many dot.com ads. It diluted our message to a certain extent. But, there are some positive developments in our research." Renee turned to page two of her report. "We found better-than-anticipated interest in our internet gift certificates. Our study suggests that the Emoney. grams could be a bigger part of our total revenue stream than we had originally assumed. And the added benefit here is that it allows customers to become familiar with our brand, which suggests that sale of gift certificates will lead to increased uptake of our core securitization business." She looked up, scanning the room for questions.

"So what does this mean?" asked John. "What is the time frame? How does it impact our expectations?"

Renee nodded. "Good question. In terms of time frame, the difficulty is that we would be relying on Christmas as the prime season for

Emoney.grams. So we may need to assume a longer interval before we meet some of our revenue goals. But, ultimately, I think the picture is very positive." John rubbed his forehead with the heel of his hand. More time was expensive, and everyone knew that they had limited cash on hand. Heads turned toward their chief financial officer.

"I looked over the projections you sent me. Given those new assumptions, we are absolutely going to need to raise more capital. My goal would be an additional five million, and I would aim to raise that money in the next three months – four at the outside." He looked consolingly at the faces around the table. "I don't foresee any problem with that."

He might not have looked so nonchalant, thought John afterwards, if he had any idea how tough the next two weeks would be. "What do you think?" asked Robin. "Is it going to be a problem?" The newspaper she hadn't had time to read was on the table. On the front page it said, "Nasdaq Falls Further on More Tech Stock Jitters."

"It's just a setback," said John. "The market has gone up too far too fast. It needed a correction." Robin spooned cold stewed chicken on top of rice and beans and put the plate in the microwave. She fished a knife and fork out of a drawer and put it down on the kitchen table, wiped clean hours ago.

"Ten percent in a week is a big correction."

"The public is losing faith in these stocks. It doesn't affect us – we're not a public company. Casual investors get hurt because they haven't done their homework, and they don't know which of these companies has something real to offer, and which ones are just quick attempts to cash in. First everyone got bought, and now everyone is going to get sold. But in the long run, what's going to matter is the quality of what you are offering, as opposed to whether or not you have the word "internet" in your business plan."

"That's fine, John, but between here and the long run, ya'all have to raise some cash, and I don't know who is going to want to give you any more money when the market is going down every day. If people start to get more skeptical, that's going to be hurting everyone."

"It will be alright." John sounded confident, but weary. "Emoney will be fine. We have a great business plan. We have some name recognition. We have a good product and a good staff and a great design team. Companies get funding based on nothing. Guys come in with a few ideas jotted on the back of matchbook and get money. We shouldn't have any problem." He reached across the table to touch his wife's hand. She still wore his old sweatpants, now with the waistband rolled over twice to keep them from falling off her narrow hips. There was no sign left of the baby weight, except for a lingering fullness beneath the soft cotton of the old white tee shirt she used for pajamas. She looked worried, or maybe she was just tired. "Don't worry, sweetheart. It will be okay. Trust me."

"I do trust you." John's certainty never failed to move her. She looked up at the clock. It was past eleven and the boys would be up by six. The thought of opening her eyes in the early morning light made her head ache. She stood up and headed toward the bedroom, laying one hand softly across the back of her husband's neck.

All the news was bad in March; John welcomed April as a fresh start, but there was no sign of improvement. After its initial plunge the Nasdaq bobbed back up like a swimmer searching for air, only to dive again, deeper. When it got to be a distraction, John stopped watching the numbers during the day, but he couldn't avoid the whispers that began to surface in the sunny common room they had fitted out last spring with a foosball table and an imported cappuccino maker. Investors were skittish. They didn't like the way the new plan relied so heavily on Christmas. The numbers for internet retail in the 1999 holiday season were not encouraging. The CFO was sleeping in his office.

A day before the May meeting news ran through the building about Inter.com, the hipster clothing site that had made a splash in December when Vogue called it "hot, hot, hot" in a holiday piece on where to shop for gifts. "Busted?" said John, amazed. "Not chapter eleven, or bought out?"

"Gone," said Haley, the graphic designer who worked down the hall. "They can't pay the bills and they can't raise a dime. A friend of a friend of mine who works there showed up this morning and they told her to clean out her desk by the end of day. Try and find it online." John typed in the address. An error message flashed across the screen.

"Wow. That's scary." John double checked the address. Maybe he had spelled it wrong.

"Yeah," Haley muttered. "That should give us something to talk about at tomorrow's meeting. If there is a meeting."

There was a meeting early the next morning. John looked at the long faces in the room and wondered how he would break the news to Robin. The CFO in his rumpled suit reviewed all the steps that had been taken, first to find financing and then to find a buyer. He spoke in a monotone and there was a sense of relief when he had finished and they could stop looking at his haggard face. The president of the company rose, and his voice comforted them with the instinctive, unforced optimism of a salesman. "I believe in the work we have done here together. I believe in the future of our industry and I believe in each and every one of you. So many of you have been here for three years, four years, five years – a couple of you even more – and you have given your heart and soul, every day. This isn't the end." That was more like it, thought John. This was the guy who had recruited him, the wunderkind with the Ivy-plated credentials, the one who could sell sand on the beach. There was a reason he had put his faith in this man. "I know you will all move on from this experience to better days and the success that you deserve. I wish to hell I had something else to tell you. I wish to hell I was anywhere else this morning than standing here delivering this news. I wish I could say we had found a way to play on, but sometimes it's not in the cards. Sometimes no matter how badly you want to win, you have to know when to fold."

There was more talk, but John barely heard it. The words moved past his ears as if they were no longer designed to take in sound. He envisioned himself waking up the next morning and getting out of bed. Where would he go? He wondered if the company's failure would make the news, because if it didn't they might be able to wait a day or two before telling Mickey and Caleb, the neighbors, Michael and Kathleen. Michael and Kathleen! John felt the acid leech out of his stomach and gnaw the edges of innocent tissue. His breath tasted sour in his mouth. They would sit there in the evenings sighing to one another over his bad judgment. *Poor Robin,*

Kathleen would say, and Michael would nod. *Up there in Boston, so far away, and now this.*

They were still talking when John left the meeting. He didn't need to hear it. Anything he needed to know would be sent to him soon enough, in great fat packets that came registered mail, as they handed over their few remaining dollars to lawyers who would document the utter worthlessness of his stake in this goddamn worthless company. Right now, he needed to get out of there, get some air, and track down a couple of cardboard boxes. Those would be in short supply too, soon.

Chapter 10

A tentative light crept in around the edges of the blinds as Robin half-opened her eyes and peered at the clock. It was six am, naturally, because she could hear Teddy starting to fuss in the other room. Ryan would sleep another thirty minutes or so, if his brother didn't wake him. Robin stirred but did not get up. Perhaps John would hear the baby and tell her to stay in bed, since she had gotten up with them twice during the night. She wouldn't feel one bit guilty, going back to sleep for a couple of hours. John lay face to the wall, his back expanding slightly with each slow breath. The crying was louder now, and he showed no signs of wakefulness, except perhaps to have receded a bit more deeply into the cocoon of covers pulled tight across his shoulder. "Don't bother yourself," Robin muttered, "I'll get him."

Teddy was already standing in his crib, holding the top rail and bouncing with impatience. He held his arms up to her with a plaintive look that broke her heart every morning, brown eyes glistening with tears that stained his eyelashes several shades darker than the wavy blonde hair on his head. "Let's get out of here, Teddy-boy," she whispered in his ear as he rubbed his wet eyes against her neck. "Let's not wake our Ryan."

She considered taking him back to their room and letting him play peek-a-boo with the comforter and the extra pillows on the big bed. Let John try to sleep through that, she thought – see if he can ignore the baby when he's climbing all over them. But she was already up and in the end, there was no use provoking John, who would only sigh and smile in that half-hearted way that made her stomach ache. He'd had a rough day yesterday, seeing the headhunter. Poor thing, she thought. He had tried to sound upbeat about how much the guy liked his resume, but she could see how glum he was. There were not enough jobs, and too many young geniuses out looking for work.

Robin closed the baby gate in the living room and put Teddy down on the floor. A bottle now and he would wait for breakfast, so she could feed the boys together. Ted crawled a foot or two and then stood up, toddling over to a bin of toys on the other side of the room. He pulled out a fire truck and let it drop, and then a stuffed gorilla, and then a whiffle bat, staggering slightly as he negotiated lifting and releasing each item in turn. A pile grew at his feet. "What are you looking for?" Robin asked, coming over to help, but Teddy did not seem to have any agenda beyond liberating the toys from their imprisonment in the box. "Have at it," said Robin, sitting down at the computer. She opened the file of photos for Lydia from the christening and clicked her way through the images, stopping at times to fuss with cropping and color balance.

The pictures had come out nicely, thought Robin. Lydia would be pleased. She would probably offer again to pay her. A few bucks would really help. Fifty dollars – just fifty dollars would pay the groceries for a week, if she used coupons and shopped carefully. Robin sighed. The photos were a gift, she reminded herself sternly. If they weren't going to ask for money from her parents or Mickey, then they certainly shouldn't take any from Lydia. The idea of it would send John over the edge.

But she could try taking pictures for money, if it wasn't for anyone they knew. Robin wondered if it was worth investigating the cost of a decent printer. Whatever it was, they didn't have it; the two of them had gone over their finances the night before and there wasn't an extra dime. If they pared down expenses to the minimum, they were alright for the summer. No dinners out, no movies, no new clothes except what was absolutely necessary for the boys. The woman who came in twice a week to help Robin with the housework would have to go. John's health insurance was good through August and then it could be extended for up to a year – for a thousand dollars a month.

At one time they had put away some money for a down payment on a house, but there was little left of that after paying for IVF, perhaps enough to cover the bills for September and October. "What about our trip home at Thanksgiving?" Robin asked. John looked stunned. "You know what, forget about it," she said. She did not want him to be forced to contemplate an unemployed Thanksgiving in Texas, watching football with daddy, avoiding the subject.

If she had a printer, she might make enough to take the boys to Dallas, but laying out the money was a risk and John was in no mood to take any risks. If it was not too expensive, she might convince her parents to get it for her as an early birthday present. But then, John would hate that like crazy and it would be a shame to make him feel worse; she could feel the skin prickle at the back of her neck, just thinking about it. He was so quiet already. She could talk to Tom at the camera shop who had been very encouraging about her work – perhaps they would set something up together. If he did the prints, she would give him a cut of whatever she made, and he could get business doing albums and framing. Robin resolved to talk to him that morning. John couldn't object to that.

But who knew, anymore? He was so touchy these days. Caleb and Mickey brought some Chinese food over one night; John insisted on sending every last bite of the leftovers home with them, including the stuff they didn't want and couldn't use. Two containers of cold rice, for God's sake – it was ridiculous. What were Mickey and Caleb going to do with all that rice? John was so vehement that even Mickey didn't dare make a joke of it, and they stood awkwardly in the hall with their jackets on as he put the half-full containers and the condiments and the extra chopsticks back into the bag.

John was working on cover letters that afternoon, so Robin took the boys with her when she went out. She leaned over the computer to say goodbye. He kissed her without taking his eyes off the screen. At Lydia's, Teddy stacked pink cardboard blocks into tall towers that Ryan gleefully knocked over while they sorted through pictures. "These are fantastic!" Lydia hugged Robin. "Thank you so much. Are you sure you won't let me pay you something? I feel guilty taking this from you."

"No, I loved doing it. She is too cute." Robin retrieved a doll that Ryan had thrown across the room and tucked the rosy-faced baby into the Mommy-and-Me Folding Umbrella Stroller. She had a doll just like that, with painted on curls and a pink rosebud of a mouth, in a box in the attic back in Texas. "I'll tell you what you can do for me – you can be my reference for all my photography customers. How's that for a trade?"

"Are you really going to make a business of it? Because you should, absolutely. You are, like, totally talented."

"Thank you. That's so sweet. I mean, it's not going to replace – it's not going to be something to live on, but I think it will be fun. If I make a few bucks, that's fine too. I worked it out with this guy at the photography store this morning. I ordered my business cards and put up a flyer, so now we are completely official."

"Isn't that great? John must be pleased too."

"John? He doesn't exactly know, yet. I am sure he will be absolutely thrilled, if he notices." The remark, which Robin had expected to sound light-hearted, rang harsh in her own ears. Stupid girl, she thought, irritated at herself. She did not want to talk about John but now Lydia tilted her body towards her in a posture that displayed concern and a willingness to hear more. All Robin's unspoken complaints seemed to hang in the air, waiting for her to give them a voice. "Of course John likes the idea. It's just that he is so busy with job interviews and all that. He's the one that's encouraged me to do this." And he had encouraged her, months ago – she remembered how enthusiastic he had been. John's eyes turned the most beautiful sea green when he was excited. The memory of it made her sad.

At home, Robin practiced what to say to potential clients. The first phone call went well; the man was friendly, and she got through talking about money without sounding apologetic. He was looking for a photographer for an anniversary party. They spoke for close to twenty minutes, and he said he would call back the next day to confirm. She never heard from him again. Still, Robin found the experience encouraging. The fifth caller booked her for his daughter's birthday party. She went early and shot the little girl in her pink party dress and her sparkly tiara. The child was turning five, and her cake was shaped like a mermaid. Robin took pictures of all the girls with their arms around each other's shoulders and Cheshire Cat grins on their faces. Half the mothers asked her for a business card.

The phone rang more often now, making it that much more obvious that John never answered it. It was one of many things he did not do, like folding the laundry or putting away toys or coming up behind her as she worked to nuzzle softly on the back of her neck. He took out the garbage every night, but seemed to tread lightly during the daytime hours, not leaving much of a footprint in the unfamiliar territory of weekdays at home. He glided noiselessly from breakfast to dinner, rarely joining them for lunch. Often he found reasons to be out of the house at midday, and Robin didn't know how he coped on those days, because there was nothing in their budget for eating out.

July was humid, quiet, torpid. John did not hold out much hope for August, when all the decision-makers were in Europe or on the Cape or picking up their children at camp. Late in the month, a friend called with an offer for a temporary position: four weeks, starting after Labor Day. "What do you think?" John asked. Would it offend him, Robin wondered, if she sounded too excited? Would that suggest a lack of confidence? She glanced at her husband, trying to guess what he wanted to hear. "On the one hand," he said, "it will cover the rent for a couple a months, plus winter clothes for the boys. You're sure they won't fit into anything from last year?" Robin paused and made an appearance of being thoughtful, as if that wasn't a ridiculous question. She shook her head no. "Okay," said John, "I didn't think so. On the other hand, they want the system up and running fast, which means I won't have any time for job hunting, so it has a negative impact there. I wish I could have done this in August when all the people I needed to talk to were on vacation." John paused. "But then again, you never know where things may lead – I guess it's better to stay in the game."

John left early to beat the traffic down to Route 128, where the new venture was setting up shop in a couple of offices sublet from a company that was downsizing. He slid his hand around Robin's waist as he kissed her good-bye, and gave each boy a poke on the way out, being careful to avoid getting any of their breakfast spattered on his clean shirt. Robin listened to the familiar ka-thump, ka-thump as he took the steps two at a time. It was nice having the house to herself. It was a different place when John was there, full of emotional microclimates that ran hot and cold, so that she had to step cautiously as she moved from the nursery to the kitchen to the bedroom. Robin let the twins kick up a ruckus in the living room while she worked on photographs. "Okay boys," she said, steering Ryan away from the Cheerios he was depositing on his brother's head, "just you let me finish this last picture and I will take ya'all to the park."

She heard John coming up the stairs around eight. She turned the last page of Goodnight Moon and put the book back on the shelf, closing the door softly on the almost-sleeping children. John walked into the kitchen holding the mail and waving the daily paper, still in its wrapper. "Didn't get to this?" he asked, grinning at her. It was a joke between them, her indifference to the news, especially when the news was bad. Robin shrugged. John stood over the salad bowl, plucking out leaves of lettuce and squares of feta cheese.

"Do you want a plate for that?" she asked, handing him a fork.

"No, this is fine." John picked up the bowl and paced around the small kitchen.

"So, how was it?"

"Interesting. They are trying to build a site for people who want to post their opinions about other websites."

"What's the point of that?"

"The point of it for advertisers is that they get the early adapters. These are folks who will use the internet for whatever they need – research, shopping, planning a trip, whatever. Plus, the site generates all this feedback about what is working and not working, and the company plans to package that information and sell it. Think about that – marketing people spend a fortune on surveys and focus groups and here we have people doing it voluntarily."

"What about the other guy – the customer? What's in it for them?"

"The user? The user gets information on what is hot and what to look out for. Plus they get to vent. Everybody likes to vent."

"They do, don't they? People can't get enough of sharing their opinions online, like writing them down makes them so much more important."

"It does makes an impact, when so may people see it."

"But it's just everybody talking at once. You can't really hear anyone. Too much all at once, and the good with the bad, like all things on the internet. How do you know who's telling the truth? I don't think I would listen to any of it. It's not like getting advice from someone you trust."

"But that's the point of these online communities. Given some time, the communal pool of experience provides a reliable sort of guidance."

"Given some time," said Robin. "Given some time. Of course that's the problem right there. The wisdom comes in time, but the decisions can't wait."

John looked at her reflectively. " I think more information is better than less information, even if you have to sift through it to get at the truth. Social networks harnessing technology for their own ends are amazingly powerful. People try and game the system, and the system adapts. It will ferret out the truth, eventually. You can't keep anything hidden, with all the eyeballs out there keeping watch." John flicked through the mail as he spoke, winnowing the junk from the bills. He pulled aside the phone bill and the cable bill, tossed a flier, and stared at the envelope beneath it. "What's this?" he asked, pointing to a familiar return address. In a font that mimicked handwriting it said *Center for Reproductive Medicine*. "What would we be getting from them now?"

"I don't know," said Robin. "Maybe it is some sort of follow-up. A product-satisfaction survey."

"It looks like a bill." John ripped open the envelope.

"What is it?" asked Robin.

John stared down at the paper, hesitating. He did not look up. He could walk over to the trash right now, he thought, and throw the letter away. He could say it was nothing. He could make it all go away if he acted quickly. Would she forgive him, if she ever found out?

"John," she said again, "what is it about?"

There were too many things to consider and no time to think. Robin stood looking at him expectantly. He paused, but it was a second too long and the moment had passed. "Dear Mr. and Mrs. Hogan," John read aloud. "We are writing in reference to the embryos currently in storage at the Center for Reproductive Medicine… IVF contract included initial two years storage fees." He paused, still staring at the paper. "I don't remember anything about embryo storage fees in the contract, do you?"

"No," said Robin. There was an informed consent, and some page beneath that, and initials here and there. "I don't really know if I ever read the contract. Go on. What does it say?"

"Annual storage rates apply after October 1, 2000. Invoice is enclosed." John's voice sounded oddly flat and strained. "If you do not wish to continue storage of cryopreserved embryos, you may opt to discard or donate them. Our donor embryo program requires the consent of both parties. Donations may be made for reproductive or research purposes. If you are interested in donation, please contact our office manager for more information."

"What is it going to cost?"

John turned to the second page. "Annual storage fee, one thousand dollars."

"Oh my God," said Robin. "That's going to blow a hole in our budget."

John looked at her, and his eyes were hard. "Robin, we can't afford it. We can't spare a thousand dollars, not if we want Ryan and Ted to have health insurance and a place to live. It could be months before I get a job – we have no money to spend on this."

"Money! John, we don't have any choice. Those are children. Our children. We can't throw them out like garbage. We can't let them thaw out and die." Robin's head was full of images of snowflakes melting. Disembodied voices called out to her. "We can find the money. We will ask my parents for a loan."

"I don't want to discuss this with your parents! Do you have any idea how pathetic that sounds? You want me to go to your father and tell him I can't pay my bills."

"We're not asking them to pay off our gambling debts, for goodness sake. We are trying to save our children."

"You try telling your father that. They won't see it that way. Do your parents even know that these embryos exist?" Robin shook her head. "I didn't think so. And if they did, they would not think of them as our children. "

"Mother and Daddy may have felt uncomfortable about IVF at the start but it's totally different now that the boys are here and they see how perfect they are. They are so happy that we have these children. They would feel the same way about the others. Those are their own grandchildren. And what if we want another child?"

"I don't want another child. I can barely provide for the children that we have." There was anger as well as anguish in his voice. "I understand how you feel. You went through so much to produce those embryos. But it doesn't make them people. They are not babies. They are a handful of cells. You can't tell your parents that they have nine unknown grandchildren sitting in liquid nitrogen at 196 degrees below zero. It is not something they can grasp. It's not something anyone can grasp."

"But what if it's true? What if each one of them is a person, with a soul?"

"If it's true, it's a sin. If it's true, it's a terrible sin because there is no way come hell or high water that we are having nine more children. But it's not true. It's a fantasy. And right now, we can't afford to throw around that kind of money so you can hold on to your fantasy. And I tell you what, I am not asking your parents or Mickey or anybody else for money. I don't need their help taking care of my wife and my children. No, Robin. No. You will not embarrass me in front of your family. I don't deserve that from you."

"I'm not trying to embarrass you." Robin was frightened, looking at him. It was hard to remember that there was a time not long ago when he was not like this, so miserable and quick to take offense. What would happen to them if it was always this hard? She pictured herself for one moment back in Texas, living alone with the boys in a dreary two-bedroom apartment. Her mother would baby sit on Saturday nights, and her father would come by to fix the squeaky doors and the clogged drains. Robin closed her eyes and willed the images away. "You can just dismiss it all you want, but lots of people believe that an embryo is a child in the eyes of God."

"Well, then people who have that belief should not put themselves in the situation of creating more embryos than they can use. We made eighteen embryos, Robin. Eighteen. Did you think we were going to have eighteen children? You had to think about this earlier. You had to say something before we got to this point. We have our boys. We are done with IVF. I would never let you take that risk again. What are we going to do, keep all the embryos on ice in perpetuity?" John's voice cracked. It was terrible for Robin to see him struggle to go on in his calm, measured way, as though if he kept talking she would not notice the tears running down his face. "I almost lost you, Robin. You almost died. You told me then that it was out of my hands; that I had already agreed." He remembered her face, pale and wan against the hospital pillow. He would not sit impotently in that hard chair again, listening to Robin suck air into her wet lungs. "This time I do not agree. No more drugs. No more doctors. No more bills. We're done. I am sorry about the embryos. I am sorry about everything. I don't want to make you sad. But we're done."

"It's my fault," said Robin. She put her hands over his and leaned forward so that her hair fell across her face in a blonde veil. "I should have known that I would feel this way and I – I didn't. I can't allow them to be destroyed. I think about them, John; I think about them all the time. I look at our boys and I think about their brothers and sisters."

John pulled Robin into his lap and folded her in his arms. "Okay. Shh, darling. Don't cry. Please don't cry. Please. Would it really help, just to know they are there? If it's that important to you, I will manage it somehow. I can find some part-time work. I'll do tutoring in the evenings. I'll get a job at the computer store. It'll be fine. Don't say anything to your parents, alright? Let me take care of it myself. I'll find the money. I'll make it okay."

Robin shook her head. She had never seen John cry; she felt unsettled, almost ill, as though she had leaned over the edge of a cliff and looked down at dark water crashing into a rocky shore, far below. The dull look in John's eyes she had grown so tired of this summer was gone, replaced with fear and tenderness and despair. She felt something in him stretched thin and near to breaking. The boys in the next room sleeping in their cribs could not grow up happy without their daddy. "No," she said, and she felt his heart beat as she lay against him. She lay a hand on his chest and met his gaze. There was color in his face again. His arm tightened around her waist. "You are right. Holding onto the embryos is not going to fix anything if we can't use them. It's just throwing the money away. We can't afford to be foolish. We have to worry about our boys. We have to think of them."

"So what do we do?"

Robin ran through the choices in her head. She pictured the clinic and the room at the back where the tanks were kept for storage. There must be thousands of embryos there, in that drab place with its whiteboard walls and hulking metal microscopes. They were sparkling bits of ice inside dark green canisters. Dr. Aylmer warned her you always lost some in the thawing. That was why it had to be done slowly and carefully. But what about the embryos nobody wanted anymore? Could she be in the room when they unscrewed the top and the cold came out like a thick, lugubrious smoke that sank when it should rise? The technicians would pull them out of the tank and toss them aside without a care, no ritual for the discarded ones, and no goodbye.

But there were other options in the letter. *Donations may be made for reproductive or research purposes.* Research! The thought stiffened her spine. What if they tore the little things apart or, even worse, let them grow until they looked like little lima beans with arms and legs and a beating heart? Please, God, keep them with you and do not let them feel any pain, she prayed silently. God would not hear her prayers if she offered up her own children for experiments. She would never know what happened to them; the dark thoughts would circle in her head on every sleepless night for the rest of her life. It was out of the question.

"What is a donation for reproductive purposes?"

"I guess that means giving the embryo to a couple that wants to have a baby."

So someone else would get their babies. Strangers would raise their children. But they would be alive. And the couples – they would want that baby so much. It would be someone like her, who had tried and tried. "We could give another couple the chance to have a child, I guess." Robin spoke slowly. John was silent. She could feel him watching her, waiting for a choice, any choice. He just wants to get past tonight and feel better, she thought. He wants it done. But what did she want? If they donated the embryos, they would be thawed slowly. The technicians would hold their breath, carrying them to the microscope, looking for signs of life. "We could give the embryos a chance to survive, even if it wasn't with us. Maybe we owe them that."

John nodded. Where there's life, there's hope, thought Robin. Something could bring them back to her. Things would be better, sooner or later. John might change his mind. How quickly did they use frozen embryos? Maybe they would still be there, waiting for them. There was really no other choice. "Reproductive donation, then," she said.

"I will call the clinic tomorrow," John replied, stroking her cheek softly as she lay her head against his chest. "I will take care of everything."

CHAPTER 11

"He's throwing the ball – it's good – oh no, the guy dropped it." Robin was sitting in the leather recliner nearest the phone. "So now it's third down."

"Fourth down," said her father.

"Fourth down," Robin corrected herself. "Fourth down and a bunch of yards. I think the kicking guy is coming out."

"How long a field goal is it?" asked John.

"Oh, they're close. It will be like twenty yards."

"Thirty four," Michael called out.

"I mean, thirty four yards," said Robin. "They snapped it – and it's through. So we're up ten points to seven. Excellent. I think the back-up quarterback is doing real well."

"At least he hasn't thrown any interceptions this time, which is a nice change of pace. Up until now, he's thrown more touchdown passes for the other team than he has for us."

"I think he's cute." Behind her, John heard the familiar squawk of the baby monitor. "I'll call you back," Robin said. "You have something to eat, okay? Do you have any of that turkey left?"

"Of course I do, Rob. You left me enough for an army. Thank you. I'll get myself something. Kiss the boys for me, alright?"

John walked from the living room into the kitchen, then back again. He sat down at the desk. He could finish this latest consulting job in a few hours – finishing the project was one of the reasons he had given Robin for staying in Boston. She hadn't really pushed him very hard. One less ticket was some money saved, and free advice from his father-in-law was not what he needed right now anyway.

John got up and wandered over to the sofa, pushing aside the clutter on the coffee table and putting up his feet. He checked his watch. Halftime should be over by now. John turned on the television, but they weren't putting Texas football on national tv during Thanksgiving weekend. He waited another fifteen minutes before calling Robin back. "John! I am so glad you called. Mother and I were playing with Teddy, and he said a whole sentence."

"Really?"

"Yes, he said 'grandma cookies.' Also, we scored."

"Excellent. Who scored?"

"Us. UT."

"No, I mean, which player? Did Williams score?"

"I don't know. Dad," Robin called out, "did you see who scored?"

"Tell John, we scored on a reverse to Roy Williams and a forty yard run." Michael looked at Robin and motioned her out of the chair. "Give that phone to me." Michael described the action with a laconic precision, and John felt he could almost see the game transpiring on the blank television in front of him. "I think the boys have it in hand now," said Michael, as the third quarter ended with another score. "Now they just have to wait and see which bowl game they are going to get."

"What do you hear about that?" asked John. "The papers in Boston don't cover it at all."

"Well, if they lost today, they were going back to the Cotton Bowl. Now they might be heading for the Holiday Bowl instead, playing Oregon."

"Damn."

"That Oregon State team is better than you think. You don't think Oregon for football but they've got some boys who can play. I know everybody always wants to play on New Year's Day, but I think the Holiday Bowl will be the better game."

"I don't have anything against Oregon. But they don't show the Holiday Bowl up here."

"Oh, sure, I see," his father-in-law said. "Can't do anything about that. What do you have – cable? Maybe that satellite television will have the game. You got a sports bar or something up there where they might show a game like that?"

"I don't know, Dad. I wish I did. I'm not quite sure where I would go about finding out. But I'll look into it. That's a great suggestion." John got off the phone and paced back and forth with a restless energy. He went into the kitchen for a beer, and the crack as he popped it open sounded oddly loud in the empty house. He turned on the basketball game. The rise and fall of the announcer's voice filled the room. John sat down at the computer and signed on. He pulled up Google and typed in: sports bar, Boston. The response line at the top of the page read "results 1-10 of 863,700."

John stared at the screen, scanning the first entries for any hint of which might be relevant. This is dumb, he thought. What were the chances that any Boston bar would be showing a UT – Oregon football game? Still, thousands of kids graduated from Texas every year. Oregon was big too. There must be other fans who had moved to Boston and would love a chance to watch their team. They could clean up catering to a group like that, if only they could find a way to reach out to them. It would be like homecoming, without actually having to go home.

You could organize things like that on the internet in a minute, thought John. You could have a site for Longhorn fans, with information about events in any city. He found the idea of it oddly exhilarating. You could link it back to the school, for team news. Merchandise. The University would love that. He knew a guy who worked in the press office back in Austin – John was sure they would welcome the chance to reach out to the alumni base. You could have message boards, so fans outside of Texas could find one another and organize get-togethers. His thoughts came with extraordinary rapidity, and each idea seemed both obvious and a revelation. Why only Texas? It was so simple. Why not organize for all the big schools? You could charge them something, some nominal fee. Sports bars would advertise – not just sports bars, but companies who made jerseys or travel agents putting together packages. ESPN would advertise.

John sat down and began to type. There were about half a dozen people he needed to call, and it was already getting late. A little research, and then he would call. He had a beer in his hand but he didn't want it anymore and it occurred to him that what he would like now was some coffee. It would feel good, layering the adrenaline rush with a caffeine buzz.

John had forgotten how staying up until four felt different than waking up at four. He lay in bed, savoring for a moment the combination of nervous energy and fatigue that animated the darkness when he closed his eyes. He would never get to sleep, he thought, and then he crashed, sleeping soundly through the morning light and waking suddenly from a dream of unusual vividness, although all he could remember was the end. He was sitting in the den in Dallas and everyone was there: Michael and Kathleen and Robin and the boys, but also Mickey and Caleb, and Haley, a girl from Emoney. They were watching a basketball game, a future basketball game, one that had not yet been played. "You can get this now," said Michael in the dream, and it didn't seem that strange to anyone. Then John had turned to Mickey and said, "It's called awaygame.com."

Awaygame.com. That was what woke him up: some barely conscious part of him saying that's the name, get up, write it down. John grabbed a pencil and scribbled it on a scrap of paper near the bed, in case the words faded away while he was in the shower like dreams sometimes did. He went towards the bathroom and then changed his mind, heading for the living room instead. He would just check if the domain name was taken.

The day went by impossibly fast. One minute it was lunchtime, and the next it was four pm and he was late for the airport. John sprinted from parking lot into the terminal, catching sight of Robin and the double stroller on the escalator just as he entered baggage claim. "Hey!" he yelled, waving his arms. Robin face lit up and she hurried toward him.

"Hi Sweetie! We took ages getting off the plane. Have ya'all been waiting here forever?"

"Not too long." That worked out well, thought John, pleased at his luck. He did not think Robin would appreciate how easy it was to lose track of time, reading articles on improving interconnectivity among users of social networking sites. Brilliant stuff. "How was the flight?"

"It was okay. They were both asleep for the landing, which was great, only it was really hard getting them off the plane. Some nice lady helped me with the hand luggage." They were heading back towards the exit, John rolling the big bag in one hand and carrying Ryan with the other. In the harsh glare of the airport's fluorescent lighting, his eyes were red and his hair was matted. "Are you all right?" asked Robin.

"I'm fine. I'm better than fine. I had the greatest idea – Rob, what would you think if I stopped looking for a regular job and started my own website? I could keep up the consulting work to have a few dollars coming in. I think I could get this moving pretty quickly – nothing like the Emoney, where we had to create and secure all the systems from scratch. I mean, that's the beauty of this, because most of the content would be generated by the users, or through links to third parties, and really the site would just be a facilitator. So it wouldn't cost much to get it started and it would just take a little time to build our on-line communities."

"John! Slow down, I don't know what you are talking about." Robin laughed, putting her arms around him. She understood nothing except that he was serious, and his enthusiasm elated and unnerved her. John took a breath and started again, explaining the concept in detail. He described the visuals as he saw them, with news scrolling along the bottom and a place to enter in your favorite team and your zip code. Robin was no sports fan; if he could sell the idea to her, then he could sell it to investors. "So, when you came back and signed in," Robin said nodding, "you would automatically get information on your own team and events in your neighborhood."

"Yes," said John, "plus you might have messages from other fans in your area and links to blogs on your teams or special offers from the school. And if you were traveling you could make those connections anywhere in the world."

"And this doesn't exist already?"

"I know; it's amazing. There's a lot of information out there but there's no community."

"So that is what you would be?'

"Partly, we would be just that. A filter to sift what you want from all the other crap. But more than that, I'd want people to go the site and recapture that feeling of being on campus on Saturday morning on the day of a big game. I want them to go on after the game and yell and scream about how we got hosed by the referees. I want them to come to us every time they think about how great it was to be young and in college."

"And you will make them feel a part of it again?"

"Yes."

"And then you will sell them stuff?"

"Well, that too."

Robin was silent for a moment as they reached the car and strapped the boys into their seats. She wondered if perhaps he was rushing into this too fast, and without enough time to consider what the consequences might be. So many things could go wrong; she couldn't even begin to think of them all. "John," she said, casting about for where to start with her apprehensions. He turned to her and smiled, too excited to wait while she searched for words.

"Isn't it great? I am absolutely certain I can make it work. I've spoken to our graphics person from Emoney and she is completely psyched. I called Jared down at UT and he is going to take the idea to the athletic director this week, just to get some feedback. Everyone was excited." He leaned across and kissed her. "I am so glad you are back."

"I'm glad you're back as well," said Robin. "I mean, I am glad to be back. And if you believe in this, John, then you should go for it. Absolutely."

Chapter 12

"Guess what?" said John, perching next to Robin on the overstuffed arm of the couch. Robin scratched ineffectually at a bright pink blotch on the faded, mushroom-colored twill.

"I'm guessing this won't ever come out." It was her own fault for trying to give Ryan something for his teething pain while he was bouncing up and down on the couch. "Why don't they make the baby medicine a more neutral color, like beige?" She looked up, sensing that more of an answer was required. John poked her. "I give up – what is it?"

"I got emails from six schools today. They're all interested in Awaygame."

"Really? From the Big Twelve schools you were talking to last month?"

"No. The whole Big Twelve is on board and will be up and running by football season. These are schools in other divisions. Five athletic directors responded to a letter I sent to the Big East and the ACC, and one email is from a guy in the PAC 10, completely unsolicited. In February they wouldn't return my phone calls, and now they are reaching out to me. They all saw what happened with Texas during March Madness."

"I saw what happened to Texas. Texas got knocked out in the first round."

"They didn't play very well, but they sold a heck of a lot of merchandise. Remember how our message boards lit up after the school sent out their letter to the alumni? We can track the traffic and see what percentage ends up buying something. It was huge. Almost eight percent of new visitors made a purchase, and a pretty good number of repeat visitors bought something too. No one can afford to turn down an opportunity like that. I bet every school from the Big East is signed up by the end of May."

"It's happening so fast I can hardly keep track."

"And you know that means?" John slid down onto the couch and pulled Robin onto his lap. "I think it would be okay to start drawing a little more in terms of salary."

"Really? God knows we could use it. The boys have hardly any summer clothes. Shall we celebrate, John? Let's get a sitter and go out. Wouldn't that be fun? I can barely remember the last time I put on something slinky."

"Go get yourself a new dress."

"Aren't you sweet? But I don't need that. Do you know what I would like?"

"What?"

"A new vacuum cleaner. This one can't suck worth a damn. No matter how much I vacuum, the boys still look like little dust bunnies when they get up off the carpet."

"You can get a new vacuum. Hell, Robin, why should you be vacuuming at all? Hire that nice lady who used to come in a couple of times a week. I don't want my wife wearing herself out." He kissed her softly and then harder. "It's gonna be great. We are going to have everything I ever promised you. Everything." He slid his hand under her shirt and felt the curve of her back between the shoulder blades. He would buy her a diamond with the first check, he thought. A diamond on a chain to lie in the hollow of her neck. He kissed her there and she arched her back, pushing against him.

The sound of the door opening made them pause. "Hey!" said Mickey, shouting from the stairs. He came in holding Ted and a large stuffed dolphin. "Uncle Mickey is home!" Robin pushed John away, smoothing her shirt. "We loved the aquarium, didn't we, Teddy?" Ted nodded. "Look at the two of you. Get a room, will you?" Behind them, Ryan pulled his hand loose of Caleb's grasp.

"Mommy we saw turtles!" he said, climbing up onto the couch and sitting astride his father.

"Did you? That's so wonderful, sweetie." Teddy reached his arms out for his mother. "Did you thank Uncle Mickey and Uncle Caleb for taking you to the aquarium? And did they buy you these animals too?"

"Fank you for the quarium," said Teddy, turning back to hug Mickey's legs.

John tossed the boys up in the air one after another, and laughed at their overtired, gleeful squealing. "Do you know what John's excited about?" began Robin.

"I'm not sure I want to know," said Mickey. "Some stuff should be private between you."

"No, stupid," said Robin, hitting him with the stained couch cushion. "He just got six more schools inquiring about Awaygame."

"Really?" said Caleb. "Fantastic. Are you offering them the same contract you signed with UT?"

"I was going to ask you a few questions about that. Do you want to take a look at it for me? I want to talk to you anyway about doing a little consulting."

"You can't afford him," said Mickey. "You might be able to afford me, but obviously you are aware that I am very, very busy, and that is why you have only asked Caleb."

"I didn't expect you to be interested, since my rights are not being violated. If ESPN tries to crush us, then I will hire you. But I was hoping Caleb would help me make some real money, so we can afford him. Let me show you." He led the way into the next room, where a long table loaded with papers fit uncomfortably between the bed and the wall. John tossed a file off the top onto the night table. "Sorry it is such a mess in here. Rob kicked me out of the living room for cursing in front of the boys."

"She's tough."

"I needed a door anyway. Ever try to get a pair of toddlers to shut up while you're on the phone?"

"I've never had the pleasure."

"Last week Ryan got hold of the sample artwork for our new logo and crayoned all over it."

Caleb laughed. "He's a handful. It was so fun with the two of them today. Ted wanted to know the name of every fish and Ryan kept escaping the stroller and running away, so I followed him, while Mickey kept Teddy safe from the sharks."

Caleb did not tell him how some woman grabbed hold of Ryan as he fled down a dimly lit corridor lined with glowing green tanks. "Are you running away from Daddy?" she asked him, laughing, while Ryan struggled to disengage himself. She smiled at Caleb, tossing her dark hair. Her lips were a bright red color that reminded him of predators. He felt as though he had been caught in a lie. Ryan wrestled himself free and ran back to him. Safely in his arms, the child turned and stared balefully at his former captor. The way his small hand rested against the back of Caleb's neck made him feel a sudden rush of love for the boy. I could do this, he thought. I would be a good father.

"Don't worry, Ryan," he said. "You're safe with Uncle Caleb." He whispered it so that the woman did not hear. To her he said simply, "Thanks. He has gotten so fast, we can hardly keep up." He kissed the top of the child's head, and turned away so that she would not see him blush.

Caleb picked up the contract with UT and looked at the notations scribbled in the margins. Awaygame amazed him. It grew like an organic thing, like ground cover spreading in the fertile soil of the internet. It followed no rules of business he had ever known, but John had foreseen it. He had offered these people something they were missing when they did not know it themselves, when it lay dormant in them like hen's teeth, some ancient, inchoate longing waiting to be given form. In Boston and Seattle and New York, the Texas fans had gathered in noisy bars to watch their team lose a basketball game and cry in the consoling arms of like-minded strangers, and then they had chugged their beers, and slapped each other's shoulders, and vowed to come back and do it again. And just like that, Awaygame was a part of their life and they couldn't do without it. "We have people," John said, "who are on the site every day. Lots of them."

"This is good," said Caleb, gesturing at the contract. "Make sure you own the rights to anything that is posted. Words and images." He paused as John searched under the bed for a pen to take notes. "Don't you think it's time you got an office?"

"Might be," said John. "I've been trying to keep the expenses down. It's getting a little crazy."

"I think you should have an office. I think you should start traveling more as well. I'm sure it's hard to be away from the boys."

"It's mostly a pain for Robin." said John.

"They're such great kids," said Caleb. His heart moved, and he could see into the well beneath it, infinitely deep and dark. He waited a moment for the sadness to ebb. "But you should be out there making contact. I think you should meet with as many of the athletic directors in person as you can manage."

"That's a good thought," said John. "I'll start setting it up."

A week and a half into September, it still felt like summer. The early morning sky showed a faint echo of starlight, and the shimmering glow of a cloudless day at dawn. John climbed into the cab, settling his suit jacket flat on the seat beside him. He was pleased with himself. He had gotten up and out without waking Robin or the boys. His flight left at 8:00, and he would be shaking hands with the athletic director at Duke by noon. Two days, three meetings, three different schools, and he would be back in the office by Thursday. He would pick up some beer and tequila for Friday afternoon, and his small staff would gather to watch the message boards light up in advance of the Saturday games. A little ritual to welcome the football season.

John was at the gate by 6:45. He considered calling home and decided against it. He did not want Robin to sense him sitting around with time to kill. He did not need to be reminded that she had her hands full. Maybe they would all sleep in. The boys had gotten shots at the pediatrician yesterday; Robin said they were cranky all evening. She had gone to bed soon after he got home. "Don't forget that I am out of town tomorrow and Wednesday," he called to her retreating back. He had forgotten to give her his itinerary. He would phone as soon as the plane landed and let her know where he was.

The sky was blue by the time of take-off, an uninterrupted clear blue for as far as you could see. John was glad he had requested a window seat. "Breakfast?" asked the flight attendant. He had barely begun to eat when the young woman was back, scooping up the remains of the complimentary bagel and grabbing the half-full cup of coffee out of his hand.

"I'll keep that, ma'am," John said.

"We need to wrap up food service, sir. Captain's orders." Her voice was sharper than he expected. Usually they oozed helpfulness, even when saying no. "The Captain is concerned about some possible turbulence." John handed her the coffee and stared out of the window. The plane turned toward the right and John checked his watch. Too early for the approach, so he must be heading west to avoid whatever was causing the turbulence. Not a single cloud hovered on the horizon.

John needed to use the washroom, but the fasten seat belt sign remained stubbornly lit. This was ridiculous. He waved at the attendants, trying to attract their attention. They stood together at the front of the plane, unmoving. After two hours, the plane began what felt like a descent. There was no announcement from the cockpit. No one asked them to put their seat backs up, or return their tray tables to the locked position. The flight attendants sat down in silence. An expectant rustle moved through the passengers. The Earth moved up swiftly underneath them as the engines roared to a stop.

Gripped with an uneasiness he could not explain, John looked left and right as the plane rolled toward the gate. He pulled out his Blackberry. The phone beeped as it powered up. John flipped it open. The screen said: "missed calls: seven." He clicked forward to see his call log. The screen read: "home, home, home, home, home, home, home." Feeling short of breath, John moved the cursor to the top entry and hit the green button. It had to be one of the boys. Or both boys. What went wrong after immunizations? It seemed to him he remembered something about immunizations, something bad that could happen. "Robin," he muttered to himself, "this had fucking better not be nothing. This had fucking better not be *where did you leave the car keys again?*"

The phone began to ring and then Robin was there, right away. "Hello?" She sounded tearful.

"Robin?"

"John!" Her voice was a weary shout. "Thank God. Thank God. Where are you? Where are you?" She sounded almost elated, and John felt fear dissolve into rage.

"Robin, what's wrong? Are the boys okay? What the hell is wrong?"

"Stop yelling at me, John." She was crying now and her words were less distinct. "I have been so worried. I didn't know what flight you were on."

"I am in North Carolina. We just landed. What happened, Rob?"

"A plane – they took two planes and ran them into the World Trade Towers, first one and then the other. They flew one into the Pentagon. Another one crashed in Pennsylvania. All hijacked planes, and they said three of them came from Boston. I saw the second one, John. It went right into the building and burst into flames. I was so afraid you were in there. No one could have survived that crash, not even before the towers came down."

"The towers came down?" John looked around him. Every person talking into a phone had the same stunned expression on his face. Their neighbors looked at them with apprehension. John glanced across the empty middle seat to a woman on the aisle. She stared at him with concern, and John realized for the first time that he was shaking. "What do you mean, the towers came down?"

"They just fell. Like they had turned to dust. Like a Bible story. I was so scared." The PA system crackled.

"Listen, hon, they are making an announcement here. I'm fine. Hang on; I will call you right back."

The pilot began to speak. "Good morning, ladies and gentlemen. Welcome to Raleigh/Durham airport. It is 10:30 local time. Folks, we're going to have to ask for your patience. We understand that there have been some acts of terrorism involving a number of aircraft in the Northeast. Because we were near to our destination, we were allowed to carry on and land here. However, I am very sorry to report that the plane will not be continuing on to Miami as scheduled. As of one half hour ago, all United States airspace is officially closed."

It was forty-five minutes before they were cleared to roll up to the terminal and exit the plane. The flight attendants moved up and down the aisles, offering apologies without answers in the wake of indignant questioning. "What about my connection to Phoenix?" asked the man in the row behind John. "I'm going to miss my flight."

"I'm sorry, sir. You can't miss your plane because there are no planes leaving. All the airports are closed."

"When will they open?"

"I don't know. I'm sorry."

"How will I get to Phoenix?"

"I'm sorry, sir. I don't know."

In the end, his own inconvenience was remarkably slight. At Duke, he huddled around a television in the coaches' office, watching hesitant news anchors speculate on how many wounded, how many dead. In Brooklyn Heights and Battery Park City, clouds of paper and ash rained down, and the fluttering scraps came from the sky like tickertape. It blew everywhere as though it carried the news of the end of an era – an era where things like this didn't happen, not here. John and the Duke coaches watched the towers implode over and over again. Information came in streams, but there was nothing to comprehend. They didn't discuss Awaygame at all, but when John said he had better get going, the athletic director hugged him tightly and said, "I will see you soon, buddy. God bless."

Earlier that day, walking off the plane with his carry-on bag, he was angry at the overheated passengers asking, *What about me? How do I get home?* What assholes, he thought. People have died today. There are people who aren't coming home at all. Still, he couldn't help but feel a bit of a pang when the schools announced that all games for the coming weekend would be cancelled. It seemed to him that a game might cheer everyone up. But he went to a vigil in Durham honoring the dead, and he stared out at the crowd, young and old, black and white, and saw the same stricken look in all their eyes. There was a girl standing next to him, nineteen or twenty, wearing pink sweatpants cropped below the knee and a tank top that pulled tight across her middle and scooped low enough in front to show off a tattoo of a unicorn on her left breast. The candlelight reflected in her tears. An older man in a polo shirt and khaki pants put an arm around her shoulders and patted her back. We were all together in this moment, John thought. It wouldn't do, right now, to divide up into teams and root against one another. They were right to wait.

John flew out on Thursday. Neither he nor Robin could sleep the night he returned. "I can barely watch television anymore," said Robin. "They keep talking to people waiting for someone to come home, and I can't stop thinking that it could have been me. It was so hard, for just that one hour. I don't know what I would have done, if it had gone on and on. So many of these people are still waiting for news."

"It must have been terrible for you."

"It was terrible for everybody. I don't know what kind of a world our boys are going to grow up in. It scares me that I don't feel like I can keep them safe."

"What bothers me," said John, "is that if someone told me beforehand about a plan to highjack airplanes with a box cutter, and use those planes to bring down two of the biggest buildings in the world – I would have said it was bullshit. A bunch of wingnuts talking crazy. If it hadn't happened, I would have said for sure that it couldn't have happened. Now I feel like this has broken down some wall between what is possible and what is pure fantasy. You start wondering about all the crazy shit you've ever heard and you have to think, well, I guess it's not impossible. I guess nothing's impossible. What are the rules, when nothing is impossible? How do you know?"

"There's no saying. It frightens me. Especially with the boys – I am always thinking of all the things that could happen to them." Robin turned and looked toward the window and the lights of the Somerville street beyond. "I don't like living here anymore. I was sitting right here Tuesday trying to imagine what we would do if you were on one of those planes." She had pictured herself a grieving widow, sleeping alone in the king-sized bed, trying to be strong for her fatherless boys. *We'll see Daddy again in heaven,* she said, holding them tight. She would take them home to Dallas, so far away from here, and the future they had planned, and her little ones, gone beyond reach of any glimmer of a hope. Would she see them again in heaven?

How would she recognize them there? "I want to find a new place," she said. "A house in a quiet neighborhood with a real yard that feels more like a proper home. I want to take the boys somewhere safe."

John contemplated this for a while. "I don't think we should move because you had a fright. That's exactly what they would want – these people who want to make the world move backwards. They can't stop the future, and we can't get rid of the past. They want to get into your head and make you frightened. We can't give in to that. But I agree it would be nice to have a yard, and some more space for the boys. Assuming things get back to normal soon, so we can play some ball, I guess we can start looking to buy a house in the Spring. Does that sound okay to you?"

"If we can do that," said Robin, snuggling next to him, "then I think we should.

Chapter 13

Meredith felt better once the phone call was made. She had known for a while that it had to be done but she kept putting it off and putting it off. Clearly, she was not going back to work in early April. How ridiculous was it that a place devoted to improving the lives of women only offered three months maternity leave? She had never realized until now what a travesty that was. Three months! She planned to nurse for a full year, at minimum. And the pediatrician said that Sophie was unlikely to sleep through the night anytime soon, unless Meredith was willing to give up letting her sleep in their bed. Which was not an option.

"It's fine with me, if it's fine with you and David," Dr. Redlands said. He was a nice man, very careful and thorough, and his waiting room was clean, with separate areas for sick kids and well kids. He didn't get impatient like some of the other doctors she had interviewed.

He answered all her questions. It wasn't too hard to reach him on the weekends or in the evenings, if things came up that worried her. She would see him later today for Sophie's first immunizations. Meredith shuddered. She had been dreading this. She had floated the idea of declining, but Dr. Redlands looked very grim. "Those side effects you hear about are vanishingly rare," he said, "and all that business about autism is a crock. A little fever for one night, and she will be fine." But Meredith hated the thought of the needle, sliding into the perfect smooth skin of Sophie's thigh. And she hated not being able to explain to the baby, why her own mother would allow someone to hurt her this way.

She got teary at the thought of it, and David reminded her that it wasn't right not to do your share, which of course she already knew. Now at least she would not be leaving her two weeks later to go back to work. She had managed to put her foot down on that, as bad as she was at saying no. It wasn't like the Center for Women's Legal Services couldn't survive. "We couldn't manage without you," her co-workers always said, but it wasn't true. They were still there; the office was still functioning. It was just a thing people said when they wanted you to feel good about doing some job that no one else wanted to do. Let someone else struggle with Alisha, who never showed up on time, or Marisol, who forgot the paperwork from her doctor. She had to think about Sophie. That was her job now. "All right, little bunny," she said. "Let's see if you want to nurse one more time, and then a nap. Sophie and Mommy have a busy afternoon."

That went well, thought Meredith, strapping the baby back into the car seat. How very different she was from the floppy bundle they took home from the hospital. Now, her legs fit comfortably on either side of the buckle that stuck up through the slit in her cleverly designed car seat-compatible travel blanket. She was awake now, and her head did not loll to one side in that precarious rag doll fashion of the early weeks, but Meredith tucked in a neck support pillow just to be safe. David would be pleased with the doctor's report. The doctor was very impressed that she was rolling over already. And her growth was perfectly adequate; no need to supplement the breast milk. David's brother Raymond had told her she was overly concerned about that when they came by last weekend, but he was a cardiologist, and of course cardiologists were inclined to think that lean was better for everyone, even babies. But no, Sophie was gaining weight. The scale in the doctor's office wouldn't lie. Meredith weighed her every day at home, but that was just the bathroom scale and those could be unreliable.

Plus, Dr. Redlands said that the little mark on her pinkie was just a freckle and nothing to worry about. David would say 'I told you so' but she didn't mind – better safe than sorry. She ran her hand over the baby's bare head. She felt warm enough, but still, it was only March and winter wasn't over. Meredith reached into the bulging diaper bag and found one of those sweet little stocking caps from the store in Brookline that sold handmade things in organic cotton. She's going to be blond, Lindsey told her, observing the absence of hair. Blond hair grows slower. Everyone knows that.

Meredith had every intention of getting in and out of the market as quickly as possible, but she had trouble figuring out how to clip the car seat into the grocery cart and in the end she decided it would be safer to go back and get the stroller. She could use a basket instead of a cart; she wouldn't have much time to shop anyway. Just get something for dinner, she thought. Fish? The salmon looked nice, but salmon had mercury and PCB's. "Excuse me," she said, "is your roast chicken organic?" She took the chicken and ordered some red lentil salad with goat feta and the woman behind the counter put it in a small brown box of recycled cardboard. The basket grew heavy on her arm and she thought about hooking it onto the stroller handles, but if the stroller tipped Sophie might be flung out despite the five-point harness. "Vegetables and we're out of here, bunnykins," she said. She put some broccoli into a paper bag, and then spilled it back out again. Broccoli in the milk would make Sophie gassy. Baby carrots were treated with chemicals. The plums were labeled organic but they came from Chile, and who knew how carefully organic farming was regulated in Chile. She settled on organic oranges from California and hydroponic lettuce grown locally. "All done, sweetheart!" she said to Sophie, who was beginning to stir ominously.

There were two people ahead of her in line, a young woman with a full cart and a gap-toothed older woman with long straight brown hair. The older woman peeked in at the baby. "So cute," she said.

Meredith smiled back at her. She only has a few items in her cart, she thought. If she asks me if I want to go first, I should really say no. Sophie's right arm had worked it's way out of the blankets and her hand had seized on the cotton cap. The baby's face registered mild surprise. She brought her arm down and the cap went down with it. The arm went back up, and the cap covered her eyes and nose. "Peek-a-boo!" said the woman in front of them. There was a small whimpering noise, slightly muffled, and her body wriggled. Meredith pulled the cap away from her face. If she asks me if I want to go first, I think I will, she thought.

But the woman was putting her things onto the belt. "How old is the baby?" she asked. Sophie blinked up at them, wide-eyed.

"Almost three months," said Meredith.

"What a darling. She looks just like you."

"Thank you," said Meredith. "People say that."

"And those remarkable green eyes! Do you think they will stay green? Does your husband have green eyes?"

"He does not," said Meredith, gesturing at the register. "I think he's ready for you."

It was funny, thought Meredith later, how much the comment bothered her. She never thought about it - never. At the initial visit, Dr. Redlands had asked all these questions about her family health history and David's family health history, and she answered them without thinking twice. "Maybe we should have told him," David said. "I don't think he was asking all those questions about our families just to get to know us better."

"To tell you the truth," said Meredith, "it never occurred to me."

At the beginning, they had assumed that they would tell everyone, naturally. When Dr. Aylmer first raised the idea of using a donor embryo, it didn't seem that different from adopting. "But there isn't the wait like adoption," he said, "and we can match the donors to your general appearance, so the child will have that identification with the family."

"If you think it is better for the child," she said, "but that doesn't matter at all to me." David didn't say anything. He was still looking stricken, poor dear. Azoospermia. That's what the doctor called it. The complete absence of sperm.

"I'm shooting blanks," he said. "That's why you can't get pregnant."

"That's only one reason," said Meredith. "My eggs could be a problem too. We just don't know." Dr. Aylmer suggested they try insemination with donor sperm, but she could see how upset the idea made David. 'Do it,' he said. But he didn't mean it. She could tell it would never be right, if the baby was hers, and not his. A donor embryo seemed like the perfect solution. Only David didn't want to tell anyone until they knew for sure she was pregnant, because bringing up donor embryos would lead to questions about why, and questions about why would lead right back to that awful word, azoospermia. After they got pregnant, it seemed foolish to say anything before they got through with the amnio. And then they started to think how if you told anybody you would have to tell everybody – and then what if Sophie found out, and not from them, at just the right time, in just the right way. It was easier to say nothing. She was pregnant. No one asked why.

And now she was here, sitting in the small nursery off their bedroom, Sophie's breath sweet and hot against her chest as she rocked. The baby had fallen asleep some time ago, but she did not want to put her down. She could hear David puttering around downstairs, cleaning up. She should really go give him a hand. But the room was dark and the baby was warm, and she was so tired.

Meredith stopped rocking and closed her eyes. She would be up again in three hours, maybe four if she was lucky. It was time to change from sweatpants into pajamas. David would be finishing his third glass of wine by now. She thought enviously of the Pinot swirling in the glass. She could taste it on his breath when they kissed. She could not have alcohol, or aspirin, or nightshade vegetables; everything passed through the milk into the baby. No bottles for her child! No formula from a can. Every cell in her child's body came from vegetables grown without pesticides and chickens that hunted and pecked in a barnyard, not a cage. Every inch of her was organic. Every cell was a labor of love. Billions of cells, and they were all from her – all of them but the handful at the start.

Chapter 14

The room under the eaves had dormer windows that looked out into the deep backyard, with a stand of birches at the back and beyond them the garish raw wood of a new cedar fence. "Eventually the boys will move up here, but not while they're so young," said Robin. "Look at all the storage space!"

"It's very nice," said Caleb.

"And the living room." Robin ran quickly down the narrow stairs, gesturing over the banister toward their old couch and chairs. "And down this way, the master bedroom. Isn't it sweet? It has a fireplace." She showed them the master bath, with its sage green walls and granite countertops. "Jacuzzi tub."

"Bubbles," said Mickey. "I love bubbles."

"You can't believe my closet. You have to see it."

"Must we?"

"I'd love to," added Caleb, glaring discretely at Mickey. "Fantastic. The built-ins are great."

"There's a linen closet too."

"It's a real house," said Mickey. "Very nice, if you like that sort of thing."

"This is the other bedroom." There were toys piled on the floor, and a dhurrie rug over hardwood floors, and two twin beds with headboards painted ocean blue. Robin pointed to a wall at the end of the corridor. "There's plenty of room in the side yard if we need more space eventually."

"Another bedroom?" Mickey asked, a question she did not answer, not even with a look. It was a subject that came up, with the boys turning three, but not for John, who was deaf to hints and insinuations. The two of them never talked about it, not since the night when they decided to donate the embryos. "It's done," he said, wrapping his arms around her so that her head rested against his heart. But it would never be done for her. Would she sense it, she wondered, if a baby was born? Once last month she heard crying in the middle of the night and went into the boys' room, but they were both absolutely sound asleep. She had wandered around the apartment looking for whatever it was that had woken her up. In retrospect she realized that it hadn't sounded like Ryan or Teddy at all; it was a wordless bleat, shrill and insistent, like a newborn's cry – loud but also weary, as though the child had been crying for hours. Her shaking woke John. "It was a dream," he said, when she wondered out loud why no one came to comfort the baby. "It was just a dream." John held her tight and kissed her damp cheeks. "Don't make yourself unhappy. Everything is fine."

Robin led Caleb and Mickey into the kitchen and through the back hall. "Mud room," she said, as they walked past a little row of hooks and a box of boots opposite the coat closet. John was sitting at a table outside on the mossy brick patio, reading the newspaper. "Where are the boys?" asked Robin.

"Over there." John waved his hand toward the farther reaches of the yard. "So you got the five-cent tour?"

"It's wonderful," said Caleb. "A great house. It's been a good couple of weeks for you, hasn't it? I loved that story out of Florida. Did the traffic on the site go up?"

"Through the roof."

"What happened?" Mickey asked John.

"Well, a coach in Florida recruited this top prospect at quarterback – eighteen years old, six foot five, all the potential in the world, and you'd would think everyone would be falling all over themselves with joy, except that their current quarterback is very popular with the faithful. Not the best arm in the world, but a tough, scrappy kid and he'll kill himself for the team. He played sick, he played hurt – hell, he came back early from his grandmother's funeral to play on homecoming – they love him on campus. And he still has two years of eligibility left, so there has been a lot of talk about who should start." John grinned. "Some reporter was pushing the coach for a comment on 'the big quarterback controversy' and the guy got angry and growled, "You been readin' the message boards on awaygame again, haven't ya son? If I catch any more of my boys readin' that chatter, ah'm gonna to start holding my trainin' camp off the grid." And good luck to him. Antarctica is a long way to go for preseason."

"I saw it on Sports Center," said Caleb. "You can't buy that publicity."

"Yeah, a number of the national news outlets picked it up. I think it played well because of the big ol' buzz-cut football coach growling about 'message boards' and 'off the grid'. Talk about dragging him kicking and screaming into the new century."

Teddy emerged from a clump of trees and ran along the grass toward them. "Momma," he called, "Ryan needs you."

"Tell Ryan he has to come and ask me himself." Robin rolled her eyes. "He is so bossy with his brother."

Teddy took a few steps back toward the trees, then stopped and turned. "Ryan needs you," he called again. He looked stricken and confused, and his brown eyes filled with tears.

Robin stood up. "I swear, that boy is the absolute king of getting his own way." Her voice was a mixture of exasperation and pride. Ted ran in front of them, his short legs pumping. They walked past a new wooden fort with a rope ladder and a slide. Behind it, Ryan half-sat and half-crouched uncomfortably atop the picket fence. He put up his hand when he saw them approach.

"I don't need any helping. I can do it myself. I can do it myself."

Robin walked over to him, ignoring his protests. "Honey, you're stuck," she said calmly. A small protruding nail caught the back of his shorts. "You are going to tear your clothes. Just wait.' She unhooked him. "Okay, now jump down from there." Ryan leaped from the fence and landed on the soft ground. Robin turned to John. "Good thing we put up the fence."

John shrugged. "Are you boys going to say hello to your Uncle Caleb and your Uncle Mickey?" The boys turned toward them, waving muddy hands.

"I was going to ask for a hug," said Mickey, "but maybe later. You want to come see what Uncle Caleb and I brought for you?"

"Presents?" said Ryan.

"Presents," affirmed Mickey. He headed back into the house. The boys waited outside until Mickey reappeared with two wrapped boxes. They set on them, shredding the paper.

"Fire truck!" yelled Ryan.

"Me too!" said Teddy.

"Actually," said Mickey, leaning in to check, "yours is an ambulance. See, there's a stretcher." The adults untwisted the tight metal ties that restrained the equipment and the little plastic men. The fire truck came with a hose and an axe, and the ambulance included something that resembled a miniature pair of scissors with big blades.

"Garden shears?" asked John.

"Jaws of life," said Mickey, consulting the packaging. "That might be more realism than we need, even from the American Heroes First Responder Series."

"Did you boys say thank you?" Robin nudged her sons, and Ryan bellowed his thanks while Ted presented his face to be kissed, first to Mickey and then to Caleb.

"Nice to see we appreciate our firefighters," said John, looking at the box. "American Heroes."

"Mickey was going to get the children the Islamic Martyr Brigade Suicide Bomber play sets but they were all out."

"I don't think any of them got sold," said Mickey. "I think they were all hauled off to Guantanamo by top secret paramilitary toy soldiers."

"Of course," said Caleb. "America the terrible. Perhaps you would like to defend them as well?"

"I would happily defend them, if the state department action figures would only grant them make-believe due process."

"You would defend the people in Guantanamo?" Robin wrinkled her nose. "You will make yourself very unpopular."

"Luckily, I am already very unpopular. Caleb, for one, is very mad at me."

"I am not mad at you. You make me sound like I'm in junior high school. I just don't think this is a great time to be suing the government. People are frightened right now and they want the government to do what is necessary to keep the country safe. It's not the moment to be insisting that political correctness trump law enforcement."

"It's not political correctness. That makes it sound like window dressing. The case is about protecting privacy. It's about thinking in advance where things will lead, so we are not always shocked and surprised when we get there."

"What are you discussing?" asked Robin.

"My law firm is representing some members of what used to be a club at Harvard, before the club was summarily disowned by the university – a club that raised money for a South American collective helping indigenous Peruvian goat farmers. Farmers of goats. They helped them feed their goats and pasteurize their cheeses. It turns out that the farm organization had a political wing, and the U.S. government in its post 9/11 wisdom has labeled them terrorists because they have occasionally supplied small amounts of food to a rebel group operating in the area."

"Those rebels are dangerous, Mickey. They're a real problem."

"Kidnapping, murdering, drug-dealing communist rebels. I'm sure many of them are terrible people. But these kids aren't murderers. They are college students who thought they were helping small farms be competitive in the global economy. And for that, they are under investigation by the FBI. It's an atrocious overreaction and a rush to judgment. And under the Patriot Act, the so-called Patriot Act,"

"Here we go," said Caleb.

"They can get their records from bookstores and libraries. They can trace their mobile phones, read their emails. check what websites they visit – all without a warrant, answerable to nobody. Every search that you make online is recorded, and the government wants unfettered access to all that information."

"Is that even possible?" Robin looked at John.

"It's easy. We track every hit on our site, so we know how many new users we have, how often they come back, what they look for, how long they stay, what they buy." John shrugged. "It's routine."

"It's a whole new world," said Robin.

"Yes," said Mickey, "with the same old people. The Homeland Security people are like kids in a candy store with all these new toys."

"But realistically," said John, "ordinary people have nothing to fear from any of this. The FBI isn't interested in what you or I are doing online. They are looking for radicals and terrorists. If you haven't done something shady, you have nothing to worry about."

"The government says they need this power and they won't abuse it. So you have to ask yourselves: do you trust them? Do you trust them to know which ones are radicals and terrorists? If criminals came stamped like meat, it would be a lot easier. In real life it's not always so obvious who are the good guys and who are the bad guys. Sometimes you don't get that sorted out until later on. For the moment, I am not comfortable that they are reliably after the right person. These kids are not terrorists. It could be anyone. It could certainly be me, since I am representing them." Mickey glanced nervously at Caleb. "Ordinary people have their own secrets."

"So you have thought about that," Caleb said, looking faintly ill, "and in the name of everyone's right to privacy, you are willing to sacrifice ours."

"It's a case with national significance. But if you want me to turn it down, I will. I mean that."

"No." Caleb smiled. "I could never ask you to make that choice and you know it. I understand that this is important to you. I know you feel strongly about privacy in theory, even if you are not so fond of it in practice. But thank you, for offering."

"I mean it, Caleb. I will say no. But that said, I do believe it's vitally important that we decide on some limits before the technology is in place, because once it is there, you know it is going to be used more broadly. That's inevitable. It's too tempting, and too easy. No one will be able to resist the opportunity to rifle through the closets of their enemies."

"If they find one thing that saves us from another attack," John began, but his wife interrupted him.

"They can rifle through my closets," said Robin. "But it will take them some time. I had three closets in the old place and I have nine here. Nine closets. Do you know how exciting that is for me?"

The voices of the boys playing hung in the air around them like birds chirping. In the neighboring yard, a door slammed. Ryan and Ted scrambled toward the fence. Ryan poked his nose through the space between the pickets. Ted turned and came back toward them. "Momma," he called, "can Isaiah come over?"

"Of course," said Robin. "The kid next door," she explained to Caleb and Mickey. "He's four. A whole year older. The boys think he's the best thing since sliced bread." She walked over and opened the gate.

"Come on in, Isaiah, it's nice to see you." Isaiah was tall for his age, with wide set eyes and an expression that was half-smiling even in repose. His hair curled tightly and his skin was a perfect café au lait. The smaller boys leaned in towards him as he sat on the grass examining their new toys.

"So you've met the neighbors?" Mickey asked Robin.

"I met Joan, his mother. She's an anthropologist. There's a ten year old daughter too. They moved to Wellesley five years ago." Robin paused. "She is very friendly. An inquiring type of woman. Most of the people I've met up here keep to themselves a bit, but not Joan. She wanted to know what did John do, and what did I do before I had the boys, and where did we go to school and how were they conceived, regular or assisted – a whole lot of questions. Maybe it's a Jewish thing."

"She's Jewish?" Mickey looked mildly surprised. "Not African-American?"

"So African-American people can't be Jewish? I am so appalled at your stereotyping." Robin poked Mickey. "No, I'm kidding. She's white and Jewish. The kids must be adopted. Can you keep an eye on them, while John and I get lunch? I was going to bring it out here, if that's okay."

"Are you alright?" asked Mickey, when Robin and John had gone inside. "You look distressed."

"What?" said Caleb. He drew his attention away from the boys where they played in the dirt. "Oh! No, I'm fine. The house is great, isn't it? I was just admiring the yard."

They heard a voice in the next yard calling, "Isaiah?" A dark-haired woman in her early forties appeared at the gate. "There you are!" She looked amiably at Mickey and Caleb, and reached over to let herself in. "I should have known to look here first." She walked briskly to where the children sat. "Isaiah, Daddy and Talia will be home soon and we are going to bike over to the Nature Center for Plant-a-Tree day."

"Can I stay here?" asked Isaiah.

"Remember, we talked about this last night, and you agreed it was very important to you to go to Plant-a-Tree day because you wanted to make sure there is lots of oxygen at the nature center for all the animals? What makes oxygen?"

"Trees," said Isaiah.

"And who needs oxygen at the nature center?"

"Frogs."

"Yes, the frogs need oxygen. And the bunnies. Do you want to pet the bunnies?"

"Okay."

"Hi!" said the woman, coming over to the patio table and putting out her hand. She wore jeans and a tee shirt with a necklace of large glass beads and silver bangle bracelets running up her arm. "I'm Joan." The men introduced themselves. "I've heard about you," she responded, with a pleased nod toward Mickey. "Harvard Law School, right? My husband teaches at Tufts, but he went to Harvard as an undergraduate. Is this your partner?" she asked, turning to Caleb. "Did you go to Harvard as well?"

"No," said Caleb.

Robin came out of the house carrying a large pitcher of iced tea. "Hi Joan," she said.

"I see Isaiah found his way over again. I hope he isn't bothering you."

"Not at all – the boys were asking for him all morning."

"By the way, I was signing Isaiah up for camp, so I got you some information. I checked with the camp director, and they still have a few spots left in his age bracket. Town camp puts the threes and fours together, which I know can be a little disenfranchising for the younger campers, but I think your boys will be fine. They're so verbal. Isaiah was exactly the same way, and he did very well last year. Town camp is only six weeks, and the private camps are seven weeks, but they cost a fortune. I'll bring over the brochure later."

"Thank you," said Robin. "That is so nice of you, but I'm not sure we were looking to send them to camp this year. They're so young still. The realtor said there was a local pond where the children could swim, so I thought the boys could go there with me."

"Morses Pond? We love Morses Pond, only be careful during the hotter weeks when it gets very crowded, because you have to keep an eye on the fecal coliform levels. They have swim lessons there during the summer – Talia took swim lessons there once, and the instructors were great, very nurturing and really empathic with all the children."

"Thank you. I will think about that. I guess the boys are getting old enough for swim lessons already. I was just going to teach them myself. I'm not trained as a teacher or anything, but I did do some lifeguarding."

"Robin swam competitively in high school and college," Mickey said to Joan.

"Really!" she responded. "At the University of Texas? That's Division I."

"I quit after my sophomore year," said Robin, waving her hand dismissively. "There were too many girls faster than me."

"Hi Joan," said John, coming out the back door with a large tray of sandwiches. "Nice to see you."

"Oh, I am disturbing your lunch! I will just gather up Isaiah and leave you in peace."

"No problem," John insisted. "Have a sandwich. Robin always makes too much food."

"Help yourself," said Robin. "There's chicken salad, and ham and cheese, and peanut butter and jelly."

"No, we'll leave you alone," said Joan. "What type of peanut butter do you use?"

"Just regular old peanut butter," said Robin.

"Do you know they sell the all-natural kind at the farmers' market on Saturdays? Isaiah loves it." Tires coming to a stop made a soft shushing noise on their driveway, and there was the thump-thump sound of car doors closing. "Oh, Randall and Talia are home from soccer. Last game of the season – let me get him; Randall would love to meet you. Randall!" she called, "come meet our new neighbors."

Randall was a big man, and he carried a little extra weight gracefully. His hair was receding, elongating his forehead, and giving it a domed shape that contrasted pleasantly with the strong horizontal lines in his face: heavy brows, thick black glasses, and the prominence of a forward-thrusting upper lip accentuated by a small, well-trimmed mustache. The girl beside him had the same slightly protruding eyes with thick lashes and heavy lids. She was a lighter brown than her father, and just a shade darker than Isaiah. Mickey turned to Robin, raising his eyebrows slightly, and she blushed a deep red.

"Hi Randall," said John, coming over to the fence to shake his hand. He opened the gate. "Come on in." Randall came over toward the table, nodding and smiling as his wife made introductions.

"Hey," said Robin to Talia, who held a small trophy in one hand, "I guess you won. Good for you!"

Talia looked critically at the shiny gold soccer ball on its white marble base. "Everybody gets one. It's for participation. We won six to three, but we don't keep score in rec soccer because the league says it is discouraging for the losing team." Talia turned to her mother. "I scored four."

"That's a lot of goals, honey. Any assists?"

"No. I passed a lot! It's not my fault nobody on my team can kick. We got one goal on a penalty and another one because a girl on their team kicked it back to their own goalie while the goalie was getting a drink. I hate this league. Next year I am doing the travel team." She turned and headed back toward her own yard. Ryan ran after her.

"Tal-ee-uh," he called in his rumbling baritone lisp. "Tal-ee-uh, is that your soccer shirt?" She wore a thin, shiny jersey that was yellow with green patches at the shoulder. "You have an eight on your shirt."

"Yup," said Talia, "that's my number." She patted his head affectionately. "When you get big you can play soccer too, okay Ryan?"

"Talia is so competitive." Joan looked significantly at her husband. "I wish she could just enjoy the game."

"It's a competitive game, Joan," said Randall. "It's not musical theater. The point is to win. I think we ought to let her play on that travel team. The coach called again the other day to ask. She is going to make our lives a misery if we don't. She told me it is not cool playing in the recreational league."

"Not cool! Fourth grade, and we are already starting with that nonsense." Joan shook her head and looked at Robin. "You have no idea. They grow up so fast."

Chapter 15

The boys moved up to the attic after they turned four. Their toys went first, one snap-top plastic bin at a time, until everything was in the room at the top of the stairs except the bedraggled plush monkeys that slept in their arms. Then the clothes went, including the Texas Ranger jerseys with R. HOGAN and T. HOGAN stitched across the backs. Robin put them on hangers and hung them on the wall like art. Finally, the beds were the only thing left. John disassembled and reassembled them; the two blue headboards side-by-side looked smaller in the big space. The boys were excited to sleep there.

Robin had a bit more time to herself these days. The boys went to preschool in the mornings, and in the afternoons those moments of peace that once seemed like mere lulls in the pandemonium lengthened into minutes and then hours when entire games were played that did not require Mommy to be a pirate or fix a race car or dispense juice with one hand and justice with the other. She was running again, four miles every morning.

On Tuesdays, they went to story hour at the library, which Joan said was very good for developing kindergarten readiness, and on Thursdays, they went to Kiddiekickers for Pre-K soccer clinic. Robin had signed John up as an assistant coach, and twice he made it home in time, and then they all went together and out for pizza afterwards.

It felt strange putting the boys to bed upstairs for the first time. Robin read their stories and turned off the overhead light. She saw their eyes dart around the room, with its unfamiliar nighttime shadows. The corners where the attic roof came low to the floor were impenetrably dark and mysterious, like the mouths of caves. She felt their uneasiness. Downstairs seemed very far away, and the fourteen steps between them like a harbinger of separations to come. But she did not want them to be fearful. Robin smiled bravely. "Off to sleep, Mommy's big boys! Dad will come and kiss you when he gets home."

John drove up around nine. He didn't come inside right away; Robin could hear him out in the garage, talking. He was still on the phone when he walked in. He held up a finger to say just one minute, and smiled at her, reaching for one of the cookies she and the boys had baked that afternoon. "No cookies for you," Robin said sternly. John pointed to the phone against his head and pantomimed bewilderment. "I know you can hear me," Robin laughed. "That's why the Good Lord gave you an ear on the other side of your head."

When he was done Robin reheated the pasta and John opened up a bottle of wine. "Sorry I'm late," he said. "We had our first live Webchat. Three Wisconsin players and their coach took questions for an hour."

"Did it go well?"

"The numbers were terrific. A couple of thousand people signed in. The questions were ridiculous. 'Coach, are you worried about the inexperience of your third-string cornerback?' and 'Are you guys excited about this week's game against Ohio State?' Jesus."

"John!"

"Sorry. Any Wisconsin player that isn't excited to play Ohio State better check his pulse. More women asked questions then you might think – lots of personal stuff. Boxers-or-briefs?" John raised his eyebrows.

"Were the guys offended?"

"They're big boys. There was one ugly moment, when a participant said something particularly unkind about a lack of balls, and it slipped past our obscenity filter. You think you've got a system in place and then – it's always a work in progress. You can't screen out all references to 'balls' in a conversation about football." John yawned. "How did tonight go with the little guys?"

"Fine," she said. He watched her wipe the granite countertop, stretching out her arm to reach across its broad surface. She had on the bracelet he had given her for her birthday, a full circlet of small diamonds set in platinum. She looked like a teenager in her tee shirt and jeans, like a kid wearing mom's good jewelry. Robin pulled her hair up off her face, slipping the length of it smoothly in and out of an elastic band. Her shirt rose with her arms, baring a small strip of bare belly.

"You look beautiful," he said, apropos of nothing.

They took their wineglasses and left the kitchen. John saw Robin glance into the empty room across the hall. "I was thinking the other day," he said, "that we might set this room up as a photography studio for you. Maybe you'd even want to do some more freelance work. We could have a guy come in and build a workspace under the window, where the light is good."

"John," said Robin, "I was thinking of something else for that room."

"Don't," said John.

"Come on, sweetheart. Wouldn't it be wonderful having a baby again? One more try for a little girl? It would be an awfully sweet room, painted pink."

John sighed. "I'll tell you the same thing I said last time, Rob. Those drugs are too dangerous. We already know how your body reacts. There's no way to be sure it wouldn't happen again."

"I might not need the drugs."

John shook his head. "I'm sorry, honey. If we could do the IVF without the drugs I would have another baby in a heartbeat. It's not that I'm not willing, not now. I know it makes you sad with the boys getting older and all. I even called up and talked to Dr. Aylmer. They won't do it. He said IVF without stimulation drugs is a waste of time. They won't even try it; the yield's too low."

"There's another possibility." She had been working on how to say this; John could tell by the way she hesitated. "It occurred to me, you never know, they might still have some of our embryos left. If we could just use our own embryos, then I wouldn't need any drugs. John, I know we signed that paper, but there's no reason for them to keep us from our own. If it's the storage fees they are worried about, we can pay them. We can pay them retroactively for everything we ever would have owed."

"There are no embryos left."

"You don't know that. I read in an article online last week that frozen embryos don't get used that much anymore, because most couples would rather shop around for eggs and sperm and make their own baby instead, instead of taking a chance on someone else's child. It turns out there are so many of those little souls left waiting for homes that church groups started campaigns for embryo adoption. Maybe all our embryos were used, but maybe they were not. Not all of them. Perhaps not all nine."

"There are no embryos." John spoke with authority, almost harshly. "I know because I asked. They didn't want to tell me anything, but I insisted. The receptionist practically hung up on me when I told her why I was calling. It took me a week to get through to the genetic counselor, and an hour to convince her that this was a reasonable request, and that we weren't going to take them to court or go postal on them or anything. She finally agreed to check the records. They were all used – adopted."

"And?" Robin's voice was choked.

"And what?"

"And what was the result? Where there any babies born?"

"She didn't tell me and I didn't ask." John looked incredulous. "I had just spent all this time convincing her that I was not some crazy stalker. I thought we had the right to know if there were any of our own embryos left for us to use. Beyond that, what good would it do us to know more? This is why I didn't tell you at the time; I didn't want you to get all worked up. I thought, it's better for you if you don't think about it."

"Don't think about it?" Robin gave a sad, exhausted chuckle. "Is that what you imagine – that I don't think about it? As if a day goes by that I don't think about those children. Our babies. How old are they? Where do they live? Are they happy?"

"Robin, I am sorry. I am so sorry. I wish things had happened differently. What do you want me to say? I can't change the past. I have tried to do my best by you and the boys. What else can I do?"

"You can agree to do IVF one more time. We can use lower doses of the stimulation drugs. We won't make any more embryos than we need. Just agree to try again and we will do it the right way this time, so that I don't get sick."

"No!" John seldom raised his voice and he was surprised by the sound that came out of him; a full-throated roar. Robin flinched as though she had been hit. "I am not going to put myself in that situation again, never. What if you do get sick? You can't control it. You could have died. You were willing to take that chance even when I begged you not to. You said in the hospital that it wasn't my choice to make. Fine. But it is my choice to make now, and I say no. I'm not willing to risk leaving those two little boys upstairs without a mother."

"Those two little boys upstairs wouldn't exist at all if it was up to you." Robin spoke in a low voice.

"That is such bullshit. Such total bullshit. Wouldn't exist if it was up to me? I did everything I could to have those children. I worked my ass off to pay for those treatments. You lied to the doctor. You lied to me. You could have died, and there would have been no Ryan, no Teddy, no us." John raised his voice, indignation settling in. "Don't tell me I don't care about my children. I care about them enough to make sure they don't lose their mother. You are unhappy because you don't have a girl and you don't get to buy Barbie dolls and pink sundresses. Don't twist this around to be about me and how I failed you. If you had a daughter, we wouldn't even be talking about embryos. You have a very good life and two beautiful sons who need a mother. It will have to be enough."

John turned and walked away. It felt strangely invigorating to be angry. *You lied to me*, he thought again. *It was not my fault you got sick. It was your fault. You put me in that untenable position and now you throw it in my face.* He willed himself not to look back at Robin as he closed the bedroom door behind him. He would not allow himself to be undone by her sadness because he was right and she was wrong, very wrong, to try and make him out to be the bad guy. There was no comfort he could offer that did not feel like atonement. I will be damned, he thought, if I let you pass judgment on me. There was a clarity in his rage that swept aside impotent misgivings.

Robin sat on the floor of the boys' old room, in the corner where the dresser had been. Her face felt heavy, as though the muscles in her cheeks did not have the strength to pull taut. She considered, almost idly, that she had never seen John so angry. The thought was a dull ache. She tried to marshal her grievances, but felt only emptiness. She was too tired for anger. John had accused her of terrible things. She tried to remember what he said, but all that she could recall was that awful statement, repeated twice. *There are no embryos.* She hated it that he sounded so certain and so final, like his was the word of God. What if the clinic made a mistake? What if they lied?

John could not simply declare that the subject was closed. She had something to say about this too. Robin raised her head. She heard a small noise that did not come from the master bedroom. She stood and drifted out into the living room. A light was on, but no one was there. She lifted her eyes to a small shape at the top of the stairs. Teddy's silhouette in the dark was infinitely familiar to her. His breath sounded raggedy in the way that it did when he was trying not to cry. She climbed the stairs slowly, wondering what he had heard.

"Hi sweetie," she said, sitting next to him. "What's wrong? Did you wake up in your new room and get frightened? Were you coming to find Mommy?"

"Daddy was yelling."

"It's okay, Teddy-bear. Mommy and Daddy had an argument, just like sometimes you and Ryan have an argument. Even people who love each other very much can have a fight and then make up."

"Mommy, are you going to go away?"

"Go away? Sweetheart, I would never go away. How could you even think that?"

"Why do little boys lose their mother? Is it because they aren't good? Ryan and I are good."

This pain was sharp and acute. Robin felt the tears running down her cheeks. "You are the most wonderful boys in the world. There is nothing you could ever do that would make me leave you. You and your brother are everything I ever wanted in my whole life."

"But you wanted a girl baby." Ted looked at her crying and hugged his mother. "You wanted a girl baby, but Ryan and I are both boys. I am sorry, Mommy." Ted started to cry. "I wish you weren't sad. I wish we were enough."

"Now you listen to me," said Robin. She pulled away from her son just far enough that she could look into his eyes. "I am so happy to be your mother. Daddy and I are so lucky to have you." She remembered that first ultrasound, when they found two sacs and two beating hearts. Nothing she had ever seen was as beautiful as those two white spots blinking like Christmas lights against the inky blackness. Then there was the other ultrasound three months later, when the technician said "boy!" and then "another boy!" Her eyes met John's across the table and she gave a shrug and a smile. Of course, she was a little disappointed at the time. She didn't know them yet, these children that she loved absolutely. She had no idea then that Teddy would have eyelashes so thick that grown women clucked with envy, or that Ryan would always glance back and make sure she was watching before he did something particularly naughty. The thought that either of them might have been different in any way made her sick. "You are a gift from God, Teddy Hogan," she whispered. "There is no other child in the world I would rather have, and nothing is ever going to take you away from me. Don't you ever worry about that again. Don't cry. I'm not sad. I won't be sad. Can you stop crying now, for Mommy?" Ted gave a hard sniff. "Good. Come on," she said, standing up and reaching a hand out to her son. "Let's get you back to bed."

Chapter 16

In the car on the way to the clinic, Robin talked about kindergarten. "The problem is," she said, squeezing the wheel of the big car nervously, "that the school has three sections of kindergarten and Joan says the youngest teacher is far and away better than the other two, but the school wants to separate the twins, so then they can't both have Miss Grey. I don't know if I should request Miss Grey for one of them, or leave it be, or ask to keep them together. Everyone asks for her, so if I don't put in a request then neither of them is going to get into that class. That's not fair to them. I think kindergarten is important; don't you think kindergarten is important?"

She paused, so Mickey said, "hmmm."

"Joan says kindergarten is significant in that it sets the tone for all of elementary school. Isaiah has Miss Grey and he is already reading on a second grade level. Joan says I should ask for Miss Grey for

Ryan because she thinks he needs a more structured classroom, but I don't know. Miss Grey seems like the sweetest one and I think Ted could use a teacher who is very nurturing. I think that might be more important at this age, when they're in school all day. It's such a long day. I wish they could just go for half a day. What do you think I should do?"

"Sure, do the half a day."

"You can't do half a day, Mickey. That's the point. They are there from eight-thirty until three. I agree with you that it's a very long day. The question is, what is more important, nurturing or structure? Maybe I should just insist that they keep the boys together. Do you really think that would be so damaging? Do you think it is that important to separate twins in kindergarten?"

"I don't know."

"You must have an opinion."

"Robin, I do not know fuck-all about kindergarten. The only thing I remember about kindergarten was the teacher patting me on the back and telling me that big boys don't cry every time that I cried. I don't know what I was supposed to take from that. I believe she thought she was being nurturing."

"Why are you so angry?"

"I am not angry. I am a little tense. I wish you would take off that ridiculous wig."

"I can't." Robin shook her head and her ersatz brown curls shook with her. "It's important that they don't recognize me. Since John already contacted them last year, they will be suspicious if they see me in there. Besides, I always wanted to try out being a brunette." She touched Mickey's arm affectionately. "Thank you for doing this. It's very kind of you."

"It's very stupid of me. Do you have any idea what kind of trouble I could get into? As a lawyer?"

"It will be fine; I promise you. If I get caught, I will swear up and down that you had no idea what I had in mind. Assuming anyone even cares. I'm not robbing a bank, Mickey. It's my own information. I have the right to know. Anyway, if there's a problem, then you just insist that you were genuinely interested in getting the information on hiring a surrogate mother. They've got no reason to disbelieve that."

"I swear, your honor, I had no idea that my sister in the wig and sunglasses was planning anything unusual." Mickey shook his head. "Yes, that will be very convincing."

"If you don't want to do this, we don't have to," said Robin.

"No. I'm in. I want to do this for you." Mickey grinned, tugging on a brown curl. "Do you know what else I remember about kindergarten? I remember how every once in a while you left all your friends to sit next to me at lunch so I didn't have to eat by myself." Plus, though he did not want to admit it to Robin, he did not have to pretend to be genuinely interested in learning about surrogacy. It would give him a chance to approach Caleb with the facts. He was always more comfortable with known quantities. Maybe it would change something for Caleb, who was turning in the most polite way possible into a miserable bastard who stared at other people's children with a look of blank resignation that made Mickey furious.

He'd had the thought two months ago, when Robin first approached him with this crazy scheme of hers. She needed to get inside the IVF clinic, although she told him in no uncertain terms that she was never going to have IVF again. She had promised to let it go; it was too upsetting to John, too upsetting to her children. But it turned out there were these nine extra embryos, siblings of a sort, siblings on ice. John believed that they were gone and she had tried to accept this reality and move on. But, as time went on, she found herself plagued by doubts. It seemed so unlikely that all nine could have been used. Robin told him it would put her misgivings to rest if only she could see it there in black and white. That was all she wanted – to take a look at her own file, and to put aside all the "what ifs" that came to her in the middle of the night.

There were just a few people in the waiting room when they walked in. "We're last, right?" Robin whispered after Mickey gave his name.

"I asked for the latest possible appointment on a Friday and they told me that was five o'clock. So we have five o'clock. That's why we had to wait two months."

"Good. You'll see, we'll sit here for a while and then we'll sit in the doctor's office for even longer. Hopefully, the office staff will start packing up soon." Robin watched the receptionist and pretended to read a magazine. The last remaining couple in the waiting room was ushered into the back.

"Look!" Mickey slunk lower in his seat and his voice became conspiratorial. "The receptionist has checked her watch at least three times in the past five minutes. Good sign."

"Stop it." Robin poked him in the ribs. "She's looking this way. I think she is staring at me."

"Possibly she is intrigued by the fact that you are wearing sunglasses in the waiting room. But I don't think so. I think she is looking at us because we are the only thing that stands between her and the weekend."

"You can follow me," called the nurse. They walked past the front office on their way to the back and Robin stole a glance at the receptionist. She was reaching under her chair for her bag. Robin's heart leaped.

Mickey had made certain to request Dr. Aylmer's partner. Robin had never been in his office before. She took a pad from her bag and sat next to Mickey. "Look," she said "I made a list of some questions to ask. I thought it might be useful."

Mickey glanced at the page with its neat, round handwriting. "*Is it hard to find a surrogate in Massachusetts?* Okay. *How many embryos do you generally transfer? What do you do with the remaining embryos? If any embryos are frozen, who has legal control of them?*" He looked at Robin. "Don't you find these questions rather embryo-centric?"

"I didn't want you to run out of things to say."

"In all the years that you've known me, have I ever run out of things to say?"

"I was trying to be helpful. Besides," Robin leaned over his shoulder and surveyed the paper, "the last question is not about embryos."

"*What will the courts do if the surrogate changes her mind?*" Mickey shook his head. "Robin, do you think it is even remotely possible I came here not knowing the law?"

"What's the answer, then?"

"In Massachusetts, the courts will uphold the surrogacy contract, unless the surrogate is carrying her own biological baby. If you don't use a donor egg, then the woman has up to four days after giving birth to change her mind."

Robin nodded. "Because it's her baby."

"She is the biological and gestational mother. Two strikes. You could end up in a custody battle. Gay men do not do so well in custody battles, not even in famously liberal Massachusetts. So it is safer to use a donor egg. Do they have a donor egg program here?"

"I don't know."

"Well then, I guess I can come up with at least one question."

"You'll think of something, I'm sure." Robin glanced at the clock. "I think I've waited long enough. I'm guessing I have ten minutes at least before the doctor shows up."

"Do you want to synchronize our watches?"

"No jokes. Keep your fingers crossed. If the doctor comes in, tell him I went looking for a bathroom."

Robin slipped out of the room. There was no one in the corridor. Muffled voices came from an examining room and she held her breath walking by the door. In seconds, she was around the corner and next to the closed door. Robin leaned into the waiting room so she could see through the glass partition into the office. It was empty. She put her hand on the doorknob and prayed that it would not be locked. It turned with a click that seemed loud in the surrounding hush.

Robin closed the door behind her. The bank of filing cabinets was labeled alphabetically. She found the drawer labeled G-I and slid it open. Hayes, Heaton, Hirsh, Hoares – Hogan. She pulled it out. It was hard to see in the dimness. It would have been a good idea to bring a flashlight. I guess I'm not cut out to be a cat burglar, Robin thought. There was a lamp on the desktop. She turned it on, arching its flexible neck downward toward the table so that only a small circle of light seeped out.

Robin opened the file. There was Dr. Aylmer's handwriting, cramped and spiky. Hysterosalpingogram. The memory of that first test came back to her, the water running into her tubes and then the sudden cramping pain so intense that she cried out. "It was like labor," she said afterwards to John, but what did she know about labor back then? Nothing. She went through the file page by page. It was like reading a horror story for a second time; the terror was more benign, once you knew how it ended.

But this was not the moment for nostalgia; she needed to move quickly. The rounds of clomiphene citrate were documented, follicles (never enough) and then the notation at the end of each page: pregnancy 0. Years slipped by under her fingers. There was a bright yellow page that marked the introduction of IVF, with its long list of drugs and a rising count of follicles that seemed ominous only in retrospect. She recognized the date of the egg retrieval – when she closed her eyes, she could picture the ultrasound machine and that long, hollow needle. Underneath, it said "ova: twenty-two."

Everything that was written there she already knew: twenty-two eggs, eighteen embryos, three transferred, nine frozen. She sifted through the pages that documented her weeks in the hospital. Nothing, nothing, nothing. The last sheet in the file said "embryo disposition." Robin held her breath. Her eyes ran quickly over the legal boilerplate. We, the undersigned, release the use of the aforementioned embryos for the purpose of: reproductive donation. Her name and John's name were printed at the bottom, and there were two signatures, both in John's nearly illegible scrawl. So this was another thing he had spared her, another thing he didn't want her to have to think about.

Robin closed the folder up and replaced it in the cabinet. She needed to get back to the room. She looked at the labels on the filing cabinets once more. Perhaps it was listed under embryo donation. She pulled open the drawer D-F. Nothing but names, endless names, one thick file after another. She looked around the room. The large drawer in the receptionist's desk looked big enough to hold files. She put one finger on the handle. A picture of a young boy in a blue frame looked out at her from the desktop. I can't just rifle through this woman's desk, thought Robin. If it is not meant to be, than it is not meant to be.

Robin was almost to the door when she noticed the small white file cabinet, half hidden under a table holding the printer and fax. She knelt next to it. This one had only two drawers, and no labels at all. She pulled open the top drawer and worked her way quickly through the files. Hogan was at the back. She opened the folder, her stomach a clenched knot. The first page was a copy of the form from their file authorizing the donation. The next two were medical histories, one for her and one for John. There was a green page marked Embryo Record Sheet. It had four columns: date; donors; recipients; # of embryos. There were only three entries, each of them identical except for the date. *Donors: John and Robin Hogan. Recipients: David Bettinger and Meredith Schuyler. Number of embryos: 3.* January 2002, March 2002, April 2002: three times three.

Robin rocked backwards on her heels. She stared at the names. She knew what the repetition meant; one failed attempt after another. Running through embryos, three at a clip, did they ever think of stopping? Did it ever occur to them that their chances were very slim, after three were gone and then six were gone? Having exhausted all of hers, did they just move on? One embryo was as good as another to them, she thought.

Robin stuck the file back in the white cabinet and stood up. She moved toward the door and then turned back into the room one more time. The ten minutes were up. She walked quickly over to the main files, pulling out the drawer marked Q-S. Schuyler. She rummaged through the names. Schuyler. There it was. She pulled it out and flipped through the lists of tests and medical history to the end. Here were the three dates again. *January: transferred 1, pregnancy 0. March: transferred 1, pregnancy 0. April: transferred two, singleton pregnancy confirmed by ultrasound 5/1/01.*

Robin's hands shook so that the paper rustled. Distantly, she heard a door open, and the sound of voices broke the stillness. The other couple – they would pass through the waiting room on their way out. There she was on the other side of the glass, on view like a fish in a fishbowl. Robin flung herself to the floor, laying her cheek against the dense loops of nylon carpeting. She lay there listening, half under the desk, her eyes locked on the small dirty wheels of the receptionist's chair. She tried to breathe more quietly. A paperclip sitting inches from her nose looked unnaturally large. This is ridiculous, thought Robin. The patients were taking their time walking out. She glanced at the file, still in her hand. Laying it on the ground, she withdrew the first page. Her eyes had adjusted to the dim light and she could just make out the names. "David Bettinger/Meredith Schuyler. 614 Tilden Street. Brookline, MA." Impulsively, Robin sat up far enough to reach the top of the desk and grabbed a pen. She lay back down. Paper, she thought. She reached in the wastebasket behind her head and pulled out a crumpled scrap. Smoothing it, she copied the names and address and shoved it into her pocket. Footsteps drew closer and she heard the door to the clinic open and close. Robin stood and replaced the file, sliding the open drawer shut.

Stepping quietly into the corridor, she straightened her rumpled clothes and blinked in the brightness of the fluorescent lighting. She was almost back to the room when the nurse walked by. "Can I help you?" she asked, sounding surprised. Her face was vaguely familiar and she stared curiously at Robin.

"Washroom?" said Robin, pointing towards the back as though to confirm that she had not found it in the other direction.

"It's right there," said the nurse.

Robin nodded her thanks. She closed the bathroom door behind her and checked her face in the mirror, relieved to see that her brown curls were still in place. She splashed a little water on her hot cheeks and headed back to the doctor's office. Mickey was talking as she stepped in. "So when I arrange for the surrogate, does the agency do the testing or do you take care of that here?"

The doctor smiled, acknowledging Robin. "Usually, the agency has done some preliminary testing early on, so they don't waste everybody's time. Most of the agencies we have worked with are very good about doing a careful psychological exam, and ruling out hepatitis, HIV, and sexually transmitted diseases."

"HIV? From the surrogate? That would be ironic. Do you test the egg donor as well?"

"Egg donor, and intended father. Infectious diseases are a two-way street. We don't want the baby or the gestational carrier to be at risk."

"That reminds me," said Mickey. "Is it possible to have more than one sperm donor? I mean, I know there is only one biological father per child, but what if my partner and I wanted to leave paternity to chance – could you use two sperm donors?"

"Sperm blending? Certainly. It's not a problem. There are some extra costs associated with testing two individuals and the additional lab work, but it is not very significant."

"What are the total costs?"

"Our fees are roughly twelve thousand dollars per cycle, but there are some variables involved in coordinating the cycles of the egg donor and the surrogate that can affect the cost. One suggestion we make at our center is to run a test cycle on the surrogate, to check how she responds to the drug regimen. That's a conservative approach, but I tell you from experience it is a good investment, because there is nothing worse than having beautiful fresh eggs all ready to go and nowhere to put them."

"What do you do then?" Mickey asked. "Freeze the eggs?"

"For reasons we don't fully understand, eggs don't take well to being frozen. We would go ahead and create the embryos. Embryos freeze very nicely. But we don't want to take that step if we don't have to, and of course freezing and storage are another expense. The costs for the gestational carrier and the donor egg vary depending on which agency you choose. All going well, you could end up spending around thirty or forty thousand dollars total. But some people pay that much just for the egg."

Mickey nodded, but Robin was startled. "A forty thousand dollar egg?" she asked.

"You hear of offers that high for girls with Ivy League credentials and the right look, the right height, the right athleticism. Of course that's not the norm." *I should hope not*, thought Robin, irritated by the idea of people who felt entitled to everything, not only to have superior children but to define what was meant by superior children. What would they do, she wondered, with the ones who fell short of the mark?

"Money aside," Mickey said, "what are the chances that a cycle is successful?"

"If the egg donor is under twenty five – and commercial donors are all under twenty five – we have about a forty percent chance of success. If the donor has a good track record, it might be as high as fifty percent."

"What about the age of the surrogate?"

"It doesn't matter, except that pregnancy is easier on women under forty. But from our point of view it's mainly in the egg. If she's healthy, we can get her pregnant."

It sounded so easy, thought Robin. Mix, stir, bake. She had a sudden, overwhelming desire to be out of this place. She looked over, trying to catch Mickey's eye. He had not run out of questions. "How often do surrogates end up carrying twins?" he asked. "If the gestational carrier has her own health insurance, will that cover her expenses as a commercial surrogate?" "Do you have agencies that you recommend?"

The doctor pulled out a sheet with several names on it. Mickey looked it over carefully. Alright, thought Robin. You've done a great job. Fidgeting slightly, she watched him slide the paper carefully into his briefcase. He did not look at her. Robin sat back in her chair. This was no performance. Robin wondered why it had not occurred to her earlier that Mickey might be genuinely interested in surrogacy. Mickey! She tried to picture him with an infant in the wee hours of the morning, but it was Caleb she saw, walking up and down the hallway in their apartment. "Do you ever work with someone who is a family member?" she asked. "A family member or a friend, rather than a paid surrogate?"

The doctor looked at her more carefully now, and Mickey stared. "There are many advantages to non-commercial surrogacy, if that is an option. Lower cost, of course. Certain individuals feel more comfortable working with someone they know, and other people are happier to work with someone who will walk away at the end of the process. In any event, we strongly recommend a full psychological evaluation."

Mickey stood up. "Thank you," he said, reaching out to shake hands with the doctor. "I can't tell you how helpful this has been. I need to talk this over with my partner and hopefully I will be in touch with you soon."

"Wonderful," said the doctor. "It's been a pleasure meeting you both."

Chapter 17

A parking attendant retrieved the SUV, and Robin slid in behind the wheel. John had chosen the Lexus, when they needed a bigger car for all the bikes and scooters and carpools. Mickey buckled his seat belt. Robin pulled out into the Cambridge traffic and headed back across the river to drop him at home. "Well," he said, finally, when it was quiet in the car and he could breathe again, "did you get the information?"

"The embryos are gone," said Robin. "I wanted to see it in black and white, and there it was in black and white."

"I'm sorry," Mickey replied. He looked over at Robin. Her color was heightened but she did not look distraught. "So, nobody saw you?"

"I don't think so. I talked to a nurse on the way back but I don't believe she was suspicious." Robin pulled the brown wig off her head. "I'm an excellent secret agent."

"You need to improve on the part where you don't draw attention to yourself. You practically volunteered to carry my child. It's very sweet, Robin, but really, what were you thinking?"

Robin made a face at him. "It just popped out, when I saw how serious you were about this surrogacy stuff. Turns out you are the stealthy one, not me. Why didn't you tell me that you and Caleb were interested in having children?"

"Because there is no use talking about it until Caleb breaks the news to his parents that he is not single because he is still pining for his high school sweetheart."

"Is that what he tells them?"

"I think that is what his mother chooses to believe. For a while he told them that he was dating a paralegal at his office. A paralegal! A pretend taboo intra-office affair. Maybe he was thinking about his secretary, because that little bitch has been after him for years. But don't you think that a person could be a bit more creative about a fantasy relationship? God. She could be an artist, or a mafia princess, or a stripper."

"A contortionist."

"Yes, perfect. A contortionist with the circus, which would explain why she was rarely around. Poor Caleb – all he wants to be is a cliché and instead he falls in love with me. Anyway, after a year or so, his folks started asking why he never brought the girl home to dinner, so he had to break up with her." Mickey grinned at Robin out of the side of his mouth, they way he used to when they were kids. "She took it well. But what about you, Rob? What are you going to do now that you have your answer?'

"I am going to go home to my wonderful husband and my wonderful boys and live happily ever after. What are you going to do about this surrogacy thing?"

"What can I do? I am going to wait; wait, and hope for change. Every once in a while I throw a temper tantrum and threaten to leave if nothing changes, so that Caleb is forced to make promises he can't keep. Sometimes I think we are on the verge of making progress. I was glad he got rid of the pretend girlfriend. She was getting on my nerves." He grimaced. "I don't know – let's just say I will not be invited to Thanksgiving at the Dunhills anytime soon. It's probably just as well. Caleb says his mother always has three gin and tonics by noon, and last year they ended up with twenty pounds of underspiced turkey jerky for dinner."

"Imagine what Caleb would say if he saw daddy out in the garage, deep frying the turkey in a garbage can."

"It would be worth the cost flying him down to Texas just to see his face. He was shocked to hear we had cornbread in our stuffing. Shocked!"

It took forever getting in and out of town. Robin was late as she pulled off the highway heading home. She glanced over her shoulder and the brown wig on the backseat caught her eye. She pulled into a gas station beside the exit and parked at the back beside the dumpster. Robin reached for the wig. She stroked the tangle of curls. It felt like a living thing beneath her touch. Her fingers tightened and the silky fibers compressed to nothing, slipping out of her grasp. On the floor at her feet it was dark and shapeless. Robin stared at the dumpster. Removing the key from the ignition, she unlocked a small drawer underneath the passenger seat. These new cars had very innovative storage features. She shoved the wig into the drawer and turned the lock.

The boys were in high spirits when she got home. They loved having dinner with Isaiah and Talia. "They ate tofu?" asked Robin, her eyebrows arching.

"They each had seconds," said Joan.

"If I made it at home, they would never touch it. Not the boys and not their daddy. Thank you so much for taking them."

"They're no trouble," said Joan.

From the couch, John waved in acknowledgement when Robin said she was going to bed. She closed the closet door softly behind her and took the folded scrap of paper from her bag. She could barely recognize her own handwriting in that awkward, hurried scrawl. Robin opened the top drawer and slid it to the back, behind the black cotton panties and the lacy thongs. She did not need to read it again; the names were seared into her memory. David Bettinger and Meredith Schuyler. What sort of people were they? She, apparently, was the kind of woman who kept her own name. Better for her at work no doubt; she probably had some high-profile job and a reputation to maintain. She put her career first, and didn't bother about children until it was too late. But now, she had both. Robin knew women like that in Wellesley; they were not around in the carpool line at pick-up time, but they came to back-to-school night in September and asked lots of questions about enrichment activities and reading readiness. These were women who were used to getting what they wanted.

All the parents were there in June, when the nursery school had a small event to mark the end of the school year. "Moving on," they called it, not to confuse it with a thing requiring mortarboards and speeches. Most of the parents were shooting video, but Robin still preferred photography. She felt time stop moving for just a second every time she clicked the shutter. The camera felt comfortable in her hand, even with the extra weight of her new zoom lens. The boys with their classmates trotted onstage after the teacher like fifteen khaki and white ducklings. The two of them stood side-by-side. Ted was doe-eyed and adorable, blonde hair clipped short for the start of summer. Ryan had already managed to untuck his button-down shirt. He bounced from one foot to the other as the piano played 'She'll Be Coming Round the Mountain When She Comes' and the children sang "We'll be Going to Kindergarten in the Fall." Robin sniffed. John put his arm around her shoulder and squeezed, gently.

There was a picnic afterwards, out on the lawn behind the school. Robin helped pour at the juice table while John kept an eye on the boys. A crowd of children were running races around the swings. Teddy moved quickly in his loping graceful style, while Ryan put his head down and ran until his legs were a blur. They were both fast, John noted with satisfaction. They came across the finish line together with a scuffle and a straight arm at the end, and the two of them went down in a heap. Ryan gave his brother an extra thump as he got back up again. Ted's eyes filled up with caramel-colored tears. "He pushed me," Ryan hollered, as he saw his father approach, his eyes blazing more darkly.

John shook his head. "I don't want to hear any complaining," he said sternly. "You do more than your share of pushing. That's enough." Echoes of his own mother lingered in the sound of his voice. *Stop your whining, Johnnie. You're no treat yourself, some of the time.* They were lucky to have one another. They would understand that, sooner or later.

It was almost time to go when Robin rejoined them. "Should we tell them now?" asked John. He'd bought tickets to Sunday's Red Sox game to celebrate the big day. "I hope they are excited."

"Of course they will be," said Robin.

"I should have gotten a ticket for Isaiah. They'd like that. I wish I'd thought of it earlier."

"They love going to the ballgame with their Daddy."

"It's more exciting with a friend."

"I'll tell you what," said Robin, "go ahead and invite Isaiah. If he can come, we'll give him my ticket."

"But I didn't mean to suggest that – this is a family thing. The boys will be very disappointed if you are not there."

"The boys won't care a bit. They have me all the time; it's having you to themselves that's a treat. Besides, I wouldn't mind having a few hours to do some shopping downtown. I haven't been to Neiman Marcus in a while."

"I should have bought Isaiah his own ticket," said John. "It would have been cheaper.

On Sunday Robin dropped John and the three boys close to the stadium and drove into Back Bay to park the car. She wandered around the stores. It was barely June, and the summer clothes were already on sale. It was oppressive the way the retailers were always rushing you towards the next season, as though September wasn't going to show up on time without them moving things along. Soon enough, thought Robin. She looked at some new running gear in a technical fabric with wicking capacity. Robin took two of the shirts and a pair of shorts to try it out.

She went to look at dresses, but everything was translucent layers and hippie-chic, not her style at all. She headed upstairs instead to the children's department. They had shorts with a camouflage print and big pockets on the sides. "Do you have these in both a five and a seven?" she asked the salesgirl.

"I'll check in the back," the girl said. Waiting, Robin sifted through a stack of red and blue polo shirts, and then her eyes strayed across the aisle to a purple-flowered shirt with a flounce along the bottom and matching lavender leggings. That is so cute, she thought. '*Girls Eighteen Months to Three*' said the sign. Robin hovered on the edge of the racks, reaching out to stroke the cotton velour of a tiny sundress. In the center of the section there was a whole row of dresses in animal prints – kittens, bunnies, panda bears. She took a few tentative steps into the thicket of orange and pink. The vibrancy of the color surrounding her felt like an alternative reality after the blues and greens and deep reds of the boy's department. Robin picked up a shirt with cherries on it; it was a size two. She held it out and imagined the size and shape of the child who would fit into that shirt. It seemed very long ago that her own children were that small. The baby could just as easily be a boy, she reminded herself. Stop doing this.

"Oh, there you are!" said the young woman. "I couldn't find you. I have both the five and the seven."

"Thanks," said Robin, putting the shirt back and taking the shorts. "Can you ring these up for me?"

"Anything else?" she asked.

"Just that."

The game was only in the fifth inning when Robin got back into the car. She drove by the stadium and then continued on, aimlessly. Much of this area was unfamiliar to her. Brookline was somewhere near here, right on the fringes of the city. They probably drove by often, with the child. Robin struggled to put the thought out of her mind. Nothing good can come of this, she told herself sternly. Not that it matters, she added, relenting. The cat was already out of the bag. She could not force herself not to know that the child existed. She could not help that it gnawed at her, knowing only that and nothing more. Anything would be easier than this, Robin thought.

The T ran above ground here, and Robin followed the tracks of the tram down a wide thoroughfare. It was quieter after a while. She turned down one of the side streets and the scene became abruptly residential. The little gardens out in front of the houses were well-tended, and tall trees thrived undisturbed in small green spaces. The sidewalks were uneven brick. Only the narrow setbacks between the houses suggested the proximity of the city. It was a quiet, unglamorous place with an air of remodeled prosperity.

Robin cruised in languorous intersecting circles, monitoring the progress of the ballgame on the radio. She followed a sign that said 'school zone 20 MPH' and found a big brick building with a small field behind it that was marked for baseball and for soccer, lines of yellow paint cutting across the infield dirt. A softball team was practicing, and younger children played on the playground next to the school. Robin idled the car by the curb, watching the children run and climb. Her eyes settled on a small boy with dark hair. He moved with an intensity that reminded her of Ryan. She watched as he charged up the ladder to the slide. The other kids his size wobbled slightly as they ran, but not this one. It made her smile. He came back around to the foot of the slide, and gave a small push to another boy who was lingering there indecisively. The boy fell. Robin saw the adults who had been hovering on the perimeter descend as the fallen child hollered. It wasn't really aggression, she thought. He was just impatient to get back up the ladder. It wasn't his fault the other child tipped over so easily.

The crying boy's mother lifted him up and retreated to a bench. A man crouched down next to the young perpetrator, holding his arm and speaking with a serious expression, although his free hand stroked the boy's back affectionately. Seen in profile, the man and the child looked strikingly alike. Robin breathed a long sigh and shook her head. Brookline was a small city. What was she thinking? Even if they lived here, even if they had not moved, her child was only one of a vast horde of two-year-olds. She was allowing her imagination to run away with her. Feeling tired and deflated, Robin put the car in drive and pulled away.

She needed to get back to familiar territory and find her way to the stadium. The eighth inning was over and the Rod Sox were down by a run, so they would come to bat in the ninth. She had maybe twenty minutes. Robin turned right; the big street with the tram tracks ought to be a couple of blocks ahead. The road curved left, so she made another right, but it brought her around to a second park. There were children playing here too, but she barely glanced at them. The street angled off to one side. I have to turn right the next chance I get, thought Robin. She drove down to the next corner but the street she was on ended and she had no choice but to turn left.

She went right again and then drove a block further, pausing at the first cross street. She looked right. There, several blocks down, the quiet street ended in a light. She could see the busier traffic beyond. Finally! She had just begun to edge forward when out of the corner of her eye she caught the name. Tilden Street. Robin hit the brakes, hard.

She sat very still in the car, her hands on the wheel numb and tingling. The Red Sox game on the radio echoed oddly in her ears. "Well, that's it for the top of the ninth," the announcer said. "Red Sox have three outs left and trail by one." With an effort she perceived that the game could be over at any moment. Robin looked again to the right, paused, and turned left. She drove slowly down the street, eyeing the houses on either side. She was at four-seventy-two, and the numbers were heading up. She could see the paper in the file as if it was sitting in front of her. *Six-one-four Tilden Street.* The leadoff hitter for the Red Sox was up now. Robin craned her neck. Some of the numbers were hard to find. There was the breaking wood sound of a ball on a bat and the crowd roared. Single. Robin went one more block. Five-eighty-six. Five-ninety-two. Johnny Damon was up. Six-zero-eight. Damon hit into a fielder's choice, moving the runner to second. Six-fourteen.

Robin parked on the street across from the house. It was bigger than most, boxy and attractive in a pale green color. The garage was closed and the driveway was bare. The man up at bat kept fouling off pitches, one after another. Robin looked at the well-kept front yard, and twisted her head around to try and see into the back. She felt contained in the still air inside the car, a silent and invisible observer. Crack! "Single to left!" the announcer blared. "That'll tie up the game. A quick throw keeps Manny on first. Single and an RBI for Ramirez."

There was a woman walking down the block, pushing an empty stroller while a small child walked alongside. Robin watched them as they approached the house. Her heart beat hard against the seatbelt strap across her chest. The boy – it was a boy – was tall for a two-year-old. She stared at him, her mouth dry. They were directly across from her now, and the mother turned her head toward the car with an inquiring glance. It was a shock for Robin when their eyes met. She felt suddenly and unexpectedly exposed. Robin looked down, and then glanced up again, surreptitiously. The woman was no longer looking at her. They were past the house and continuing up the block. "That's a hard line drive, but right to the shortstop. He throws to second. The play at first – out! Double play!" the announcer on the radio blared. "This game's going to extra innings."

The spasm in Robin's chest eased and she breathed deeply, almost panting. The oxygen reaching her brain was like a spell breaking. She couldn't sit there waiting to be seen. Robin put the car into drive. She went several houses up the street before pulling into a driveway to turn around. She headed back the other way, only slowing infinitesimally as she passed the big green house. She was halfway down the next block when she saw the other car. It was expensive-looking, something recent and foreign and solid, and a dark-haired man was driving. He sat alone in the front like a chauffeur. In the seat behind him a woman was turned so that Robin saw only the back of her head. She was looking into a child's seat set facing forward, the way they were after the children reached a certain size. Her hair obscured Robin's view like a curtain. As the two cars passed, she settled back into her seat, and Robin caught a fleeting view of a small face.

Just keep driving, thought Robin to herself, but she came to the intersection and turned around. She paused, watching the car ahead of her. It moved forward steadily, without concern, going neither slowly nor quickly. It turned into the driveway at six-fourteen. Robin, following behind, willed herself not to slow down more as she passed. The woman was out of the car, bending in at an open back door. She pulled out a small blonde girl and set her down. Even from a distance Robin felt a jolt of recognition. Teddy's face. Teddy's face at two, just waking up from a nap, eyes half shut. Grasping the woman's hand, the little girl walked around the back of the car. She was close to the street as the car drove by, and Robin could see her mother's hand tighten as she tugged the child away from edge of the drive. At the pressure from her mother, the girl looked up. Her eyes, luminous and green, followed Robin as she rolled slowly and steadily past.

⚯

CHAPTER 18

There was a McDonalds east of Wellesley, just far enough out of town that Robin felt in no danger there of running into anyone she knew. She had gotten into the habit of stopping for coffee after dropping the boys off at camp, and using the restroom to put on her wig. The worst part was hovering in the toilet stall, breathing in all the nasty smells that lingered beneath the thick, faux-pine fog of industrial disinfectant, until she was absolutely certain no one would have seen her go in as a blond and come out as a brunette. The first time she got the thing on askew and a heavyset woman in a floral blouse gave her the fisheye as she washed her hands and tugged discretely at her hairline.

As a rule, it was past ten before she arrived at the house in Brookline. She always went around the corner to park. Sometimes she brought Jack, the dog they had gotten the boys for Christmas.

Still a puppy, he tripped over his floppy ears with enthusiasm every time someone came home. She didn't like to leave him alone when she was gone all morning. She walked him up to the end of Tilden Street and back. There was nothing to draw one's attention about a woman taking a walk with her dog, or stopping to linger for a moment or two while the dog sniffed at the dirt. If she paused by the tree nearest their house, she could often hear voices coming from the backyard.

Once Robin and Jack wandered by just as the woman walked backwards out of her front door, hovering in front of the child as she made her way down porch stairs. "Carefully, Sophie!" the woman called. "Go slowly! Let Mommy help you get in the car." Robin's heart gave a flutter. Sophie Bettinger. She hustled Jack back to the Lexus and followed their car to a playground a mile or two from the house. It was a quiet, secluded spot, with thick rubber mats cushioning the ground beneath the swings and a big wooden structure that had both turrets and a steering wheel, like a castle that was also a mobile home. The play area was surrounded by a low stone wall, and beyond that was a rocky hillside with tall oaks that shaded the children and their caregivers through the morning hours.

Jack stood on the rear seat and put his paws up against the window, making the funny little wow-wow-wow noise that he used for a bark. "Not today, buddy," said Robin, regretfully. She pulled over and stroked the dog to quiet him, watching the child from a distance. Sophie was struggling to get out of the stroller even before they were through the gate at the entrance to the playground. *Sophie.* Robin breathed the word, feeling the softness of its consonants. She said it out loud, stretching it to three syllables the way they would back home. So-ah-fee. It was nice; it was a nice name. Sophie kicked and wriggled in the grasp of her mother, who was attempting to put sunblock on her face and the back of her neck. The woman had on green cotton pants that were rolled up to below the knee. Her gauzy white top had wide sleeves that dragged in the dirt as she ran lotion along the girl's legs and on the tops of her feet and between her toes. Robin could tell the child was hollering from the twisted arc of her back as she strained to get away. She cracked the window just a few inches, making sure that Jack could not leap out and create a spectacle. "No,

Mommymommy!" the girl cried plaintively, "I said no thank you Mommy for the lotion. I said no thank you."

Robin giggled and sniffed, wiping her eyes. "Wow-wow-wow" barked Jack. Quickly, she closed the window and put the car into drive. It was time to go home. She slowed as they rolled by the spot where the woman had parked her car. It was a dark blue Audi. A bumper sticker on the back said: "More TREES/Less BUSH." Oh, she's one of those, thought Robin. It was a small miracle the child wasn't named Clementine, or Serenity. Or some old fashioned New England historical name, like Bitsy, or Abigail. In the boys' class at school, there were two girls named Abigail and one named Priscilla.

The silence was broken by a muffled chirp. With her free hand, she rummaged through the white leather bag that took up most of the passenger seat. The phone had stopped ringing by the time she located it. Robin glanced at the missed call message. Her mother. She wanted to talk to her mother; she wanted to tell her everything. She wanted to tell her how much Sophie looked like Ted, with her cupid-bow lips and the long eyelashes that everyone always said were wasted on a boy. She wanted to tell her how she felt like crying every time she heard the little girl's voice. But she could not tell her mother about Sophie Bettinger without telling her how they came to have more embryos than they could use, or how they came to give those embryos away. Robin put the phone down. She could not call her right now, and chat about nothing.

It occurred to Robin, and not for the first time, that the person she ought to inform was John. Regularly, she had resolved to tell him everything. Often at night she imagined that he would overhear her thoughts, they were so loud in her ears. It amazed her, lying next to him, that he did not just roll over and say, *Tell me about the child.* Instead, he stroked her hip and turned her body towards his, looking into her eyes with an intensity that bore right through her and saw nothing. Lately, she felt loneliest when he held her. When they made love, she shut her eyes and pretended it was a stranger.

It would better for her if John knew, but that didn't mean it would be easy to tell him. He was going to be angry that Robin had involved Mickey in the visit to the clinic, angry that she had ever gone to Brookline, angry that she had indulged herself by going back to check on the girl. And Robin didn't think she could stand it if John saw the child only as a problem, as a threat to their peaceful existence. He would blame her for that, as if she had created the situation rather than discovering it. As if Sophie wasn't there whether they knew about her or not.

Robin knew it would be almost impossible to make him understand that finding the girl had been an accident. To her it seemed clear that fate had brought them together; it made her wonder if there was a reason. Why did God lead her to her daughter if they were destined to spend their lives apart? Daily, she resolved to stop visiting, to stop thinking about her, to stop daydreaming of tearful reunions. Sometimes when the boys were playing and not fighting, in those moments when watching them side by side flooded her with a kind of happiness that was almost painful, thoughts would come into her head unbidden. *You have a sister. You don't even know her.*

Whatever God intended, there would be no more visits for a while, because summer camp was almost over. Robin contemplated all she needed to do in the three weeks that remained until the start of kindergarten. The boys needed clothes, backpacks, lunchboxes. She wanted to bring them over to the new school to play, so that the place would be familiar to them on the first day. Joan had suggested that she start early getting them up and dressed every morning at the right time, so that it wouldn't come as a shock to their systems when the school year began. Joan was a big believer in ritual. It made sense to Robin, although it hadn't worked out so well for her friend. Both Joan's kids had developed school day rituals of their own: Talia's involved finding things in her backpack that should have been attended to the night before, while Isaiah almost always decided at the very last minute that he was wearing the wrong socks. Some mornings, Robin could hear the shrieking from her kitchen window.

Joan wanted to carpool, but Robin didn't feel her boys were ready for that, not quite yet. She thought that they would be more comfortable pulling up to the school with her, and getting one last kiss goodbye before they ran off into class. It was hard to imagine putting them into Joan's car and then retreating into the echoing quietness of an empty house. Thank heaven for Jack, thought Robin, reaching behind her to ruffle the dog's ears.

Drop-off on the first day went smoothly enough. The boys' classrooms were next door to one another, which was reassuring to all of them. Ryan saw a friend from camp across the room and bolted with hardly a backward wave. Teddy grabbed her hand after his brother left. Robin put her arm around his shoulder and felt him leaning back hard against her as he walked across the threshold, as though his torso declined to follow his legs into the classroom. She gave him a gentle push. Ms. Grey was dressed with an endearing frumpiness that suggested muppets, or church picnics. "Hi, Ted!" she said, sticking a name tag with a smiley face onto his shirt. "C'mon in and sit down. Thanks, Mom! We'll see you at pick up time!" She looked at Teddy. "Wave good-bye to Mommy!" Robin lifted up the camera slung around her neck and snapped.

She walked slowly out of the building and back toward the parking lot. Neither of them had cried. That was a good omen. Robin sat in the car, making a mental list of everything that needed to be done before three. Groceries, dry cleaning, calls for the PTA membership committee. All of that would take only an hour or two. It was a beautiful morning. A good morning for the park, thought Robin, if she had somebody to take. She felt her pulse race slightly. It had been weeks since she'd gone to Brookline. Next Thursday, it would be a full month. She lay the camera on the seat next to her. She could be there and back by lunchtime.

There was no car in the driveway at the house, so Robin drove by without stopping and headed to the playground. It was only ten o'clock, but already steamy. She parked the car several blocks away and walked. The camera bag bumped against her hip. She heard Sophie's voice before she saw her. Robin strode past, just barely glancing over the wall into the playground. Beyond the gate, she saw a path that led up into the trees. She climbed up the hillside, grateful to be in the shade. Robin left the path when it turned to the right, negotiating the grassy slope to follow the arc of the wall. She pushed branches aside and climbed over rocks and tree roots until she reached a large boulder with a fine view of the playground just below. The boulder got no morning sun, so it was dimmer and cooler there.

She pulled out her camera and peered through the viewfinder. It was a pretty little place, this park. Robin found Sophie and centered the picture. She was in the sandbox, smiling. A bigger boy poured sand from a bucket. Robin increased the zoom. She took a dozen pictures, each of them eerily familiar. There was Sophie in profile, so much like the picture of herself that hung at the top of the stairs in her parent's house. Tendrils of hair, fine as cornsilk, escaped the elastic bands of her pigtails and hung curling gently against her cheek. Sophie threw back her head, laughing. There was nothing of Ryan in her; she was like Robin, and like Teddy.

From her spot in the woods, Robin could hear the nervous inflection on the second syllable as the woman called out, "So-fee! So-feee!." Sophie turned her head, scanning the row of mothers on the benches across from her. She faced the hillside full on now, and her serious expression at full zoom filled the frame. Staring, her eyes were green and sparkling, like ocean water, like John's eyes when he was happy. Robin breathed hard and clicked.

The woman came over and lifted Sophie out of the sandbox. She pulled out a pack of wet wipes and cleaned the child's hands, shaking her head no when Sophie pointed back into the sand. "No." Robin could read her lips. "Dirty." She led Sophie over to the swings and gave her a push. Sophie's laughing face swung in and out of the camera frame. Robin lowered the camera and waited. You could see the child wanted to go higher. She doesn't look like Ryan, Robin thought, but she is just as fearless. After a few minutes Sophie started wriggling, and half turned around in the swing seat. The woman stopped pushing immediately. She caught the swing to stop its motion, and lifted the child out. They walked together toward the climbing structure. There was an older girl there, an Asian girl, and Sophie reached out for her and climbed with her onto a bouncy bridge that spanned the soft sand moat around the castle.

The Asian girl jumped up and down, and then Sophie jumped up and down. They ran together from one side of the bridge to the other. Robin thought she could never get tired of watching her face as she ran and squealed. She took picture after picture. After five minutes or so Sophie was bored with the bridge and began to climb up the castle. She clambered onto the first rung of the ladder and reached for the next. Robin waited for the woman to swoop in and scoop her up. Robin glanced around, but she could not see her, only an unfamiliar woman, standing beneath Sophie on the bouncy bridge looking uncomfortable in her high wedge heels. Robin wondered who she was. Her hair was chin length and sleek, and she wore a short skirt and sunglasses as big as bug's eyes.

"Ahem." The noise behind her startled Robin, and her head swiveled. The woman, Sophie's mother, stood behind her at the base of the boulder. "Excuse me," she said. Her tone was courteous but not friendly. Robin's heart pounded. She glanced down at her camera, as though still half expecting to find the woman safely there, in the viewfinder, where she belonged. Robin looked up again. The noise of the playground seemed suddenly very far away, and all she could hear was the sound of the other woman breathing. Meredith Schuyler. Robin's scalp prickled beneath the brown wig.

"Hello," she answered hesitantly. The woman was staring at her strangely. Did she recognize her resemblance to the child? Had this drawn her here? Robin felt exposed, as though everything she had ever done or desired was transparent to this stranger.

"I'm sorry," said Meredith, in a tone that suggested that she was not at all sorry. "Were you photographing my daughter? I don't mean to pry but I believe you were taking pictures of my daughter earlier, and then again just now by the castle. Of my daughter. There." Meredith pointed toward Sophie, and Robin turned to look.

"I was taking pictures," said Robin. "I didn't mean to frighten you. I'm sorry." Her mind raced furiously. Why would she be here, in this awkward spot, in the woods above the park? "I was taking pictures of different areas of the playground because – I am a photographer." She reached down and grabbed the camera bag, holding it up as though it were evidence. "I was scouting for locations – lighting. Angles." Robin looked into the bag as though it would give her inspiration. Stuck in the bottom was an old, worn business card. She pulled it out. "Here," she said, handing it to Meredith. It had her name, and their address from Somerville, and underneath it said "Family photos, birthday parties, all events." Meredith's face softened.

"I'm sorry," she said, sounding sincere this time. "Of course I didn't know – it seemed odd – I just thought I would check." She looked embarrassed and Robin felt a rush of sympathy for her.

"No need to apologize. I understand. I understand completely. I have children too, so I understand. Boys. Two boys. She's real cute, your daughter. She's a beautiful girl."

"Thanks," said Meredith. They stood facing one another for a few seconds more, and then Meredith turned to go. "Sorry to bother you," she said again. She climbed over a rock and then paused, looking back over her shoulder. "Excuse me," she said, glancing down at the card and then up, "Robin? Do I know you from somewhere?"

"No!" said Robin. "No. I don't think so. No. I get that all the time."

Meredith stared at her for just a moment longer. "Bye," she said, waving. She walked off down the hill, flip-flops skidding dangerously down the slippery slope.

Chapter 19

"Well that was exhausting," said Lindsey, settling down on the big leather couch in Meredith's kitchen. "No wonder I don't do it very often."

"Going to the playground is supposed to wear the kids out, not the moms," Meredith replied. "Perhaps if you wore more comfortable shoes."

Lindsey examined her feet. "You can't limit yourself that way if you are going to be serious about your footwear. Wedges aren't so bad, as long as you keep your balance. It's all in the core. You should try pilates. It does wonders for keeping you centered."

"I am very centered," said Meredith, sounding slightly aggrieved. "Working part time, being with Sophie, I feel like I'm in a really good place right now. I know you probably think I should be working full time, but I'm happy like this."

"What are you talking about? Why would I want you to work full time? David makes plenty of money. They don't pay you worth a damn at that center for wayward girls."

"Center for Women's Legal Services."

"Whatever. I don't think you should work more, Merrie. I was just talking about. abdominal muscles. Nothing metaphysical." She glanced over at Meredith, who was getting blueberry-pomegranate juice out of the refrigerator for the girls. "I don't suppose you have a diet coke?"

"No," said Meredith sternly. "I'm sorry. I don't buy anything with artificial sweeteners. I wish you wouldn't drink that stuff. It will kill you."

"You have to die of something. I guess for me it will be aspartame and caffeine. At least I will be awake while I'm still alive."

Meredith got Lily crayons and colored pencils and paper, and she sat cross-legged at the kitchen table to draw. Sophie climbed up onto the chair next to her. "Is it for me?" she asked, pointing to the picture.

"You can have it," Lily said. "What should I draw for you?"

She is such a great kid, thought Meredith, gazing at her fondly. Lily's hair was cut at a blunt angle that framed her face in black. She concentrated hard as she drew, looking simultaneously serene and fierce. "Draw a duck," said Sophie. Lily drew a curved head and a broad beak and wavy blue lines where the bird sat on top of the water. It was strikingly good, for a child of six.

"Is Lily excited about starting first grade?" she asked, coming over to the couch.

"I think so," replied Lindsey. "She is nervous. A new school is always a little scary." Lily's score on the entrance test for elementary school had risen dramatically once she decided to start giving the answers out loud instead of just thinking them in her head, and Lindsey had moved her to a school for gifted children that emphasized learning through the arts. "I think she will like it there. I'm sure she'll fit in better than she did in her last school. She will be with her own people."

"Are there a lot of Asian kids?"

"I have no idea. But there are lots of eccentric children with esoteric hobbies and an inability to make eye contact. I don't think selective muteness will strike them as out of the ordinary. They definitely thought she was weird at her old kindergarten. Do you know, last May, her teacher called me on the phone at work just to tell me that she had said 'don't cry, it's okay' to one of the other girls. She called me at work! For four words – like I needed to know immediately. The night before that, at dinner, Sophie said, 'Mommy, I love my imaginary friend Petunia. Petunia is so noble and so sage.' But four words in school and it was a veritable news flash. I don't know. Do you think I should be more worried?"

"I don't think it is such a big deal," Meredith said in a soothing tone. "So she's a little shy. You were a funny kid too. Remember in second grade, how you insisted on wearing white go-go boots every single day for an entire year?"

"Oh my god, yes, it drove my mother insane. We had a huge fight when I insisted on wearing them for Christmas dinner, with the red velvet dress. She said, 'You are not going to wear go-go boots to your grandmother's house!' And I was screaming at her: 'White goes with everything!!!' I was actually holding onto the boots because I thought she might rip them right off my feet, but luckily for me, my dad called her an hysterical bitch, and they got into it and she forgot all about my boots until it was time to leave. By then she was drunk enough that she didn't care anymore." Lindsey chuckled. "That dress had white smocking on it. It was short, like a baby-doll. It looked great with those boots."

Meredith looked over at Lily, still happily drawing, and imagined her in a short red velvet dress and white go-go boots. It would look good on her. She was adorable today, in khaki cargo shorts with big pockets and a simple little tank top in dark purple that probably cost an arm and a leg. The new school started tomorrow. First grade already – it seemed like yesterday that they were in China. "Do you ever hear from any of the other families from the China trip?" she asked.

"I got a note once from the couple from North Carolina – you remember Charles and Linda?"

"Of course."

"Linda said that Kaylee was doing wonderfully, and that the whole congregation was praying for her. I'm not sure why she needs all that prayer if things are going so well."

"Sounds a little ominous."

"Also, they are taking her to a specialist in Durham, because the Lord works in mysterious ways, some of which are only known to specialists."

"And Mary and Louisa?"

"I get an email from Louisa now and then. They split up. Louisa says it was amicable, but she also says that she has sole legal custody, since the adoption was done in her name only."

"That's too bad, but I am glad it was friendly."

"So she says. But I didn't like the way she said 'sole legal custody.' Sounds like a woman who has been spending some time with her lawyer."

"But it would be a terrible shame if Mary lost contact with her daughter over a technicality. I am sure the courts wouldn't let that happen."

"I don't know. The courts are not so well equipped to deal with situations like this – it's all too new. I don't think they have the best tools in their toolbox to deal with new shit, at least not right away. It's like that story we ran last month in the magazine – the billionaire from Oklahoma who married a Playboy playmate when he was ninety-three and she was twenty-four?"

"I must have missed it."

"They had a pre-nup, so she was only supposed to walk away with half a million dollars, plus the opportunity to restyle herself as Mrs. Oil Baron. But the little cat got a doctor to auto-extract his sperm after he was dead, and she showed up for the reading of the will knocked up. Now she's claiming a full share of the inheritance on behalf of that fetus, or whatever it is. He's got three other kids, not one of them under sixty."

"You can get sperm from a dead guy?"

Lindsey nodded significantly, arching her perfectly groomed eyebrows. "Yup." Her voice sank to a whisper. "You use a cattle prod." She looked down her nose with great distaste. "Ninety-three year old sperm. That can't be good."

"Is she going to get the money?"

"I don't know. It isn't resolved yet. But the point of the article was that there is no – what do you call that, when the court learns from the past?"

"Precedent."

"Exactly! There is no precedent. The judge will have to figure it out based on things that are similar like – I don't know, what the hell is similar to that? Normally, any kid that can prove paternity has a legal claim, but that makes sense. The dad may not have meant to get the woman pregnant, but he did the deed, so he has to put his money where his dick was. This guy was dead. He wasn't careless. He didn't spread his seeds around. He didn't have any say, because he was no longer conversant."

"He married her. That has to count for something."

"Very true. You do get the feeling, though, that he did not envision starting a family with Mrs. Thirty-four Double D when they tied the knot. Still, it is hard to prove. I don't know if she has to prove he wanted a child, or if the rest of the family has to prove that he did not. The whole thing's a conundrum."

Yes, thought Meredith. It was a strange story and for some reason it made her terribly uncomfortable. She was sad, too, about Mary and Louisa. The idea that Mary might be separated from her child made her heart ache. She did not want to think about it anymore.

"How's Rick?" she asked, and leaned back into the warm embrace of the couch.

Chapter 20

"I saw Lindsey today." Meredith spoke loudly over the sound of running water. "She took off the whole day to spend with Lily before she starts school. We met in the playground with the girls."

David kicked off the shoes he had worn to work, and lay down diagonally across the bed. He watched his wife, crouched by the bathtub, pouring water from a cup into a bucket to amuse the child. "I do it myself," said Sophie, snatching the cup.

"Didn't school start today?"

"Not for Lily. She starts next week. She's in this accelerated program now. Lindsey says it will be marvelous for Lily because next to these other children, she is hardly weird at all. She says that in the land of the blind, the one-eyed girl is prom queen."

"Sounds like Lindsey. How did Lily seem?"

"I always think Lily is wonderful. Sophie just adores her. How was your day?"

"Well, good and bad. The bad news was that we got a delivery of Spongebob Squarepants backpacks, and Spongebob is pink instead of yellow. Ten thousand backpacks. It's amazing. There are whole factories in China that have done nothing but produce the likeness of this one smiley-faced, yellow sea sponge with brown pants for five years, and suddenly someone decides to make him pink. Why? It boggles the mind."

"I'm sure it was an honest mistake. I hope no one gets in trouble."

"I imagine someone in China is going to get in a lot of trouble when I tell them they have to take all this shit back. Maybe they can sell it there. Maybe they can find some child who watches tv in black and white and doesn't care if Spongebob is pink."

"What is the good news?"

"My public relations firm, to whom I have paid an obscene amount of money for several years, informs me that they have finally done the impossible and gotten us onto Oprah's Christmas list. Unconfirmed. No promises. But I think so."

"Wow. What was the secret this year? How did they do it?"

"Actually, there was no secret at all. We just had the right product. It's fancy version of a lunchbox. Extremely Earth-friendly concept, and designed for grown-ups, so they don't feel self-conscious toting their lunch to the office. Plus, it's that upscale robin's egg blue and chocolate brown color combination – nothing neon, nothing pastel. Oprah colors."

"That's wonderful, honey."

"It is sort of a big deal. It's not saving the planet, but it's not bad and it could be a lot of money. I'll get you a couple; you can use them to take food to the park."

"Oh!" said Meredith. "The strangest thing happened today at the park. It frightened me half to death. Lily was playing in the sandbox, and you know I hate her playing in the sand; it's full of germs. So I went to get her out, and one of the other mothers pointed at this woman, sitting on a big rock in the trees above the playground, taking pictures of the kids. A little while later we were by the climbing castle, and I looked up and there she was again. And, you know, I had the strangest feeling that she was photographing Sophie. It seemed like she was following us. Lindsey thought so too."

"Did she?"

"Well, she didn't disagree. Naturally, I thought about pedophile rings. A little blonde girl with Sophie's looks – she'd be an obvious target."

"Meredith, do you really think there are pedophile rings grabbing children off the streets of Brookline and we don't hear about it? Practically all child abduction cases turn out to be by a family member. Besides, no one could steal Sophie – you never take your eyes off of her. Did you actually confront this woman?"

"I went to talk to her. It turns out she was a photographer scouting locations in the park. I felt so silly. She was very nice about it. I think I kind of scared her."

"You are so terrifying."

"No, but I surprised her."

"She'll recover. I wish you wouldn't get yourself so worked up."

"Listen, if you were there, you would have thought it was odd as well."

"Maybe."

"David." Meredith's voice deepened and softened. "Earlier tonight, just now, when she was with you, did Sophie fall?"

"Not that I noticed."

"Did she cry?"

"No." David picked up the newspaper. "She was fine."

"She has a big bruise on her leg."

"Kids get bumps, honey."

"No, this is big." Meredith turned Sophie around, slippery with soap, to reach at her back. "and there is another one here. David, come look at this."

"Sweetheart, I'm sure it's nothing. You can't worry about every scrape and freckle."

"This isn't a scrape or a freckle. I am going to call the doctor."

"You shouldn't bother the pediatrician after office hours about a bruise. Honestly, Meredith, he's going to stop taking your calls."

Meredith ran a wet washcloth along her daughter's arms and legs, rinsing her clean. Sophie, laughing, grabbed the cloth and put it on her head. "Hat," she said.

"There's another one here," said Meredith, retrieving the washcloth with a reflexive smile at the baby. "Come and look."

"Okay, just a second," said David. He folded the newspaper neatly and laid it on the chair.

"Daddy!" yelled Sophie, "I am in the bathtub. Come and see."

"Coming darling," said David. He stood beside Meredith at the tub. "Let's see this bruise," he said, kneeling down. It was dark and purple, two inches around, inky and opaque like something infinitely deep, like the sky without stars or the ocean at night. Meredith turned the child around, holding her gently. The two marks on her back were smaller with the same eggplant hue, stark against the paleness of her skin.

"I am sure these weren't here earlier today," said Meredith. "I don't remember her getting hurt. I can't believe she would hurt herself this badly and not even cry. I know you think I am over-reacting, but this is not normal."

"Call the doctor," said David. "Call the doctor. Now."

Chapter 21

Leukemia. Meredith did not hear the word so much as feel it. It wrapped around her like a thing with tentacles, squeezing her tight. Her hands were clammy, and that was leukemia, and there was a cramp in her belly and that was leukemia, and her heart beat so hard she thought it would wake Sophie, who was asleep in her arms. Bile rose in Meredith's throat. The young oncologist looked at her with warm brown eyes and continued to talk. Her voice was matter of fact. "Leukemia is the most common of the childhood cancers, and one of the most curable." There was more, but Meredith did not hear it. She was suffocating. She needed to make it stop, this incessant repetition of the word.

"But it isn't necessarily cancer," Meredith interrupted. She felt herself struggling, as though she had to physically push the sentence out against a terrible weight. "You said earlier that there were other tests that needed to be done, for confirmation. So it might be something else."

Doctor Coben looked sympathetic. "Mrs. Bettinger," she said, and Meredith did not correct her, "I need to be very clear about this. I know it is difficult to hear. Further testing will indicate what type of leukemia Sophie has. Then I will be able to tell you more about a treatment plan and a prognosis. But Sophie does have leukemia. That is what is causing these bruises, and that is why she is so pale."

"We use a lot of sunblock," said Meredith. "I think that is why she is so pale. I am really diligent about it."

The doctor continued talking. Results from the bone marrow testing done yesterday would be available later this morning. Even before the results came back, Sophie would have a medi-port placed beneath the skin on her chest, which would make it easier in the coming months to access her little veins, for blood draws and chemotherapy. Meredith noticed that David was writing down everything in a new blue spiral notebook. "Will Sophie require sedation again for that, like she did for the bone marrow sample yesterday?" he asked.

Sedation was yet another needle stick. Sophie cried so hard when the needle went into her arm. "Shh, sweetheart," Meredith whispered, "don't cry. It's okay. It will be over soon." But it wasn't over. It felt like it would never be over.

"No," said Doctor Coben. "This is a bigger procedure and it will require general anesthesia. I'll get her on the table as soon as possible, since I know she is going to be hungry when she wakes up, but she can't have anything to eat until after the operation. Once the port is in, we can begin the first phase of treatment, the induction phase. Our goal now is to get her into remission. That's step one."

"And then?" asked David. He wrote down the word 'induction.'

"And then we are going to get her healthy. It's a long, tough battle, but the odds are good. We'll know more as we get back test results and see how she responds to the initial doses of chemotherapy."

"How long does induction take?"

"Generally, we can get a child free of visible signs of disease in about four weeks. Unfortunately, she is going to have to spend much of that time in the hospital."

"Will she lose her hair?" It shocked Meredith that her own voice sounded almost normal. I am not having this conversation, she thought. How can I be having this conversation?

"Usually the drugs will have that affect after a couple of weeks." The doctor paused. "It will come back."

Meredith stroked the blonde head lying against her chest. It seemed to her so grossly unfair that Sophie would lose her hair when it had only just begun to grow in earnest. She had never even had a haircut. Now every passer-by would look at her and know that she was a cancer patient. All the ladies who came up to admire her in the supermarket and the park would look at her beautiful face and her bald head and pity them both. It was more than Meredith could bear.

David was writing furiously. Meredith thought back over the past twenty-four hours, wondering where he had found the time to get his hands on a notebook. He had come with her to the pediatrician – they couldn't be squeezed in until the afternoon. Doctor Redlands had a long-suffering look on his face when he came out to meet them in the waiting room. "Okay, let's see these bruises," he said, as they ushered Sophie into an examining room. But his expression changed when he saw her back. Now there were tiny marks running down her arms as well, a spray of dots lurking just beneath the surface that shone red through the translucent upper layer of her skin. "Petechiae," said the doctor.

"What's that?' asked David. She could picture how lost he looked yesterday, with nothing in his hands to record the answer.

"They are from the breaking of capillaries, the tiniest blood vessels. It may be nothing, but we had better take some blood and check on her platelets." The doctor stared at Sophie thoughtfully. "Would you say that she seems particularly pale recently?"

"Sophie is very fair-skinned," replied Meredith. "We always, always use sunblock."

They waited a few minutes in the room by themselves, and then the blood work came back, and Doctor Redlands looked increasingly grave and sent them directly to the hospital for more testing. David held her hand as the technician slid the thick needle into their daughter's hip. There was no notebook then either. It was almost eight before they got home, and David lingered downstairs to reheat some food while Meredith put Sophie to bed. He had just turned the oven on when he heard a long, shuddering groan. He raced up the steps two at a time. Meredith was standing in the bathroom, crying as she dabbed at Sophie's mouth with a washcloth. "I just wanted to brush her teeth," she choked, pointing to the child's size toothbrush with its bristles stained pink.

Sophie seemed stunned to silence by her mother's sobs. She fingered the band-aid on her arm, looking sleepy and hollow-eyed. "Do you want to sleep in Mommy and Daddy's bed tonight?" Meredith asked, and the child nodded. Meredith curled up next to her.

After a while, David came in and shook her shoulder gently. "Food's ready," he whispered. Meredith shook her head. He came in a little while later and said, "Raymond is on the phone." David's brother lived in Marblehead, north of Boston, but his practice was in town. "I called him to see if he knew any of these pediatric oncologists that our doctor recommended. Do you want to talk?"

"No," said Meredith.

Perhaps Raymond had told David to get a notebook. That would be his type of advice: write everything down. He had always been a very meticulous student; he was always perfect like that. It drove David crazy. David said Ray would meet them at the hospital later today.

Doctor Coben came by after Sophie was back from recovery. "Hi, Sophie!" she said, pulling back the bandage on her chest to take a look at the newly installed port. It was a small, neat protrusion, as though someone had slid a quarter beneath the skin. "Looks great." The doctor turned to face David and Meredith. "We got results from the tests. Sophie has acute myeloid leukemia. AML. So, now we know what we're up against." She spoke briskly but her eyes were sad. "I am very hopeful. We will start chemotherapy first thing tomorrow."

"AML?" said Raymond, when he arrived. "Not ALL? I think AML is the rarer one."

"Is rarer worse?" asked Meredith.

"Perhaps a little – trickier. I'm sure the long-term success rates are good in either case."

"Fifty to seventy percent," said David. "They have a computer with internet access in the lounge. AML survival is fifty to seventy percent, and ALL is seventy to eighty."

Meredith and David exchanged a look. Fifty percent seemed infinitely more uncertain than eighty.

"Don't get obsessed with the numbers," said Raymond.

"Easy for you to say," said Meredith.

"No, it's not." Ray spoke thoughtfully. "It is not easy for me to say. It would be easy for me to say that I know everything is going to be all right, but that would be a lie, and I'm not going to lie to you."

"I'm sorry," said Meredith. "I didn't mean to snap at you."

"Don't apologize," said Raymond. "Here's some more medical advice, while I'm giving it out for free. Don't apologize, don't be a saint, and don't be a martyr. Let people help you if they offer. Have you eaten?"

"I couldn't."

"Don't stop eating! What good will you be to Sophie if you get sick? Tell me, what is Sophie's favorite food?"

"Burritos," said Meredith. Raymond looked quizzical. "Don't ask me," Meredith shrugged. "The child has always loved burritos."

"Okay. I am taking David and going out for food. I will drop him and the food back here. You hang in there, and I will be back tomorrow."

The week passed in a blur. "Hi darling," said Lindsey, when she came by on day five. She hugged Meredith, and they sat together on the foot of Sophie's bed. "You know I would have been here earlier, but I was worried that Lily might have been exposed to chicken pox,"

"Chicken pox!" cried Meredith, pulling away involuntarily.

"It's all right! That's why I waited. The exposure was three weeks ago, and she has no sign of spots, so I have the all-clear from the pediatrician. But I couldn't take the chance."

"No! Of course not. I am glad you waited. Sophie will be so excited to see you."

Sophie stirred and opened her eyes. "Hi, Sweetheart," said Lindsey.

"Is Lily here?" Sophie asked groggily.

"Yes, I can see she is so excited to see me," Lindsey laughed. "No, Sophie, Lily isn't here. I will bring her soon, if it's allowed. She helped me pick out this." She handed Sophie a fluffy stuffed dog with a zipper down it's back. "It's a doggie that's a purse," she explained. "It's got puppies in its belly, and you can pull them out this way." Lindsey unzipped the bag and removed a small ball of fluff with eyes and a tail. Sophie wrapped her arms around the dog's furry neck and peered into the cavity in its back, pulling out three more puppies.

"Not a very good anatomy lesson," said Meredith.

"Anatomy is overrated," said Lindsey. "It's a sample. I got it from an editor at Child World doing a piece on new toys for Christmas '04. She promised me that it will be the hot toy for girls this year. It's the Doggie Doodle line. This one is Mommie Doodle. They have one with a stethoscope and band-aids that is called Doctor Doodle, and another one with make-up and a tiara called Diva Doodle."

"Cute," said Meredith.

Lindsey lowered her voice slightly and muttered conspiratorially, "I told them they should make one with little sex toys and call it Dildo Doodle. I told them I would feature that in my magazine. We have twice the circulation of Child World."

"Did they think you were funny?"

"No, no one at Child World ever thinks I am funny. It's such a damn serious business, child-rearing." Lindsey paused, glancing at Meredith. "I'm sorry. I shouldn't be joking."

"Please, joke away. I could use a laugh."

"Yes," said Lindsey. "You look like hell."

"Thanks."

"I can't lie to you, girlfriend. You need concealer and a manicure. Have you been out of here at all?"

"I can't leave." Meredith spoke definitively.

"You can't run away, but that doesn't mean you can't leave! Where's David?"

"He will be here in a half an hour or so. He goes to the office in the afternoons to get some work done – or so he claims. I think he spends all his time there on the internet. He keeps proposing alternate treatments to the oncologist."

"Okay, when he gets here, you and I are going out for dinner and a drink. A stiff drink. No arguments! I will bring you back, even if you beg me not to."

"I can't go, Lindsey. What if the doctor comes by while I am out? We are waiting to hear if they have the cytogenetic test results back."

"David will listen carefully to the doctor and give you a full report. You need a moment out of this place." Lindsey looked around her and shuddered. "Sophie will be great with Daddy, won't you Sophiekins? Do you like the doggie?" Sophie nodded. "I am glad! Lily will be glad too."

"I have a port," said Sophie.

"A port! Let's see." Sophie lifted her hospital gown and showed the round bump beside her heart. "Looks like they've installed an on/off button. I've always wanted one of those for Lily. Can I turn you off if I press your button?" Sophie nodded no, vigorously. "How about if I press this button?" Lindsey reached beneath her gown and touched her belly. Sophie giggled. Lindsey looked at Meredith and smiled wearily. "So that's a port, huh? Any port in a storm, I guess. What a trooper she is."

It took David and Lindsey together a half hour to persuade Meredith to go. "Where do you want to eat?" asked Lindsey, as they exited the building.

"Anywhere. So long as it's close." The air outside the hospital felt good.

"There's a place near here where Matt Damon came last year with Ben Affleck and the two of them got so drunk they made the bartender set up beer pong on one of the tables. It's always crowded, but I think I can get us in." Lindsey pulled out her cell phone.

"Anything quick."

Over dinner, Meredith explained the concept of sanctuary therapy to Lindsey. "David says the cancer cells are like a zombie clone army. They look like immature white blood cells, the way that zombies look like humans, except they have been reprogrammed and instead of developing into normal cells, they just reproduce and reproduce. Right now her blood is thick with them, and the first round of chemo is like blasting into a crowd with a machine gun – you can't miss. The tricky thing is to chase down the last few, and if you don't get all of them, they just come back stronger." Meredith's voice thickened. "So, it turns out cancer cells like to hide in the brain, because regular chemo drugs can't pass through the blood-brain barrier. That is their sanctuary."

"Like enemy combatants hiding in a church."

"Exactly. Because of this, once a week for the next few weeks they are going to inject drugs directly into her spinal fluid. These drugs are so powerful that they could kill her, so they have to use a second drug to stop the process after it's gone far enough. It's like they set the church on fire to get the bad guys out, betting they can put the fire out before the whole structure burns down."

"Poor baby."

"They're trying so hard to save her. It's like they are at war, the doctors and the cancer, and my little girl is their battleground. It's such a cruel disease. There's so much damage being done to her, and you can't even worry about it, because everything now is life or death." They were arguing about whether or not there was time for dessert when Meredith's cell phone rang. "It's David," she said. Lindsey paid up while Meredith took the call outside.

Lindsey walked out of the restaurant, closing her bag. She saw Meredith standing out front, the phone pressed to one ear and her free hand over the other. She had lost weight in the last week, and the skin hung loosely on her cheekbones. Her eyes looked gothic and huge with black half moons below them. She stood in the middle of the sidewalk, nodding leadenly, oblivious to the steady flow of pedestrian traffic that diverted right and left of her. A heavyset older man in a suit came up to her, leaning in close. "Can you please take your cell phone conversation elsewhere," he said, putting so much emphasis on the word 'please' that his jowls quivered with disdain. "You are inconveniencing everyone."

"Oh! I am so sorry," said Meredith, stepping awkwardly to the side, and bumping into a person on her left. The fat man glared at her indignantly and walked away.

"Hey!" Lindsey shouted after him, "Who the hell are you? You think you are saving civilization, one asshole comment at a time? Mind your own business. You take up quite a bit of the sidewalk yourself." She threw her arm around Meredith's shoulders. "Let's get you back to your girl."

Days bled, one into another. On the fourteenth day of treatment, they took a second bone marrow sample. Sophie did not cry this time as they wheeled her off into the procedure room. She is resigned to it, thought Meredith. It seemed to her like the only thing worse than tears.

They met with Dr. Coben to review the results. "Let me start with the good news," she said. "Sophie has come through the first two weeks in great shape. No fevers, no infection – she seems to be tolerating the drugs very well."

"The bruising is entirely gone," said Meredith. "That's got to be a good sign. The nurse said Sophie is a tough little bird, and that is what it takes to beat this thing,"

"The staff loves her." Dr. Coben exuded warmth, but there was a hesitation to her smile, a holding back that suggested fatigue, or reluctance. It reminded Meredith that she was 'starting with the good news.'

"What is the bad news?" she asked.

"It's not bad news," said the doctor, "it's just not the best news. Sophie's bone marrow sample showed a vast decrease in the total number of cells. So the chemo is working. Still, twenty percent of the remaining cells are blasts – cancer cells. We'd be happier if that number was lower. But we have two more weeks. Hopefully the number goes down far enough, and we can continue with the next phase of chemo. However, I have to be honest with you here and tell you that I am a bit concerned."

"Damn," said David. "Shit. I don't know; I was sure she was responding."

"She is responding. She is definitely responding. A little slower than we like, but if the numbers are on target in two more weeks than it shouldn't change our prognosis at all."

"So she still has the same chance as anyone else, fifty to seventy percent?"

"That's probably reasonable. Sure. But I need to give you one other piece of information. The cytogenetic results are back." David and Meredith sat up straighter. They had been anxiously waiting for the laboratory studies of Sophie's tumor cells. What had happened, to turn them from friend into foe? "The lab noted one significant change in virtually all of the tumor cells tested," Dr. Coben continued. "In a normal cell, Sophie has two of each of her twenty-three chromosomes, one from mom and one from dad." She nodded at each of them in turn. "But in the tumor cells, there is only one copy of chromosome seven. We call that monosomy seven. The 'mono' part means one."

"Is that bad?" asked Meredith.

"It's not the news that we had hoped for. Statistically, monosomy seven is associated with a higher incidence of relapse, and a slightly lower five-year survival rate. That said, and I know how upsetting this is, many children with monosomy seven get better. You have to remember that. But sometimes our kids with monosomy seven do not respond as well to chemo. That may be why we are not seeing as robust a response as we would like."

Meredith began to cry. David laid his hand against the back of her neck. "There's got to be something else we could do," he said. "If the chemo is not that likely to succeed we should be looking at other things."

"Right now," said the doctor, "the chemo is our best bet."

"What about a stem cell transplant? I've read that many AML patients require stem cell transplantation. Why aren't we discussing that?"

"It may be that down the road we do consider that option. But transplants are difficult and dangerous and not without consequences, including morbidity. Without an exact match, it is possible that the cure may be even worse than the disease."

"Then shouldn't we be looking for a match? Nobody has tested us. Perhaps one of us is a match for Sophie. Or someone else. I don't care what it costs."

"Mr. Bettinger, I assure you that if I thought transplant was the best thing for Sophie I would say so, regardless of the costs. At this stage, we don't recommend transplant for children with AML unless there is a sibling match. The proteins that mark the surface of her cells are unique. You and your wife have each contributed three of the six proteins that make up Sophie's cellular signature. Every parent matches their child at three out of six markers, but three out of six for our purposes is not enough. I'm sorry. If there were a sibling, it might be different. As it stands, our best bet is the chemotherapy."

"And if there was a sibling?" Meredith's voice had a calm urgency.

"But there isn't a sibling."

"But what if there were?"

"Hypothetically, we would test them." Dr. Coben looked confused. "But it has got to be a full sibling. Only a full sibling. If there was a match, we would go to transplant."

"And Sophie would have a better chance?" The doctor nodded. Meredith turned to look at David, her eyes shining beneath their damp glaze.

"I believe it is possible," said David, his voice like gravel, "I believe it is virtually certain that Sophie does have at least one full sibling."

Chapter 22

John glanced at the front page of the newspaper before starting as usual with sports, even though every story in the sports section was ancient history by the time it got into print. The Patriots were favored to beat the Cardinals tomorrow – naturally the Boston Globe went with the local team. You wouldn't know from the Boston papers any team other than the Patriots even existed – the Pats and whoever they were playing that week. The Red Sox had taken one from Yankees, so of course the newspapers were covering that like the end of World War Three. The great rivalry – it got into your blood if you lived up here.

The Yankees may have lost yesterday but they were still two and a half games up – September heroics in Boston were just another way to suck the fans in, so that the team could break their hearts again in October. Red Sox Nation knew that better than anyone else by now.

But they couldn't help themselves. Once in a while John wondered why the fans didn't just wake up one morning and tell the Red Sox to fuck themselves, declare their allegiance to some other team, and move on. Why was it so impossible? What invisible threads bound them to this luckless franchise? It wasn't your family. You didn't owe them eternal loyalty. You chose them – you made a choice to plant a piece of your heart in this rocky soil and then suddenly that weedy patch of earth owns you, tapping into some part of your brain that is ancient, ancient like hunting in packs with spears and stones, ancient like hunting in packs with fangs and claws, ancient like your life depends on it, and now you would give your last ounce of blood to watch these guys hoist a pennant, when it wouldn't get you so much as a free peanut. You would imagine people might think very carefully before raising their children to be Red Sox fans, but nobody ever did.

John was two sips into his coffee when he heard a knock and the simultaneous click of the back door opening. "Hell-lo!" Joan called out, her voice low and slightly nasal. "Robin?"

"She's not here," John responded, not getting up. He had never quite gotten used to the unfettered coming-and-going between the two houses, but Robin told him not to fuss about it. It was good for the boys, Robin said. "She just left to do some grocery shopping. Can I give her a message?"

"Darn." Joan looked dismayed. "I thought maybe she could help me out. Isaiah needs a photo for his travel soccer ID card right this minute and I can't find anything more recent than last December. Robin and I were at the park a couple of weeks ago and she was taking pictures of the boys, so I thought she might have something I could use. I have to get it in this afternoon or he can't play in the first game next week."

"Can't he play without an ID for one day?"

"No one can play without an ID! These people are soccer Nazi's."

"They're six-year-olds. What are they worried about?"

"I guess they don't want a team bringing in some star player from another league, or a boy who is older. Anything that would gain them some sort of unfair advantage in the level of competition."

"Bringing in ringers in the first grade? I guess I will have to be on the look-out for scouts at the kindergarten soccer clinic tomorrow."

John chuckled. "Well, Robin won't be home for a while, but maybe I can dig something up for you. I wouldn't want to see Isaiah miss his first game."

"If you could find anything it would be such a help. Anything with a little picture of his face I can cut out to fit the space on the card – it's small." She held her thumb and forefinger about an inch apart.

"A thumbnail. Got it. I'll see what I can do." Joan looked like she was going to take a seat at the table, so he added, "I'll bring it over. Quick as I can." John was still grinning to himself as he walked into the spare bedroom. Six-year-olds! People took themselves so seriously. There was probably no one on that team better than Ryan.

Robin's laptop was lying on the long table they'd bought after the boys moved upstairs. John flipped it open. A small box popped up on the screen, blinking "password?" Damn, thought John. He tried her cell, but the call went to voicemail. Robin never picked up; it was hardly worth paying for the phone if she wasn't going to answer it. He would have to take a stab at guessing the password. He tried the boys' birthday, and ryanteddy. Nothing. He tried rhogan and robinandjohn. No. John drummed his fingers on the white plastic casing. She had chosen the password for their first computer, the one they had shared. What was it again? He typed in dallastexas and the screensaver popped up, a shot of the boys on their first birthday.

John opened the editing program that Robin used for photos. He looked at some of the files that had been opened recently, toggling impatiently through the images. He didn't see anything with Isaiah in it. Perhaps she hadn't edited that bunch yet. Maybe it wasn't even on the computer. If it's still in the camera, he decided, Joan was just out of luck. He left the editing program, searched for all images and sorted by date. There were lots of picture files, including a number that had been downloaded recently. He clicked on a folder marked "september2004." It had forty or forty-five jpegs, nothing labeled, nothing marked. That was so Robin. He opened the first. There was Ted, brandishing a stick as if it was a sword. It was recent, and taken in the park. He clicked open another. He could see Isaiah, behind Ted and Ryan. But he was too far away; his head was the size of a pea.

The third picture was just Ryan and the fourth was of Isaiah, but he was hanging upside down. That might do, thought John.

They could turn it around so he was right side up; who would know? John set the print options for the photo printer and hit return. The machine buzzed and hummed like it was waking up from a nap. John opened more pictures while he waited, looking for something better. There were the boys on the monkey bars, first at a distance and then close up. Robin was playing with that new zoom. She pulled in so tight you could see dust on their eyelashes, and the picture quality was still perfect.

The next picture was a shot of a sandbox. Their boys hadn't gone near a sandbox in ages. He stared at it for a minute. He didn't see anyone he knew. This didn't even look like their park. He opened the next file. Same unfamiliar park, same unknown sandbox, this time closer up. There was a little blonde girl staring off into the distance. Cute kid, he thought. Why did they have a picture of her? Was Robin still dreaming dreams of little girls? She hadn't said a word about it since the night they'd had that terrible fight.

He opened a third picture of the sandbox and then a fourth. Slowly, John became aware of a tingling sensation in his hands. There she was again, the blonde child. Now in the sandbox, now in the swing, now climbing up some castle-like thing. There was something eerily familiar about the girl. John fought to place the resemblance, but he couldn't think clearly; there was a tightness in his chest and suddenly the room felt warm and airless.

You do know who she is, he thought. He stared at one of the pictures again. Robin had zoomed in tight here, and the child was smiling. It nagged at his brain like something just past the fringes of recall; like a word on the tip of his tongue. She looked – she looked a lot like Ted, he thought. Like Ted, except for the green eyes. He pictured Teddy's eyes. They were a soft brown flecked with gold, a color like caramel. Robin's color. They moved him to distraction. But Robin always said she was disappointed that neither of the boys had his color. She said she would never have fallen in love with him if it weren't for his green eyes.

Green. His head swiveled back to the picture on the screen. She looked just like Ted, except for her green eyes. Her green eyes that were his green eyes, staring back at him as though the picture was a mirror. In the gentle hollows of his receding hairline, he felt a prickling where the hair that did not exist anymore seemed to be standing on end. The sensation was strangely specific, like the pain of a phantom limb.

Oh Robin, he thought, what have you done?

He looked again at the close-up of the girl in the sandbox. She wrinkled her nose when she smiled, and a small spray of freckles was visible against the whiteness of her skin. His heart leaped in an unbidden rush of joy. Robin must have looked just like this as a child. John pulled down a menu and hit print. Then he closed the picture files one by one. He went over to the printer and slipped the photo into his pocket. The picture of Isaiah lay beneath it – he had nearly forgotten all about that.

John had no idea how much time had gone by since he had walked into that room. Most likely, Joan would show up again any minute. He took the picture from the tray and walked out the back door and through the small gate. He didn't have time to knock before she yelled, "Come in!" Their back door opened directly into the kitchen. "Did you find something?" she asked anxiously.

"Just this," he said, handing her the picture. "I know he's upside-down, but if you trim out the face and turn him right-side-up, I think it will pass for normal."

"Sure," said Joan, "that will work. Thanks so much, John. This is fantastic." She inverted the photo and looked at it carefully. "If you didn't tell me," she said with a laugh, "I would never know."

John said nothing to Robin when she got back that afternoon. She was sitting at the kitchen table after the boys went to bed, sorting through paperwork for the PTA. "How's it going?" he asked.

"Okay," Robin answered. She was in charge of PTA membership for kindergarten, which meant calling everyone to ask them to be sure and send in their checks. "It's not the job I wanted. Joan told me I should sign up to be grade mom, because that gives you a better sense of what is going on in the classroom."

"So why didn't you do that?"

"Well, they asked about this, and I didn't want to say no. Probably somebody already signed up to be grade mom ages ago."

"Robin," said John, "I found the pictures of that girl."

"That girl?" John could not tell if Robin was feigning ignorance, or challenging him to identify the girl more precisely. He saw the color rise in her cheeks. She was waiting to see if he would use the word. *Oh, our daughter? Is that who you mean?*

"Joan came over all worked up about how she needed a photo of Isaiah right that minute or he would never play soccer in this town again, so I agreed to look through your picture files. She couldn't wait until you got back."

"Did you find something for her?"

"Yes, I found something for her. And I found some pictures of a little blonde-haired girl in a park. I know who she is, Robin." John's voice was calm. "How did you find her?"

Robin spoke after a pause, and the words came tumbling out. "I only wanted to make sure they weren't lying to you – the people at the clinic. I thought they might have lied about the embryos, just to get you to go away. I went to get that information, and the rest of it was just there."

"You went to the clinic? You just waltzed in and took a look at their files?"

"No, I went with Mickey. Do you know Mickey and Caleb are thinking of having a child? I went with him when he interviewed the doctor about surrogacy. No one was in the office, so I took a look at our files. Their name and address was there."

"No one was in the office?"

"It was a Friday afternoon. You know how they go home early on Friday afternoon."

"So Mickey just happened to schedule a visit to our clinic for Friday afternoon and you just happened to go with him? I can't believe you got Mickey to participate in this. Robin, it's illegal. It's breaking and entering. You broke into their files. You could get in trouble. Mickey could get into more trouble – my God, you could ruin his career."

"Nothing happened. Nobody saw me."

"Does Mickey know about the girl?"

"No! He has no idea."

"It won't take two minutes for them to put it all together if you get caught." John pointed to the laptop. "You are stalking the girl."

"I wasn't stalking! I didn't even set out to find her. I got lost in Brookline one day and drove right by her house. As soon as I saw her, I knew. I knew – the same as you, John. It was the most incredible coincidence." She stared searchingly into his face. He was frightened, but not angry. "Oh, sweetheart, you should see her. She is so beautiful. Isn't she beautiful?"

"She is unbelievably beautiful. She looks just like you." He shook his head, speaking almost grudgingly. "I understand how you feel, but she is not ours. Don't you see what a dangerous game you are playing? Naturally, I am concerned about the consequences if anybody finds out. I am worried about me, and my business, and the boys, and Mickey and Caleb. But mostly, I am worried about you. You are going to get hurt, Robin. If you can't stop thinking about this girl, it is going to break your heart. I know it's hard. Robin, love, I know it is hard. You need to walk away."

"I know that," Robin answered softly. "I already decided that I would never go back. After that day in the park – John, she saw me."

"Who saw you? The child?"

"No. The mother. She saw me in the woods and I guess I sort of freaked her out. She came creeping up behind me and asked me what I was doing taking pictures of her child."

"Oh, Jesus. What did you say to her?"

"I told her I was a photographer scouting locations in the park for family photos and whatever. Don't worry, John, she totally bought it. She apologized and everything." Robin paused. "But there is this one other thing. This was real stupid, but I was surprised."

"What did you do?"

"I gave her my card. I had this old business card in my camera bag with our address from Somerville, so I gave it to her. What I thought was, she will see that I am really a photographer."

"So now she has our name and our address."

"Our old address! It probably doesn't matter. They will have never given her our name. She will never think to bring this up with the clinic. They are the only ones who could make the connection."

"But if she did – are you sure she didn't recognize you? The girl – she looks just like you."

"Sophie. Her name is Sophie. No, I don't think so. I don't think it occurred to her. And she only has the old address."

"If they have our name, they can trace us here. Okay." John exhaled. "Okay. Hopefully, we'll dodge the bullet. Oh, Robin," John hugged her, "I swear, sometimes you are like a child, not thinking a minute ahead. I know this is hard for you, but you need to forget you ever saw that little girl. Do it for Ryan and Ted, okay? Because how are we going to explain it to those boys if the police are here looking for their mother?"

"I promise you, John. I'll never go there again. I'll try not to think about her. But I'm glad you know. It's a relief to me that you finally know." She clung to him. "I was so afraid you would be angry."

John felt a surge of tenderness for his wife. "Of course not. Don't worry – it will be alright. I'll make sure it's alright."

They did not speak of it during the following week. Robin did not raise the subject. She knew John never would. It was hard for her not to talk about it all the time, now that he knew. Thursday marked the end of the first full month of kindergarten. She pulled into the driveway after pick-up, both boys talking at once as they tumbled out of the car. Robin sifted through the mail as she listened to their tales of the day. "I was line leader," said Teddy. "We went to library."

"We went to library yesterday," said Ryan. "Next week we get to bring home a book if we sit quietly and listen. I didn't get any time-outs today, Mommy."

"That's good, honey." Ryan had gotten an alarming number of time-outs in the first two weeks. His teacher told her that he was just getting used to the routine. She seemed to like him. She said he had a 'wonderful, exuberant energy.' That sounded like something good, but Robin wondered if exuberant energy was some sort of kindergarten code word for ADHD. She would have to ask Joan. Isaiah had been on Ritalin for eight months now. He took it every morning, with his organic cheerios and his hormone-free milk. The school was very pleased with the improvement in his behavior.

The first thing she noticed about the letter was that the name and address were handwritten. Not the fake handwriting of computer-generated script, but handwritten, messy, but still legible. It was a business-size envelope, and it didn't look like an invitation. Robin glanced curiously at the return address. Cambridge, it said. She turned the envelope over. Center for Reproductive Medicine.

Robin caught herself on the near edge of panic. It could be nothing, she thought. It could be a routine follow-up. They could be interested in the health of the boys. Her hands shook opening the envelope, and it tore in a jagged edge. The note inside was brief:

Dear Mr. and Mrs. Hogan,

A situation has recently been brought to our attention regarding your embryo donation of September 2000 that we would like to share with you. As you know, our center is committed to protecting the privacy and confidentiality of our patients and donors. However, there are some unusual circumstances involved which I believe it would be best to discuss in person. Can you please contact our office to schedule a meeting? There is some urgency involved and we would like to meet with you as soon as possible.

Thank you for your consideration of this unusual request. I hope that you will give us the opportunity to explain the facts involved. I feel certain that when you understand the potentially serious implications, you will agree that our decision to contact you was justified.

Thanks again,
Fred Aylmer

She stared at the spiky script of the doctor's signature, which brought back memories of prescription slips and order forms for procedures and bloodwork. She was aware of the boys, still clamoring next to her, but their voices sounded far away. Mechanically, she set out cheese and crackers and sliced an apple, opened their backpacks and checked for notes. The memory of lying on the office floor with her face pressed against the dirty carpeting made her cheeks burn. Still, she thought, she's my daughter. How could they blame me for wanting to see her? Wasn't that the most natural feeling in the world?

Thursday was John's busiest day of the week during football season. Robin was already in bed when he got home, lying awake with her eyes closed. In the morning, Ted and Ryan were fighting over the last slice of French toast. John gave her a commiserating glance as he ran through the kitchen and out the front door. "I won't be late," he shouted over his shoulder.

"You're very quiet," he said that evening, as they carried their dinner plates to the sink. John refilled his glass with red wine and headed into the living room. Robin grabbed a sponge, but John took it and tossed it back on the counter. "Come and watch the game with me," he said. "I'll get this later." Jack followed them into the living room. Robin listened to John's plans for an interactive feature that would complement the ESPN college game of the week. "What do you think about a guy from each school blogging the game in real time? People could send texts for color commentary. Maybe pictures of themselves, little alumni gatherings. It would be great."

"Honey," said Robin, hitting the mute button, "I've got to show you something."

John stared at the letter for a long time. "It doesn't sound hostile," he said, finally. "Do you think it could be about something else?"

"What else could it be? They probably don't want to start out sounding accusatory. I think they're trying to sound like they are not taking sides. What do they mean by 'the facts involved' anyway? They don't know anything. What facts could they have?"

"Are you sure that no one recognized you at the clinic?"

Robin concentrated. She saw herself slipping in and then out of the office door. "There was a nurse I ran into on the way back to the room," she said. "She looked familiar. She might have looked at me funny." Robin paused. "I don't know. I thought it was okay at the time and I just don't know why I should be in any trouble. That's my file. It was our embryo. I had a right. Don't I have a right to the information in my own file?"

"It was all in our file? Their address, and the information on the baby – that was all in our file?"

Robin had a sharp image of herself in the darkened room, pulling out the drawer marked Q – S. "No," she said. "No. I looked in her file. Oh shit. I forgot about that."

"So if that nurse recognized you,"

"Then they could prove I had gone into her file. Oh, John! Do you really think they would go after us that way? I don't want to embarrass you or the boys – or get Mickey in trouble. Oh, my Lord. I will never forgive myself if I have harmed Mickey. I need to talk to him. I need to tell him that I am so sorry."

"What you need," said John, "is a lawyer."

They had agreed on their next steps by bedtime. John liked to have a plan in place. They called Mickey and Caleb and arranged to meet them for lunch the next day. Robin needed to explain what had transpired after that day at the clinic, and to apologize. John wanted to know if they should be worried about criminal charges. "Don't fret to much," he told Robin. "Mickey will forgive you. I don't even imagine he will be so surprised. He knows you pretty well."

"I don't believe it would ever occur to him," said Robin. "The idea that an embryo turns out to be a baby – it's not real to Mickey, the way it is real to me."

They would ask Mickey and Caleb for the name of a lawyer. John wanted to talk to someone before responding to the clinic. If the lawyer approved, they would schedule a meeting for early next week. John removed his watch and wallet, putting them into a tray on the top of his dresser. He was supposed to go to Nashville on Wednesday; he could change that to the following week. He hung his pants on a hanger, shaking out the loose change from his pockets. He pulled open the top drawer. He kept a glass dish there, where coins accumulated. To the left of his socks and in front of the binoculars, the picture of the child stared out at him. Sophie. He picked it up, one finger gently tracing the white border along the edge. Carefully, so it would not get bent, he slid the photo to the back of the drawer.

Chapter 23

"Mr. Rose," said John, "it's a pleasure to meet you in person. Thank you for doing this on such short notice."

"Please, call me Greg." He folded his ample frame into the Lexus. Greg Rose had reddish hair and a broad face with a square chin that provided a solid bulwark against the encroaching fleshiness of his thick neck. He sat hunched slightly forward, his briefcase on his lap, as if to demonstrate a willingness to take up as little space as possible, so that he looked oddly cramped sitting all by himself in the expansive back seat of the SUV. "I am delighted that you called. It's a fascinating case." His blue eyes assessed them with a cool intelligence that belied the diffidence of his posture.

"You were recommended to us by Robin's brother, Mickey Hanley. I guess you guys went to law school together at Harvard." John did not mention the argument that erupted when Caleb brought up

Rose's name. According to Caleb, he specialized in advocating for the rights of the unborn. The very idea of the unborn having rights gave Mickey fits.

"An unborn child has a soul," Robin reminded her brother. "A person with a soul should have rights."

"I know what we were brought up to believe," he replied, "but the popes themselves have changed their minds more than once about when ensoulment takes place. You can't expect the courts to protect the current doctrine of the Catholic church just because it happens to suit your interests at the moment."

"It's not a matter of what suits my interests, Mickey. It's a matter of right and wrong."

"I know you want to believe that, but the reality is it's not so simple. The law cannot recognize a fetus as a human being with all the same rights as its mother. Hell, even you wouldn't do that. If you had to choose between the life of one of your boys and the life of an embryo, you wouldn't hesitate for a second. They're not the same thing. You can't make them the same under the law. You can't put a woman in prison for having an abortion, or call a pregnant woman a child abuser because she has a glass of wine, or for God's sake, chemotherapy. It doesn't make any sense. You know that. You are the one who made extra embryos and then froze them and then gave them away. How can you go and say they're people?"

Caleb looked at Robin's trembling lower lip and added, "Of course that doesn't mean that the fetus has no rights. You would think that the law could be subtle enough to recognize a special category of protections for unborn persons. Most people would agree to that. It's just that the way we argue about it, there's no room for middle ground. And I admit, Greg Rose is not into middle ground. But, he is smart as a whip, and he would take a very personal interest in the case."

"I don't give damn about the man's ideology," said John. "We need someone good who has experience in this area. If this guy is smart and he understands the issues, then I'm fine with that. It he's interested, better yet."

Caleb nodded. "You can't deny that she got the information, so you have to explain her actions. Anyone can sympathize with her attachment to those embryos, but you need someone who is able to present a legal basis for it. You need someone motivated to be zealous in her defense."

"If you need a zealot, then Greg Rose is your man," said Mickey. "Be sure and say I said hello. That will surprise him." When they got up to leave he hugged his sister tightly. "It will be okay," he whispered.

"Mickey said you would find the situation intriguing." Robin smiled wanly at the lawyer in the backseat. "He spoke very highly of your enthusiasm."

"It was kind of him to think of me. Tremendously bright guy, your brother, very bright. We had our differences of opinion, of course." Greg gave an unconvincing laugh. "I guess he remembers a couple of those friendly debates we had working together on Law Review. Well, about the case. I considered the principal facts after we spoke on Sunday. Here's what I see as our main argument. When you agreed to surrender the embryos, you did so because you unable to pay the storage fee of..." Greg checked his notes, "one thousand dollars. Is that correct?"

"Yes," said Robin.

"Money was one issue," said John. "There were other issues as well."

"Let's concentrate for the sake of argument on the money. If you had easy access to a thousand dollars, you would have paid the storage fee, correct?"

"Yeah," said John, "That's probably true."

"Well, no court in the country would allow you to irrevocably lose your parental rights because you didn't have a thousand dollars at hand. Imagine the outcry if a hospital said 'you can't pay your bill, so we are keeping the baby.' Adoption law in all fifty states specifically protects the mother from being bribed or enticed to give up her child."

"But this wasn't an adoption," John countered mildly. "When we signed the papers, there was no baby."

"That is how they will try to represent it. You consented to the transfer of property. But you could not have consented to the termination of your parental rights, because according to the law, that consent cannot be given under duress. The legal framework of the donor program denies the humanity of the embryo. They do not recognize the continuity of life from embryo to newborn. And yet, what difference does it make that the consent process occurred some months before the child was born? The effect is the same. You are denied the right to parent your own child because of a paper signed with a gun to your heads. The consent is void."

"Yes," said Robin, "That's exactly the point. I never stopped thinking of myself as the mother of those embryos. Still, I don't entirely understand how this helps me, if they are accusing me of illegally accessing their files."

"That was your daughter's file. You had every right to it. You have every right to a relationship with the child."

"I think we are getting well ahead of ourselves," said John. "We don't even know yet what they are asking of us. If they only want Robin to avoid any contact with the girl from this point on, then we have no cause to get confrontational."

Greg looked momentarily crestfallen. "That depends on your goals," he said. "What are you hoping for as a result of this action?" He addressed himself to Robin.

"Our goal," said John, "first and foremost, is to make sure that Robin is in no legal jeopardy and that she has not, completely unwittingly, implicated Mickey in any illegal act."

"What is your goal?" Greg asked Robin directly.

"I don't want Mickey to be in any trouble." Robin's eyes were rimmed with red. "That's the most important thing to me. Besides that – I don't know. I want them to understand that I never meant any harm. Of course I only want what is best for Sophie."

"And do you see a relationship with you as something that might be best for Sophie?"

"That's not relevant," said John.

"Yes," said Robin. "At least, I would like her to know that we exist. I would like her to know that Ryan and Teddy exist. She ought to know that at least, John. Then she can choose for herself what she wants, when she is old enough to choose."

"So, visitation?"

Visitation. The word dangled in a mist in front of her eyes, and her mind echoed with images she had pushed forcefully aside: Sophie, swimming towards her in the pool, or standing side by side with her brothers, or perched on phonebooks to take her place at the Thanksgiving table back home. "Maybe," she said.

"Robin, no." said John. "We're not here to make trouble. We're here to avoid trouble. The idea that we could have a claim on the child might be something they should know. If they want to make trouble for Robin, everything is on the table. But please, let's see if we can handle this without getting hostile. Before this letter came, we were not thinking about going after that child. We were just hoping that they would never come looking for us."

"As your lawyer, I would advise you not to offer that information to anyone. Unless you are asked under oath, do not volunteer a statement along those lines, which undercuts any argument you may wish to make regarding your intended relationship with Sophie."

"I have no intended relationship with Sophie," said John, sounding irritable. He gave a warning glance to Robin. "The last thing we need is to turn this into a legal battle. If we can settle it quietly, that is what I want. That's what is best for our family."

When they got to the clinic, John gave their name to the receptionist. She did not ask them to sit down, but escorted them immediately down the corridor to a room with a small kitchenette in one corner and a large table in the middle. A lab tech in a white coat eating a sandwich cleared his things away with a mumbled apology. Dr. Aylmer came in a moment later. "Mr. and Mrs. Hogan, thank you so much. You look well. Feeling fine, Mrs. Hogan? Wonderful. Thank you for coming. My apologies, but we thought the lunchroom would give us more space." The doctor stared briefly at Greg Rose, and then stuck out his hand.

"Oh," said John, "Sorry. This is our attorney, Greg Rose. Greg, Dr. Aylmer."

"Of – of course." The lawyer's presence seemed to throw the doctor off stride. "Well, won't you all sit down? Please, let me explain why we asked you to come today. As you no doubt suspect, this matter relates to one of the embryos that you generously donated in the fall of 2000." Greg Rose stirred but did not speak. "In January 2002, use of your embryo resulted in the birth of a child." Dr. Aylmer looked at John and then at Robin. Why is he telling me this, Robin wondered? Why is he telling me this, if he plans to accuse me of knowing it already? "That child, a girl, is now two and a half years old."

Robin watched him intently. His manner was solicitous and confiding. Was he trying to lull her into confessing? Did he think that she would blurt out some incriminating remark, like the villains in the old tv shows? *Yes, I know, Doctor. Sophie Bettinger, 614 Tilden Street, Brookline, Mass.* "Last week, the girl's parents approached us with some very disturbing information," the doctor continued. Robin's heart beat faster. "Their daughter has been diagnosed with leukemia."

Doctor Aylmer glanced up at Robin and John with a pained expression. They returned his gaze with blank faces. This can't be a trick, thought Robin. No one could make up something so awful. "Oh my God," said Robin, after a pause, "that is terrible." She glanced over at John. He shook his head, as though he were warning her.

"Naturally, her parents are distraught. The child was diagnosed almost a month ago, and she has already undergone one round of chemotherapy. According to her doctors, her odds of survival would be vastly improved by a bone marrow transplant. So perhaps you understand why we have contacted you."

"Of course!" said Robin. "She needs to get bone marrow from a family member. I've heard about that. I would be happy to donate – I'm sure we both would." She looked at John, who nodded vigorously. "You did the right thing, coming to us. We want to help."

"Thank you," said Dr. Aylmer, "but unfortunately neither of you are candidates for bone marrow donation."

"But we are her parents," said Robin.

"And, as her biological parents, you would each be a partial match. A full sibling, however, has a chance, a one out of four chance, of being a perfect match."

"The boys," said John.

"I understand of course if you wish to consult with your attorney." Dr. Aylmer stared curiously at Greg Rose.

"That's not necessary," said John, looking embarrassed.

"No, not at all," said Robin. "We will test the boys. Only – is it painful? Is it in any way dangerous for them?"

"To check for a match is just a blood test. If one of them becomes the donor – I think it is a very safe procedure. But you had better get those details from the oncologist herself. Perhaps the girl's parents could give you more information. They are anxious to meet with you, if you are comfortable with that."

"Are they here?" Robin felt her cheeks turn suddenly pale. She glanced sidelong at her husband, searching for a way to say no that would not sound strange or abrupt.

"They are in my office. We didn't feel it was appropriate to introduce them without your permission. But since you have so generously offered to help, why don't I let them come in now? They'll be very anxious to express their gratitude." Dr. Aylmer slipped quickly out of the door. Greg, John and Robin all rose, but none of them spoke. They looked at one another in confusion as the doctor left the lunchroom.

"I'm sorry," said John to Greg. "This is not what we had anticipated. I don't know what to say." He turned to Robin, "Do you want me to go tell the doctor that we don't wish to meet the parents?"

"I don't know. Maybe we can't avoid it if we are going to be there for Sophie. John, she needs us. She needs her brothers. I can't worry about anything else right now."

The doctor returned before John could respond, holding the door for David and Meredith. Robin took a step behind her husband as Dr. Aylmer introduced them. "Meredith and I have been trying to think of how we could begin to thank you," said David, "first, for your generosity and compassion, in helping us to have our daughter, and now for agreeing to have your children tested as donors. We don't know what to say. We owe you so much."

"Yes," said Meredith. She hugged John and then Robin, barely glancing at them from beneath lids that seemed weighted with sorrow. "We want to thank you on behalf of our little girl."

"How is Sophie?" asked Robin. Dr. Aylmer looked over at her in surprise.

"She's hanging in there. It's been very tough. But she has an unbelievable spirit and she bounces back – the medicines knock her out, so sometimes she gets listless and sad for a while, but she always bounces back again the next day. Officially speaking, she is in remission as of two days ago,"

"Thank God!" said Robin.

"Yes, said Meredith, glancing at her briefly, "Thank goodness for that. So she has a few minutes to recuperate and we will do this testing, and then if there isn't a match," Meredith's voice quavered and they could see that she finished the sentence with an effort, "then we will start the next round of chemo. And she is just going to have to be a brave little bunny."

Robin began to cry. "Poor little darling," she said. Meredith hugged her again. She looked into her face more closely this time. Her expression changed and she wiped her eyes with the heels of her hands.

"Have we met?" she asked, her voice still shaky. "You look very familiar."

Robin sniffed. "No. Perhaps I look familiar to you because of Sophie. She looks a lot like me."

Meredith drew back. She stared at Robin appraisingly. "I'm sorry," she said, "but I wasn't aware that you had ever seen Sophie." She peered at her, and Robin could see the bruised look in her eyes harden into something more stony. "I do know you. You were that woman in the park the other day – the photographer." She cocked her head sideways. "You've changed your hair, but I recognize you. You're not a photographer. You were taking pictures of Sophie. Have you been following us?" There was a sort of horror in her voice.

"I think you must be mistaken," Robin said. Her face was crimson. Meredith picked up her chin, breathing softly through her mouth.

"That's my child" said Meredith "You have no right.." She did not finish her sentence.

Greg Rose spoke for the first time. "Robin, there's no need for you to respond to that."

David looked at his wife in amazement. "Please," he said to John and Robin. "We're all a little emotional right now. We just brought the baby home yesterday, and my wife has barely been out of the hospital for weeks. I can't tell you how difficult this has been."

"I understand," said John. "just tell us what we need to do to have the boys tested."

"Here," said David, handing him Dr. Coben's card. "perhaps it is better if you work directly with the oncology people. They will arrange everything. And of course, we will cover all the costs of testing."

"You don't have to concern yourself about that. I can pay for the testing. We just want to do whatever we can to help the child get well. I assure you," said John, "we have her best interests very much at heart."

"I am certain," said Dr. Aylmer, "that everybody in this room just wants to help Sophie."

Chapter 24

"Are you sure?" asked David. "Are you absolutely sure?"

"David, I am not crazy. I am not hysterical. I know what I saw."

He hesitated. For weeks she had slept no more than a few restless hours a night, and yet it was not like Meredith to make accusations casually. She sat bolt upright in the passenger seat, breathing deeply. There was a spot of color in her cheeks, a pink stain against the drabness that had come to inhabit her face, as though the harsh fluorescence of hospital lighting followed her everywhere. She looked at him dry-eyed.

"That woman is obsessed with our child. You heard her! *'Ya'll know how Sophie looks just lie-ack me?'* Disgusting. How could she say that to me? It had to be her. How else would she know?"

David nodded thoughtfully. "I guess that makes sense. And it is strange that they had a lawyer with them. Aylmer was surprised too

– did you see his face when he told us they had their attorney in the room?"

"Sweetheart, don't you understand? They had their lawyer there because they are thinking of challenging us for custody. What other explanation can there be?" Meredith gave a strangled gasp. "What if they plan to use the bone marrow? What if one of the boys is a match for Sophie, and they won't let him donate unless we give them our baby. Can they do that? Do you think anybody could be so cruel?"

"No. no," said David. "Calm down."

"Don't tell me to calm down! I am not hysterical!"

"Calm. Down." David shook his head vigorously, as though he wanted to clear her words out of his ears. "You are getting yourself upset for nothing. How would they even have known Sophie was sick?"

"She was following us. She could have known. She probably did know. How else can you account for the lawyer?"

"I don't know." Anxiety rumbled in his belly. "One step at a time. We need to assume they are reasonable people. There is a fifty-fifty chance one of those boys can help our child. Until we find out otherwise, we have to keep on good terms. Don't pick a fight. We need them."

"What we need," said Meredith grimly, "is a good lawyer."

David considered this in silence. He dropped Meredith at home, where they had left their sitter perched on the edge of her chair, eyeing Sophie with a vigilant expression as she lay on the couch watching cartoons. "Go on in," he said in the driveway, "I'm going to run over to work for a couple of hours." Meredith squeezed his hand and slid quickly out of the car. David flipped open his cell phone as he backed out of the driveway.

He called his publicist and left a message. "She'll get right back to you, Mr. Bettinger," said the receptionist, oozing helpfulness The light in front of him turned red. Was it possible that Meredith could be right? It seemed like craziness. Sophie was not an infant. She was two and a half; she had never spent a night away from them in her life. He had held Meredith's hand and run a damp washcloth along her forehead as she gave birth, for God's sake. The car behind him beeped, a short irritable staccato. He looked up and the light was green. "Calm the fuck down," he whispered hoarsely. It was craziness; this was all craziness. It was so hard to find the fine line between the craziness that was ridiculous and the craziness that was real.

His phone trilled. "David!" said Angela. "Babe, how are you? I heard the news about your little girl – horrible, terrible. Olivia didn't know; she should have interrupted my call. Is there anything I can do? Anything? Because whatever I can do, it's yours, you know that."

"Thanks, Angela. I appreciate that. Actually, there is something you can do, if you would. I need some information. I know you have a friend who works for The Globe. Can she do a little checking for me, in confidence?"

David could sense her hesitation. "Is it medical information? Because if you need medical information, it would be much better for you to talk to my cousin at Dana Farber; he'll give you the scoop…"

"It's not medical. I don't mean to be mysterious, Angela, but – it's a very long story. I don't think it will take her more than a couple minutes."

"But you can't tell me what this is about?"

"No," David admitted. "I can't. Only – it is for my daughter. We're fighting for her life here. Can you help me?"

Angela sighed. Favors were worth more than money, in her business. "I'll try. I don't know. Ellen may not say yes. Reporters are inquisitive. You're going to have to give her more than you gave me." She groaned quietly. "Let me call her first. I'll email you her name and number."

Angela must have been persuasive, because Ellen called him right away. It was easier talking to a stranger. She was a very good listener. "How terrible," she said. "How unfair." David was grateful to her for understanding. "Do you really think they would try to take the child away from you?" asked Ellen. "Are they monsters?"

"They seemed nice enough, but I don't know. They had a lawyer with them. That's what made us suspicious. Greg Rose. I thought if we knew more about him, it might be a sort of window into their intentions. That's why I called you. Can you find out something about him? Maybe he's just a friend who came along for moral support. I don't know. It could be nothing more than that. It would be a big favor if you would do just that."

"So you want to know what sort of legal work he does?"

"Whatever you can find out." She didn't seem hesitant at all, David noted with relief. "I can't tell you how much I appreciate it. And of course I have to ask you to keep this all private."

"No problem. I can check into the couple as well. Why don't you give me their names? I'm happy to do it for you. So sorry about your kid."

"John and Robin Hogan," said David, gratefully. "I didn't get their address. Whatever you can find out about them would be great as well."

Maybe it would be better just to disappear, thought Meredith, sitting in the kitchen, watching Sophie whirl and bob to the tinny music that came out of a toy giraffe. Throw some things in a suitcase and take off. How wonderful it would be to wake up Monday morning at the beach. Or perhaps in Disneyworld. Meredith had never been to Disneyworld, never had any intention of going to Disneyworld, but now it called out to her like a memory of happier times. She wanted to sit in a pink teacup. She wanted to meander down a fake river in a slow moving boat.

But on Monday, they would be back at the hospital. Normally, the doctor explained, they would already have done the tests to determine whether or not a bone marrow transplant was available. But this was a new circumstance, unprecedented. Dr. Coben had promised to expedite the boys' results, but in the meantime Sophie would start her second round of chemotherapy – an even more terrible ordeal than the first, a scorched-earth approach by which the gains of round one could be consolidated and kept. They could not afford to wait and do nothing. It was a restless monster, this disease, and it must be kept at bay. A few days to recover and then it began again.

It was going to be nearly impossible to go through the motions on Monday morning: get her dressed, put her in the car. Meredith wondered what she would say to Sophie, when the child found out where they were heading. What can I offer her, she wondered? What wouldn't we trade, if we did not have to go?

But on Saturday evening Sophie was flushed, and by Sunday morning she was shaking and feverish. So much for running away, thought Meredith, as they headed into the emergency room. A staff member at the hospital tracked down Dr. Coben on the sidelines of her son's soccer game. "It's fine; don't worry about that," said the doctor when David apologized. They could hear the shouts of the game behind her. "We'll admit her now, and if we can get the infection under control quickly, we can still begin chemo as scheduled tomorrow." They hung up the phone and the game was gone, like a window closing.

Their new room was in the corner, with a second window that gave them a little extra daylight. An Eastern exposure, Meredith realized ruefully at six am. She got up from a blue vinyl chair that lay stretched almost flat into a narrow bed. She stared down at the sleeping child in the dirty morning light and ran a hand softly across the soft, naked skin of her scalp. Her face looked wan and pale, with no sign of yesterday's fever.

Mid-afternoon, Sophie's favorite of the young nursing assistants poked her head into the room. "Mrs. Bettinger?" said the girl, a slip of a thing, with big eyes and a brown pony-tail. Sneakers peaked out beneath the dragging bottoms of her pink scrubs. She looked like a child dressed as a nurse for Halloween. "There's a lady here? She says you know her? Robin?" Meredith involuntarily laid a hand across Sophie's chest. Sophie stirred but did not open her eyes. She was often listless after chemo, waiting for the anti-nausea drugs to kick in.

Meredith went out into the hall where Robin stood in gym clothes, track pants and a jacket in some grey synthetic that slid along her body without clinging or creasing. A ribbon in her hair matched the pink stripes on her pants. Meredith felt suddenly aware that the old green cotton sweater she wore was unraveling at the hem, and the jeans she never bothered to shorten dragged on the floor behind her. She tucked her wavy brown hair behind her ears and stared at the other woman defiantly. "I brought the boys in for their tests," Robin said. "They are with their Daddy, getting a little treat at the coffee shop next door." She attempted a small grin. "They were real brave."

Meredith stared at Robin blank-faced, remembering Sophie's look of resignation as they reattached the IV drip to her port. Robin's uncomfortable smile faded. She really was exceptionally pretty, thought Meredith, with an odd sense of detachment. "So," said Robin, when Meredith did not speak, "I asked downstairs and they said you were up here. They said Sophie came back in yesterday. Is she alright?" her voice deepened with concern, and Meredith counted three full syllables in the word alright.

"The fever is gone," she answered automatically. "But she's back on chemo now."

"Oh," said Robin, looking sad. "I brought her this." She held out a small disposable plastic tub. "It's cupcakes. Red velvet. That's my boys' favorite. Ryan noticed right away when I put some aside, but I told him they were for the special little girl who is sick, and he was happy to share them with her."

"Thank you," said Meredith woodenly. She looked down at the tub in her hands.

"Does Sophie like red velvet cake?" asked Robin.

"I don't think she's ever had it. We don't – we try to stay away from processed sugar."

"There's cream cheese in the frosting," said Robin. "And it's not from a mix or anything. I made it from scratch. It's my mother's recipe."

"It's chocolate, right?"

"Yes. Cocoa. Does Sophie like chocolate? She isn't allergic or anything, is she?"

"No. Sophie loves chocolate. I was just wondering – what makes it red?"

"Oh, that's just food coloring. I don't know why we add it. Just tradition, I suppose." Robin paused, eyeing the closed door behind Meredith. "I was wondering – do you think it would be okay if I said hi? You wouldn't have to explain anything. I thought, maybe, I could wish her good luck. Because I'm just sure it's going to work out with one of the boys, and then she might want to know who gave her the bone marrow. And then you could say – the lady who said hi that day, it was one of her sons. She might like that."

"No," said Meredith. "No. I'm sorry – it's not a good idea. Sophie just had her chemotherapy this morning. Her immune system – colds and viruses – it's not a good time for her to have any non-essential visitors. She's not feeling well at all. Not now."

"Okay," said Robin. "Another time then."

"Alright, well," Meredith nodded toward the plastic tub, "thank you. And thank you for bringing the boys."

"Of course," said Robin. "I'll be praying for a match."

Oh please, don't let there be a match, thought Meredith, and then a horror seized her and she said, fervently, "Yes, we are all praying for a match." She turned abruptly and slipped inside the door. Sophie was awake now.

"My feet are cold," she said in a small voice.

"Mommy will rub them." Meredith settled in beside her. "It will make them feel warmer." Please, she thought, let there be a match.

Meredith recounted the story indignantly to David when he got to the hospital after work. "Cupcakes! Exactly what Sophie needs right now. White flour, and some toxic red chemical stuff. 'I made it from scratch,' she says. As if homemade poisons were so much better."

"I know," said David. "I know how upsetting it is. But she was trying to be nice. Be careful. We can't afford to fling her cupcakes back in her face."

"I didn't! I was nice. I was perfectly friendly."

"I'm sure you were."

"I didn't let her in to speak to Sophie though."

"I don't think that would have been a good idea."

"No. 'You wouldn't have to explain anything,' she says. Explain what? That she is Sophie's real mother? That's what she meant. She was tossing me a bone – *You wouldn't have to explain anything*. Not yet."

"Sshh," said David, drawing Meredith farther away from the bed, where Sophie slept fitfully.

"They didn't have any business telling her that Sophie was here. They're not supposed to release that information to non-family members. Which is what they are."

"You're right. I'm going to speak to them. We'll remind the hospital staff that no one is to be given access to Sophie or her medical records without our specific approval."

"Won't that raise some eyebrows? I don't want them asking questions. I'm always around. I can deal with it."

"You could doze off. You could go to the bathroom. I don't care what the staff thinks so long as they follow our instructions."

"Okay. You tell them, alright, sweetheart?" Meredith glanced fearfully at the door and her spine stiffened. "Food coloring," she muttered darkly.

On Tuesday, Lindsey brought Lily in to cheer Sophie up. "Look Sophie," Lily whispered, with a glance at the nurse who was still in the room, "I made you a picture."

"Is that your house?" asked Sophie, staring at the paper.

"No, that's the school. All the kids are outside because it's recess."

"Sophie doesn't know about recess," said Meredith. "She's never been to school. Not yet!"

"I go to school," said Sophie stubbornly.

"Not yet," said her mother. "Someday."

"I go to school now. This one is me." Sophie pointed at one of the girls on the page.

"But she has dark hair and dark eyes like mine," said Lily. "You have green eyes and yellow hair."

"I do have dark hair!" screamed Sophie with sudden intensity. "I do go to school!"

"Okay," said Lily, looking concerned but calm, "you can go to school. This girl is you." Lily pointed to a girl with light hair and a jump rope. Sophie pushed the picture away.

"She doesn't have dark hair."

"But you don't have dark hair either."

"Will you make me dark hair?" asked Sophie.

"Okay," said Lily, pulling crayons out of her school bag. She took the picture and drew in a smaller girl with short, dark hair. Lily made the eyes big and round, and colored them in with green. "There you go," she said.

Sophie shook her head. "Make me dark hair," she whimpered.

"I did," said Lily. "Look! This girl has dark hair."

"No," said Sophie, "make me dark hair." She pointed to her chest. Lily stared at her questioningly.

"I'm sorry, Sophie," she said, "I don't know what you want."

"She wants you to make her some hair," said Lindsey, putting one hand on her daughter's shoulder, "but you can't do that with crayons. Hold on, Sophiekins. I have an idea." Lindsey pulled out her cell phone. Meredith looked at her apologetically. "Right! No cell phones. God, I hate hospitals. Listen Lily can you stay here a minute while I run and make a call?" Lily nodded. "I'll be right back."

Meredith, watery-eyed, gave Lily a small smile. "Don't take it personally," she said. "They started her on steroids today. It's another kind of drug, and it makes her sort of crazy. She's been a terror all afternoon."

"I'm hungry," whined Sophie.

"Also she's always hungry," continued Meredith, pulling out a shopping bag from the small closet. "What'll it be, Sophie?"

Lindsey came back ten minutes later. "Okay Sophie, " she said. "Don't you worry. Auntie Lindsey, stylist to the stars, is on the job." She turned to Meredith. "Do they have limits on visitors? Do you need us to leave?"

"Leave? No – they don't like too many visitors at a time, but David won't be here for a couple of hours."

"You're not expecting someone else?"

"No."

"Because while I was coming back down the corridor, there was a woman in the hallway asking the nurse which room was Bettinger."

Meredith's eyes narrowed. "Now? Just now?"

"Yes, just now."

Meredith moved quickly to the door and stepped outside, looking left and right. The long hallway was quiet. At the far end, a woman with dark hair that rimmed her ears in tight round curls sat with a nurse on hard plastic chairs, leaning their heads together as they spoke. The nurse stood up when she saw Meredith. "Do you need anything, Mrs. Bettinger?" she asked in a bright voice. The other woman kept her head down, writing diligently in a small notebook. Meredith's heart went out to her.

"No, I'm fine," said Meredith, retreating back into her own room. "I don't know what that was about. There's no one out there."

A half an hour later, there was a knock on the door. "Excuse me!" The nurse with the chirpy voice called into the room. "There's someone out here looking for you, Mrs. Bettinger."

Meredith stood up from her chair with an irritated shake of the shoulders. "What now?" she asked. Lindsey smiled at her stiff back and followed her into the hall. A girl of twenty-five or twenty-six stood there holding a large cardboard box.

"Hi Lindsey!" the girl said. She looked out of place, in lipstick and three inch heels, like an exotic bird dragging it's colorful plumage across the drab speckled landscape of the hospital floor. "Found them! They were in the studio room closet, just like you thought. Is there anything else you need today? Because some of us girls were going to go, like, to this pedicure place that serves cocktails."

"Sounds great," said Lindsey, accepting the box.

"Yeah. Tipsy Toes Tuesday. Love it!" The girl glanced awkwardly at Meredith and with half a wave, clip-clopped down the hall toward the elevators.

Meredith followed Lindsey back into the room. "Sophie!" Lindsey said, "did you want Lily to make you some dark hair?"

"I want yellow hair," said Sophie.

"You want yellow hair on your head?"

"Yellow hair."

"I think we can manage that." Lindsey rifled through the cardboard box and extracted a long blonde wig. "How's this?" she asked Sophie. She put it first on her own head, and then on Meredith. Sophie reached out both hands. Lindsey took the wig and put it carefully on the little bald head, then lifted Sophie up and carried her into the bathroom to look in the mirror. Sophie grinned from ear to ear. "But we have more, Sophie. Look." Lindsey pulled out a short black wig with square cut bangs and a longer one with red curls. "All for you! Light brown short hair, dark brown shaggy hair and of course," Lindsey pulled the final wig from the box, "dreadlocks! Shall we put that one on your mommy?" She put it on Meredith's head and Sophie and Lily shrieked with laughter.

David arrived as Lindsey and Lily were leaving for dinner. "Can we have Chinese?" asked Lily, waving good-bye as Meredith blew grateful kisses.

"Lindsey was so great," Meredith said, explaining about the wigs. "When the girl arrived with the box, I was sure it was her again." Meredith gave a significant nod toward the door. "Lindsey thought she overheard someone earlier, asking for the Bettinger girl. I checked, but I didn't see her. I don't know. Maybe you are right. Maybe it is all in my head."

"No," said David. "It's not all in your head. I had a friend of a friend of mine do some checking and I found out some interesting things about Mr. Greg Rose."

"The attorney?"

"Yep. Harvard Law School, class of 1998. A couple of notable cases. In 2002, he represented an anti-abortion protestor who was driving around to clinics and schools in a truck covered with big, nasty pictures of dismembered fetuses."

"Ugh."

"When the protestor was asked to leave a middle school campus, he sued the principal for violation of his first amendment rights, with Greg doing the honors. Then in 2003, Rose defended a pharmacist from Western Massachusetts who refused to sell the morning-after pill to some young lady with a prescription because he believed he shouldn't have to give out pills if it violated his conscience. Didn't believe in using contraception that might harm a fertilized egg. She ended up getting an abortion later on, and sued the pharmacist for the expense and emotional distress."

"So Mr. Rose is an anti-abortion lawyer."

"He wrote a Law Review article condemning stem cell research because it was based on the slaughter of untold innocent souls."

"But where does that fit in here? We didn't slaughter any embryos. We adopted one."

"Well, if embryos have rights like children, then so do their parents."

"Oh, for heaven's sake. So now what do we do?"

"We get a lawyer with experience in reproductive rights. I called Edward Zamotas this afternoon. Do you remember him? He did some pro bono work at your Women's Center a few years ago."

"Zamotas?" The name was familiar.

"He defended that pregnant girl whose boyfriend had her arrested for child abuse because he thought she might be drinking."

"Yes, I remember." Meredith recalled Edward now. He was a thin man, intense, humorless. "That girl was definitely drinking. She used to tell the counselors about it all the time."

Cindy Wilder – that was her name. She had driven the staff to distraction. She laughed at them when they told her to cut down on the booze, to stop bingeing. "I will tell you the truth," she said, her eyes heavy-lidded and defiant. "Everybody else jus' lies, but I will tell you the truth. Sometimes I have got to have me a drink."

"The father of the baby wanted to get her committed to an alcohol abuse program. He went to Family Services and they told the police. The prosecutor was this young guy who wanted to get his name in the papers, and he pressed charges. Zamotas said that there was no baby yet, so there couldn't be any child abuse."

"And he won," said David.

Meredith nodded. "And the prosecutor got himself elected Attorney General. Family Services took the baby away after he was born. Cindy used to come by the Center sometimes after her mother kicked her out again. I don't know what happened to the little boy. I asked Cindy once, and she said she had no idea." She was a tough one, thought Meredith, remembering her smirk.

"I spoke to Edward this afternoon. He knows Greg Rose. He believes Rose will be trying to establish a new precedent for the treatment of frozen embryos."

"I don't care about frozen embryos." Meredith spoke bitterly. She hated them all equally, Greg Rose and Edward Zamotas and Cindy Wilder and the prosecutor who put her on trial. None of them knew or cared what it was like to watch your baby suffer. "Sophie is not a frozen embryo. She is a child who has never spent a night without her parents. They can't take her away from us. That's not reproductive rights. That is human rights."

"Of course it is. I know we are doing the right thing, sweetheart, but I bet that girl's boyfriend thought he was doing the right thing too, when he went to the police. We need someone who understands the law and will make it work for us."

"Daddy," called Sophie in a sleepy voice, "look at me." She pulled on the short black wig. "Lily has black hair."

"Yes she does, sweetheart," said David, lying down next to her. Sophie took up hardly any space at all in the narrow bed.

"My next hair might be black."

"No," said David, "I don't think so."

"Why?" said Sophie.

"Because you are a blonde-haired girl. That is what you were meant to be. And blonde-haired girls don't grow black hair. But you can wear your black wig if you want."

Sophie stared up at him. "I'm hungry," she said, starting to cry. "I want a burrito."

Chapter 25

It was 'K' week for the kindergarten classes. The boys were building kites and coloring kangaroos, and for snack Robin got kiwis and Kit Kat bars. "K was a tough one," she said to Joan. Robin was driving Isaiah and Talia to school all week, because Joan needed to get the next chapter in her book about bi-racial children to the publisher by Friday.

"I remember K week from last year," agreed Joan. "I sent knishes."
"Is that right? I can never get my kids to eat fish."
"Knishes are potato."
"Oh! Well, that's nice. I thought everybody would send Hershey's kisses. That's what I thought of first. How's the writing going?"
"Pretty well. This chapter, really, is the key to the whole book. This is where I explain why early adolescence is the best time for a bi-racial child to choose a racial identity. I'm calling it, 'I Choose Me.'

Of course, people will take issue with the timing. I'm prepared for it to be wildly controversial. You have no idea."

"Do they have to choose?"

"Of course they do. As children, we are defined by our families and then as we get older, we need to identify ourselves as a part of something larger – at some point, you have to know who you are in the world. When children get to a certain age, they need to know their identity."

"I wouldn't want them to take sides," said Robin.

"See, that's my point – choosing one race is not a rejection of the other; that's an old idea that has no currency anymore. If we separate the internal, self-identification process from the externally defined categories of racial identity, than we liberate the concept of race from the narrow biological imperatives of tribalism."

"It sure is a good thing that you are writing this book," said Robin. "It is going to help so many people."

Robin skipped her run that morning, and she didn't go for groceries even though they were out of milk. She sat outside in the sun, with the back door open so she wouldn't miss the phone if the doctor called. She stirred her tea absent-mindedly. If there was a match, they might be needed at the hospital right away. A fifty-fifty chance there was no match, she reminded herself firmly. The warm sun on her face made her sleepy. A vision rose in her mind of a small, stark, white room with two children side by side in narrow beds. There was Teddy, looking brave and pale and interesting against the pillow. And next to him, the girl, a little thin and scared but looking better already.

She did not leave the house until pick-up time. The line at the school was everlasting. It took fifteen minutes to get up the drive and around the loop to the spot where the boys stood with Talia. "Hop in," she said brightly. "Quick, quick."

"I'm not going home with you," said Talia, "I have a play date with Kate."

"Your mommy didn't tell me that, sweetheart." Robin pulled out her phone. "I'll have to check." The assistant principal came over to the window.

"Keep the line moving, please, Mrs. Hogan."

"One second, Mrs. Roscoe. I am phoning Talia's mother, one second. I'm sure it's just a miscommunication. Won't take a moment."

"If you want to make a phone call, you are going to have to pull over and park." Mrs. Roscoe smiled harder. "Have to keep the line moving!"

"Damn, damn, damn," Robin muttered under her breath. She reached Joan on the fourth ring.

"Oh, did I forget to tell you? Sorry! Of course she is going to Kate's. I was sure I had mentioned that this morning."

"Probably you did," said Robin, who was certain that she had not. "No harm done." She inched her way back into the slow line of traffic departing the parking lot. They got home at three-thirty. There were no messages on the phone.

After snack, the boys settled on the couch to watch Animal Planet. Robin checked her watch. Four o'clock. In fifteen minutes they had to start getting ready for soccer. When the phone rang at ten after four, she darted into the kitchen to answer it.

"Hello," she said breathlessly.

"Mrs. Hogan? This is Doctor Coben."

"I was hoping that would be you! Do you have the test results?"

"I do." Dr. Coben paused. "We have good news. Your son Ryan is a perfect match for Sophie."

"Ryan? Are you sure?" Robin felt flutters in her chest.

"Yes, quite sure," said Dr. Coben with a laugh. "Are you and your husband still prepared to go ahead with the stem cell donation?"

"Of course," said Robin. A bark of complaint came from the living room, and she leaned out of the kitchen to check on the boys. Ryan, growing restless, was imitating a woodpecker with his index finger on Teddy's upper arm. "Ryan," she said, "stop tapping your brother." Ryan put his hand down. "Move over." He shuffled a few inches to the right. "Further," she said. He wriggled down half a foot. She frowned at the dog, who leaped off the couch with a look of shame.

"I am so sorry," said Robin, returning to the phone call, "of course we want to help Sophie. What do we do next? Do Ryan and Sophie have to go into the hospital right away? I know we need to move fast."

"We do want to move quickly, but there's a bit more to the process than that. First, we need to get Ryan started on a drug that will stimulate his bone marrow to make extra stem cells. The more he has circulating in his blood, the less harvesting we need to do."

"Harvesting?" said Robin. The word tasted sour in her mouth.

"The easiest way to get at the stem cells is to take them right out of his blood. It's much less invasive than taking out the marrow." The thought of removing marrow from Ryan's bones made Robin's stomach clench. "After five days on a growth stimulating factor, we will do a small procedure to put in a central line."

"What kind of procedure?"

"A small surgery."

"Oh. We didn't know – what is a central line?"

"That's a tube we put into his chest in order to get access to an artery. We will give him general anesthesia, and he won't feel a thing."

"But he will have a tube sticking out of his chest? How will he go to school like that?"

"We'll have it out again as soon as we finish the harvesting. While that's going on, we're going to need him here most of the day, so realistically he's going to miss a few days of school. As soon as we have enough stem cells to complete the transplant, we will take the line out. That's very easy, just light sedation, and he should feel good as new in a day or two."

"But how do you get the cells out? How do you do the – harvesting?"

"We attach a tube from the central line to a special machine. As his blood circulates, it runs through a filter in the machine that removes just some of the cells, including the stem cells, leaving the rest, which go right back into Ryan."

"Does that hurt?"

"He can't feel the filtering but there are some side effects during the process. He is likely to feel a little light-headed. Sometimes, a donor might have a little cramping. All those things are transient, and once it's over he will feel better right away."

"I guess it's easier for him than for Sophie."

"Much easier."

"And the stem cells go into Sophie. I guess she is hooked up to the machine as well?"

"Oh, no. After the stem cells are collected – that will take two or three days, four at the outset – they have to be concentrated and processed. We won't do the transplant for another couple of days."

"You mean Sophie won't be there with us?"

"The recipient comes to the hospital once the collection is complete to undergo what we call a conditioning regimen – she will be getting high doses of chemotherapy and radiation that will eliminate her own bone marrow and make room for the donor cells to engraft and grow."

"That sounds awful."

"It is pretty awful," Dr. Coben admitted. "We can't risk starting that until we know we have the stem cells in hand. Can you come down to the hospital tomorrow morning so we can begin the neupogen therapy?"

"Can't I just pick it up at the pharmacy?"

"Neupogen is an injection, not a pill. We can show you how to do it. If you want to make arrangements with your pediatrician, I am sure you can get the shots done there instead. That might be more convenient for you."

"I don't think we want to bother our pediatrician," Robin answered quickly, thinking in passing of all the questions better left unanswered. "I can do the shots. I have lots of experience, y'know, from the IVF. I just need to be home by four tomorrow, because the boys have gymnastics on Tuesdays."

"I have to warn you that Ryan might not feel up to gymnastics this week, Mrs. Hogan. The neupogen has some side effects as well, unfortunately. Muscle fatigue, bone pain, sometimes headaches or nausea."

"Oh poor Ryan!"

"I'm sorry." Dr. Coben paused. "I know this is a lot to absorb all at once. But it is a wonderful thing that your family is doing for Sophie. A year from now, that little girl may well be alive only because of you."

She already is, thought Robin.

"But you're sure?" Dr. Coben pressed.

"Sure of what?"

"You're sure you are willing to go through with the donation? You, and your husband? Maybe you would like some time to think this over before you say yes. It would not be good for Sophie if we were to start the process and then were unable to proceed with the transplant."

"No – of course. We are both committed to doing this for Sophie, to make her better. I'm certain it is what Ryan would want as well, if he were old enough to understand."

Robin hung up with the doctor and went back into the living room. The dog had returned to his sofa cushion, and Ryan was walking along the back of the couch as though it were a balance beam. "Get off!" she cried, and Jack jumped down. Ryan looked at her, and took a couple more steps toward the end. "Climb down from there," she said, trying to look stern. He leapt off, sticking his legs out straight in front of him, and then pulling them down sharply to land on both feet.

"That's a pike. We did pikes in gymnastics last week. Tomorrow we are going to have a handstand contest."

"Oh, baby," said Robin, pulling him towards her. He leaned away from the hug, laughing. From the couch, Teddy watched with a wary eye. She reached for him, and her embrace encompassed them both. "Okay, the two of you," she said, "let's get your cleats on."

They arrived at soccer practice before Robin had finished explaining. "Go!" she said, opening the door so they could tumble out. "And don't talk about this with anybody, alright boys? This is just a private family matter."

The phone was ringing again as they walked in the door after practice. For a moment, Robin wondered if it could be them, calling right away to say thank you. Maybe they wanted to make sure Ryan knew how much they appreciated everything he would be going through for Sophie's sake. She wondered if they might think it was a good idea for the two children to meet. She had thought about that herself, that it might help Ryan to understand.

But the woman's voice on the phone was unfamiliar. "Is this Mrs. Robin Hogan?" she asked. "My name is Ellen Gordon, with the Boston Globe. Could I have a moment of your time, Mrs. Hogan?"

"We already get the Globe," said Robin as politely as she could.

"I'm not selling the newspaper, Mrs. Hogan. I am a reporter. According to information I have obtained, you and your husband are planning to allow one of your children to be a bone marrow donor for a biological sibling that was adopted as a frozen embryo. A savior sibling. Would you be able to confirm that for me, Mrs. Hogan?"

"Who told you about that? How did you find out about it?" Robin felt like something very large was bearing down upon her, moving quickly, so that she could not see the thing in its entirety but only felt the enormity of it.

"So, can I take that as a confirmation?" said Ellen Gordon. "You have twin boys, right? Have either of your children tested positive as a match?"

"That's none of your business," said Robin. "This is a private family matter."

"It is my understanding that the hospital staff has been instructed not to allow you to have any contact whatsoever with the sick child. Do you have any idea why her parents would feel the need to do such a thing?"

"The staff told you that?"

"Are you unhappy about this restriction?"

"No. I mean, I don't think what you're saying is true."

"Is it true that you made an earlier attempt to get into her room?"

"I went to see her, but it's not like I was sneaking into her room, not the way you make it sound. I asked the mother. It wasn't a good time, is all."

"Mrs. Hogan, people have suggested to me that you and your husband intend to ask for custody of your biological child."

"What are you talking about? Who said that?"

"Have you made a formal request for custody?"

"No!"

"Not yet?"

"No!"

"Do you intend to withhold the bone marrow donation if you are not given custody of the child?"

"Why are you saying these things?" asked Robin, whose voice was shaking. "I just wanted to see her. She is our own flesh and blood. We would never do anything to put her life in danger. We are saving her life. Her brother is saving her life. You make it sound like something terrible, something ugly." Robin hit the red button on the phone. "I'm not talking to you anymore," she said to the lifeless receiver.

John had already spoken to Greg Rose when he got home an hour later. There was nothing to be done, the lawyer said, unless they could identify the source of the leak. The hospital had an obligation to keep their patients' information confidential, but that complaint would have to come from the Bettingers. Robin and John could sue the newspaper if they printed anything that was not true, strictly speaking. "I asked him if we should call her back," said John. "Maybe we should make a definitive statement that we are not seeking custody, not in return for the donation nor in any other circumstance."

"What did Greg Rose say about that?" Robin asked. She found herself oddly reluctant to consider such an option.

"He said perhaps that is exactly what this was meant to achieve. He thinks maybe they put this story out there to intimidate us, in case we were going to try to establish parental rights."

"How dare they! Ryan is going to have five days of shots and days of harvesting after that, and a surgery – you'd think they would be grateful. I don't know what kind of people these Bettingers are."

"I didn't know this donation thing involved a surgery. Nobody mentioned any surgery. I don't like the sound of that."

"A small surgery."

"I don't want him having any goddamn surgery."

"But we have no choice, John."

"I hate this," said John. "Alright. We have a responsibility to the child. I guess Ryan will understand that when he's older. I don't have the faintest idea how we are going to explain it to him now."

"It would help if he could meet Sophie, and see how sick she is. That reporter said the Bettingers told the hospital staff to keep me away from Sophie. She said, "What did you do to make such a step necessary?" I didn't do anything, John! I baked some cupcakes for a sick little girl, to make her feel better. Is it so unnatural that I care about her? I almost wish we did insist that they let us see the child in return for our cooperation. A lot of people who give up babies for adoption, they have that relationship. They get to see the child once in a while. And they weren't pushed into giving their child away, not the way we were. Greg Rose is exactly right about that."

"Robin," said John, "this is not the time. Maybe we can talk about that when she is feeling better. I want to know her too. I really do. My heart turns over inside my chest when I think about that child. But I don't want to get her parents more upset. This is a hard time for them. I don't want them to get angry and start making accusations. It seems dangerous to me. We're doing everything we can for her. She doesn't need to know who we are."

"Maybe not now, but in the future she will. It's in her best interests. When children get to a certain age, they need to know more about their identity."

John looked at her strangely. "Rob, if you are suggesting that we take Rose's advice and go after visitation, you had better think a damn site harder about that before you screw up our lives completely. I'm not so sure Rose didn't plant this story himself, to get us riled up. He wants us to go to court. He wants a fight. He was on it again today about how the laws need to acknowledge the rights of embryos. He's aiming to strike the fear of God into the IVF clinics. You know what? I think he wants to shut them down entirely."

"Of course he doesn't, John, don't be ridiculous. Nobody is against IVF."

"The Church is against IVF."

"Well technically, yes." In her heart, Robin had always believed that the Church's position on IVF was more pro forma than sincere. "But they are not against the children. As soon as the embryo exists, it is a child in the eyes of God, like any other child."

"I know how much you want to believe that those little specks are children just like Ryan or Teddy, but if that is the case you can't be creating them or freezing them or sizing them up under microscopes to decide which ones to implant. That's the mess you get into when you insist that every embryo is a child."

"And this is the mess that you get into when you insist that they are not. You can't deny that she is our daughter now, can you John? I am not going to walk away from her."

"I'm not asking you to walk away from her. I couldn't do it myself, not now. I'm asking you to think critically about this Greg Rose and keep in mind that he has his own agenda. To tell you the truth, the guy makes me nervous." John reached out to run one hand along the side of her face, "You don't even know what you want, you only know how you feel. He wants the drama. He wants to use our story to make a bigger point, but I'll be damned if I am going to be held up to the world as the man who sold his unborn children for a thousand bucks. We are going to be judged, Rob. We are going to be judged by people who have never stood a day in our shoes."

Robin stared unhappily at the floor. "I don't care what other people think of me," she muttered to herself, although the idea of walking into the boys' school with voices buzzing all around her filled her with dread. What would she tell her parents? But there was no reason anyone in Texas had to know what was in the Boston Globe. She would ask Mickey not to mention a word of it back home. "Let's not say anymore now to that woman from the paper, okay?" she said, after a pause. "I don't think I gave her anything today that she could use. I told her that we wanted to help Sophie. What could be so bad about that? There's no story there – if people find out about the embryos, then so be it. We didn't do anything wrong. We gave them a chance, that's all. Someday, when Sophie is all well again – perhaps we can make them understand that we belong in her life. Because we do." She looked coolly at John, and her voice grew in confidence. There was doubt in his eyes and none in hers. "We do. I would rather work out something amicable. But if they keep on treating us like dirt, and spreading lies, with all that we have done for them – then I am going to let them know that we have rights to that child. Our boys have a right to know their sister. She is our child too. She needs us now, and she may need us later. And if Mr. Rose knows how to make that case for us, then I think we should let him do his job."

Chapter 26

Fearful But Desperate, Parents of Child Adopted As an Embryo Turn to Biological Family For Help
by Ellen Gordon
Globe staff / October 12, 2004

It seemed like the perfect solution when Meredith Schuyler and David Bettinger of Brookline had difficulty conceiving: using a donor embryo, one of hundreds of thousands of cryopreserved embryos languishing in IVF facilities nationwide. Then last month came the crushing news that their daughter Sophie, now age two and a half, had cancer. Fighting to save her, the Bettingers reached out to the people they need and fear the most — the biological parents, John and Robin Hogan of nearby Wellesley, whose twin sons may hold the key to Sophie's survival.

Given their genetic relationship, the odds were fifty-fifty that one of the Hogan boys would be able to provide their biological sister with the bone marrow donation that doctors say is her best chance of beating the disease, a rare and unusually aggressive form of childhood leukemia. The twins' mother declined to comment on which of the boys is a match. "That's a private family matter," said Mrs. Hogan. However, she did confirm that the transplant will take place. "Her brother is saving her life," Mrs. Hogan explained.

The Bettingers made the difficult decision to contact the donor family despite the fact that both sides were promised anonymity at the time of the embryo donation. Bringing in the Hogan family has raised painful issues for the adoptive couple, who never anticipated a role for them in their daughter's life. Attempts by Mrs. Hogan to visit the child have been rebuffed. "I just wanted to see her," said Mrs. Hogan. "She is our own flesh and blood." According to the hospital staff, contact between Sophie Bettinger and the Hogan family is currently off-limits at the request of the parents. "We are not allowed to let her in there, even if she is the child's biological mother," said one hospital staffer, "and if she asks about the medical records or the child's condition, we are supposed to refer the matter to our supervisor and inform the parents. Usually we release certain information to family members only, but in this current situation we are going to say nothing to anybody."

Asked whether the stem cell donation might be contingent on an agreement granting them access to the child, Mrs. Hogan said only, "we would never do anything to put her life in danger." According to Mrs. Hogan, they have not yet made a formal request for custody or visitation. The Hogan's attorney, Greg Rose, has been a frequent advocate of increased protection for embryos. In a 2002 article on the use of embryos for stem cell therapy, Rose wrote, "The characterization of embryos as property that is our current legal standard denies their essential humanity, even in cases such as embryo adoption, where the intention of bringing the embryo to term requires us to consider the embryo as a person and not as a possession." Asked about his client's intentions, Mr. Rose declined to comment.

In silence, Meredith passed the paper to David. He read through the article once and then a second time, forcing his mind to focus and strip meaning from the blur of familiar names and phrases. "Shit!" he shouted, flinging the paper down. "Damn that woman."

"I told you, she's a threat," Meredith said ominously. "She's a crazy woman and a stalker and a religious fanatic and a Texan. You can't reason with those people." On a toy stove that filled one corner of the breakfast nook, Sophie cooked a pretend egg in a purple plastic frying pan. "Our own flesh and blood," Meredith repeated, looking at the child. "Please. What century is this?"

"What?" said David, looking momentarily confused. "No – not her. I meant Ellen Gordon, the reporter from the Globe. I am going to ram this paper down her fucking throat."

"David, stop," said Meredith, glancing significantly at Sophie. "I don't understand how the reporter found out any of this. Do you think the Hogans told her? Why would they do that?"

"Toast," said Sophie, handing David a piece of plastic bread.

"Thank you," said David. "No, it wasn't them. Meredith, I'm sorry, I talked to that reporter. Off the record! I thought she was just doing me a favor." Briefly, he told her of his contact with Ellen Gordon. "I am going to have a conversation with Angela this morning. And somebody at that hospital is getting fired, or they are going to hear from our attorney."

"David, you can't be serious, picking a fight with the hospital. Not now, when Sophie is about to go in for her transplant."

"Hopefully, she's about to go in for her transplant. Hopefully. If the Boston Globe hasn't fucked everything up with their goddamn article." David slammed his hand against the table. "I can't believe I spoke to that woman."

"What do you mean, fucked everything up? Why should the article change anything?"

"Do you think the Hogans are going to be happy about this? What if it scares them away? I've seen it a hundred times – bad press at the wrong moment screws the deal every time. Maybe I should call them today and apologize."

"Don't say a thing!" The thought of David apologizing to Robin Hogan made her nauseous. "Please. They don't have any way to know it was you. She obviously spoke to that reporter herself. They are probably thrilled to have their fifteen minutes of fame. It sounds to me like she is enjoying herself, playing the hero. 'Oh, we would never do anything to put her life in danger.' No demands for custody!

"Not yet." Not while, 'her brother,' Meredith scratched at the air to put the words into virtual quotation marks, is saving her life." She breathed a deep raggedy sigh. "Okay. If her life is saved, it is all worth it, no matter what happens. That's what I keep reminding myself."

"Fruit salad," said Sophie, handing her mother a bowl containing a single plastic strawberry.

"Thank you, darling," said Meredith.

"I promise you," said David, "I will not let them hurt our family. I'll meet with Zamotas today. As soon as the transplant is done, maybe we can get an order of protection. I appreciate the help that their kid is giving us. But if they come after my daughter, there will be hell to pay. I would never let that happen to you."

"It isn't about me," said Meredith. "This is about what is right for Sophie. She needs us."

The phone rang, and David stood up to leave. "There's going to be a lot of that today," he said, gesturing at the receiver. "I'll call you later, okay? You'll be at the hospital?" Meredith nodded. She had to take Sophie in for an echocardiogram and a pulmonary function test, the first of many tests in preparation for the transplant.

"Meredith!" Lindsey's voice was raspy in the morning. "Embryo donation? Are you serious? Just when were you planning to tell me?"

Lindsey met her at the hospital later that afternoon to talk. "I didn't mean to keep it a secret," Meredith said beseechingly, reaching out to touch her friend's hand. "It was just that one thing led to another. But it never seemed to matter very much that she wasn't our biological child. And then, suddenly, it was the only thing that mattered."

The two women sat together on a vinyl couch near the outpatient procedure room. "Well," said Lindsey, "I have to say you surprised me. I wouldn't have thought you had it in you."

"To use a donor embryo?" asked Meredith.

"To keep a secret. Did anybody know?"

"No. Just David and myself and the people at the IVF clinic, of course. We were going to tell everyone once we had told Sophie. We didn't want her to find out by accident, from some random remark."

"That's why the adoption people go on and on about telling them the whole story from day one. The secret-keeping gets you in trouble."

"I suppose I didn't anticipate that my daughter would get leukemia."

"No, I guess not," said Lindsey. "It's hard to imagine something like that happening. But good news about the sibling, right? Have you met him? What's he like?"

"I don't know and I don't care," said Meredith. "He is seeing the doctor today. I just hope I don't get a call from her saying the whole thing is off."

"Why would they do that? That would be horrible."

"Because they were upset about the article. I don't know. Because they found out that David told the reporter who they are. Because she doesn't like the thought of her little boy hooked up to a machine for ten or twelve hours while it filters his blood. She thought her boys were 'real brave' just for getting their blood tests done. God! Does she have any idea what Sophie has been through?"

"No," said Lindsey. "She doesn't. How would she know? But why do you hate her so much? Is she that much of an asshole?"

"I didn't tell you," said Meredith. "Do you remember that day in the park with the girls? She was the photographer in the woods. I recognized her when we met at the clinic. That was her taking pictures of Sophie. All dressed up in some stupid wig."

"Wow," said Lindsey. "That is creepy. Do you really think they would try to challenge you for custody? That's crazy, right? No court in the world would take that seriously."

"One would think that the consent form they signed when they gave up the embryos would be the final word. But our attorney is not completely confident about it. The law makes it difficult for a mother to sign away her parental rights before the child is born – that's to make sure that nobody takes advantage of pregnant girls, who may not understand what it will mean to give birth."

"But you gave birth," said Lindsey, "not her."

"Yes. That should help. Still, it's hard to predict how a court will rule when there is no precedent. David has been doing some research. There are several surrogacy cases where they ruled that the surrogate's consent for adoption before the pregnancy wasn't valid if it violated mandatory waiting period laws after birth. And there was another case here in Massachusetts of a surrogate who gave birth using someone else's embryo and our State Supreme Court ruled that since she had no biological tie to the child, the genetic parents were the legal parents, and their name went on the birth certificate."

"God, Meredith!" said Lindsey, "you are making yourself crazy over this. Half of Hollywood uses donor eggs and donor embryos and surrogate moms. What you should be reading is People Magazine, or Us Weekly. When the celebs divorce, it's always mom and dad slugging it out for custody, not bio-dad and gestational mom. Let's be realistic. They do not have a shot in hell."

"I wish I could feel so sure. You know how fanatical these people can be. Zamotas thinks their lawyer will go after the consent form, because that's his agenda – he's out to make a point about embryos. He wants to invalidate any legal document that treats them as property. You see, if embryos are not property, then they are people, and they have rights. And you have to think about their rights, and their best interests and take care of them like a patient. Plus, there's the possibility that one of them will come back and sue you. And that liability just might lead IVF clinics to decide that they should not be freezing embryos in the first place, which is exactly what Mr. Greg Rose wants to see."

"Well that's a terrific idea," said Lindsey. "Let him go after the whole IVF industry. Let's see how that works out for him. Meredith, please. Everybody does in vitro. They are not going to stop freezing embryos."

"They did in Italy. They just changed the law this year. Zamotas told us. You can't make more than three embryos anymore and each one of them has to be implanted. So now, the Italians are going to Spain for their IVF."

"Oh, medical tourism! Cool. We are doing an article on medical tourism. We did nose jobs in Buenos Aires and liposuction in Mexico. The procedures are so much cheaper there that you get a vacation for free, and you still save money overall."

"Lindsey," said Meredith, "please tell me that this is an expose. Please tell me you are not writing a puff piece on surgery in third world countries."

"The piece is balanced. We give safety tips. We suggest bringing a friend along and wearing compression socks on the plane ride home. Plus, we advise people to avoid areas with high rates of malaria. Nothing complicates a post-op like malaria."

"Seriously, Lindsey. I know you think this is funny, but I am really scared."

"I understand that you feel threatened but I don't think I can make you feel better by validating all your fears. Merrie, seriously, just worry about Sophie. You can't believe that a court is going to take her away from the only parents she has ever known, in favor of a couple who gave her up willingly when she was a ball of cells."

"My lawyer doesn't think it is a joke. The reporter didn't think it was a joke. David is ready to kill her, by the way – he had no idea she would do this after he said it was all off the record. He talked to Zamotas about it this morning. He said when you look at the article, she doesn't actually quote him and she has other sources for everything she writes – Robin, and someone from the hospital." Meredith lowered her voice conspiratorially. "The hospital is doing an investigation. They promised us that if they find out who spoke to her, that person will be fired. But the damage is done. Can you believe that reporter would do this to us?"

"David went to her with the story," said Lindsey. "He got her name from his publicist, for god's sake. What did he think a reporter would do? Publicists give them stories. They write them up. It's a business, not a public service help line. David, of all people, should appreciate that."

Meredith stared indignantly at her friend. "This reporter violated our privacy, embarrassed us, took advantage of what she learned from David in confidence and may have imperiled the well being of our child. That's appropriate journalism?"

"Yes it is," said Lindsey. "And how did that article embarrass you? It's Robin who comes off sounding like a bit of a nut job, to tell you the truth. Are you so embarrassed to have everyone know that you are adoptive parents? Is that the issue?"

"No!" said Meredith. "I never felt ashamed of that, not for one moment."

"Not ashamed at all," said Lindsey. "You were perfectly fine about it, that's why you kept it a secret from everyone, even your best friend."

"Oh, Lindsey. You have every right to be angry. I'm sorry, okay? I apologize. It's just that – it's so hard. There's no chapter on this stuff in the parenting guides. There's no roadmap at all. You step off that main trail and you are in the woods by yourself, stumbling around in the dark. And then some woman at work says, 'she looks just like you,' and you don't know what to say, so you thank her, and that is like you have told a lie. And then your eighty-year-old aunt says, 'I wish your mother had lived to see this day, because she was so afraid you would wait too long and never have children of your own. She would have been so happy.' And so you say you are happy too, and that is another lie. And you are trying to go straight ahead on your path but there are all these twists and turns, and you get farther and farther into the woods, and with every lie you tell, the thicket around you gets denser. And then the lights come on, and you are in this place, and you don't have any idea how you got here."

The door opened and a nurse came out. "Mrs. Bettinger?" she said, smiling at Meredith. "Sophie is asking for you. Do you want to come in? We are almost done."

Meredith rose. "Wait!" said Lindsey. She threw her arms around her friend and squeezed tight. "I have to go, okay? Can I reach you later?"

"Sure," said Meredith. "We get to take her back home tonight. I'm sure we'll be watching the game."

"Oh, right. The American League Championships!" said Lindsey. "Yankees-Red Sox. Can you believe it? That should be a good distraction."

"No, it will be horrible," said Meredith. "I can't believe it's this week. Just when I can't take another thing going wrong, I'm going to have to watch the Sox lose to the Yankees yet again."

"We could win," suggested Lindsey, without conviction.

"Yeah," said Meredith. "Maybe this will be the year the Sox beat the Yankees and then win the World Series. I've been feeling lucky."

"Why don't you try rooting for the Yankees?" said the nurse. Meredith stared at her dumbfounded. "Well, you want to win, right?" She looked in exasperation at their blank faces. "Oh well, suit yourselves. My husband says I just don't get baseball."

Chapter 27

"What are you doing home?" said Robin. She never expected to see John before eleven on a Thursday during football season, and especially not this week, when the quarterback Vince Young from UT had agreed to make himself available for a Thursday night live webchat. John had been so excited when they first got it on the schedule. They sent a whole crew to Austin to make sure it turned out well: two in technical support, a media person to help the young star with his answers, and Alex, the best of the interns, to filter the questions. John had been thinking about going down there himself, a few weeks ago.

"They didn't need me," John replied. If Robin had to ask, she had not been watching the webcast. She had obviously missed the spirited online discussion of whether or not the "flesh and blood" daughter of Awaygame.com founder and UT alum John Hogan counted as a Longhorn legacy despite having been adopted as an embryo by Northerners. "I bet she's rooting for you," one fan gushed to Young.

"We appreciate everyone's support," the woman at the keyboard typed as Vince Young shrugged. "We know our fans are not going to be happy without a BCS bowl game and that is what we are focused on right now."

"WHAT THE FUCK," John texted Alex.

"Srry" he typed in return. "was busy deleting remark: 'lucky girl gets donation of orange-and-white bone marrow.' Vince thinks he sounded like a dick. Wants to shout out best wishes to sick girl. ok?"

"Do whatever," John responded. There was no point in irritating Vince Young or his handlers. The damage was done.

"Did the webchat go alright?" Robin asked.

"Fabulous," said John. Robin did not lift her eyes from the computer screen. "What are you looking at?"

"I've been reading the comments page from where the Globe story was picked up by Yahoo news."

John groaned. This is what the press does, he explained to her when the article first came out. They twist everything around to make it more sensational. Ignore it, and it will all go away. Don't talk about it, don't think about it, and don't answer any more questions from reporters. For a happy moment, Robin seemed to agree. 'For the sake of everyone's privacy, especially the children, we simply cannot discuss this matter at this time' – that was all they needed to say.

"Look at this one," said Robin. She turned the screen toward him.

Of course she needs her REAL family. This shows how wrong it is to adopt children and take away their rights to know about their heritage and medical records. I was adopted and I know how hard it is to live with that rejection from your OWN FAMILY. These people should welcome the help of the biological parents because only they can fill that hole in the child's life.
Stillsearching

John's eyes continued on down the page.

@Stillsearching that is the stupidest thing I ever heard. How can you feel rejection from parents who never knew you and never even saw you? She was adopted as an embryo not a baby, you moron. Her "real" mother gave birth to her. Now she is struggling with a sick child and on top of that she has to

worry about losing her child. This is SO UNFAIR. These people don't have the right to tear another family apart. That is disgusting to me. **Evelyn**

I agree. I guess she didn't have so much interest in her "flesh and blood" when it was frozen in a tank. Now she thinks she is the mother because her son is giving bone marrow. He can save the girl so it is the Christian thing to do. That woman should be grateful to the other family who rescued her "flesh and blood" when many embryos never find a home before they reach their "expiration date" and get flushed down the toilet. **nofreckles**

"Damn fools," he muttered. No matter how many times he saw it, the vitriol of the web chatterers never failed to astound him. "Don't listen to these sanctimonious assholes."

"But look at this," Robin insisted.

I don't know why you are attacking this family who is only trying to help. First they donate their embryos instead of allowing them to be destroyed, which is "the Christian thing to do." Now they are giving her the gift of bone marrow which I believe is a very painful process and maybe even dangerous I don't know. But the other family does not even want them to see the girl or say thank you very much. This would be very difficult for most people but still they are doing everything they can to save the child. **Lisa476**

"Some people do take the time to try and understand. And other people are so cruel. Listen," Robin read aloud:

"Funny how everybody has an opinion about what is the Christian thing to do. Maybe they should have thought about that before they made these embryos. People with money to do IVF think they can arrange the world to suit themselves and then call it God's will. Maybe God's will was for them to adopt the children who need homes in this world instead of asking modern medicine to give them a "miracle." Miracles only come from God. People playing God create these situations. Maybe that is why the poor little girl has leukemia. **Godlislove972**"

"Alright, stop," said John. "Shut it down. We're not reading any more of these. It's just noise. We don't need to find out what all the lunatics of America think about our situation, okay? It's not illuminating."

"I don't care what people say about me. I just pray to God we are doing the right thing. I wonder sometimes if God is sending us a sign, bringing us together with Sophie like this. I wish I knew. I thought I might learn something from all this, but most of it is so mean-spirited. Still, there are a lot of people out there offering support and good wishes."

"And I appreciate that, but I don't really want to hear from them any more than the others. None of these people knows our story. What right do they have to judge?"

"As much right as anybody, I guess."

"Fine. Let no one judge."

"Joan says," began Robin.

"I especially do not want to hear what she has to say!"

"But Joan was just explaining to me," persisted Robin, "that in Muslim societies they believe you can raise another man's child but you can never change the child's last name. They have to know their lineage."

"Are we going to bring the Koran into this as well? I don't want anybody telling me whether or not I am a good Christian, and I don't give a damn whether or not I am a good Muslim."

"I don't think that is what she meant."

"What she meant is to stick her nose into our business and get all the gory details so she can explain what went wrong and why she knows better. I'm sure she thinks that the solution to everything is years of therapy, for all of us, including the boys. I'm sure she knows exactly what we should do. Maybe we can go on Oprah and she can be the expert."

"John, I don't know why you are so angry."

"I don't know. It's been a long day." With a twinge, John remembered that Robin had begun the day hours before him, when Ryan woke up crying about the pain in his legs. "How's the boy?" he asked, jerking his head in the direction of upstairs.

"He's alright. I'm keeping him home for the rest of the week. I spoke to his teacher. She says the other children all have some idea that he is giving part of his blood to a sick girl and they are not talking about it much except to wonder whether or not it will hurt. I have to assume the parents are being careful in how they explain this to their children. His teacher wanted permission for the class to make him a card, since she thought they needed a chance to express their concern."

"That's nice of her," said John gruffly.

"Mommy!" A wail came from the top of the stairs. Robin checked her watch.

"Time for more Tylenol," she said. "It was so terrible giving him that shot again tonight. He started crying and I started crying."

Ryan felt no better the next morning, so Joan offered to drive Ted to school. "Thank you so much," said Robin, detaching Teddy's hands, which were clasped tightly behind her neck. "Stop it," she said, as he leaned his head against her arms while she tightened his seatbelt.

"Mommy, where's my lunch?" asked Ted plaintively.

"Oh, darn it, I forgot," said Robin. "Can you wait one second?" she asked Joan. She ran back into the kitchen and grabbed the brown paper bag. "I'll be right back," she said to Ryan, who lay sprawled on the couch. His eyes followed her as she sprinted down the front walk.

"Isaiah and I were talking last night," said Joan, as Ted grabbed the lunch and his mother's hand, clutching them both, "and I want you to know he really envies Ryan this chance to do something so special for another person. We think he is like a superhero, right, Isaiah?"

"Does Ryan get to stay home from school all week?" asked Isaiah.

"My stomach hurts," Teddy whimpered.

"You're fine," said Robin. "Ryan is staying home because his legs are sore from the medicine, Isaiah. On Monday, he has to go into the hospital in the morning to start taking out just the special cells that will help the little girl get better."

"He's going to have a tube sticking out of his chest like a straw," said Teddy.

"Ew," said Talia.

"Cool," said Isaiah. "But does that mean he can't go to soccer on Saturday?"

"Not this week," said Robin, regretfully.

"I'm sure Ryan is very proud of what he is doing," said Joan. "This is an amazing experience for your whole family. I hope you are keeping a journal." Joan looked significantly at Robin. "You should write everything down. I think it would make a really powerful article about modern parenting. I would love to work with you on that."

"I don't think we are interested in any more publicity."

"Wouldn't it be great for you and John to have a chance to affect the paradigm for how these thing are handled institutionally? We could always do it anonymously."

I am not so sure about that, thought Robin. Anonymity was what the other side had, the readers and writers of commentaries and blogs, while people like her were stripped naked and lit by the unflattering glare of a hundred thousand opinions. "I have to get back inside. See you at three o'clock." She touched Teddy's head lightly and he pouted back at her.

John had rigged up caller ID, so that when the phone rang mid-morning she was able to tell it was her mother. "Leave it be," she said to Ryan, curled up next to her on the couch. Her mother had scared Ryan half to death last time they spoke. "Brave little lamb," she called him. "Brave little lamb, letting them suck your blood out with that machine. Bless you, baby. Grandma is going to send you some cookies to make you strong again." It had taken Robin two hours to get him calm.

In retrospect, Robin and John both thought the conversation with her parents would have gone better if they'd had a little more time to organize their thoughts. But Robin's college roommate Dina had a friend in Boston who had sent her an email, and Dina forwarded the link to her mother, who reached Kathleen by eight-thirty that morning. John was still at home when their phone rang. "Well, I appreciate why you froze them in the first place, in case the IVF didn't work," said her father. "You couldn't be taking any more of those drugs. What I don't understand is how that clinic could be allowed to give away your embryos."

"They don't give them away," said Robin. She could hear John sigh on the other extension. The background noise was loud with all four of them on the call.

"I told you!" said her mother. "I told you they don't give those babies away. I'm sure they get good money for them. I saw in a magazine that some couple paid a college girl twenty-five thousand dollars for her eggs. Imagine what a whole embryo is worth. Especially your child, from a good family like that."

"Mom," said John, "they can't sell embryos. That would be like selling babies. That's against the law. They donate them to infertile couples."

"Well, they're not theirs to give away," said Kathleen indignantly.

"We sort of gave them permission to give them away."

"Because otherwise they were going to destroy the embryos," said Robin. "I didn't want them used for research purposes."

"I should think not," said Kathleen.

"Kathleen, let her finish," barked her father.

"And I didn't want them thawed and thrown away, so we had to donate them. That is how they ended up with our embryo. She's a beautiful girl."

"I thought these people wouldn't let you in to see the child," said Michael.

"We saw pictures," said John. "She looks a lot like Robin."

"Well, I can't wait to see her," said Kathleen.

"Mother," said Robin, "you have to know that's not going to happen anytime soon."

"Well, I got the impression from the article," Kathleen began,

"The article," said John, "is trash. Don't pay any attention to that article. The reporter took everything Robin said out of context. We don't have any intention of taking this girl away from her parents."

"You are her parents as well," said Kathleen.

"They're not her parents," said Michael. "That's all they need, taking possession of a sick child with all sorts of medical issues. I don't know why you agreed to do the transplant in the first place. They've got no right to ask you. Bone marrow transplant is a very risky thing."

"It's risky for the recipient," said John. "It's not a risk for the donor. Ryan starts his neupogen shots tomorrow,"

"Oh, poor little lamb," said Kathleen.

"And then he goes into the hospital on Monday for a small procedure. It will all be over by Wednesday or Thursday."

"It will all be over until this girl needs something else. Next thing you know, they'll be knocking on your door asking for a kidney."

"We won't let them take Ryan's kidney," said John. I would give her a kidney, thought Robin. I would do it in a heartbeat.

"But Daddy, " said Robin, "we couldn't refuse to do the transplant. We were the only ones that could help her."

"Well, maybe." He gave a low growl of disgust. "Looks a lot like Robin, does she? What a mess. You keep your feet on the floor, alright Robbie? You take good care of my grandsons. They keep you busy enough. You don't need another child."

Well, they certainly do keep me busy, thought Robin, brushing the curls from Ryan's eyes as he lay on the couch watching a rebroadcast of last night's game two between the Yankees and the Sox. "I think the Red Sox will win this time," said Ryan. "We would definitely win this game if we had Pedro Martinez pitching. Pedro Martinez is so good. He's my favorite pitcher."

"What if Pedro Martinez got traded to the Yankees? Would he still be your favorite pitcher?"

"No." Ryan looked at his mother quizzically. "Then he would be a Yankee." Robin glanced mournfully at the television. The Red Sox were going to lose again, three to one. John had stayed up until the end to watch. The phone rang, and she checked the caller ID. Private number. That was Mickey.

"Hey!" she answered.

"Hey yourself. I called to check on my nephew, the savior."

"Ryan's okay. He's got some pain in his legs and I think last night he had a little fever. I've got him home today."

"And you?"

"Everyone keeps asking me. I don't know. How am I supposed to be? I am worried about Ryan; I am worried about Sophie. One of our parents wants me to make believe the child doesn't even exist, and the other one is expecting a visit from her at Christmas."

"But you understand that this is impossible?"

"Impossible? I've got no opinions on what is impossible anymore. All I know is that nothing is possible unless the transplant works. I don't even know how likely it is that she will survive. Naturally, we get no information from them. We are just the donors. Just a source of tissue. It's not as though we have feelings."

"They're scared of you, Robin."

"I haven't done anything to them. They don't try to understand."

"Understand what?"

"Understand what it is like for me, to know that I have a daughter who is a complete stranger to me. I can't help her; I can't comfort her. It's like a hole in my heart. At times I think I feel the way she will, after the transplant, when she has that little bit of someone else inside of her. It doesn't go away. She's going to struggle with that her whole life. She will have to take all these drugs to suppress her immune system so it doesn't kill her trying to go after that other piece. It goes against the laws of nature. That's how I feel. A little piece of me is gone. It feels wrong."

"Perhaps you should try drugs as well."

"Very funny. But Mickey, something in me will always cry out for that child. And I think something in her will always cry out for me."

"Kids grow up all the time not knowing their father. They are resilient. They do alright."

"You don't think those children are looking for a father?"

"Of course – for child support. If you were a guy, that would probably be your biggest concern."

"If I were a guy," said Robin, "maybe it wouldn't hurt so much."

"Maybe. I wouldn't say that in front of Caleb. I don't think he would appreciate it right now."

"Is everything alright, Mickey?"

"I don't know. Ever since he and I talked about our little escapade in the fertility clinic, he's been awful. It's Caleb, so there's no drama. He just sits in a chair, quietly miserable. I think it has finally dawned on him that this maze we are in has no way out, not short of rejecting all the pretenses he has so painstakingly established. He thinks he can never be a father. That's very hard for him to accept. I can't fix that for him unless he can find a way out of his box."

"Caleb would be such an amazing dad."

"As opposed to me, you mean."

"I didn't say that!"

"No, but it's true. Babies are messy, and children are boring. Then, right about around the time they start having something really interesting to say, they stop talking their parents altogether."

"Mickey, you don't mean any of that. I heard you asking those questions about surrogacy. You were serious."

"I was serious! Of course I'm serious. I want a child. I want it for him, so he can be happy with me. He's not happy now."

"Are you fighting?"

"No. We never fight. Caleb was always easy, and now he doesn't argue at all. I don't think he cares enough to bother, anymore. He doesn't care where we go to dinner. He doesn't care what movie we see. I took him to a documentary even though he hates documentaries and he didn't even bother to whine about it. I'm not sure he noticed. The other day, we were talking about where to go on vacation and he said, 'you spend all this time planning a trip and then it rains; it always rains.' He's so bitter. Caleb was never bitter. You have no idea what it is like, watching someone you love turn into a different person."

"I think I do know something about that, Mickey." Robin was quiet, remembering John's face lit from above in their old kitchen. *I don't want another child. I can barely provide for the children I have now.* The memory stung like salt, cleaning and purifying. "Do you think he is unhappy enough to leave?"

"Caleb won't leave. He wouldn't hurt me, not even to save himself. He won't hurt anybody. Not me and not his parents. He will kill us all with his kindness, and he will never choose. No. I think I would have to be the one to go. I just don't know if I can. I love him enough to stay, but I don't know if I love him enough to leave."

Things change, thought Robin. Things change, and it is hard to predict how you will feel. She felt exhausted by his logic, and his certainty. Mickey always saw the future as though the path you chose was a tunnel that led inevitably from here to there. Leave, or suffer. She would never be able to convince him that there might be middle ground. Her heart sank. It did not seem inevitable to her that Mickey and Caleb should be unhappy, or that they should be apart, but it took more energy than she could muster to argue with her brother. She did not have time for it right now. In the living room, Ryan was moaning as the Yankees scored again. "What difference would it make if you left?" she asked, sounding more irritated than she had intended. "For Caleb, I mean. It would be the same thing with the next guy."

"If there was a next guy. It's possible that if I were out of the way, he might be able to find that girl he's been pretending to date all these years."

"The contortionist?" asked Robin wearily.

"The contortionist, yes." Over the phone, she could not tell if he was smiling or crying. "I'm not saying it would be perfect. But it might be good enough. And then he could have the whole nine yards of picket fence. It's not just his parents' dream, you know, it's his as well. But it's asking a lot of me, Robin. Just offering to go will never be enough. That would be like blackmail. I will have to insist, do you see? I will have to leave without giving him a choice. I will have to break my own goddamn heart. Do you think I am strong enough to do that?"

"You can get up the nerve to do anything," said Robin, "but that doesn't mean you will be able to live with the consequences. I really don't want to see anything happen to the two of you. Don't rush, Mickey. Not unless you're sure."

Chapter 28

"John?" called Robin, "aren't you coming to bed? We have to get up early tomorrow."

"Yeah, in a minute. Bottom of the ninth and the Yanks are up by one. The Red Sox are about to lose game four."

"Well, that will make for a nice change of pace." Robin wandered into the living room where John sat in front of the television with his laptop open next to him. "Didn't they lose last night too?"

"This is for the sweep. Three more outs and the Yankees are going back to the World Series."

"Oh, poor Boston. Couldn't they even win one game? The boys are going to be so disappointed."

"It's a life lesson." John smiled, a little sadly. "In the end, the Red Sox always lose. It is a pity it had to be the Yankees again. The whole city will be in mourning tomorrow."

"And he walked him!" said the announcer. Boston's manager trotted out to home plate.

"What's he doing?" Robin asked.

"Putting in a pinch runner. They are playing for the tie, trying to get one run across. It's because it's against Rivera, right? And he doesn't give up many runs. If they can score one and take it to extra innings, Rivera will be out and maybe they will have a shot."

"Do you really think they can win?"

"Probably not. It's a minor miracle if they take the game, and then they are still not going to win the series. The Sox are down three games to none. No team in history has ever come back from that."

"The runner is going," said the announcer. "Posada throws. He is safe!"

"Look at that," said John.

Robin stood up. "I'm going to bed."

"With a runner on second and nobody out?"

"But you said it doesn't matter, even if they win."

"No, not in the long run. But it will make Ryan and Teddy happy in the morning."

"That would be nice. Remember we have to leave here by six-thirty. Joan is taking Teddy."

"I'll be up." John's blackberry chirped, and he dug it out from under a cushion.

"Who's calling this late?"

"It's a text from Alex. '$5 on sox to win.' Okay, I'll take that." His eyes moved from the larger screen to the smaller one for just a second as he tapped out a response with both thumbs.

Crack. The sound of the bat on the ball broke through the hum of noise from the crowd. "That's going to get through," said John. The runner broke from second and was around third before the centerfielder reached the ball. He threw it in to second base, conceding the run. "Tie game. Damn!"

The next morning, Robin was done showering by six am. Fatigue made the air around her feel thick, and she stared jealously at John, inert and snoring. The alarm rang, and John slid a pillow over his head. "How did the game turn out?" she asked, lifting the edge.

"Sox won. Bottom of the twelfth, walk-off homerun. It was amazing."

"Well, good for them! You can be the one to tell the boys."

"I can be the one to wake the boys, you mean." With a feral noise, John pulled himself to a sitting position. "Okay. I'm up. I'll get them going."

Ryan was quiet in the back of the car, so quiet that Robin thought he must be dozing but when she turned to look his eyes were wide open and alert. She could feel his apprehension as they entered the hospital. When she reached for his hand, he slipped it into hers without resistance.

They put him into a bed with wheels on it like a cart, and the nurse swung up the heavy metal arms that clicked into place on either side. The doctor injected something into his i.v. and suddenly he was half asleep, staring glassy-eyed as they rolled the bed toward the door. "I'll be right here, darling," she said. He looked so small under the sheet, insubstantial, not at all like the sturdy presence he was in a crowd of kindergarteners.

John pulled a second chair into the cubicle and they sat there, waiting. Robin practiced deep, cleansing breaths, in and out, in and out – eight, nine, ten – and that was one minute gone. Forty-four more to go. John's cellphone rang. "I have to take this, okay?" he said. It was not really a question, and she did not bother to answer. He headed out to a quiet waiting room down the hall. When I was Ryan's age, thought Robin, that would have been a place where you could go to have a cigarette. She could picture anxious fathers with no Blackberries pacing up and down, breathing smoke like dragons, in through the mouth, out through the nose.

The nurse, when she came, reported that everything was going well. He was awake, she said. They would bring him back in soon. Ryan was sound asleep when they wheeled him in, with his i.v. pole, and a large new patch of gauze taped across his chest. The hospital gown was faded blue, a cool color that brought out how pale he was – like his father, pale by mid-October while she stayed sun-kissed through Thanksgiving. The machine above the bed clicked and whirred. She rested her hand on his head and he did not stir.

"John," she said, as he came back into the cubicle. He bent down close, pulling lightly on the gauze to peer under it. "Don't," she said. John stood and put an arm around her waist. Ryan's mouth hung open and drool hung from his lower lip, puddling on the pillow beneath. "Why doesn't he wake up?" she asked. Robin searched her memory for details on the risks of anesthesia in children. The doctor had reviewed it with her last week, and then again this morning before she signed the consent. Rare. They were all rare. That was all she could remember. Rare meant things could happen, but they never did. Rare meant, don't worry about it.

The nurse came in and raised the head of the bed, so that Ryan no longer lay flat. "How are you feeling?" she asked, when his eyelids fluttered. "Could you have a little drink?" Ryan shook his head. A noise came out of his mouth that was neither a word nor a groan. It sounded like "urrrr." Robin looked nervously at the nurse, who appeared unfazed. "Try and get him to take a little juice, if you can," she said. She pointed to a small bottle on the stand near his bed.

"It's orange," said Robin. "Ryan likes apple. Can we get apple?"

"I'll check the kitchenette," said the nurse.

"Mah," said Ryan.

"I'm here, sweetie pie. Not going anywhere." She made an effort not to sound like she was going to cry.

The doctor took out the i.v. when she came by half an hour later. Ryan was sitting up now, his legs curled under him. Robin saw him eyeing the buttons on a machine that was temptingly close. One hand rested on the top of the metal side rail. "You look like you're ready to make a break for it!" said Dr. Coben. "Do you think you could take a walk?" Ryan nodded and with a quick leap swung himself up and over the rail, his bare feet resting against the side of the bed while he hung from the bar, examining the floor below for a clear landing spot.

"Not like that!" laughed the doctor, scooping him up. "You are supposed to be woozy. Do you feel sore?" Ryan nodded. She placed him gently on the ground. "I want you to go with Mom and Dad down to the cafeteria and get some lunch. Can you do that?" He nodded again. "Wonderful. You are a champ. Do you want to see the central line?"

"Yes," said Ryan.

She peeled away the gauze so they could look at the soft plastic tubing flowering from his chest. It had two branches, like a 'y'.

"Cool," said Ryan.

"When you finish lunch," said the doctor to Robin and John, "can you come up to the cancer clinic, where we met last week? We have a room near there set up for harvesting the cells. It's got a television and a dvd player, Ryan. You brought a movie, right?"

"I have a whole bunch," said Robin, gesturing to an oversized handbag on the chair.

"I want to watch the Red Sox game," said Ryan.

"That's not on until later," said Dr. Coben. "We'll get you home by then. But that's a nice quiet activity for you tonight."

"Not the way he watches it," said Robin with a small laugh. "He likes to keep them company running the bases."

"If the Red Sox win today," said Ryan, "then we only have to win two more games in New York and then we will go to the World Series."

"Is that all?" said Dr. Coben.

"Yup. And then they have to win four games out of seven and then they are the world champions."

"Well, you are already my champion, because you are doing a wonderful thing for someone else who is sick and needs help."

Ryan nodded. "My mom told me that already."

"Are you very proud of yourself?"

Ryan nodded. "I'm getting rollerblades."

After lunch they took the elevator to the second floor. The cancer clinic was through the sunny atrium, down a long corridor and to the left. They walked up to the nurses' station, which stood in the center of a long room. On either side, curtains divided the space into eight little pup tents of space. Several were closed, and as they stood there they could hear the murmur of voices behind the gently fluttering walls. One boy of maybe ten or twelve sat by himself, the curtain three quarters open, and a dull, bored look on his face. He wore earphones and his bald head nodded rhythmically up and down. One sneaker tapped against the metal frame of the bed.

"I'm Mrs. Hogan," Robin said to the nurse.

"Ryan Hogan? Come this way." The room around the corner had a bed and two chairs, and a large box in a non-descript color that was neither tan nor grey but some metallic shade in between. The front of it was covered with dials and switches, and threaded with plastic tubing that snaked in and out of the machine. Reflexively, Robin reached down and restrained Ryan. He took two steps toward the machine, pulling his mother with him.

"It's pretty neat looking, isn't it?" asked Dr. Coben, coming in behind them. "Come and look." She lifted Ryan up onto the bed. "Are you nervous about this?" Ryan shrugged. "You don't have to be nervous. It will all be fine. It's a loop. You know about loops, right?" Ryan nodded. "Your blood will go through the loop into the machine and then out again, and right back into you. That's why you have two tubes. This one is in." She connected a long plastic tube to one side of the y-shaped central line. "And this one is out. Ready?" Ryan nodded again. Dr. Coben attached the second line, and blood shot into the clear tube, coloring it red. Their eyes followed the leading edge of the red line as it sped twisting and turning through the tubes until it disappeared into the box.

"Cool," said Ryan.

"Now watch," said the doctor. After a few seconds the blood reappeared, racing through the clear tubing like it knew the way home. Ryan stared down at his chest in wonder. "My blood is fast," he said.

"Even your blood is fast," said John. "Good job, kid." He put up his hand and Ryan slapped it hard. In a clear plastic bag hanging on a pole behind the machine, a few bright red spots appeared.

"He was so great," Robin told her mother that evening. She sat on the couch between the boys. It was the bottom of the fifth inning, and the Red Sox were up, two to one. "He played cards with his daddy, and then we watched a movie. He didn't complain, not once. John complained more than he did." John grimaced. "The nurses wouldn't let him use his cell phone so he was working away on that Blackberry."

"My thumbs got tired," said John.

"Poor baby," said Robin. "He's going back to the office tomorrow, and I will take Ryan in myself."

"You're going back again tomorrow?" Teddy whined.

"I don't have to go in so early tomorrow," said his mother, in soothing tones. "Ryan and I can drop you at school before we go."

"I don't want to go to school tomorrow. It's not fair. Ryan never has to go."

"Now Ted, you have nothing to complain about, with all your brother's been through in the past week. Do you want to have shots in your leg and needles in your arm? Do you want to have surgery to put tubes in your chest? This was no picnic for him, buster."

"I had a needle too."

"That was the easy one," said Ryan. "You were lucky your blood was not perfect enough. I had to miss soccer, and everything."

"My blood is perfect enough." Teddy looked like he might cry.

"Listen, mom, I had better go," said Robin. "Love to daddy!"

The Yankees got back-to-back singles in the sixth with one man out. "Uh oh," said John.

"Pedro Martinez will get them out," said Ryan confidently. "He will throw the ball right past them." He demonstrated Pedro's leg kick, standing on the couch.

"Sit down," said his mother.

The next pitch hit the batter square in the back. "Put a fork in him," said John. "Because he is done. And Jeter's up. Christ."

"John, I wish you wouldn't," said Robin.

"Sorry," said John, as Jeter doubled, bringing all three base runners home and putting the Yankees up, four to two. "Okay, I guess that's it. You boys ready for bed?"

"It's not over," said Ryan, and he was still awake when the Red Sox tied the game in the eighth, but both boys were sound asleep on the couch in the bottom of the fourteenth when David Ortiz muscled a single into the outfield, bringing the winning run home for Boston. Still shaking his head, John carried them up to their beds, one by one.

There was no time for jubilation on Tuesday morning. Traffic was bad, the nurses were busy, and already Ryan was worried about game six, which would be played that night at Yankee Stadium. "Daddy says Curt Schilling shouldn't be pitching at all because he's hurt. He broke something in his foot, and the doctors stapled it back together just for this game. He's our second best pitcher after Pedro Martinez." Robin watched the clock tick with growing impatience.

She wanted to get out of the hospital in time to pick Teddy up after school. It seemed a little inconsiderate to make them wait, when they were the ones helping someone else. Finally, Dr. Coben came in.

"Day two!" she said in a cheery voice, though she looked worn. "Sorry for the delay. It's been an eventful morning." Robin remembered the young boy she saw the day before, the one who had not bothered to close the curtain. She would pray for him on Sunday.

They were halfway through the first movie when Ryan started feeling ill. "My mouth feels funny," he said. Robin could see him shivering.

"Do you want some juice?" she asked. He shook his head. Robin pushed the button to summon the nurse. Five minutes later, a round-faced, middle-aged woman wearing a pink top stuck her head in the door.

"Everything alright in here?" she said.

"He's got the chills," said Robin, "and a tingling around his mouth."

"I'll be right back," she said. Robin ran her hands down Ryan's legs to quiet the shaking, carefully avoiding the tubes that snaked in and out of the bed. She looked at the bag hanging on the pole. It was only half full.

It was ten minutes before the nurse returned. Behind her through the open door, Robin could see a couple sitting on a bench in the corridor. His arm was around her shoulders and the woman, who was thin with dark hair, cried great shuddering sobs. "Let's see what we can do for you," said the nurse. "I'm going to slow the collection rate down a bit and see if that helps. You lose some electrolytes in this process, and sometimes that can make you feel a little sick." She adjusted several of the dials on the front. "Let me know if that doesn't do the trick."

A few minutes later, the nurse opened the door again. "He's doing better," said Robin. "Thank you for checking. We're just fine."

"Oh good," said the nurse. "I have a phone call for you at the nurses' station. Can you come pick that up?"

Robin looked doubtfully at Ryan. "Will you be alright by yourself for a moment?"

Ryan frowned. "How long will you be gone?"

"Just one minute, sweetie. I'll be right back." She slipped out the door and hurried down the hall and around the corner. "There's a phone call for me?" she said to the nurse at the desk. The woman handed her the phone and pressed a button. "This is Robin Hogan," she said.

"Mrs. Hogan," said a high voice, that was both chipper and regretful. "This is Ms. Grey, Teddy's teacher. I just wanted to let you know we had a little incident here today."

"What happened to Ted?" said Robin. "Is he hurt?"

"Well, no." She paused. "Actually, he hurt someone else. Ted pushed another child at recess. The boy fell on a rock and cut his knee. There was quite a bit of blood."

"Ted? My Ted? He pushed somebody? It must have been an accident."

"No, it was no accident. He was angry. The playground monitor had a pretty good view of the whole thing."

"Do you know why he was angry?" Robin felt a prickle of apprehension, as though she sensed a blow coming from behind.

"I understand that the other boy said something to him about the girl. Your – the one with cancer. The girl your other son is donating for."

"I know which girl you mean. What exactly did that child say to Teddy?"

"I wasn't there, Mrs. Hogan. I can't say exactly. We've talked to the children, and from what we understand, this boy asked Teddy why he wasn't giving blood like his brother, and Teddy said it was because he wasn't a match. And then the boy said they should both be a match because the sick girl was their sister, and Teddy said that the girl was not their sister. And then the other boy said she was their sister, and that you and your husband wanted her back, and Teddy said that his mommy and daddy only wanted him and his brother."

"Sweet Jesus," said Robin. She heard her own words like an echo in her ears: *"you and your brother are everything I ever wanted in my whole life"*.

"As I understand it, Teddy insisted that he didn't have a sister, and then the boy said something else, and then Teddy pushed him."

"What else did this child say?"

"I'm not certain. I really can't be sure."

"You seem to have a pretty good handle on the rest of the conversation."

"I only know what the children have been repeating. They could be entirely mistaken."

"Ms. Grey, are you going to tell me what that boy said to Teddy?"

"According to the children, as I understand it, he said his mother told his father that with two boys at home you were probably good and sorry you had given away the girl."

"What! He said that in front of everybody? Of course Teddy was angry. I can't believe that any child would be so hurtful."

"Now Mrs. Hogan, I know you are concerned, but please understand, children say these things all the time…"

"This situation comes up for you all the time, does it?"

"No." Robin could feel her take a breath. "Not this particular situation."

"How's Teddy? Is he okay?"

"I haven't spoken with Ted. He was sent to the principal's office for pushing."

"They are punishing him? After what that child said?"

"The other boy was hurt, and his mother is very upset. I understand how you must feel about this, but Ted did break the rules."

"Ms. Grey, with all due respect, I don't think you have any idea how I feel about this. And if that boy's mother is upset now, just you wait until she hears from my husband. I would like you to go in and tell my son that I am on my way. It may take me a few minutes to get there, but I am coming to get him." Robin steadied herself against the desk. "In the meantime, I don't want anyone else to discuss this issue with my child. Not one word. Alright?" The nurse did not look up as Robin handed her back the phone.

Robin walked slowly back toward the room. Dr. Coben's voice came from around the corner. I need to speak to her, thought Robin. Then a second woman spoke. She knew that voice as well. "Shh, shh, darling," said the second voice. "It's okay." There was a low whimpering sound. Robin's heart jumped. It was a bad time for this. She needed to speak to Dr. Coben; she needed to focus. The thought of seeing Sophie made her breathless, and she wondered if she would ever get a chance to tell her about everything they were going through right now and how it was all worth it to make her well. Not now, she thought. I can't do this now. She backed quickly into an open exam space and pulled the curtain shut, perching on the edge of the gurney inside.

The two voices were louder as they turned the corner. "Go ahead and put her in exam two," said Dr. Coben. The curtain to her left billowed slightly, and she heard a rustle and a creak. It was quiet for a moment and then Dr. Coben spoke. "Her temperature is a hundred and one. If we start her on antibiotics right away, I think it will probably resolve by tomorrow and then we can go ahead with the preparation for the transplant."

"I don't know," said Meredith, "I want her to be strong going into it. Do you think this could be her body telling us that she needs more time to recover, before we start with the drugs and the radiation? Are you sure she is ready?"

"She is as ready as it is possible to be. If we wait, we run the risk that her remission fails." They both inhaled deeply. "Let's keep her here tonight. I can check on her in the morning, and if the fever is gone we can finish the testing and be ready to start her conditioning phase as soon as the harvest is completed. Let me see what she has left." There was the sound of papers rustling. "Just the renal clearance test."

"Another biopsy?" Meredith sounded weary.

"No. Very simple. Just a single injection of a marker, totally harmless, and then serial blood sampling over the course of several hours. We like to see how fast the kidneys can clear the marker out of her blood. We can do it all through her central line and she will barely notice."

"Why don't you start her on antibiotics and let me bring her home until Thursday. We can do the test after that." There was a pleading quality to her voice.

"It just means a delay. She's already here, and I'd like to keep an eye on her overnight. Then we can get started tomorrow."

"Can't we wait until the harvesting is done?" She was frankly pleading now. "I was hoping not to be in the hospital while they were here. It makes me anxious, and I don't think that sort of negative energy is helpful for Sophie. What if we ran into the boy? Who knows what his mother may have told him. You saw the article. You understand how they are trying to insinuate themselves into her life. This is not something a two-year-old can be expected to handle. I'm trying to protect my daughter. Don't you see how terrifying that could be for her, to be accosted by strangers? It's a very toxic situation, and that is the last thing she needs right now."

It seemed to Robin like an eternity until Dr. Coben replied. "I can only speak from my own experience, so I can't tell you what is best for your daughter psychologically. But medically, the best thing for her would be to do the test as soon as possible. It's possible the donor won't need to come back tomorrow, if we do well enough today." She sighed. "How about this: I will check if I can get you into a room on the other side of the atrium, in the adult cancer patient wing. Alright? There will be no reason for your paths to cross. Let me see if I can make those arrangements."

When she heard Dr. Coben walk away, Robin slipped out and around the corner, hurrying back toward the room. How long had she been gone? She walked in, and Ryan glared at her with damp eyes. "You said you would be back in one minute!" he shouted hoarsely. His lip trembled, and his legs were shivering again. "I was here by myself a long time."

"I'm sorry baby," she said, hurrying over to him. Reaching across to grab the call button, her hand bumped one of the tubes.

"Ow!" said Ryan.

"Sorry," she said again. "So, so sorry, darling boy." She pushed hard on the button, twice. She went back to the door and stuck her head out into the hall. "Can you please tell the doctor that I need to see her pronto?" she called to a passing orderly.

Fifteen minutes later, Robin and Ryan were in the car. Dr. Coben had begged to finish up, but Robin was resolute. "If we have to, we'll come back tomorrow," she said, spitting out the words syllable by syllable, and Ryan howled. He was still sniffling in the back. "You have been such a brave boy," Robin said. "We need to go get your brother now. How about this: we will get a pizza, and you boys can both stay up and watch the game tonight. As late as you want. Pepperoni pizza. How about that?"

"Al-right," said Ryan, his breath wheezy with unshed tears. Teddy was still in the principal's office when she got to the school. She could see the indignation in his face, and the shame. He climbed silently into the car. Only Jack was cheerful as they made their way into the house.

"I am every bit as angry as you are," Robin said to John later in a low voice as they stood in the kitchen. It was the bottom of the third, no score. "But you can't act like it is fine to hurt another child. You can't condone the behavior just because you sympathize."

"I didn't!" John said, with his wide-eyed look. "I was very clear that it was wrong to hit first, even if he was provoked and even though the little shit totally deserved it."

"John, you brought him home a present. That is not discipline. That is not even a mixed message. I know you are proud of the boy..."

"I wish I had it on tape," said John, admiringly.

"That's not right." Robin shook her head warningly, but the phone rang.

"Can you get it?" said John, escaping back to the couch.

"Oh, Mickey," said Robin gratefully. "I am so glad it is you. You cannot imagine the day I have had."

"I bet. I'm sorry Robbie; I really can't talk right now. I need to ask you a question. Have you by any chance heard from Caleb?"

"No. Is everything alright? Why isn't he with you?"

"No reason. It's fine. I'm sure he just went down to see his folks and forgot to leave a note, that's all. Go back to your boys!" How strange, thought Robin. A roar from the other room interrupted her thoughts.

"What's going on?" she asked.

"Home run Red Sox!" shouted Ryan.

"Wait, Ry," said his father, "they are arguing the call."

"Why are they conferencing like that?" said Robin. "When did baseball get so complicated?"

"When they added video replay," said John. The umpire came back onto the field, and twirled his arm in a circle above his head. John and the boys slapped hands, and Ryan jumped up and down on the couch.

"Sit down," said Robin.

Schilling, playing for Boston, was pitching brilliantly despite the torn tendon in his ankle. The pain was etched in his face, but his delivery looked free and easy. There was no saying how far he could go, the announcers cautioned, over and over. He would not be on the mound at all except for the fact that his doctor, in desperation, had stitched the injured tendon directly to the deep muscle below. It was a new procedure, and no one could predict long it would hold. There was already blood on his sock. Who knew what damage there might be in the long term? Robin wondered if doctor had warned him about the risks. They watched the circle of red expand, inning after inning. It was four to nothing after six.

Schiller left the game in the seventh. "Amazing," said John. He limped back to the dugout. The boys were wide awake in the bottom of the eighth, when the Yankees scored to cut the lead to two. They got two more on base in the ninth, and the winning run came to the plate with two men down. "One more out and we win," said Ryan.

"But a single ties it," John pointed out. "And a home run wins the series for the Yankees. This is probably it. This is the moment when the Red Sox fans get their hearts broken yet again." Teddy sat in his father's lap, staring at the screen.

"Full count!" said the announcer, "and the pitch…"

"Strike three!" yelled Ryan.

"Swing and a miss," said the announcer. "Ladies and gentlemen, we are going to game seven."

Chapter 29

All he wanted was one night to celebrate together. Mickey clung bitterly to this thought as he paced up and down the narrow hallway. He had every right to be happy. He had won his case. Justice had been served.

It should have been a great day. It was a big win for a sweet girl from El Salvador who had come to the States five years earlier to visit her cousin and fallen in love with a local Joe – a U.S. army private from Worcester who was, in fact, actually named Joe. As his wife, she applied for citizenship. During the years it took them to process her application, she worked at his cousin's bakery. Joe went to Afghanistan. They had a boy. Joe went to Iraq. She was five months pregnant with their second child when his Humvee overturned. Given notice of his death, INS dismissed her application, claiming that she was no longer a spouse.

This morning the court had ruled at last, dismissing the government's assertion that she was not an "immediate relative." She would not have to take the baby home to El Salvador, to her mother's house, where there were already too many mouths to feed. She would not have to leave Joe Junior here, to grow up with his cousins and play soccer on Sunday afternoons with no one to watch. She would not have to live hoping for occasional telephone calls and the kindness of aunts, and perhaps a visit once a year from her son with the precious blue passport, who could come and go if he chose, if it still mattered to him. She cried in her mother-in-law's arms when she heard the news.

Mickey called Caleb from the courthouse. "Let's go out tonight," he said, forgetting just for a moment that Caleb was not in the mood for exuberance. He felt the hesitation on the other end. "Do you have other plans?"

"No," said Caleb. "Sure, let's go out. I can meet you at seven." There was a pause. "Better make that eight. I don't know how long these depositions will last. Can you leave a message with Roseanne to tell me where you want to meet?" Roseanne, Caleb's assistant, usually let Mickey's calls go to voicemail.

"If it's too much trouble, we can just skip it."

"Would you mind?" Caleb sounded grateful, as though Mickey's offer had been genuine, and not a reproach. "I'm swamped. Congratulations. You must be pleased."

Miserable fucking son of a bitch, thought Mickey, but his anger had faded, and with it the indignation that had fueled him all afternoon, while he packed his suitcases and put books into cartons. I can't make him happy, he thought, folding old button down shirts and jeans. He felt energized by his certainty. If he was gone by seven, there would be no confrontation and he could not be talked out of it. At six-thirty he was nearly packed. I am doing the right thing, he thought, looking around the living room. The painting of the tree stared back at him reproachfully. He picked up the car keys, and took a few steps toward the door. He looked back at the painting. "It's for the best," he said. As he lifted the bigger bag it occurred to him that in fairness he should leave a note. He glanced furtively at the clock.

You are weak, he told himself, standing in the kitchen, looking for a pen. Weak, he thought, scratching out a few lines slowly, listening for the sound of steps in the hall. Weak, like that little boy who cried every time he got hit. "Punch him back," his father said, but he never did. He wasn't even angry at the boys who teased and pushed and punched. He was angry at himself for being weak enough to care what those damn fools thought of him. Why could he not cease caring? Why was he continually a hostage to needs that made him miserable? He was no longer a child. He was someone else now, an opponent to be feared, an intimidating presence in the courtroom, a person to be relied upon, someone not to be crossed. The person he had become was strong; that person would leave for Caleb's sake if not his own.

He straightened up at the sound of a key in the lock. Caleb walked in, tired, grey-looking, carrying a bottle of champagne. "It was over a little earlier than I thought," he said, and then his eyes lit on the two suitcases by the door. "Mickey," he said. Mickey crumpled the note in his hand. "Are you sure?" There was nothing Mickey could say in that silence. Caleb surveyed his anguish, shaking his head slightly side to side. "Would you leave?"

"Caleb," he said, "you deserve more." The sentences that had shape and form within his mind died on his lips.

Caleb shrugged sadly. "We all do." He came over to the table where Mickey stood. "Are you really so unhappy?"

"I don't believe I was designed for happiness," said Mickey. "My life is pretty good. It's not the nightmare it would have been fifty years ago, right? I am very grateful for that, and I am happy enough in my own way, or I would be if you were alright. But you are a mess. You walk around like pieces of you are missing and you ignore the wounds and soldier on. I don't want to drink champagne and make small talk and watch the Red Sox lose to the Yankees yet again while you bleed all over our Italian leather couches. And for what? It's a whole new world. It's a whole new century. Wake up. It's not against the law anymore. We live here, in Massachusetts, not Afghanistan. We could be married."

"Is that what you want?" Caleb asked eagerly. "Why didn't you say so? We can get the license this weekend. I didn't know it mattered to you."

"It doesn't matter to me! I don't care about getting married. Don't you understand? It matters to you. It all matters to you. The wedding. The house. The children. You need that. Either make a choice to have it with me, or I will leave so you can find it with somebody else. I am not going to stay here and watch while you politely bleed to death."

"It's so simple for you," said Caleb. "Go tell your parents and then everything will be perfect. Never mind that my father will never speak to me again. Never mind that my mother will wear out her knees praying for me to recover. Never mind that I love these people and don't want to cause them pain. I know you feel my parents are monsters but you have to meet them halfway. You can't be so judgmental. This is how they were raised. They believe it is wrong."

"I believe they are wrong. And I have every right to judge them when they are ruining our lives. There is no halfway. This is who I am. It makes them sick. Am I supposed to find that halfway alright? I am done with that. I have done nothing wrong. They can meet me here. What are they afraid of? Ask them what it is they are so afraid of."

"They are afraid that God and the world will condemn their son. It is only natural for them to try and protect me."

"To protect you from yourself?"

"Even from myself. Wouldn't you protect me from myself, if you could?"

I wanted to, thought Mickey, but I did not. It was more than I could manage, as it turned out. He looked at Caleb, weighed down with misery, and felt ashamed. "Sometimes, people do change. We might be able to make them see things differently."

"I don't know if that is possible."

"If they can't, then they don't deserve you."

"They are my parents. They don't have to deserve me."

Caleb grabbed the keys that lay next to the blank pad.

"Are you going to tell them?" asked Mickey.

"I don't know."

Mickey inhaled and exhaled, slowly, deeply. "I have always believed that they already knew."

"It takes a great effort for them not to know. They work hard at it. That's how much they love me."

"It's very touching, but I don't know if you can call it love. Caleb, be a man. Go to your parents. Give them the chance to do the right thing, and if they cannot accept us, then wash your hands of it. But stop making excuses for them. It's disgusting. It's pathetic actually. And stop apologizing for yourself, you fucking coward. Tell them to go to hell. Or don't, if that is what you choose, and I will leave, and you can marry Roseanne. Poor girl. She's been in love with you for years."

"Don't be cruel," said Caleb. "That's not funny."

"I wasn't joking."

"I have to think," said Caleb. "You have to give me some time to think. Don't go! Wait for me here. I'll call you."

"Where am I going to go?" said Mickey out loud to no one, as Caleb slammed the door behind him. "You have the car." Mickey wandered restlessly from room to room. He searched half-heartedly for some food in the kitchen, finding an open package of crackers in the cabinet. The clock on the mantle ticked loudly and the phone on the end table tugged at him like a leash on a dog, tethering him to his own simmering discontent. His suitcases lay where he had dropped them, near the door. On the television, cheerful fools were talking about the coming election: more polls, more evidence of polarization. Mickey wondered where Caleb would go, if he did not go to see his parents. He used his cell to call Robin and left the other line free. There was a noise like cheering behind her; the boys were watching the Red Sox, of course. He switched on the game. The Sox were winning. Ryan and Ted would be happy. To lose the boys would be such a blow to Caleb. They would miss him too. They would ask for him at first, and Robin would shush them, and then after a while they would forget him. For the first time that evening, his eyes filled with tears. Robin wanted to talk but he cut her off; he needed to get off the phone.

By eleven, Mickey decided that Caleb must have gone to Connecticut. It was three hours drive to his parents' house. Perhaps it was a good sign that he had not called – they could be talking; he would not interrupt. If it went well, Caleb would let him know. If it went badly, he would be home again. Mickey lay down on top of the covers. He dug out a brief from one of his boxes. *Whereas the petitioner's entry* *visa was unreasonably delayed...Endless delays tantamount to denial... First Amendment rights explicitly intended to protect minority beliefs...*He put the papers aside. The earliest Caleb could be back was two. The clock read 1:58, but that clock was always five minutes fast. He watched the red lights on the dial as they changed. When it turned to 2:17 he stood up and went back into the kitchen.

By three am, Mickey was convinced that Caleb was gone for the night. It was too late now to call. Perhaps Caleb stopped at a rest stop and fell asleep in the car. There might have been a good reason why he had not called. If Mickey sent a text, he would probably respond. Unless he was asleep, and didn't get it until morning. He could be soundly and peacefully asleep, at his parents' house, or at a hotel, or even at Roseanne's. It might be that Caleb did not call because there was nothing left to say. The wrenching pain in Mickey's gut that had subsided flared again. He would not send a text. He did not want Caleb to know he was up worrying at this ungodly hour. He was not interested in apologies, or the heavy-lidded sincerity of sad eyes, if Caleb was resting peacefully somewhere right now.

At four, Mickey sent a text. "Where the hell r u? r u ok?" There was no response.

Mickey was certain that he had never closed his eyes, but when the phone rang it startled him the ways calls do when they come in the middle of the night, and he woke with his heart thudding and panted in the dark wondering why, until consciousness caught up with him, and he recognized the sound. It's okay, he thought. It's the phone. It's Caleb. Be calm. "Hello?" he said, trying to sound wakeful.

"Mickey?" It was a woman's voice, not entirely unfamiliar. He grunted an affirmative. "It's Roseanne. Did they call you?"

The clock read 6:15. "Did who call me?"

"Oh God." She was crying; Mickey could hear that now.

"Roseanne, what's wrong? Are you okay?"

"Something's happened. Caleb's mother called me."

"She called you?" Perhaps it was Caleb's father. Maybe the news did him in, the old buzzard. "Why didn't she call here, if she was looking for Caleb?"

"She's not looking for Caleb, Mickey." Mickey sat up. Something had happened. Roseanne was crying. Don't say it, he thought. Stop talking. He wanted to reach through the phone and put his hands around her neck so she could not say another word.

"What happened?" he said. There was a hollow space in the middle of his chest, and his feet and hands grew cold.

"He went there last night, out of the blue. Maybe he was drunk; I don't know. His mother said he arrived in a state, talking absolute nonsense. They tried to reason with him, and he got angry and he left. He must have been on his way home. The car hit the guardrail and went off the road. The state troopers called them a couple of hours ago."

The state troopers called them. Why them, he wanted to ask her; why them and not me? It was a stupid, petty question, and he could not ask it; he would have to ask the other one, the one that stuck in his throat. "Is he – is he okay?"

"I think it was pretty bad. She told me the troopers said he wasn't wearing his seatbelt. It doesn't make any sense, Mickey. Caleb is always so careful. When she said that, for just a moment, I thought that's it, it's just a mistake, this didn't happen to him. But his mother is there at the hospital. I asked her if there was anything we could do and she said pray for him. Ask anyone who cared to pray for him, she said."

"Do you know where he is?"

"In Hartford. I took the address to send some flowers. I can give it to you."

"Roseanne?" She was a pretty girl who wore silk blouses in dark jewel tones with bows that tied at the neck. Caleb bought her earrings once, for Christmas. Every time Mickey saw her, she had them on. She always looked right through him when he came by the office. "I need to get there. Please. I need to get there right away." He could not remember that they had ever spoken more than a word or two. "Do you think you could do something for me? I don't have a car."

She answered quickly, without hesitation. "You can take mine. I'll pick you up if you want. You can drop me at the T."

It took an hour and forty-five minutes to get to Hartford. Roseanne drove a Subaru, not new, but neat as a pin. It smelled of her shampoo, something with an undertone of raspberry. Mickey sipped his second cup of coffee. He would make an effort with the Dunhills.

Caleb needed them both; they had to act as a team. That was his opening argument. He rehearsed it as he turned south onto 91.

The lady at the desk said the ICU was immediate family only, so he answered "I am his brother," and she said second floor, and down the hall. The rooms had glass walls, and the nursing staff could look in as they passed. "Caleb Dunhill?" he said to a man standing near the desk, and the man gestured down the corridor to the far room on the right. He recognized the thin woman with ash blonde hair who stood by the door. She had Caleb's face, but older and pulled taut. He had not noticed the likeness when he saw her the first time, or in the pictures on Caleb's dresser. How had he missed it, that familiar face? She did not look imperious here, but frail and lost. Mickey felt the strongest desire to comfort her.

She looked up at him, approaching with purposeful strides. "I'm Mickey," he said.

"I know who you are," she answered. Her mouth twitched. "You have some nerve, coming here. You've done enough harm already."

"I am sorry you feel that way." Her eyes were Caleb's eyes, red-laced and shining with a hostility that unnerved him. Mickey rummaged in his mind for the words he had pictured himself saying in the car. A team; they should be a team. "Caleb needs both of us," he said. He shuffled to his left, angling for a glimpse into the room. He could see tubes, and an IV, and monitors that blinked red and green. The figure in the bed did not move. It could be anyone. With an effort he returned his gaze to the older woman standing next to him. "For his sake, we should work together."

"Caleb does not need anything from you." She drew back her shoulders and led with her chin. She looked less frail now, and her voice was animated, as though the prospect of a fight had fueled her own recovery. "He has his family. You have no right to be here, no right at all. I will take care of my son."

So she is fighting for her boy now, thought Mickey. Now she is the mother lion. Where were you last night when he needed you to understand? Ready to throw him out of the pride then, were you? With an effort, he spoke in a low and level voice. "Mrs. Dunhill, you don't have to accept our relationship but surely in common decency you will respect Caleb's wishes at a time like this." Do not plead, he told himself. Do not let her smell weakness. "You know it's what he would want."

"Don't you come lecturing me! Caleb doesn't need your type of help. There are no more parties or nightclubs for him now. You can just go back where you came from and let him be. He's got no use for any of you people now. Stay away from my boy."

Parties? Nightclubs? Mickey stared at her quizzically, the old bird. That was easier to believe, was it? That it was all an artifact of intoxication and depravity? That in the shadow of some drug-fueled binge Caleb had accidentally gone home with a partner of the wrong gender? Ah, the decadent gay lifestyle. He could have laughed. She should see them on a Saturday night: him begging to go see some movie with subtitles, and Caleb arguing for Chinese take-out and a bottle of wine at home. There were so many things he wanted to say. That their nephews called him Uncle Caleb. That the knee he hurt playing football still ached on cold, rainy days. That when the moonlight fell across his sleeping back at the right angle he looked like one of the statues they had gone to see in Italy, and that Mickey would lie awake just to watch him there, remembering all the sleepless nights of his childhood, when he had tried and failed to imagine having a life like this.

Mickey wanted to laugh out loud but there was no time. If only he could plead his case in front of a judge and a jury of his peers. They would dismiss her charges out of hand. But it was only the two of them, no one else to witness, and no one else to tell him what he needed to know. "Please," he said, "how is he? Is he going to be alright?"

"We don't know," said Mrs. Dunhill, looking startled, as though the question had taken her by surprise. "Now that's really all the information I am going to give you. I would like you to leave."

"Can I see him?" asked Mickey, weighing the risks of pushing by her into the room.

"No, I don't believe that is a good idea at all."

"Mrs. Dunhill," Mickey spoke slowly and clearly, "you do understand that when Caleb wakes up, he is going to be very upset and angry that you refused to let me in. Are you sure that is what you want?"

"If Caleb wakes up I am certain he will want his mother." The word "if" sent a chill down Mickey's spine. "If he wakes up, he is not waltzing out of here. Is that what you want to know? If he wakes up, he will be a cripple in a wheelchair. Who will take care of him then? You? I don't think so. Just go."

If he wakes up? *If?* If his legs did not work, what did that mean about the rest of him? She did not use the word paralyzed. Did she mean paralyzed? Paralyzed, so that Caleb's body would no longer respond to his touch? Caleb's mother was staring at him with disgust as though she knew everything he was thinking. Thoughts flashed through his mind of hospital beds and catheters and doughy legs like pork sausages lying inanimate next to him. She had asked him to leave. No one would blame him if he went. I wasn't the one who wanted a goddamn baby, Mickey raged, suddenly angry. I don't like taking care of people. "I love your son, Mrs. Dunhill. I will always love him. I want to be with him no matter what." Mickey took a breath. "I'm not going anywhere," he said, quietly. "I'm not leaving him. I can't. Please."

She did not speak, but the coldness of her glare wavered. Mickey, his eyes fixed on her, sensed hesitation.

She is considering me, he said to himself. Reasonable doubt.

"She told you to go." Mrs. Dunhill drew herself up at the sound of the voice behind her. George Dunhill stood in the doorway, still solid at sixty three, the erectness of his bearing providing the illusion of a power that he no longer had. His careful enunciation of each word projected a subtle menace. "I believe she asked you to go. Are you going to respect my wife's wishes, or do I need to call for security?"

Mickey looked at him warily. Professions of love would not sway this one; any displays of sentiment would only confirm his darkest suspicions. Mickey threw back his own shoulders in an unconscious imitation of the older man's rigid posture. "Mr. Dunhill, let's be reasonable. I don't think some sort of embarrassing scene in the corridor is in your wife's best interests, or your son's. Think about it. Battles like this can be very ugly and very public as well. I am a lawyer too; perhaps Caleb mentioned that?"

"I know all about you," he growled. "I know where you work. I know where you went to school." Ah, thought Mickey, so you have discovered Google. Good for you. "So that's the kind of friend you are to Caleb? You're going to go to court, are you, and embarrass my family? Don't come here and threaten us." He took a step closer to Mickey. "I know your type. You probably threatened Caleb as well. I saw it last night. He was frightened of something. That wasn't him talking. You put him up to it, didn't you, with your threats? Couldn't even stay, he was so frightened of what you might do. Couldn't look his mother in the eye and say he was sorry. Well, you're not going to frighten me. Caleb isn't concerned about your threats right now, not when he is fighting for his life."

"I am his life," said Mickey.

"Get out, " shouted Mr. Dunhill. "Get out."

Chapter 30

"Teddy!" Robin called, "Joan is waiting. Let's go." Teddy, who had progressed no further than the bottom stair, screwed up his face with a determined poutiness. "Young man," said his mother, "school time. Here's your lunch." She waggled the paper bag enticingly. Teddy wrapped his arms around the newel post. His brown eyes were stony. Robin looked at him and sighed. "What's wrong, Teddy Bear?"

"I hate Harrison."

Of course you hate Harrison, Robin thought, that mean-hearted little spawn. "Teddy, we talked about this. Harrison doesn't know anything about our family. When you talk about something without knowing the facts, then you are ignorant. He's just ignorant, and his family is ignorant. It doesn't matter what he says. But that doesn't mean it was right for you to push him. You can't hit people."

"Unless they hit you first." Ryan was lying on the couch where his father had deposited him before leaving for work. "Daddy says if someone hits you first, then you can go ahead and hit him back, harder."

Harrison was a small boy with a loud, piping voice who wore polo shirts tucked neatly into his sweatpants. She could not picture him throwing a punch. "Nobody is hitting anybody," Robin said. "Miss Grey is going to speak to all the children about respecting people's privacy and not using hurtful language. You apologize to Harrison, and he will apologize to you, and it will all be over." Teddy, his head wagging, took a firmer grip of the post. Robin sighed. "Wait right here," she said to them both.

Joan's car was idling in the driveway. "You'd better go," said Robin. "Teddy's got himself chained to the staircase like he was Martin Luther King at a sit-in. I'm going to have to drop him off myself, or else take him with us to the hospital."

"Take him," said Joan cheerily. "Everybody needs a mental health day once in a while."

"Sounds good to me," said Robin. "I could use a mental health day myself."

"I need a mental health day every day," said Isaiah.

Robin had a bag packed with movies and a small bottle of red Gatorade. She went back into the bedroom to get her phone. She had forgotten to charge it and the battery was low. They weren't supposed to use cell phones in the hospital anyway. She turned the thing off and slipped it into her pocket. "C'mon boys," she said.

Ryan whimpered as his feet touched the floor. "I can't walk," he said, taking a few tottering steps toward the door.

"You are walking right now," said Teddy darkly.

"I'll carry you," said Robin, putting the bag over her shoulder and heaving him up. His weight was heavy against her shoulder.

"I want daddy to carry me!" Ted called, the pitch of his voice rising.

"Teddy-boy, you are riding on my last nerve," said his mother. "Daddy is meeting us at the hospital around lunchtime. Do you want to come to the hospital? I will let you come, but only if you promise to be no trouble at all. We can all come home together after Ryan has his line taken out. I'm telling you right now, this isn't going to be fun. It's boring at the hospital. You can't run around or disturb the other patients, or bother the nurses. But if that's what you want, get up on your feet and stop this whining. I swear, if I hear so much as one sniffle, I will carry you myself – I will carry you right into that school and put you down at your desk, and you can be someone else's problem."

Dr. Coben looked very pleased to see them, and she clucked sympathetically when Robin reported that the pain in Ryan's legs was worse. "Can you do this one more time, champ?" she asked him, and Robin gave him a beaming smile when he nodded yes. Teddy climbed into her lap and hid his eyes as the blood began to flow through the tubes. Robin detached him long enough to start the movie. It was something they had seen dozens of times before, a hockey movie about a team of underdogs who make good.

"How much longer?" asked Ryan, after a minute.

"The doctor said maybe three hours." On the television, the ragtag hockey team got new jerseys, with their names written on the backs.

"I want to play hockey," said Ryan.

"Me too," said Ted.

"We can go ice skating," said Robin. "We can go this weekend. As soon as your legs feel better."

"I don't want to go ice skating." Ryan looked indignant. "I want to play hockey on a hockey team."

"I'm hungry," said Ted.

"You should have eaten your breakfast," said Robin. "It's not even eleven."

"I'm hungry," Teddy whimpered.

"I will take you down to the cafeteria as soon as Daddy gets here."

"No!" Ryan objected. "You promised me you wouldn't leave again." His voice sounded shaky and the skin around his lips looked pale.

"Okay," said Robin, "I won't leave. Daddy will take Teddy." Teddy made a small strangled noise but said nothing. "Are you feeling okay, Ryan? Drink some Gatorade."

"I don't want anything."

The kids in the movie were playing a game against the mean boys from the next town. The rag-tag team had skinny kids, and fat kids, and a girl, and one large brooding-looking boy who appeared to be homeless. The boys on the other team all looked alike. "I want to be on a hockey team," said Ryan.

"I'm hungry," said Teddy. "I want some Gatorade."

"You can't drink the Gatorade," said Robin. "Your brother needs to keep his fluids up."

"I don't want any Gatorade," said Ryan. "My stomach hurts."

"My stomach hurts too," said Ted. "I'm really hungry. Why didn't you bring me some Gatorade?"

"I didn't know you were going to be here." Robin looked around at the bare walls and scouted through her bag. Snacks would have been a good idea, had she thought of it. "Ryan, do you mind if I take your brother down to the vending machines for just one minute?"

"You promised you wouldn't go!" Ryan looked near tears. "You promised me."

"Okay! I was just asking."

"I want to go to the vending machines," said Teddy.

"I can't take you right now. Daddy will be here soon."

"I'm hungry! You didn't bring anything for me to drink. I want to go to the vending machines. I can go by myself."

"It's all the way back near the elevators. I don't think you should go there by yourself."

"I can go by myself."

"Are you sure?" asked Robin.

"My hands hurt," said Ryan.

"I can go by myself," said Ted. He sounded very certain. It was only down the corridor and into the atrium, Robin thought. It would keep him quiet until John got there. John was forever telling her that she babied the boys. Here was Teddy acting brave all of a sudden, and it might be a mistake to discourage him. Robin pulled out her wallet.

"Do you want something too?" she asked Ryan.

"I'm not hungry," he said miserably.

"Teddy, you go just past that nurse at the desk, and make a left. Do you know which one is left?" Teddy nodded, raising his left hand. "Good. Then go straight down into the big room with the glass ceiling.

The machines are in the corner there. They work just like the machines at Daddy's office. You can do those by yourself, right?" Teddy nodded solemnly. "Buy one drink and one snack and then come straight back. Got that? I'll leave the door open." She watched him from the door as he walked down the hallway and turned the corner.

Ryan whimpered softly as he watched the rag-tag kids celebrate their first win. He didn't smile, and under the covers his legs were shivering. "Are you getting those chills again?" she asked. His lips were blue. Robin checked her watch. It was almost twelve.

John arrived as she was reaching for the button to call the nurse. "I'm so glad you are here," she said.

He laid a hand on Ryan's forehead, which was suddenly damp. "Hey, buddy," he said, and he glanced significantly at Robin. "Have you spoken to Mickey?"

"Mickey? Not since last night." What an odd conversation that was, thought Robin, who had not remembered it again until this minute. "Why?"

"I think he's trying to reach you. Look." He showed her a text on his Blackberry: 'does robin have her phone?'

The cellphone took forever to turn on. Then it flashed, and the little window on the front said 'check messages'. In the inbox, there were two unread texts. She opened the first: "Caleb hurt. Driving to CT. Will call later." Her fingers were shaking. John took the phone from her and punched the green button a second time: "Bad news. Pls come. I need you."

"Mickey," said Robin, staring at the screen. John slid one hand under her arm. She reached for her bag. "I have to go."

"Mommy!" said Ryan. "Go where? You said you would stay."

"Ryan," said Robin, leaning in close. "I know I promised you I wouldn't leave. Sweetheart, sometimes things happen that we never could have expected. Do you understand? Your Uncle Mickey needs me a lot right now. I think he might need me even more than you. And you have your Daddy here, and Uncle Mickey is all alone. Do you think you can you share your Mommy with him, just for a little while?"

Ryan nodded. Robin kissed him on the forehead, gently, and then kissed John and squeezed his hand. "He should be pretty close to done, but ask the nurse. She'll come by – I pushed the button twice. I will get back as soon as I can."

"Send me a message," said John, pointing to the Blackberry strapped to his belt.

Returning down a long corridor that had not led to the big room with windows in the ceiling, Teddy walked by the nurse at the desk for a second time. He did not look at her. Don't bother the nurses, his mother said. The grown ups walking past talked in quiet voices and their shoes made loud squeaking noises on the shiny tile floor. Teddy said nothing. He was being good; he was not disturbing anyone. Still, his mother might be angry with him, because he did not go straight to the vending machines and come straight back. He stared down at the green wall where it met the speckled floor. The first hallway he went down looked like this too.

Fighting the urge to cry, Teddy peered out from under his eyelashes at a man coming out of a room. He wore a white coat like the doctor who connected Ryan to the machine that took his blood. Teddy did not like seeing blood in the tubes. Perhaps doctors were not like regular strangers, and it would be okay to ask them for help. Find someone in uniform, his teacher said. He eyed two women in white coats up ahead. They were walking briskly, moving away from him, and next to them, moving even quicker, was a flash of yellow hair against a familiar red jacket. Mommy, thought Ted.

It occurred to Ted that his mother must be going to look for him. He had been gone a long time. He trotted after her, breaking into a little half jog to keep her in sight, even though she had warned him not to run in the hospital. She was moving fast, like she did when she was angry. He wondered if Ryan was crying because their mother had left the room. If Ryan was crying when they got back, she would be even angrier at him. Teddy trotted a little slower. Ryan felt sick, and it was all because of this little girl, who was not his sister. Harrison was stupid, thought Teddy. That girl could not be his sister. If she was his sister, his mother and father would never have sent her to go live with someone else. They never left him or Ryan. Mom wouldn't even leave Ryan for a moment now, because he was being brave and doing this special thing for the girl who was sick. She would never leave me, Teddy thought, even if she was very angry.

His mother turned the corner, so Teddy ran a bit, just to keep up. Now he was in the big room. He walked over to where the vending machines were, but there was no one there. He looked back the other way. The red jacket was farther away now, just going out of sight through the door on the other side. Ted headed back that way. The people in front of him moved slowly and he pushed past them, the tail of a man's raincoat slapping him in the face as he went by. "'Scuse me," he said, his voice muffled by the thick fabric.

He peeked around the corner and she was there, down the hall, by the elevators. There was a grimness about her face that frightened him. I'm sorry, he wanted to say. I didn't mean to take so long. "Mommy?" he said softly, but she did not hear him, and in a second the elevator door opened and closed and she was gone. Teddy stood and watched the elevators for a time but she did not come back.

He walked very slowly into the atrium. The three dollar bills were clutched tight in his hand. He went into the corner where the vending machines hummed quietly. Tears trickled down his face as he stared at the drinks through the glass window. He recognized Pepsi and orange soda. His mother liked it better when he had juice. If she came back, and he had juice and not soda, she might say 'there's my Teddy-bear' and scoop him up in her arms. Carefully, he slid a dollar bill into the slot and pushed the button next to the box with pictures of apples and raspberries. Nothing happened. He pushed the button again, harder.

"You need another quarter," said a woman who was watching him as she walked by.

"My Daddy has this machine at his work," said Teddy, still sniffling. "It costs a dollar for juice."

"Sometimes machines have different prices," said the woman gently. "Are you alright? Do you want some help? Where is your Mommy?"

"She left," said Teddy. "I have another dollar." He held up his hand with the two remaining dollar bills.

"Slide one in," she said, "and then push the button again." The juice box fell to the bottom with a small plunking sound. "Now take your change." She fished out three quarters and handed them back to Ted. "Do you want something else?"

Teddy nodded.

What a beautiful child, the woman thought. The shape of his face was familiar to her, the wide-set eyes and the long blonde lashes stained dark with tears.

Teddy looked up cautiously. Her eyes were dark, and so were the circles beneath them. She looked serious but friendly, like the teachers at school. "I want Sunchips," he said. She slid the money into the other machine and showed him which buttons to push. He opened the little door and extracted the bag.

"Now where do you need to go with that?" asked the woman, with a quick glance at her watch.

"I don't know," said Ted. "My brother was here with my Mommy, but my Mommy left. Maybe my brother left too, because he wasn't feeling well and he wanted to go home. The doctor said he was being very brave."

"I bet your brother is very brave and you are too. It's not easy being sick."

"Oh!" said Teddy, "he is not sick. A girl is sick. He is giving some cells to a girl because she is very sick." The woman made a small sound and did not answer. Teddy looked at her, concerned. "Don't be sad," he said, "she's going to get all better. The doctor said Ryan's blood is the perfect type to make her better."

"What's your name?" asked the woman. Her voice sounded funny.

"Teddy Michael Hogan."

"My name is Meredith," the woman replied. "It is nice to meet you."

"It's nice to meet you too," said Ted.

He smiled Sophie's smile, and she fought the urge to dry his damp cheeks with her fingertips. This is how she feels, Meredith thought. This is what it is like for her, when she sees Sophie.

"How about we get you back to your brother's room?" she said. "They will be missing you."

"I don't know," said Ted. "I saw Mommy go in the elevator." He looked confidingly at Meredith. "I don't want to go in the room when Mommy is not there. Ryan's blood is showing."

"I'm sure she won't be gone long," said Meredith. "Did she want you to wait here for her?"

"I don't know," said Teddy unhappily.

Meredith stared at his round brown face and pink stained cheeks. This is the color Sophie would be, if she didn't wear sunblock all the time. If she could go outside, where the sun shone.

"Can I wait here with you?"

"I'm not sure how long I can stay," said Meredith anxiously, taking a second glance at her watch. "My little girl is expecting me."

"Is she sick?"

"Yes, she is," Meredith replied slowly. "She's very sick. Just like the little girl your brother is helping." Meredith hesitated, and Teddy looked up at her, his eyes liquid and unsuspecting. Meredith felt uncomfortable, as though she were lying to the boy. "In fact," she continued, "it is my daughter that he is helping. That's my little girl who is going to get those cells from your brother."

"You are her mommy?"

"Yes," Meredith said.

Teddy nodded with a look of satisfaction. "I told Harrison that she was not my sister. Harrison, a boy in my class, said she was my sister. That's stupid. He said my Mommy and Daddy gave her away. Don't you think that's stupid? Mommy says Harrison is ignorant."

"I think your mommy is exactly right."

"Because she can't be my sister if you are her mommy." Teddy smiled at her as though they shared a joke. "What is her name, your little girl?"

"Sophie."

"Is Sophie going to get better?"

"I hope so. What your brother is doing is going to help a lot."

"I was sick last summer. I threw up for three days."

"Not much fun, is it?"

Teddy shook his head. "My brother had to have shots every night with a big needle. Mommy said, 'One more time. One more time.' It made his legs hurt."

"That's terrible," said Meredith.

"He will feel better soon. We are going to go ice skating, when he is better."

"But not today."

"No! Today is the last game of the Red Sox against the Yankees. The Red Sox is my and my brother's favorite team."

"Me too! Do you think they will win?"

"Daddy says the Yankees always win, but Mommy says sometimes miracles can happen. The Red Sox won three in a row. We have Big Papi. He can hit the ball" – Ted swung an imaginary bat, his face a corkscrew of concentration – "so far."

We might just win it, thought Meredith. It would be a miracle. "Anything could happen," she said. "Look, I really have to get you back to your own room."

Teddy's voice warbled and tears filled his eyes again. "I am waiting here for Mommy. Mommy's coming back soon." He sat down in one of the dull grey chairs and grabbed tight to the armrest with both hands. "You could just stay right here while I wait for mommy."

Meredith sighed. "Well Teddy, I don't want you to be all by yourself, but I can't leave Sophie alone either." Teddy's fingernails grew white as he clutched at the upholstery. "How about if I get Sophie and bring her back to the atrium? We can wait here with you together."

"She isn't too sick?"

"She is more like herself, today." Teddy looked very small and forlorn, sitting in the big chair. "I bet she would really love to meet you," Meredith added. "Would you like that?" He nodded his head, up and down. "Wait here." She opened his chips, and stuck the straw into his juice box. "Keep an eye out for your mother."

Chapter 31

The door was unlocked. Robin let herself in. Mickey did not get up. He was lying on top of the covers, fully dressed. She lay down next to him. "How is he?" she asked.

"Ah," said Mickey, "Exactly. Question of the day. How is Caleb?"

"Mickey, please." Robin's face was pale and white. "Don't play games with me. I can't take it right now. Just tell me if he is going to be alright."

"I wouldn't know. The ugly trolls that guard the bridge wouldn't let me in."

"Seriously? The people at the hospital wouldn't let you in?"

'I convinced the hospital staff that I was his brother, but I couldn't get his parents to fall for it. They requested that I leave the premises."

"Are you kidding me?"

Mickey smiled ruefully at the indignant flare of her nostrils. "His mother said that he was going to be in a wheelchair and therefore he would no longer have any use for me." Mickey did not repeat that terrible word, "if." "There are no homosexuals in wheelchairs, you know. It's like atheists in foxholes." His voice was clipped and rough-edged, a brittle facsimile of its usual languid self. "I got some information out of Roseanne when I returned the car. There is a head wound, and an injury to the thoracolumbar junction of the spine. Complete paralysis below the waist, if not worse."

Like something out of the Bible, Robin thought. She said nothing. "Assholes probably think it's divine retribution," Mickey snarled. "Meanwhile, he is unconscious, and until he wakes up, compos mentis, his parents are in charge, and I am officially persona non grata."

"Did you explain who you are to the doctor?"

"Who I am? I am nobody. I am not his next of kin. I am not a family member. I am an unwelcome guest. I was begging them for information. I was pathetic, Robin, you should have seen me. The nurses wouldn't speak to me at all. Do you think they are going to side with me against the grieving mother? They can't, and they won't. 'Please don't make things difficult,' the doctor says, as though things were not difficult already. I said, 'that's my job, you know. I am a lawyer; I make things difficult for a living.' Not a very productive thing to say, but I did manage to make him look a little nervous. God, doctors hate lawyers. Still, it was just a bluff. Empty words to make me feel better. Legally, I don't have a leg to stand on. Just like Caleb." His face twitched in the direction of a smile. "I've got to let it go. It's hopeless. I can't start a battle with his folks that I am going to lose. It's not like we're married. If we'd gone ahead and gotten married, it would be different. I could be a test case, just like you. Do you think our mother could live through it, having both her children be test cases? What would the neighbors think?"

"Don't joke, Mickey. It's so terrible. Believe me, I know how you feel, getting shut out of that room. This is exactly what I have been going through."

"No, it is not, really," said Mickey. "That little girl doesn't even know you. She is not going to wake up broken and battered and in pain and lie there wondering why you have abandoned her."

"Well I did not mean," said Robin, and then she stopped, because she could not think of what it was she had intended to say. "Poor Caleb," she continued, "it is all so unfair. Do you think his parents will at least tell him that you wanted to be there?"

"Our understanding of one another left something to be desired, but I would have to guess not." Now Mickey sounded a little more like himself. "I would really like to be in that room with him. Isn't that stupid? I should be running in the other direction. I should take my opportunity and bow out gracefully. He's so helpless, Robin. I can't make it better. But I want to be there. I want to take care of him. I want to hold his stupid hand and dab at his forehead with hot washcloths or cold washcloths or whatever it is you are supposed to do."

"When he wakes up, he will ask for you, and the hospital staff will have to let you in."

"I am not so sure." Mickey's dark eyes grew bleaker still. "If I were Caleb, I would never want to see me again. It's all my fault. His father told me Caleb looked terrified when he came to talk to them. He was scared because of me. That's the only reason he went."

"His father has no idea how Caleb feels about you. They don't understand anything. What do they know about your lives together? Nothing. Caleb loves you."

"He wasn't ready, Rob. I said some terrible things."

"Mickey, he had an accident. You can't spend your whole life blaming yourself for an accident."

"I am going to have to beg to differ on that, sis. I imagine I can spend my whole life blaming myself for an accident. But not without him. Not alone." Mickey's voice cracked. His wet eyes reminded her of childhood, when he cried easily out of pain or rage. How many years it had been since she had seen that familiar, contorted expression on his face as he wrestled for control? She could still hear her father, shouting 'Can you stop blubbering, for Pete's sake.'

"What if he dies, Rob?" Mickey moaned. "What if he dies and I never get to tell him I'm sorry?"

"He's not going to die," said Robin. She glanced around the room. All the evidence of Caleb's existence seemed to mitigate against the possibility that he could be gone. There were cufflinks and shirt tabs neatly arranged in a leather box on the dresser, and books on the bedside table. She recognized Tim Russert's book about his father; she and the boys had bought it for John for Father's Day. That was the stuff Caleb liked, plain-spoken and informative. A card from Mickey and Teddy was taped to his mirror. HaPPy BiRthDay UncLe CaLeB, it said on the front. They loved him so much. He could not possibly be dead.

The thought of the boys brought her abruptly back to the present. The harvesting must be done by now. She looked sidelong at Mickey. His dark eyes gazed into the middle distance. "I know Caleb needs you there with him. You cannot give up so easily. What about Greg Rose? Maybe he can help."

"So you think Greg Rose will help me?" It was a relief to see a mildly amused expression pass across his face. "Aren't you sweet? No, the law is on their side. Mr. Rose will be only too happy to tell you that."

"I know he would want to help," said Robin. "He's a compassionate individual. He called last night to see how Ryan was feeling."

Mickey roused himself onto his elbows. "Ryan! He's still doing that blood collecting thing, isn't he? You'd better get back to the hospital. Poor little guy. He will want his mommy."

"I can stay," said Robin. Her voice was a question mark.

"Go," said Mickey. "I'll be okay. Go take care of your boys. Tell them Uncle Mickey and Uncle Caleb love them very much." He drew himself up on one elbow. "And Robin," his voice thickened, "I want you to promise me something."

"Anything."

"Promise me you will not try to separate that woman from her child." Robin stared back at him, saying nothing. "I know what the girl means to you. But those people are a family. It's not the same as your family, but you have to respect it for what it is. Please. For me."

"It's so sad, John," she said when she got back to the hospital. "He's so upset. I don't believe he's thinking clearly. I feel like going down to Connecticut and pleading with Caleb's parents myself. How can they do this to him?" She looked around then, at the empty room. "Where is Ryan? Did everything go alright?"

"Everything went fine. He finished up with the harvesting right after you left, and then as soon as he felt better, they sedated him for the procedure to remove the line. He's down there now. I think he will be back anytime. I tell you, Robin, that's a tough kid." John's voice was hoarse with pride.

Robin looked around the room again, as though registering its emptiness a second time. "Where's Teddy?" she asked.

"Teddy?" John looked blank. "Isn't he at school? Or with Joan? Didn't you say she was picking him up?"

Robin stared at him, first in rage and then in horror. "Vending machines," she said, racing out of the room.

John's voice came floating after her down the hall. "Robin, what are you talking about? Where's Teddy?"

She skidded around the corner into the clinic and grabbed hold of a young nurse. "Have you seen my son? Not the one giving blood; the other boy. Teddy. He was here earlier, a couple of hours ago?" The nurse shook her head, pulling free of Robin's grasp. Robin saw herself in the girl's eyes, pale and wild. Calm down, she thought, calm down. She took a deep breath and felt her heart thudding.

The nurse at the desk turned toward her. "Are you looking for a little boy, about four or five? Blonde hair like yours?" Robin nodded, her eyes filling with tears. "I saw a child like that playing with a girl in the atrium maybe half an hour ago." Without a word, Robin dashed off. People stared discretely at her as she raced down the corridor.

She saw him almost right away, across the atrium, his head peaking out from behind a couch. He was laughing, and his face was dirty. After a second, he ducked back again behind the thick brown cushions. "I see you!" yelled a small girl. She charged after him, pushing an iv pole in front of her. A bag of clear fluid dripped through a line that tucked into the front of her hospital gown. "Sophie," whispered John, who had materialized at her side. "That's her, isn't it?"

"John," panted Robin, "I forgot to tell you that Teddy was here. He didn't want to go to school today. I let him come with us to the hospital."

"So I see." John put an arm around her shoulder. He smiled, glancing at Teddy, and then his gaze returned to the girl.

After a few minutes, Teddy saw them too. "Mommy!" he said, running toward her. "You came back!" She nodded mutely at him. "This is the little girl! She is the one who is getting Ryan's blood. She is not so sick today." Sophie came towards them dragging her pole, still giggling. Behind her, Robin saw Meredith rise from the couch.

"We didn't know where you were," said Robin, kneeling down to put her arms around Ted. She smiled at Sophie, who stared back at her, suddenly shy.

"I was waiting here for you. I saw you go away in the elevator. I was waiting for you to come back. I'm sorry, Mommy, for not listening." He peered at her face, like she was a puzzle he needed to solve. "You're not angry anymore? I waited right here. Meredith and Sophie waited with me so I wouldn't be all by myself."

"That was very, very nice of them," said Robin, looking up at Meredith. She was standing near them now, and Sophie had moved over next to her mother. "Thank you."

"It's alright," said Meredith. Her eyes were red but she did not look sad, not like she had on the day they met in the fertility center. "He was wonderful playing with Sophie. I think this was the best time she has had in ages."

"Sophie is funny," said Ted, making faces at her. "And you know what? She is a Red Sox fan."

"Go Big Papi!" shrieked Sophie with a manic glee.

"I hear the boys are both big Red Sox fans," said Meredith. She laid one hand against the child's bald head and felt her almost vibrating with happiness. "Perhaps you would like to come by Sophie's room this evening and watch some of the game with us? Sophie would be very excited to meet Ryan, and I know she would be thrilled to see Teddy again. It's going to be the last good night. Now that the cells are in, they will start the conditioning tomorrow, to get her prepared for the transplant. She's not going to feel so chipper, once they begin knocking out her bone marrow." Meredith paused, and then continued. "Teddy told us how hard this has been on Ryan. David and I, we would like the chance to say thank you to him – to all of you."

Apprehensively, John glanced at his wife. "Are you sure?" Robin asked Meredith. "We wouldn't want to intrude on your time together as a family."

"I am sure," said Meredith firmly.

Epilogue

The big kitchen at the back of the house was full of people, and it felt overheated despite the three tall, narrow windows wedged open to let in the cool October air. The room smelled of lemon and olives and some foreign spice that Robin thought might be from India, or Morocco, or Turkey — the sort of spice you would expect to find in food cooked slowly in pots made out of clay. Meredith wandered through carrying trays of toasted bread with goat cheese and honey, the embroidered sleeves of her tunic top fluttering behind her as she maneuvered through the crowd. Everyone but the children spoke in quiet voices and drank wine or seltzer from round wine glasses that had no stems.

The party didn't change much from year to year. Many of the faces were familiar now to Robin. There was David's brother Raymond and his wife Jocelyn, nice people; she liked them both, especially her. Raymond was more courteous than friendly, the way your doctor might be when you ran into him away from the office. He asked a lot of medical questions too. "What a shame it was," he said, "that John's mother died so young and never got a chance to meet the boys. Remind me what she had – was it coronary artery disease or arrhythmia?" It was meant to be subtle, Robin thought.

There were always quite a few people from that women's center where Meredith worked, mostly staff, but once in a while one of the women they had helped. Grace, who always came, told Robin she had turned to Meredith for help time and again, making her way through a cosmetology program while raising five kids: two of her own, and three more she inherited when the state declared her sister unfit. She was devoted to Sophie, for whom she babysat every other Saturday. "She's so smart, that girl,' Gloria told Robin the first time they met. "Nothing wrong with her at all, God bless her soul." Robin liked the idea that Grace put Sophie to bed at night now and then. She would be sure to see her say her prayers.

There were always a lot of people from the neighborhood there, more names than Robin could remember, although they all knew hers. The first year, one woman had stared at her until Robin's face grew hot, but she had not been back again. The next-door neighbor she knew for sure was Janet, and there was a woman from down the block named Dinah who informed her that she was a herbalist. People would look at you kind of strange if you called yourself that in some parts of the world.

Lindsey was in the corner talking to Meredith's Aunt Evelyn. Robin moved over and stood in the periphery of their conversation. "Yes, seventh grade already," said Lindsey. "You're right; it does go quickly." She gave a friendly wave when she saw Robin. "Hey! Come here, stranger!" She kissed her twice, the way the Europeans did. "You know Robin?" she said to Aunt Evelyn.

"Of course! Delighted to see you again, my dear. So pleased that you could join us." She said the same thing every year, with a big smile for Robin, and then never another word.

"Thank you," said Robin. "It's lovely to see you as well."

"I'm going to get some coffee," said Aunt Evelyn.

"So how are you?" said Robin. She gestured at Lindsey's finger, which sparkled with something oversized. "I hear congratulations are in order."

"Yeah, Rick and I finally decided to make it official. Lily is very pleased. She was always a bit put off by our scandalous lack of a ceremony. They're so close, Rick and Lily. I think he wanted it more for her than for me. He was so busy when his own kids were growing up. Raising Lily is virtually a new experience for him. He even likes the oboe recitals."

"Do his own kids mind that?" asked Meredith, who was passing by with the appetizers.

"His kids are happy for him – they don't mind anything, so long as I sign the pre-nup."

"And how is Lily enjoying junior high school?"

It's alright," said Lindsey. "She likes it well enough, but she's still pining for that crazy elementary school we sent her to, the Greater Boston Academy for the Sartorially Challenged."

Robin laughed. "Poor kid. It can be hard starting at a new school. Has she tried joining a club?"

"It's not that simple. You are underestimating the level of culture shock. Last June, at their graduation, the sixth grade class did an interpretive dance version of *A Tale of Two Cities*. One kid recited a timeline of French historical events, and a small boy did multiplication on a chalkboard in the corner to represent the rising toll of death."

"Well, that certainly is unusual," said Robin.

"Yes. Lily was particularly moving as the crazy knitting lady. Now, I ask you, can you replace that with chess club or debate society? No, you cannot. But we're trying to move on. She stays busy. There's the oboe, of course, and gymnastics. She's thinking about taking Chinese."

"David thinks everyone should speak Chinese," said Meredith.

"It's not on my agenda," said Lindsey, "but if she wants it, that's fine. I can't commit to speaking Mandarin at the dinner table anytime soon. I'm a busy woman."

"I know! Meredith told me on the phone that you had a new television thing in the works. What is it, a style segment?"

"No, it's a nationally syndicated show," said Lindsey. "It's on the Gossip Channel. We look at fashion hits and misses for several celebrities every week. Thumbs up, thumbs down. And then we drop in on clubs all over the country and stage impromptu contests for the kids, to pick out the best and the worst outfits of the night. I'm the regular judge, and we get a different fashion designer to work with me every week. Last week we had Jason Wu, who did Michele Obama's gown for the inaugural. We're calling it, *You Wore What???* The network loves it! On the air in January. You'll see the promos soon."

"How wonderful, said Robin. "I can't wait. I bet it's a big hit."

The insistent clink of a fork against a wine glass filled the air, taking up many of the unoccupied frequencies higher than human speech. It was a noise that climbed into crevices although it was not loud, and all the hum of conversation quickly died away. "Thank you," said David, when it was quiet. "Thank you all for coming. I wanted to take just a moment to express one more time our gratitude to everyone here who helped us during that difficult period five years ago. For what you did for Sophie, for what you did for us – we remain eternally grateful." There was polite applause. "Also, I get to announce the happy news that we just completed our annual screen and Sophie is officially five years cancer-free." The response in the kitchen was more raucous this time, with stamping of feet and pounding of tables. "To normal!" said David, raising his glass.

"Let's go sit at the table," said Meredith. They made their way to the far end of the room, past the couch where Sophie and Lily sat side by side watching High School Musical Two.

"You must hate those tests," said Robin softly to Meredith.

"Sophie pitches a fit every year. You know how she is about needles! She's had enough of them to last a lifetime, thank you. I'm okay. It's hard on her."

"It's hard on both of you," Lindsey interjected. "I know you're always anxious."

"When they call with the results, I have a little panic attack," admitted Meredith, "but most of the time I don't think about it much. It's the truth. I have this certainty that she is going to be fine. When the Red Sox won the World Series on transplant day, I thought, well, alright, it really is going to be okay. What a day that was." Her eyes caught Robin's across the table. "Sophie was sitting in my lap with this red stuff that looked like kool-aid dripping into her, and I was thinking, it can still go badly, the Cardinals might rally, we might lose four in a row. I lived through Buckner and the ball between the legs; you don't have to tell me that anything can happen. Then suddenly it is the last out, and nobody drops the ball, and the team is celebrating on the field. And I thought, we've done it, we've got our miracle." She glanced at Sophie, who was singing loudly and out of tune, while Lily nodded her head encouragingly. The blond pony tail she would never let them cut hung down between her thin shoulder blades. "I just knew we had our miracle. That's what kept me going. Superstition. It's way better than anti-depressants. Superstition kept me from going crazy those next few weeks, waiting for the cells to engraft so she could have bone marrow again.

"That was a bad time," said Robin.

"Bad! Remember? She had that terrible pneumonia, and she could hardly breathe. Her mouth was full of sores. I still cry every time she gets a canker sore."

"Does she get them often?" Robin asked with concern. "Teddy gets them all the time. It's awful."

"Please!" said Lindsey, "don't even talk about canker sores in front of the mother of an oboist. In my household, canker sores are a disaster. They are the Hurricane Katrina of mucosal disorders. Lily got one last month, just before the try-outs for All State band."

"She made it anyway," said Meredith brightly.

"But the hysteria!" said Lindsey. "The banging of doors. The stoic lack of crying. The drama of seventh grade despair. I couldn't take it; I left her with Rick. Thank God for mid-week charity events with an open bar."

"Thank God for Rick," said Meredith, frowning at her and turning to Robin. "How are the boys? They've gotten so big."

"They are growing up fast."

"Sophie is still tiny."

"It'll happen." Robin saw concern flit across Meredith's face. "What do the doctors say?"

"They say she might always be small, because of all the chemo."

"Well small is nice," said Robin. "I always wanted to be small, so I could be the girl on top in the pyramid. But I was a cheerleader. I bet Sophie doesn't want to be a cheerleader?"

"No," said Meredith.

"That's too bad. I guess it wouldn't really suit you, to have a cheerleader."

"No," Meredith admitted.

"I understand," said Robin.

The sliding door to the backyard opened, and Teddy and Ryan made their way inside, bringing with them the sweet musky scent of late October. Dead leaves crunched beneath their feet on the terracotta floor. It was still light outside, but only a fraction of the early evening sun made its way into the kitchen, and the boys blinked in the glare of the large flat screen across from the couch. "I know this next one," said Sophie, taking a firmer grip of the plastic chicken drumstick she was using as a microphone. Lily, who had perfect pitch, sang the instrumental parts out loud.

"Sophie," said Ted, "come play soccer in the backyard. I'll be goalie. Ryan will be on your team."

"After this song," said Sophie.

"De du de du dat. De du de bom bom," sang Lily.

"I'll let you score," said Teddy. "I'll only block Ryan's shots."

"Okay," said Sophie.

"So they are soccer players?" Lindsey asked Robin.

"Teddy plays soccer and baseball. Ryan plays soccer and hockey, but I think he is going to make his Daddy happy one of these days and switch over to football. John will be just wild to watch him hit somebody other than his brother."

"Where is John?" asked Lindsey.

"He'll be here soon."

"I want to pick his brain a bit on social media. We're working on a plan to go after that young adult demographic for TwentySomething. Most of the traffic on our website now is still generated by the magazine. I need to get to the girls who haven't bought a magazine or a newspaper or anything printed on paper in years. You know – the girl who has a closer relationship with her phone than with her boyfriend. I want to get her hooked on TwentySomething.com. Because the magazine itself is going to go away."

"Oh no!" said Meredith. "It looks so good."

"Even the cutest dinosaurs went extinct. The whole industry is dead. They just don't realize it yet. They're like glossy paper chickens with their heads cut off, making a few more trips around the barnyard."

The loss of all those magazines she never read made Meredith feel mournful. She would miss them if they disappeared from the racks by the check-out counters, where yesterday's headlines screamed out at her in bold fonts. Sometimes she glanced through a story or two while she waited, always putting it carefully back into the right slot when it was time to unload the cart. "But you must be so sad," she said to Lindsey, "You built that magazine from nothing."

"I built a brand. Evolve or die. The people imagine that they don't want to see anything change, but it is the customers themselves who are driving the process forward. We are not dragging the audience along; we are barely keeping up with them."

"I think it's a shame," said Meredith.

"You will adjust," said Lindsey.

"That's just the way John thinks," said Robin. "He says people get all nostalgic about familiar things, but then they go with what works. You should talk to him. Call him at the office and set something up. He's got more time for that sort of thing since the merger. Sports Illustrated does almost all of the day to day work now."

"That must be nice for you," said Meredith.

"It is," agreed Robin. "John coached Teddy's baseball team last spring, and we spent four weeks this summer at a lake near Dallas. He can work from anywhere, nowadays. It was nice to spend some time with my folks. They're not getting any younger."

The doorbell rang, and David waved over at Meredith, pointing his wineglass towards the front of the house. "I'll get it," he said.

"It's going to be John," said Robin, getting up from the table and following him into the hall.

David opened the door, and the two men shook hands. "Hey buddy," said John, "I am sorry to be late. I was hoping to get here earlier."

"It's fine," said David. "Don't worry about it." He looked away quickly. He never looked John in the eye, Robin thought. Perhaps it was the familiar green that unsettled him.

"Hi sweetheart," said John, kissing his wife.

She put an hand on his arm to keep him there as David headed back into the kitchen. "What took you so long?" she asked. "Is everything alright?"

"It's all fine," said John. "It took forever to fix the damage Mickey did trying to take apart the crib before the movers came. It's a damn good thing the Justice Department isn't asking him to use a screwdriver. Your brother is a menace with a tool in his hand." He paused. "Caleb was a little emotional."

Robin nodded. It had been five years for him too, five long years of rehab, and patient, endless negotiations at home and at work, but he had gotten himself a wheelchair accessible office and a cordial relationship with a kind-hearted woman from Ohio, who gave birth to their baby, three months old already. Five years. A long time -- and then, not so long, now that there was time enough to think about all the years ahead. Robin could remember when the past was nothing but yesterday or the day before, just a few steps that brought you to the present, and the present itself was merely a bridge to the future, where your real life lay. Now she stood poised between the two, looking forward and backward in equal measure. She was getting older. She could not run toward the future like the boys did, discarding the past without a thought, like the wet towels and dirty clothes she collected from the floor of their room every day.

Five years was nothing, or an eternity. Time, Robin thought, was about the only thing that grew more elastic with age. It might have been yesterday that she was in the hospital waiting room with Mickey, keeping him company for a little while as he sat in a hard plastic chair the color of sherbet and tried to work, cursing at the sim card in his laptop when the internet connection went out, again. It was an eternity, but it did end. It had to end. For a month Caleb's parents did not so much as acknowledge his existence, did not even admit to knowing he was only two floors away. Then one day the mother came creeping down from the ICU. Of course she knew he was there all along. She did not tell him why she came, and Mickey did not ask. Perhaps the vigil got to her, or fear crept in, as Caleb inched toward lucidity. Maybe she couldn't stand it anymore, the way her son's eyes reached for the door every time the knob turned.

She asked him to come only when her husband wasn't there. Mickey did not fight with her; it would have made Caleb unhappy. Mr. Dunhill pretended not to know, right up to the day Mickey drove down in a rented car and took Caleb back to Boston, to a rehab facility just outside the city. It was on the T, so Caleb's mother could get there by herself, if she took the train in to town. She was always gone by the time Mickey arrived after work.

It was two more years before Caleb felt comfortable enough with the hand controls in the new van to drive himself back to Connecticut. Robin asked him once how that went and he said, "Okay." He did not elaborate. He was working again by then, and the fogginess of the early days had lifted. He took up wheelchair basketball, and forced Mickey to drop every one of the lawsuits he had begun over ramps and curb cuts. The boys climbed all over him and he waived Robin off when she tried to pry them away. "I'll do it," he said, when they asked for juice, or a snack or a ride to the movie theater. It was more than being nice, she realized after a while. He was testing himself. He was making sure.

"Guess what?" John said. "The Dunhills are taking the baby for the week while Mickey and Caleb get settled in Washington."

"No!" said Robin. Her face glowed pink with pleasure.

"Never underestimate the power of grandchildren," said John.

"So your brother took the job in DC?" asked Meredith. "How wonderful to work in this new administration."

"It'll certainly be a new experience for Mickey," said John, "working for the government, and not against them."

"But everything is different now, with Obama," Meredith insisted.

"Oh, well, we'll see. They did sell Mickey on the idea that change is coming. It might be too much change for me, but it will never be enough for Mickey, not while the human race is in charge. He promised them two years. I think he'll manage that without getting himself run out of town or blowing the place up, so long as they don't let him have any power tools."

"What will Caleb do?"

"He's going to take a leave of absence and stay home with the little guy. The timing is pretty good. Then they'll come back here and Caleb will go back to work, so as not to let that ramp they put in go to waste."

"That's great," said Meredith. "I'm glad. Now, John, you should get yourself something to eat." She took his hand and leaned forward, lowering her voice. "Can you all stay a few minutes at the end? David and I have something we need to talk to you about."

After the rush and flurry of good-byes, the room seemed not only quiet but still. "I can think again!" said Meredith. "Thank you for waiting." David opened one last bottle of wine, and poured four glasses.

Sophie and the boys were watching preseason basketball. "I am really good at basketball," said Sophie. "I am going to play on a real team this winter."

Ryan smirked at her. "You're pretty short," he said. "I could put you in my pocket."

"I can get the ball all the way up to the basket," Sophie insisted.

"Let's go into the living room," said Meredith. She sat next to David on the couch, and Robin and John took chairs that were side by side. Robin waited for one of them to start. The silence ran on a beat too long, and Meredith looked up to the ceiling, as though she had written something there that would tell her what to say. David looked at her with a small smile, and Meredith lay her hand over his. "David and I have been talking about Sophie a lot since this last check up. About her future."

"We didn't do that for a while," said David.

"No," said Meredith. "We didn't dare for a long time. You know, she is doing really well. But there are a few consequences of her treatment. She struggles with some things in school. Math."

"Oh, I could never do math," said Robin, "and I didn't have chemotherapy or radiation."

"That's the thing," said Meredith. "It doesn't really matter. We can get her through math. I can help her."

"And when it gets too complicated for Meredith, we can ask Lily," added David.

"She'll be fine. But the thing is – well, you know, she's never going to have any children. I mean, not her own children. Not the traditional way."

"We wondered about that," said Robin.

"The doctors warned us that would happen," said David. "The chemotherapy destroys the eggs. It's not something that can come back."

"So we were thinking about what it would be like for her when she grew up – if she didn't have children, or if she adopted. Either way, because of us, there would always be the lack of a biological connection on either end. She would never experience that. No blood relatives." She stopped.

"Except you," said David.

"In fact, you are the only blood relatives she will ever have," Meredith paused, "and while I believe that Sophie is a very happy and secure little girl, it seems to us that feeling closer to you and your family might be important for her, long-term. So she could have that in her life."

"Might make the whole situation easier," said David.

"Yes. Might make it easier for her, someday, when we have to tell her about the infertility." Meredith stumbled only slightly on the last word. "So we were wondering, if it were okay with you, if Sophie could get to know the rest of her biological family a bit better. Maybe spend some time with them. Thanksgiving, or a holiday. A vacation." She paused. David squeezed her hand softly. Neither of them spoke. "I realize it's a lot to ask," she added.

"You can say no," said David. "We would fully understand."

"We don't want to say no," said Robin. The words rushed out, one on top of the other. "Sophie is welcome with us anytime. We would love to take her down to Texas." She looked over at John, who nodded slowly. "She could come and meet my cousins." Robin's voice grew thicker. "And her grandparents. But only on one condition."

"What's that?" said David.

"You come too." They started to object and Robin shook her head. "If this is Sophie's family, then I guess it must be your family too. You come down to Texas for Thanksgiving. All three of you." Meredith and Robin were both crying now. "But I have to warn you about one thing." Her voice cracked. "My Daddy,"

"Your father will be fine," said John impatiently.

"My Daddy, he fries the turkey in a garbage can out in the garage." Robin took a shaky breath. "And we always have cornbread in our stuffing. And that's just the way it is. That's just the way it is, back home."

Acknowledgements

I am infinitely indebted to a number of people whose support, advice and encouragement helped produce this book. To all of you who read and re-read: thank you. A special thanks to Sally Cohen for her endless enthusiasm and to Annette Patterson for her tough love (you were right; it wasn't good enough). I am so lucky to have both of you in my life.

For Howard Appelbaum: thanks for having so much faith in me, and for all your interest and eagerness to help. You are a positive presence in my universe. And much love and gratitude to Pamela Bensimhon, who never gets tired of helping, despite all the helping that she does.

Thanks to Ann Patty, who liked in the book enough to take it apart, and to Victoria Skurnick, whose cynicism was tempered by hugs, kisses and exclamation points. I appreciate all your efforts on my behalf.

To my husband, who is the chief nurturer of all my aspirations, intellectual and otherwise: this book is the latest and the least of what we have *built together. Thank you for not editing. So much love to my children, who are always my inspiration and will be terribly embarrassed to see it here in print. Devon, James and Dylan: without you, there is nothing. And thanks to Cruskaia and Anna, who have taught me that it is love and not trees that grow a family.*

A kiss to my father, who believed this to be the best novel he had ever read – a low bar indeed. Thank you for reading, Daddy. I miss you.

This book is for my mother.

Made in the USA
San Bernardino, CA
11 June 2013